Skipper's Oath

The Frank Mattituck Series, Book One

WITHDRAWN

by

P. Wesley Lundburg

Gaslamp Scriveners Press

This book is dedicated to Tania Gavino:
Thank you for being
an amazing wife, best friend,
partner, and inspiration.

This is a work of fiction. Names, characters, businesses, places, events and incidents are either the products of the author's imagination or used fictitiously. Any resemblance to actual persons, living or dead, or actual events is purely coincidental.

Gaslamp Scriveners Press
Saint James, New York

Prologue

Expert Rifleman

The seas were getting rough enough that Yakutat Police Officer Wayne Barrett began to question his decision to get underway on his own. He frequently did this, but the seas of the Gulf of Alaska could be unpredictable, so Wayne normally followed the conventional wisdom of always having somebody else on board in rough seas. If you slipped and hit your head, or fell overboard, there was a chance of survival. Alone . . . well, the odds were not in your favor.

The 28-foot harbor patrol boat was a retail craft with an aluminum hull and a pair of Honda 250 outboards. It was a fast boat, but the hull design left it a tad squirrely in a crossed sea—a current-pushed swell under a wind-driven surface chop, each with a different direction. When Wayne had turned the vessel out of the harbor and opened throttle to muscle over the rising seas of the open Gulf, there had only been a low swell of 4 or 5 feet. Now it had picked up to a solid 8-foot swell, coming from directly south, and an easterly gale had kicked up a 2-foot chop crossing these swells at a 90-degree angle.

The little boat was starting to buck side-to-side while clambering up the face of the swells and dropping

2

down their backsides. Wayne half-thought about turning back, but the reports of a problem Bayliner drove those thoughts away. Wayne's thoughts returned to the call that had come in an hour before.

"Yakutat Harbor, Yakutat Harbor," the voice had said. "Fun N Games on channel 16, over."

Millie Crawford, the dispatcher, had answered the call on VHF marine radio while Wayne continued filling out the day's log.

"Fun N Games, this is Yakutat Harbor," she had said, her older voice graveled but steady. "Go ahead."

"Yakutat Harbor, yeah . . ." the voice had begun, uneven, as if the speaker were turning his head away from the mic. "We got a boat out here acting a little crazy. He's making us a bit nervous."

Millie had looked around to Wayne. He gave her an upward nod, indicating she should continue with the call rather than hand it over to him.

"Fun N Games," she had said into the mic, "does it seem the vessel is in distress?"

"No, Yakutat. No . . . he's just circling around us, round and round. Anytime I try to steer into port, he cuts me off. He's trying to keep us out here, I guess. Dunno why."

Millie's hand had been busy writing notes.

"Roger," she had answered. "How many people on your vessel?"

"Two. Me and the wife."

"And what's your position?"

After getting the details of the 45-foot cruising yacht, she had asked for details on the Bayliner. Wayne had stopped making entries in the log and joined her at the radio. He had hunched over the chart table, finding the coordinates the Fun N Games had given and noting their speed and direction. He quickly plotted a course to intercept them, in case he needed to get underway.

"He's got a gun, it looks like," the Fun N Games reported, the man's tone rising an octave. "Sweet Jesus, Yakutat, he's got a rifle out."

Wayne had now stepped over, and Millie had handed him the mic. She looked relieved to pass it along.

"Fun N Games," he said, "how many are on board the Bayliner?"

"Two, far as I can tell." There was a brief pause as the man unkeyed his mic, then came back on. "Yeah, my wife says there's two. A tall skinnier one, and a shorter, stalkier type. The short one's got the rifle."

Guns on boats were not unusual in Alaska. Many hunters took boats to remote hunting grounds, and halibut anglers often used handguns to kill the big fish when they pull them up alongside the boat. A hunter would have a rifle for when he got on shore for hunting, but a sport fisherman would never use a rifle to shoot a halibut; the long barrel would make it almost impossible. A handgun was the thing. But the fact that the Fun N Games said the other boat had a rifle out was troubling. There could be no reason Wayne could think of for a rifle being out on the open Gulf, except for no good.

Millie was studying Wayne's face. They'd been working together for over 15 years, since Wayne had been hired out of the Seattle Harbor Police. Millie had been the Yakutat Police and Fire day dispatcher for 25 years. She knew Wayne well, and could easily recognize concern in his eyes and brow.

"What are you thinking, Wayne," she asked, her voice revealing her own concern.

"This ain't right," he said. "Something's very wrong out there. I may need to get underway."

"Seas are supposed to pick up," Millie cautioned. "Want me to call Jake in to go with you?"

Wayne shook his head.

"No. No time." He turned a stern eye on her. "Something's really wrong out there, and I suspect it's about to get worse."

He'd gone to the gun locker then while Millie kept talking to the Fun N Games, getting the play-by-play on what the Bayliner and her two crew were up to. He had donned his bullet-proof vest, pulling his Police jacket over it, and palmed the Glock on his hip, reassuring himself that it was there. He then pulled the Yakutat Police ball cap over his balding head and strode quickly to the door. He paused and grabbed the keys to the boat from the hook behind the service counter before passing through the door, Millie's voice and the VHF radio echoing in the large room as he had left.

He had the boat underway in less than three minutes. He had barely passed the breakwater when Millie called him on the Police VHF frequency. Wayne reached to the radio mic above his head, and pulled it to his mouth.

"Yeah, Millie, what's new?"

"Well, Wayne, I've lost contact with the Fun N Games. I've tried hailing him a few times now, but there's no answer."

Wayne had let his body sink back against the backrest, thinking.

"What was the last thing you heard?"

"The short guy was still on the back of the Bayliner with the rifle. He appeared to be trying to get a good look at the Fun N Games. Or," she said, her voice turning lower, "where the people on board were."

"And that was the last?"

"Yep," Millie said, a finality in her tone.

"Okay, Millie. Thanks."

"Wayne, I called Jake. He'll be in within 15 minutes."

"I can't wait for him, Millie. Something's haywire out there, and I aim to get on scene ASAP."

There was a pause.

"Okay, Wayne," came Millie's gravely, even voice. "Please be careful, Wayne. I'll call the Coast Guard."

"Roger, Millie. Good move on calling the Coasties."

"Call me every 5 minutes, Wayne." Millie rarely took a commanding tone with him, but now was one of those moments.

"Roger, wilco," he returned.

Millie was putting him on what the Coast Guard called a radio guard, where he would report his position at the appointed times, and she would track him on the charts.

Wayne sat straight again and pushed the twin throttles forward. Instantly, the props on the massive twin Honda outboards bit at the sea, churning white froth out the stern and lunging the aluminum boat forward at a startling speed. He set his eyes on the magnetic compass on the dash as his left hand reached for the GPS, resetting the screen to punch in coordinates.

Knowing his tendency to get too caught up in the details of the GPS and radar, he glanced out the windshield to make sure nothing was in his course. The boat was screaming along at close to 45 knots now, the hull coming completely out of the water as it hurtled over the swells, then slamming back into the cross-chop and careening crazily from side-to-side as the hull sought its keel track.

Jake would be proud, Wayne thought. He was always criticizing Wayne for getting too caught up in the equipment and not paying enough attention to the "real seas in front of you." Wayne smiled at the irritation in his partner. But now Wayne was watching the seas and leaving the GPS and radar alone. Normally, he'd be programming in waypoints, trajectories of the last known position of the Fun N Games, and plotting a course to steer to get there. But he was just steering the boat now, admiring how the vessel barreled over the seas.

That was another thing Jake criticized: Wayne's joy in running the boat fast over rough seas. It was dangerous, Jake claimed. Nonsense, Wayne would retort. They make boats for this nowadays.

Wayne adjusted the radar screen to a six-mile distance, hoping to pick up the blips of the Fun N Games and the Bayliner. Nothing. Just sea static as the radar picked up the face of the oncoming swells. He got curious about the distance to the Fun N Games, and looked into the GPS screen. He gauged the distance to the Fun N Games---

The deck beneath his feet lurched, buckling his knees and spinning him to the right. The deck shifted as the boat hit another wave in the cross-chop and pitched upward, forcing his body down toward the dash. His right hand slid off the helm and into its spokes as the wave gripped the boat and turned it hard to port. The sea's force now caught hold of the outboards and forced them to the left, causing the helm to spin to port. The spokes tore at his wrist and pulled his hand with it in its fast spin.

"Ahhh!" he screamed with pain as he pulled his body back, trying to free his hand.

The spokes beat his fingers as his hand passed out of the helm's center, breaking the middle and pinky fingers.

"Ahhhh! Aaahhh!" he screamed again. "Fuck! . . . Fuck fuck fuck!!!!"

He was on his knees now, gaping at his twisted fingers. He touched them, confirming they were broken. Bone protruded from the pinky, the finger that bore the brunt of the helm's spokes.

He got his left foot under him and started to stand. Looking out, he could see the boat had gone completely off course, and was now running between the waves. The starboard side dropped as the boat crested each wave, and seemingly slid sideways down the backside of the wave. He looked out the starboard window and saw the next wave bearing down on the small boat.

It looked like an angry grey mountain, crashing down on a nuisance ant.

Wayne grabbed the helm with his left hand and spun it to starboard, into the wave. The boat began to turn to take the wave from the bow, but it was too late. The wave threw the boat sideways, tipping it dangerously to the left. Wayne toppled and rolled against the port bulkhead, hitting his head hard on the aluminum cabin wall.

He must have lost consciousness for a moment. It seemed that time had skipped a chunk, and jumped him ahead to a moment of realizing he'd been lying flat. He struggled to his feet as the boat slid easily down the back side of the wave. He gripped the helm and forced it to the right, his right hand screaming pain as he held tightly onto a grip on the starboard bulkhead.

He sat in the seat, trying to collect his thoughts.

Millie's voice on the radio pulled him to a more lucid reality.

"Yeah, Millie. I'm all right."

"You missed your call-in," she said, worry in her voice.

"I'm all right. Just took a nasty roll." He touched his temple with his right index finger and pulled it away, blood on his finger. "Any more contact?"

"No," she said. "You should be about there," she added.

Wayne looked at the radar screen and saw two contacts, a half mile ahead. The Bayliner was alongside the larger cabin cruiser, the Fun N Games. He could see a figure moving from the interior of the Fun N Games to its aft deck. There was another figure on the Bayliner, a taller man. The shorter, stalky man on the Fun N Games appeared to be handing something over.

Food. It was food. Boxes and canisters. And cases of beer.

"Jesus," Wayne muttered. "Is this about a fucking robbery?"

He reached down to the dash and flipped on the blue light bar above the cabin of the Harbor Police boat, then flipped on the siren as well. Instantly, both men's heads turned toward him.

"Millie," he said into the radio. "It looks like a robbery. Two men passing food and beer from the Fun N Games to the Bayliner."

"Does the Bayliner have a name?"

Wayne reached for the binoculars and placed them against his eyes.

"I can't see from this angle," he said into the mic.

Now he could see the men clearly as they scrambled. The taller one looked older. He ditched into the cabin of the Bayliner, presumably to get it ready to make a run for it. The other man, surprisingly, had turned again to the cabin, out of view.

Now Wayne could see the couple sitting low on the aft deck, probably on a bench or chaise below the gunwales. They appeared alive and okay. Probably tied up, or at least ordered to sit still.

The short man appeared again, a handgun drawn. He said something to the couple, and the man got up and led the short man into the cabin. A moment later, they reappeared, the older man first. The short man had something in his hand. A pouch. A money pouch.

He then raised the gun and aimed it at the old man. The gun kicked and the man dropped out of sight. Wayne could see the woman screaming hysterically in response as she got up to approach her downed husband. The handgun kicked again, and the woman dropped out of sight.

"Millie, one of these guys just shot both the Fun N Games' owners."

"What?" she replied immediately. "Did I hear you right? He shot them? As in, just now? You saw it?"

"Yes, just now, and I watched it. I'm approaching them now."

He was intent on the tethered vessels as the short man jumped the gunwales back into the Bayliner. He quickly unwound the line securing the boats together, and shouted at the taller man inside. Slowly, the Bayliner spit out white water and separated from the Fun N Games.

Wayne had no choice. Much as he wanted to pursue the Bayliner, he needed to see to the downed couple.

"Millie, the Bayliner's cast off the Fun N Games and is getting underway. I'm going to board the Fun N Games and ascertain the condition of the owners."

"Roger," Millie replied. "I'm calling the Coast Guard and the State Troopers."

"Roger. I will report back to you within three minutes."

The Bayliner was 50 yards away and gaining speed to the west as Wayne came alongside the Fun N Games and cut his engines to neutral. He ran the three steps back to the aft deck and grabbed the beam line and wrapped it around a cleat on the gunwale of the Fun N Games. Without hesitation, he jumped aboard and dropped onto the aft deck of the Fun N Games.

The couple were lying side-by-side, pools of blood gathering together and already sloshing on the deck in the pitching seas. Each, lying face down, had a dark hole in the center of the head. No doubt they were dead, but he quickly checked for pulses anyway. Feeling nothing, he jumped back aboard the Harbor Police boat, cast off, and ran to the helm, throwing the throttles forward as the light boat jumped forward and quickly gained speed.

As he steered toward the receding transom of the Bayliner, he picked up the binoculars and checked for a name on the stern.

"Millie, the Fun N Games folks are dead. I'm in pursuit of the Bayliner. It's medium length, a little more than 30 feet, maybe 35 feet. Blue hull and white superstructure. No name or homeport on the back. I can't see any registration numbers." These would be on both sides of the bow, well out of sight from where he was.

"Copied," Millie replied.

"I'm gaining quickly. I should be able to intercept," he added.

It occurred to him he didn't know exactly how to intercept a larger, heavier boat by himself. He might be able to fire off shots at them, but to what purpose? Maybe it'd be better to back off and hold in pursuit, and wait for backup. He radioed to Millie his intentions to follow the boat and update his position until backup could arrive, most likely from the Coast Guard.

He pulled back on the throttle, and with the radar, ensured an even distance of 200 yards.

"This should be plenty safe in these seas," he muttered to himself. "Nobody I know could shoot with any accuracy at that distance."

He maintained his distance behind the Bayliner for a quarter hour before the Bayliner altered course. At first, she seemed to simply be making an adjustment. But then she cut sharply to starboard, coming around fast. Wayne lifted the binoculars to see if a closer look would give him any clues. He trained them on the Bayliner as she showed her starboard beam to him, and could see the shorter man had a rifle in his hands.

Wayne was considering what they might be up to as the Bayliner continued to turn starboard.

"What the--?" Wayne muttered.

The Bayliner seemed to be turning around. They couldn't be thinking of turning themselves over, could they? He shook his head. No way. Not after what they'd just done.

He pulled the binoculars to his eyes again and peered to see if he could spot the men and what they were up to. He could see the tall man at the helm, but he'd lost track of the short man. The two vessels were steering almost straight at each other. Vaguely, Wayne realized he'd missed his chance to get the registration numbers off the bow and radio them in.

Just as he tried to read them now, he detected movement on the flybridge of the Bayliner. He re-trained the binoculars to check on the movement. It was the other man, and he seemed to be leaning low. But in what direction was he facing? It looked like he was facing aft, away from Wayne.

He peered to see what the man was doing as the Bayliner approached. It looked like . . . it looked like he was--- yes, Wayne realized. He *was* facing Wayne. And he had something--- something pointed---

Wayne realized too late that it was the rifle, taking aim on him. He saw a flash, and the windshield shattered in front of him, the glass falling on the dash and helm and floor at his feet. He began to duck as he reached for the Glock, but he seemed to slide into a world of slow motion. His hand moved toward the Glock, but then fell listlessly downward. Wayne felt himself sliding, his ass slipping off the seat. His arms were numb as he continued to slide.

It was then that he realized he couldn't breathe. A gurgly sound emitted from his neck as he tried to draw breath. He reached up with his right hand, the broken fingers no longer throbbing, and touched his neck. It felt like his thorax was gone, a flap-rimmed hole where it should have been. He pulled his hand away. It was covered with blood.

Sliding further, the front of the seat now at the small of his back, he reached for the VHF mic. The white plastic turned red with his touch. He keyed the mic and tried to speak, but only sucking and gurgling emitted.

Jesus, he thought, *how the fuck did that guy hit me from that distance? On pitching seas . . . ?*

Wayne felt tired as his body slumped to the deck. He could hear Millie trying to call him on the VHF. It seemed so distant, like a TV nobody's watching in an adjacent room. He tried to draw breath, but couldn't even expand his lungs. His muscles felt depleted. Utterly spent. He was getting more and more . . . tired. So tired. Tired and numb and now . . . cold. He shivered, and his spirit dropped into a deep dark void.

Carl Elkins stood in disbelief at the helm of the Bayliner as it pitched over the rough Alaskan seas. He had heard the pop of the rifle and then watched the front windshield of the Harbor Patrol boat shatter and drop. The cop had disappeared, probably taking cover.

Carl shook his head.

That crazy fuck, he thought to himself. He hardly knew the guy, but what he did know, he didn't like. At all. Carl had been running shipments for the Seattle drug ring for almost two years now, all done by sea. He would pick up shipments at one or the other shipyard in Puget Sound, then run them up to Alaskan port towns – occasionally Anchorage as well. He was always set up with a pleasure boat, arranged for the purpose of the run. Two or three times, he was on the same boat. It all depended on whether the feds were onto The Ring or not.

Usually he made these runs by himself. He had been an experienced 1st mate on sea-going tugs who killed his company career with beer and vodka. Increasingly unable to control his consumption, it had become harder and harder to find spots on tugs. His drunken reputation began to precede him everywhere. He'd been approaching rock bottom when The Ring offered him a dream job, running shipments from Seattle to Southeast Alaska and Southcentral Alaska. It allowed him to be on the sea, alone with his alcohol, his boat and food all paid for.

This time, though, he'd been told Norm Peck was going to ride with him. For what purpose, Carl had no idea. The guy was useless at everything except barking orders and killing people. It didn't just make Carl nervous, it scared the be-jesus out of him. This was way out of his league, whatever was going on. But there was nothing he could do. Just keep on captaining, not crossing the crazy ass nor balking at his orders. His primary hope was that he would come out alive on the other end.

"Come along side him now," Peck said as he re-entered the cabin from the flybridge.

"What?" Carl asked, incredulous. "That's a cop, Norm—"

"Peck," the stocky man said irritably. "Fucking Peck. I've told you a hundred times. Call me Peck."

"Okay, okay. Sorry. But that's a cop, Peck. He's trained with a gun. These other people were just old people. Defenseless duckees in a shooting gallery. But what we want in coming up all bold on a cop?"

"He's dead."

Carl blinked. "What?"

"He's dead. I picked him off." The man suddenly became elated.

Carl looked at him.

"Fucking-A," Peck went on, his voice rising to match the grin on his face. "I picked him off from 200 yards in rough seas! In rough fucking seas!"

The man was genuinely happy and excited. It seemed he had no understanding that he'd just taken a life. His excitement had the innocence of an 8-year-old boy being told he was going to Disneyland.

Carl shook his head and kept his mouth shut. If he said anything that sounded to Norm—er, Peck that sounded like a judgment . . .

He's fucking loony, Carl thought.

But he revealed nothing of his thoughts. He held a steady line for the Harbor Police boat. He noticed that its outboards were now idle, allowing the vessel to drift with the seas. That would make it tougher to come alongside, but well within the ability of a former tugboat operator.

"You sure he's dead?" he ventured.

Peck stepped forward and planted his feet against the pitching deck, squarely facing Carl. Carl could feel the man's eyes boring into the side of his head. Peck held the icy gaze to drive home his point.

Finally, Carl nodded acknowledgement.

The tension eased as quickly as it had come on.

"Can you believe that shot?" Peck asked.

"No," Carl said drily. "Pretty amazing."

Inside, a nervous coldness gripped his heart as he drew a deep breath to calm himself.

Skipper's Oath

Chapter One

Frontier Angst

Frank Mattituck's past often sneaked up behind him at the bar like an unwanted conversation, at first whispering in his ear imperceptibly until it had his subconscious ear, then permeating this thoughts to nearly complete dominance. It had nothing to do with sitting in a bar—in fact, it was far worse if he were sitting at home watching a baseball game, or running his boat, the DeeVee8, to the Gulf on a fishing charter. The latter frequently happened, as it was a lonely time of routine. His clients would be talking excitedly on the way out in the morning, and sleeping on the way back in after maxing out on halibut, Pacific Cod, and the occasional ling cod or yellow-eyed rockfish.

But this time, it happened when he was sitting in The Crow's Nest, sipping a Guinness. He hated drinking alone because when the hauntings did occur, they came while he was at the bar alone. Like the running time on charters, it was a time of being completely alone in the midst of buzzing voices and laughter all around. Mattituck sometimes wondered if it were that contrast that triggered the hauntings. Like his life, it was a density of joy and activity surrounding a tiny, insignificant void in the middle. The contrast accentuated the existence of the void.

A hand clapped him on the back, breaking him from his despondent musings.

"Frank! How the hell're things?"

Mattituck smiled as he turned to see Jim Milner beaming his bright white incisors. The whiteness of his teeth and beard always surprised Mattituck, due to the sharp contrast with his deep tanned face.

Another contrast. This one not as sharp as Mattituck's emotional one.

"Good, good," Mattituck smiled back.

Jim slid onto the stool next to Mattituck and signaled to the bar tender.

"Day off?" Jim asked.

"Nope. Just back early. Clients only wanted halibut and maxed out early."

"What about the sea lions?" Jim asked, knowing that whenever Mattituck maxed his clients early, he would swing them by the sea lion colony on Glacier Island or other sightseeing ventures. It was one of the many things that made him stand out from other charter boats.

Another contrast that set Mattituck apart.

"Weren't really interested. They wanted to get back here and celebrate. They're sitting right back there," he added, gesturing toward a particularly loud table of six men with heavy southern accents.

Jim resisted the urge to count the number of empty Budweiser bottles on the table. At least they had enough class to drink the long neck bottles.

The group was clearly drunk, and Jim could hear they were telling stories of their day on the water to the people at the table next to them.

"Wait . . ." one of the people at the next table said back, "which charter boat was this on?"

Jim recognized Toby Burns, the supposed up-and-comer on the Valdez charter boat scene. Rumor was the young man had been set-up by his banker dad from Michigan to pursue his dream of being a charter boat captain.

"Sound Esh---er, Sound Eshperinch . . . Uhh . . ." the man's glossy eyes fell into silence, then refocused on Mattituck. "Shee-it, he'sh riiight over thear," he added, pointing.

Toby followed the man's finger, and grinned.

"Matty!" he blurted at Mattituck.

Mattituck turned slowly, clearly not in a mood for conversations across a bar room. He nodded to Toby with indifferent courtesy and turned back to his beer.

"Matty!" Toby shouted again, nudging the man sitting next to him. "Finally made some clients happy, eh?"

Mattituck held up his right middle finger without turning around. He stared out the window behind the bar, looking at the boats in the marina below.

"What the fuck, man?" Toby shouted, feigning surprise. "Be friendly with a dickhead, and that's what you get back."

Mattituck raised the jutting finger higher as if raising the silent volume.

The table of southerners had fallen silent, the men unsure of whether these were locals giving each other a hard time, or if what they were watching was serious.

Toby got up and approached the bar.

"C'mon, Matty," he said, hands stretched out to the sides. "It's all in good fun."

Still Mattituck stared at the boats in the harbor.

"Not in the mood, I guess, Toby."

Toby reached forward and gripped Mattituck's shoulder.

"Let it go," Jim inserted, a look of warning on his face.

"Fuck you," Toby said.

Mattituck stiffened visibly. He turned and faced Toby, his jaw set under clenched teeth.

Toby flinched for the briefest of seconds under the cold blue glare Mattituck set on him.

"Apologize," Mattituck said flatly.

Toby stared him down, unmoving and silent.

"You need to respect your elders, Toby," Mattituck added.

"Fuck both of you, fucking geezers."

Jim broke into a chuckle, dismissive of any tension.

"Geezers?" he laughed. "Me, maybe, but Frank here's got no more'n ten years on you."

"Looks like a fuckin' geezer to me," Toby replied, "all craggly faced and shit. . ."

Toby Burns was relatively new in Valdez, having come from Michigan two years previously with a flashy 32-foot charter boat, the Halibut Orca, to establish himself in The Last Frontier. He was young, in his upper twenties, and had the ego and hot-temper that often came with youth. And wealth. His father was a successful banker who had decided to invest in an Alaska charter boat company. Run by his son, of course. A spoiled son with a dream.

Mattituck held him in his icy gaze.

"Everybody here's waiting to see what you'll do, Toby," Mattituck said, his voice low and growling. "Respect your superior, or do something stupid." His eyes moved enough to take in Toby's red face. "My money's on something stupid. You just have that look about you," Mattituck said, his face easing to something between angry and bemused.

Laughter erupted around the bar, led by the southerners' drunken high volume.

Toby's eyes slid side-to-side, taking in the laughter at his expense. His face deepened in redness.

Suddenly, his fist shot in a tight, forceful jab. Mattituck saw it and ducked to the left, but was too late. The blow caught him on the ear. Mattituck felt the burning on his ear, and the deep cartilage pain that only comes with blows to the ear. He sprang off the stool toward Toby, but was caught by a burly arm.

"Ain't worth it," Jim said loudly, pulling Mattituck back toward the bar. "He ain't worth it. He's just a fucking greenhorn."

Jim turned to Toby.

"You got your shot in, schoolboy," Jim said. "Now do what's right—sit your ass on that stool right there and buy him a beer. That's the right thing to do."

"What the—" Toby started.

"*That's* the right thing to do," Jim cut him off. "Buy him a beer, and you say you're sorry without saying you're sorry."

Toby looked incredulous.

"You got a thing or two to learn about how we live here in Valdez," Jim said. "We disagree, we argue . . . hell, we may even fight. But in the end, this here's our community, and you're either in it or you ain't. But we don't end with this kinda bullshit." He nodded toward the stool. "Now sit your ass down right there and buy the man a beer."

Toby didn't move.

"Old man, you're as stupid as you look. Next thing, you'll be telling me to suck his dick!"

In Mattituck's mind, the room went to a deafened silence. Time slowed and seemed to stop altogether. The words *suck his dick* echoed through his mind like sound waves among stalactites, trickling lower as they receded in the darkness. His eyes were unfocused for a moment, reverberating in his memory.

Frank Mattituck had been watching a Mariners game, killing time while Janelle was out with her friends. Frank, being more of a loner, didn't care much for kicking around town with friends—not that he had all that many friends. And certainly not the party-types who bounce from night club to night club. Janelle and he had been together over two years now, with a recently sealed full engagement on, and they had long since learned to respect each other's distance. The differences between them didn't affect their love for one another, and Janelle was fond of saying that nothing could tear them apart. Ever.

He loved her. She was fun, caring . . . mindful. He loved her personality, and the way she could be light-hearted, but turn serious when someone was being treated unfairly or was hurt. And she was certainly an amazing-looking woman. He loved her long blonde hair, straight except for an upturn at the ends, reminiscent of the popular style of the 1960s. A retro thing. Janelle always had been into the latest styles, and the money she'd grown up with ensured she would always be drawn to the ways of her upper Bellevue family. Upper middle class, although it felt to Frank that was clearly in the upper class range. Her father owned a shipyard and four freighters, always expanding his shipping line between Seattle and southeast Asia. And the man loved his little princess. In fact, the spoiled attitude in her occasionally irritated Frank, but her smile and warmth always drove that away.

Frank was Janelle's diamond in the rough, her mother always said. He was an outdoorsman, always on adventures—a sharp contrast to her daughter. But their love for each other outweighed all that. Everybody knew it. Even Frank.

His heart lifted when the third baseman drove a gap single to left-center, giving the pinch-runner on second plenty of time to trot in to home. It being the bottom of the 9th, it was a game-ending shot that put the Mariners up, 3-2.

His cell pinged a new message, and he set his beer on the coffee table as he retrieved the phone. His heart lifted again. It was a text message from Janelle. He loved when she texted him while out on the town—it made it clear she was thinking of him, missing him.

He was still smiling as he pressed his thumb to the fingerprint-reader, accessing the message. She had sent him a picture. Probably of her smiling in a bar, surrounded by her BFF's. He tapped her name on the text message screen, and the image opened up.

An intense weight pressed in on his chest. His eyes strained to make out what he was looking at. It was the side of Janelle's face, that much was clear. But the rest was . . .

He shook his head, trying to refocus his unseeing eyes on the TV screen in his living room, then looked down at the image again. Janelle's smooth cheek and jawline. Her eyes closed. Her mouth open. Something was in her mouth. He blinked in disbelief.

A shaft. A skin shaft. The shaft of a penis. Another man's penis.

Frank dropped his phone. Even if it were his cock, there would never be any pictures of it. And this picture had been taken by someone else. No way to take a selfie of that.

He couldn't believe—didn't know what to— he turned the phone and tapped the typing screen.

"???" he sent.

What the hell could this be? Some joke? What the fuck kind of joke—

His phone pinged. Another image. Janelle's mouth was farther out the man's cock, the sharp rim of the head of his dick just appearing at the corner of Janelle's mouth.

"Jesus . . ." Frank whispered.

Janelle's eyes were half-open in this shot, a look of near ecstasy on her face.

Ping. Another image.

This one showed her kissing the tip of the dick, the mushroom end glistening in the dim light where the pictures were being taken.

Frank's phone hit the carpet by his feet. What--? He didn't know what to think. His mind reeled. Were these old images? It couldn't be that—

His thoughts stopped there.

No. It was pretty clear these were real-time shots, and whoever's dick was in Janelle's mouth—right at this very moment—was the guy sending the pics. Someone who knew Frank was her boyfriend. Which meant this was probably not the first time she'd sucked his dick. Not that it mattered. Once was enough.

Mattituck's eyes refocused on Toby Burns, the younger man's last words still reverberating in Mattituck's mind. *'Next time,'* Toby had said, *'you'll be telling me to suck his dick.'* The image was poignant and painful, and the image of Janelle flickered like an old movie, strobing in his mind's eye.

Toby gestured at him. "C'mon, fucking geezer. I am *not* buying you a beer, and I am *not* going to suck your dick!"

Mattituck stood upright, coming off the stool. It was a feigned move that caused Toby to believe it was a lazy move, not a fighting move. Inwardly, he relaxed. It was a reaction that multiplied the effect of the blow that came. In one swift move, Mattituck used the momentum of coming off the stool to propel his torso so that his arm shot up in a hard uppercut. The blow cupped Toby's mouth shut, making a loud snap as his teeth came together.

Mattituck wasted no time, his inner rage fueling him. He came at Toby with a left-right-left set of jabs to the chin that added to the backward momentum from the upper cut. Each quick blow snapped Toby's head back, and the younger man's body weight went beyond a retrievable point. He hit the floor hard on his back, knocking the wind out of him.

Mattituck stepped in, hovering over Toby as the downed man struggled onto his stomach, then lifted himself upright. Mattituck held in a slight crouch, waiting for Toby to fully regain his feet.

Jim Milner pulled his shoulder, but Mattituck shrugged him off, intent on Toby. In Mattituck's mind, Toby might as well have been the man with Janelle, as the images had merged in his mind. He made a half lurch forward to regain his position over Toby as the man got his knees under him and began to lift to his feet. Mattituck wanted him full upright before he let loose on the sniveling bastard.

Jim slipped around in front of Mattituck, his face coming into Mattituck's view. The old man's white beard and its sharp contrast with his dark skin grounded Mattituck's mind, and he came into realization of where he was and what he was doing.

"Frank – it's not worth it. Let it go. He's just a greenhorn."

Mattituck's eyes focused on his friends'. The pupils of his older friend drew him, as he saw the firm rationality of him. He was right. Mattituck pushed the images of Janelle from his mind and drew breath.

"You fucking snake!" Toby yelled. "I will sue your fucking ass! I'm pressing charges!"

He turned and strode out of the bar toward the parking lot.

"Hot damn," Jim said. "I'da thought you was going to pound his face in."

Mattituck fell back onto the stool, quiet and still brooding.

"What the hell set you off? I've never seen you that wild-eyed before."

Mattituck looked at him, then turned and grabbed his Guinness. He said nothing until he'd down several gulps.

"I don't know," he said finally. "He just set me off is all."

"I'd say," the bartender said. "I've seen quick jabs before, but damn—that was something. You used to fight or something?"

Mattituck closed his eyes and wiped his forehead. He'd broken out in a sweat.

"He's got him a martial arts background," one of the southerners had said. He was flanked by three of his friends.

"We was about t' come beat his ass," he continued.

"No way we'da stood by for that shee-it," another said, an overweight man with a scraggly beard. "You da man! We gotchyour back, uh-huh."

"Thanks," Mattituck said genuinely.

"C'mon," Jim said. "Let's have us a beer or two on the Kimberly Marie."

Mattituck nodded and turned to pay.

"On me," the bartender said. "Both of you. You for good fighting," he said to Mattituck, "and you for stopping the fighting," he said to Jim.

Todd Benson sat across the counter of the Valdez Law Enforcement Center, listening to Toby's complaint. He shook his head.

"What?" Toby said, surprise in his voice. "Aren't you going to arrest him?"

Todd shook his head again. He was the sole Alaska State Trooper in Valdez, and was assigned to Fish and Wildlife on Prince William Sound, the body of water between Valdez and the Gulf of Alaska, 80 miles to the south. He operated with an office adjacent to the Valdez Police Department, and shared the dispatcher and front counter with them. Today was his turn for counter duty.

"Listen," he said to Toby. "Don't be an idiot. I know Frank Mattituck very well, and if you got your ass beat by him, you probably deserved it."

Toby started to protest, but Todd cut him off.

"Did you throw the first punch?"

"Hell no . . ." Toby said, losing resolve under Trooper Benson's eyes.

"Don't give me any bull, Mr. Burns. Mattituck never throws the first punch. Never." He had known Frank Mattituck since he'd been assigned to Valdez. As the Fish & Wildlife Officer, you get to know all the charter boat captains pretty well. Frank was consistent in catches and never broke the law. To a fault. And the word was that Frank's charters were the best for families. He engaged the kids and made everybody feel comfortable. In Todd Benson's mind, that spoke to the character of the man.

He went on, looking Toby Burns straight in the eye.

"I bet if I go down to The Crow's Nest and talk to witnesses, I'll find that trend of never throwing the first punch is still true of Frank Mattituck."

Toby visibly caved.

Frank Mattituck was as good a guy as Todd had known. A bit misunderstood at times, and maybe a bit rough around the edges at times, but definitely a stand-up guy. Over the years as a Frontier law enforcement agent, Trooper Benson had utmost confidence in his ability to read people. Frank could be trusted. Toby Burns, on the other hand, was a rich little hothead from Michigan who thought he could storm onto the great Alaskan outdoors and conquer it. And its people along with it.

"My advice to you," Todd said, "is that you speed up your learning how to get along in this town. This is not the Lower 48, and people live by the rules of this land. You want to survive here, you'd better learn the ways of the land."

"And those are?"

"That we cover each other's backsides, and don't pick unnecessary fights with our fellow locals."

"Some say Mattituck's an asshole. Don't sound like he lives up to your rules," Toby said, regaining his confidence.

"Don't believe everything you hear. And never assume that what you see on the outside is what's in a person. Especially up here," Todd concluded. "Now, about your visit here today . . . I can't tell you not to file a complaint or press charges. That's up to you."

He held Toby's gaze, unmoving.

Several moments passed.

"I won't press," Toby said finally.

"Good. Now I'm sure you have charters lined up in the morning and have no time for nonsense." Todd got up from his seat and started for his office. "See you on the water," he said without turning around.

Fuck, Toby thought, realizing that the rumor of friendship between Trooper Benson and Frank Mattituck was clearly true. *Guess I can expect more boardings now.*

Skipper's Oath

Chapter Two

An Unfortunate Meeting

The Kimberly Marie was a proud 72 foot cabin cruiser that Jim Milner had been chartering since his wife had died in 1991. Not much of a fisherman, Jim had opted for what at the time was a new kind of charter— almost a scaled-down private cruise boat.

On this late June Tuesday, Jim cast off from his slip in the Valdez Harbor as he thought about the contrast with his friend, Frank Mattituck. Frank was the best Jim had ever known at the fishing charters. He admired the younger man, and saw much of himself in him. As the Kimberly Marie drifted from the dock, her motors humming below deck, his mind wandered back to the evening before, after the fight between Frank and Toby Burns.

He and Frank had come back to the Kimberly Marie and claimed chairs on the big cruiser's aft deck. Jim had grabbed four Killian's Reds from the galley fridge and joined Frank as he settled back and gazed at the evening sun shining on Sugarloaf Mountain.

"No Guinness," Jim said, setting two of the Killian's in front of his friend. "Hope Killian's is okay."

Frank smiled and reached for the nearest bottle.

"Thanks for being there, Jim," he said.

"Aww," Jim guffawed. "You handled yourself just fine."

"Just this side of jail," Mattituck corrected. "If you hadn't been there, I might well be in jail right now."

Several minutes passed as both men quickly emptied their bottles.

"You were wondering what set me off," Mattituck said unexpectedly. Jim had always known him to be a very private man.

"Only if it's something you want to share," Jim replied.

Mattituck seemed lost in his thoughts. Then he told Jim about his engagement four years previously. He told Jim how he and Janelle had met years before, prior to his moving to Valdez. He told Jim how he had pursued his dream up here, and after a six-month breakup, they'd gotten back together and he wintered with her in a swank downtown Seattle condo that overlooked the waterfront. He told about how she was going to move up to Valdez to be with him in the spring when he returned to get the charter company up and running for the season.

"Said she couldn't be without me," Mattituck said. "That's how she put it. She had found in our break-up that I was the only one for her."

"So what happened?" Jim asked, careful not to pry too much.

"We'd been back together for about two months," Mattituck began, then paused to take a few sips from the Killian's.

Mattituck then told him about the night he had been watching a Mariners game in their condo while she was supposedly out with friends on a girl's night. He told

Jim how the Mariners had won in a come-back 9th inning, and how he was feeling on top of the world. Janelle's text had come right then, right when he'd felt the world was a wonderful place. Nothing could go wrong. Then he told Jim about the pictures sent by her old high school sweetheart, of her sucking his dick. Sent from her phone.

Jim was stunned. He listened intently, feeling the pain this must have caused his friend. Frank fell silent.

"How do you know it was her high school sweetheart?" he finally asked.

Frank took two deep gulps off his next Killian's and set the bottle carefully on the table between them.

"She tried to text later that night to tell me how much she missed me. I'm guessing the bastard erased the pictures as soon as he sent them. He must have taken them without her knowing—the pictures were in semi-darkness and her eyes were mostly closed, except the last one where her eyes—" he broke off and drew breath— "they were half-closed, like she was . . . really enjoying it."

He was quiet a moment, and Jim waited.

"Point being," Mattituck continued, "she obviously had no idea he was taking pictures. With her phone."

Jim waited a moment, then asked, "So she didn't know about the pics later when she tried to text you."

"Right."

"What did you do?"

"I sent her the pics. No words. Just the pics." He stared off at Sugarloaf and downed the rest of the bottle, then got up and headed to the galley. He came back with four more Killian's. "Okay if we have more?" he asked Jim.

"You know better'n to ask that," Jim replied.

Mattituck sat down and twisted the cap off, then took two deep drags off the sweaty bottle.

"I did sent her some words after she tried to call several times. She finally texted '*Frank, I'm so sorry. It was just a one-time thing. We were drunk, and I bumped into my old high school boyfriend . . .*' or some such shit to that effect."

"And you answered with words then?"

"Yep. One short message: *This is what happens when you lose track of your phone. Goodbye.*"

Jim had to suppress a laugh. Even in a moment like that, Frank's sharp wit shined through.

Now, the next morning, as Jim ran the Kimberly Marie through the harbor entrance, he grinned at Frank's retort to Janelle. He was indeed a complex man, that Frank Mattituck. The grin faded as he entered again, through his friend's memory, that fateful night in Seattle. He felt the pain of such a situation. He'd never experienced pain like that with his Louise. Of course, her death had devastated him, but in her death as well as her life, she had been faithful and dedicated. He couldn't imagine what it had felt like to get those pictures.

As he cleared the jetty, Jim nosed the Kimberly Marie toward Entrance Island, thinking he might stop off in Growler Bay, Glacier Island, to pay respects to his beloved Louise. Growler Bay had been the site of their first overnight on the Kimberly Marie, less than a year after they'd married, and where she had always asked that he spread her ashes, should she be the first to go. She had been the first to go, and so he had. Neither of them could ever have guessed she would have contracted breast cancer and cut their wonderful life together so short.

Jim had never remarried. He'd never even been interested in another relationship. Like mallards, he and Louise were the only possible partners for each other.

With his life plans with Louise in remnants, only the love he had for this land—for Prince William Sound—remained alive. There was nothing else he wanted, so he started the charter cruise business. It had grown quickly, largely because his passion for what he showed his clients was contagious. Soon he could afford a crew, and he had taken on a cook for most runs, and always had a single deckhand as well, mostly to help with the lines, even though the cabin cruiser was a slow motor yacht that was easily run by a single person. Jim, however, preferred not only to have the help, but also the added the safety for his clients of having another person aboard who could get the large boat safely to port should something happen to him.

Over the years, word had got around about Jim's cruises, and he'd built up a loyal clientele who readily told friends about their experience aboard the Kimberly Marie. The vessel had four large, comfortable cabins, each with its own head. He could accommodate three clients—couples or singles—or a family without anybody feeling on top of one another. His tours now even attracted some Hollywood personalities who had heard about Jim Milner and his rustic voyages, and who enjoyed the ability to 'get away from it all.' And without cameras or other tourists invading their respites, Jim's charters had built a solid reputation. For well over a decade now, he had been booking charters one to two years in advance.

But when he had a few days between charters, he often took a solo voyage with the Kimberly Marie and explored new possible land stops, or visited old favorites just to enjoy them again. He enjoyed the solitude of those trips, thinking always of Louise and what could have been. More than that, he thought of what was, and what they had shared. And missed her.

After he cleared the jetty by a quarter mile, he set the auto-pilot and stepped off the flying bridge to regain the helm in the main cabin below, smiling as the vessel plodded along at twelve knots toward Valdez Arm. Once he was sure the auto-pilot would hold the course steady, he remained below deck to enjoy the morning ride in the warmth of the cabin. While she would likely drift off course with the current, he knew the auto-pilot would correct as needed to keep the heavy vessel bearing on Entrance Island. He would have plenty of time to drop into the galley and grab a cup of coffee.

At the Kimberly Marie's slower cruising speed, it took an hour to pass Entrance Island and cross into Valdez Arm, the narrow passage at the southern end of which the ill-fated Exxon Valdez had run aground on Bligh Reef, straight across the Arm from where Louise's ashes had been spread over calm, serene Growler Bay. It took another two hours to enter Columbia Bay, the tall jutting peaks of Glacier Island on the left and famous Columbia Glacier far up the inlet to the right. The massive glacier had receded several miles just in Jim's tenure on the waters here, a sad marking of time that seemed significantly accelerated from the receding rate prior to Louise's passing. All the hub-bub of climate change and global warming was, to Jim's thinking, ridiculous. Anybody who could watch what he'd watched would give no argument in the glaring evidence of Columbia Glacier's retreat.

Jim took a deep gulp of the fresh mid-morning air, and turned the helm to steer the Kimberly Marie into Growler Bay. The blunt bow of the wide-beamed cruiser sliced the serene waters with only a whisper from the saline waters as they parted to allow the vessel to pass through, her twin diesels humming exhaust out the stern. Jim let the peace wash over him as he drank down the last of the pot of coffee he'd consumed since leaving Valdez three and a half hours earlier. He eased back the throttle to five knots and locked the helm on course, then made his way forward to ready the anchor.

Anchoring the day and maybe the night with Louise's ashes and memories suited Jim just fine.

As he came abeam of the point of land jutting into the middle of the bay, he noted a mid-sized Bayliner halfway up the gravelly beach to the starboard. The Kimberly Marie purred quietly, but with enough sound in the tranquil air to capture the attention of the two men inside the Bayliner. Upon emerging and seeing the Kimberly Marie, they began waving their arms wildly.

They were in trouble, Jim could see. In these parts, one always came to the aid of a person in trouble.

Jim turned the helm to point the Kimberly Marie toward the Bayliner. He could see now the vessel was hard aground, high enough that it looked like they must have run it up the shore intentionally, and at a high speed. He quickly came astern the vessel some two hundred feet before Jim brought her up and dropped anchor. He would not chance running the Kimberly Marie aground, nor get her too close to rocks. He would launch the dinghy and see how he might help these folks. He could see that the Bayliner had been run a good distance up the beach and was listing heavily to her starboard side. They must have been taking on water and had run her up the beach to save her and themselves.

Jim didn't bother to mount the nine-horse kicker he usually used on the dinghy after putting it in the water. With such a short distance, he opted to row ashore and rowed toward the Bayliner. The two men jumped off the Bayliner onto the beach and sat on rocks on the beach, awaiting Jim's arrival. He rowed evenly in the quiet of the approaching noon sun, reaching shore to the two men wading out into the water to assist him.

"Thank god," the older of them hollered as Jim's dinghy approached. "We've been here five days."

The other man, quite a number of years younger as well as shorter, remained silent, allowing the elder to do all the talking. From Jim's guess, they might be father and son.

"Lucky for you I come to this bay now and again," Jim replied. "The strait out there sees a lot of traffic, on account of the glacier, but not many venture into these inlets."

"We wouldn't have either if it hadn't been for our boat springing a leak," the elder man said.

Jim looked the shorter man over. He was of a stocky, muscular build, like one of those gym people. He had a military-style haircut, although it was growing out, but what caught Jim's attention was his eyes. There was a hunger there, or anger. Not all that unusual in Alaska, but the man had a tenseness about him that made Jim feel uneasy. The sharp scar along the man's jawline added to the uneasiness Jim felt.

"Did you hit a rock or something?" Jim asked across the water as he stowed the oars along the gunwales and let the momentum take him the remaining distance.

The two stranded men looked at each other.

"Uh, yeah," the younger man said. "We hit a rock, I guess."

"Or a dead-head," the older man said.

Jim sensed something and looked back at the elder, just as the man caught hold of the forward line on the dinghy and began to pull it in to shore. The younger man was on the opposite side of the bow, his right hand behind him as the dinghy slid abreast of him.

"Hey, what goes on here?" Jim asked, suspicion rising.

The younger man stepped forward and swung a wrench up and over toward Jim. Jim ducked to the left, but the hard steel made contact, glancing off his temple and hitting hard on his shoulder. Jim's 68-year-old frame dropped to the bottom of the dinghy and he struggled to get back up on all fours, his head reeling. He turned toward the younger man just in time to see the wrench falling fast toward him again, then all went black.

Frank Mattituck turned the 36-foot aluminum DeeVee8 northwest toward Hinchinbrook Entrance, some 80 nautical miles south of Valdez. It had been a great day on the Gulf, with all six clients maxing out on halibut and three of them landing some very nice ling cod to boot. The smallest of the halibut was 85 pounds, and the largest just under 180 pounds. None of the clients were derby ticket holders, so none were concerned about not having the largest halibut thus far on the season. Four of the clients were Fairbanks people, a customer-base that was far more interested in the quality of the meat than the size of the fish. The best eating halibut were in the forty- to sixty-pound range. Although they had said at the outset that they wanted "chickens," the Alaska knick-name for the less-than-sixty pound halibut, he smiled that none were complaining at the larger fish they'd reeled in on this fine, sunny day.

Mattituck's fishing charter business, Sound Experience Charters, had drawn a loyal clientele among Alaskans due to his unusual philosophy of chartering. Most charter boat captains took the attitude that they knew what was best for their clients, running them through rough seas deep into the Gulf of Alaska in pursuit of the large, derby-winning halibut. Mattituck, on the other hand, prided himself on delivering for his clients precisely what they wanted. He offered two types of halibut charters: the "Gulf Experience" for the derby-ticket types seeking the big fish, or the "Sound Experience" for those who sought the best-eating fish. The choice was always appreciated by clients, and the fact that he cared about them having a good time resonated well with novice anglers.

In less than six seasons of operation, his Sound Experience Charters had gained an excellent reputation, particularly among the Fairbanks crowd. He had grown the company from one boat, the Knot Skunked, to a two-boat operation within three years—a clear sign that Mattituck's philosophy rang well with the clientele he'd tapped into. Additionally, he'd become known as the most family-friendly charter out of Valdez, and so the Knot Skunked and the DeeVee8 enjoyed a high number of kid-laden trips, often seeing dual-families and single-families booking the entire boat.

Now, as the DeeVee8 passed Hinchinbrook Lighthouse, sleek and defiant against the often-unforgiving Alaskan seas, Mattituck felt the vessel begin to rise with the high, distant-spaced swells of the open ocean compressed into a narrow passage. The DeeVee8 slowly rose ten feet, then gently dropped again only to rise slowly once again as she barreled along at a clip of 34 knots, her comfortable cruising speed.

Mattituck's crewman, Ernie, kept the clients happily stocked with coffee, tea, soda, or water. Or any alcoholic beverage they themselves had brought on board. He also made sure there were plenty of snacks available for the long ride home. The Gulf-to-Valdez run typically took three hours each way, even with DeeVee8's good speed.

"How about seeing some sea lions on the way home?" Mattituck asked. "We maxed early, so we have time." The two families he had on board today quickly agreed.

Mattituck noticed a sizeable cabin cruiser southbound as the DeeVee8 neared the north exit from the Entrance, just north of Zaikof Bay. The vessel was moving slowly, perhaps entering the bay. Not many cabin cruisers that size, Mattituck thought, and he wondered if Jim Milner was taking clients out to Montague Island. He normally didn't venture this far south, as the ride for his clients could be rough, and with less scenery, but he did venture to Montague for deer hunters.

Mattituck reached for the mic on the VHF radio mounted on the headboard above the windshield.

"Kimberly Marie, Kimberly Marie, this is the DeeVee8, channel one-six."

He waited for his friend to respond on the hailing and distress channel. After a few moments, he tried again.

"Kimberly Marie, Kimberly Marie . . . DeeVee8, channel one-six, over."

No reply.

He pulled the binoculars from their case on the dash, and trained them on the vessel. That was her, all right. He knew the Kimberly Marie's superstructure very well.

VHF radio reception could be funny, though, and it was not uncommon for a captain to be paying more attention to his clients than the radio, so Mattituck let several minutes pass by. The massive cruise ship that had entered the Entrance ahead of him now lay to the port quarter, a good three miles away. The Kimberly Marie was past the DeeVee8's port beam.

"Kimberly Marie, Kimberly Marie, this is the DeeVee8, DeeVee8. Come in, Jim," he added.

No answer.

Ah, well, Mattituck thought. Jim was maybe getting hard of hearing. He smiled at the thought of the old mariner. Many times, Mattituck ribbed the white-haired salty captain for pushing himself well beyond retirement age.

"What the hell else am I going to do?" Jim would quip back. "Got no woman, got not grandkids – or kids for that matter. All there is to do is show people this amazing Sound."

Mattituck watched the Kimberly Marie as she slipped in the distance along the port side, more than three miles away. He could now tell by her angle that she was indeed headed into Zaikof Bay. He really wanted to talk to Jim, and would have tried to call by cell phone, but this far south in the Sound, the cell coverage was spotty at best. He called Ernie, his crewman, for a cup of coffee and set a course on the GPS for Bull Head on Glacier Island to show his clients the three-hundred-strong colony of sea lions that always gathered there.

Todd Benson, the lone Alaska State Trooper assigned to Prince William Sound, had noted the DeeVee8's call to the Kimberly Marie while he was on patrol. So the next day, when the call had come from Anchorage that Jim Milner and the Kimberly Marie had been reported missing, Todd immediately decided to check with Frank Mattituck as his best lead.

As always, Mattituck was on a charter. For at least the past two years, Todd knew Mattituck to be running charters almost seven days a week throughout the peak fishing months. And that was just on the DeeVee8. The guy had expanded to two boats now, and was running both full-time. As Trooper Benson understood it, Mattituck had no family other than a sister and a nephew in Anchorage. He lived alone in a nice ranch-style house in the Robe River subdivision, six miles out of Valdez. Normally, contacting a busy charter boat captain would be difficult, but Todd knew Mattituck fairly well, as they were acquaintances, and he knew where Mattituck tended to be fishing. For the past couple of seasons, Mattituck's boat was a good contact if for no other reason, the use of the DeeVee8's head . . . something Todd's trooper boat lacked. When Todd's crewman—hired usually from the Valdez kids home from college for summer—was female, he needed to tap into the head-system of friends on the water when the crew needed to use the bathroom. Even with males, including himself, there were times that they needed to use a real head, not merely urinate over the side.

When Todd was unable to reach Mattituck by cell, he tried VHF radio from port. Not getting a response, he decided to get underway and do some fisheries checks, and try to reach the DeeVee8 from the Sound.

He followed the route fishing charters almost always took, cutting through Tatitlek Narrows, across the wide inlet of Port Fidalgo, and through the narrow passage between Knowles Head and Goose Island before crossing Orca Bay to Hinchinbrook Entrance. Beyond that lay the Gulf of Alaska, the promised land of halibut, but a dangerous place for boaters who didn't know what they were doing.

As Todd emerged from the south end of Tatitlek Narrows into Port Fidalgo, he picked up the VHF mic and checked the squelch.

"DeeVee8, DeeVee8, this is the Happy Fitzgerald, do you pick me up?" Todd used the fake name when he was calling those few vessels he used for information, not wanting to attract attention as AST 32067. Everybody tuned in when the State Troopers or the Coast Guard were hailing a vessel.

A minute or two later, the reply came.

"Happy Fitzgerald, DeeVee8. Channel 68, Cap'n?"

"Roger that. Six-eight."

When both were tuned and had established contact, Mattituck asked Todd if he needed the head, a tone of banter in his voice.

"No," Todd replied, crackling over the distance. "Just wanting to follow up on a call you made yesterday. Have you seen Jim?"

Eight miles due west of the state trooper, Mattituck's face was visibly concerned. Normally Todd would use the vessel's name outright, so why Jim's name—and that without the last name. The Todd must be working on something related to Jim.

"Nope, sure haven't," Mattituck replied. "Not in the last few days, anyway. Last I saw him, he looked like he might be headed into Zaikof. I tried calling him, but he must not have heard me."

Just then, both vessels picked up a call on channel 16 on their secondary radios for AST 32067. Mattituck heard Todd reply and switch to HF radio, which Mattituck didn't have. Not that it would have done any good; the frequency the troopers and the Coast Guard used were not advertised and changed frequently, and both agencies had encryption capabilities. Mattituck waited for Todd to come back on channel 68.

"Well, Frank. I'm being diverted. Do me a favor, will you? Let me know if you see Jim and have him give me a shout, would you?"

"Definitely. Roger Wilco," Mattituck returned.

"Happy Fitzgerald, out," Todd said, signaling that he was switching away from the frequency.

Mattituck was sitting with clients in the morning sun, off the eastern point of Smith Island, a very nice and reliable spot for yellow-eye rockfish, commonly called Red Snapper in Alaska, although not really a Red Snapper. But a definite favorite of anybody who knew fishing in Alaska. His clients wanted to target them while hoping to grab a few chicken halibut in the effort. Mattituck turned his face up to the sun while sitting on the gunwale of the DeeVee8's ten foot fish deck. His clients were one party of five, two sisters and their husbands from Fairbanks, and the 14-year-old son of one of them.

Just a couple of years older than his nephew, Derek Vincent Mattituck, the boy's mannerisms reminded Mattituck of Derek. The plan was that when Derek was old enough, he would be Mattituck's crewman. While he only saw Derek occasionally, the boy was like a son to Mattituck—especially since the boy's father had never been on scene. The DeeVee8 was the other great joy in Mattituck's life, and so when he expanded Sound Experience Charters from the Knot Skunked to a two-boat operation, he had named the brand new vessel after Derek. Mattituck had purchased the vessel a week after Derek's eighth birthday, and Mattituck and Derek had come up with the name DeeVee8, Derek Victor 8, on the vessel's first overnight trip – a trip Mattituck and Derek had shared.

An urge to see his nephew gripped him and he pulled out his wallet to look at Derek's school picture. He smiled at the image and decided he needed have his sister and Derek come over from Anchorage for a visit. He started to fold the wallet, and stopped. He slid Derek's picture to the side, revealing a picture behind it of Monica Castle. He realized it had been a while since he'd looked at this picture. She was beautiful. Dark smooth complexion and jet black hair, brown eyes. A smile that curled at the corners of her mouth. This was the look for him. Something about her had always struck him as perfect, even though he knew many might not agree. To him, though, she was precisely the right look. More importantly, she was the right person. He had never felt so comfortable with anybody, as though he were hanging with a female version of himself.

Janelle paled in comparison. He'd met Monica more than two years after the break-up. She had been the first—well, the only—serious relationship after Janelle.

He thought of the last time they had been together. He'd run the DeeVee8 down to Cordova to prep her for the upcoming season, and they'd spent the day together on a drive and hike around the Million Dollar Bridge. Her smile filled his memory and he felt a yearning rise deep in his chest. Why had he let so much time go by? There really was no reason. He'd told himself he was just busy—there's a lot of work getting a two-boat charter company up and ready for the season. But he knew that was just an excuse. The reality was there was no reason. He just hadn't called her. And the weeks had slipped by.

As he watched the rods of his clients, alert for signs of nibbles, his thoughts drifted back to Jim Milner and where he might be. Why was Todd looking for him? It couldn't be good, if Todd were calling him under cover of the Happy Fitzgerald and avoiding the name of Jim's boat on the radio. Something was amiss. He decided that if his clients maxed out early, he would return them to port without the usual sight-seeing excursion, fuel up and head down to Zaikof Bay. If he ran down that way in the evening, he could check on Jim. He had a rare day without clients the next day, so the timing was good. He could take the extra day to locate his friend if he needed to.

Skipper's Oath

Chapter Three

The Mystery Bayliner

Todd was running the AST 32067 at her full speed of 53 knots, rounding the southwest corner of Bligh Island. When he broke out onto the open Sound, the three foot swells slowed him down. The wave frequency – the distance between them—in a 32-foot vessel at that speed could beat the boat up in a hurry, to say nothing of Todd and his crewman, Jessie. He steered a course to take him northwest to the inside passage between Glacier Island and Columbia Bay.

The report was that a Coast Guard C-130 had been doing a routine flight from Kodiak to Valdez, except that the pilot enjoyed low altitudes and flying between peaks. Glacier Island had a nice V to fly through at the island's narrowest point, some 800 yards across with 1200-foot mountains jutting up less than a half mile from each other on either side. It made for a fun banking turn through the short gorge that especially thrilled the younger airmen.

As the C-130 had cut through this V from Chamberlain Bay on the south to Growler Bay on the north, pilot and co-pilot had simultaneously seen a small sport cruiser aground on the sandy beach near the head of Growler Bay. It was not the kind of boat you put up on shore to do some beach-combing. They had banked a tight turn over Columbia Bay to make another pass and had radioed the sighting to Air Station Kodiak. As they had approached the beached vessel from the north, they had seen it was high up the beach, but not so high that a super high tide had pushed it up.

The pilot had dipped the wing on the right to gain a better view as they flew by, looking for signs of anybody on board or on shore. They had seen none. The boat appeared not to have been there long, and they had guessed that it had been run up onto the beach intentionally. Perhaps it had hit a rock—the fiberglass hull would not tolerate a jolt on the Alaska rocks—and had beached it to keep from sinking. This was not an unusual strategy when a boater hit a rock and was taking on water. But why wouldn't they have radioed for help?

The C-130 had made two more passes, hoping to see the occupants of the Bayliner. They had kept very close watch on the tree and foliage line behind the beach, but had not seen anybody.

They then relayed all the detail they could to Air Station Kodiak and were told to make wide passes around the island, cutting through the V on each pass until a surface vessel arrived.

Todd and Jessie could see the massive Coast Guard cargo plane flying low around the Growler Bay area as they rounded the northwest edge of Glacier Island. When the seas laid back down and Todd could see they were clear of the iceberg trail from Columbia

Glacier on the north, he opened the throttle and quickly gained speed to 50 knots. The rigid hull vessel seemed to fly across the surface of the smoother water, throwing a low rooster tail shouldered by a sliver of a wake as she sped along.

As they came abreast of Growler Bay, Todd turned the boat into the bay in a wide arch, maintaining speed but watching the GPS very closely for any shallow areas hidden beneath the surface. He told Jessie to stand in the forward cabin hatch, where his eye level would be a good four feet higher than Todd's, and keep watch for any deadheads or other hazards in the water. He reached to the dash and turned on the flashing blue lights on the mast head to signal he was an emergency vessel on a call.

As they neared the end of Growler Bay, Todd slowed the vessel and rounded a point to the starboard, and within a minute they sighted the beached vessel.

"Looks like about a 30 or 32 foot Bayliner," Todd said.

"Not a good boat for these parts," Jessie said, young but no new-comer to Prince William Sound. He had grown up in Valdez, and had fished the waters with his dad since he was five.

"Nope. Sure isn't. Always amazes me how many I see, though."

Todd had slowed to 5kts as they approached the beach, and Jessie went forward onto the bow. He found the end of the bow line and readied himself to jump off as soon as the rigid hull bumped the sandy bottom. Todd heard the splash and watched Jessie's head moving over the bow.

"We'll need the anchor," he shouted to Jessie.

Jessie acknowledged him with a nod as he walked the line up to the beach.

"Tide's rising, remember," Todd added. "I'll need you to keep watch and move the anchor up with the rising tide." This would keep AST 32067 accessible for them when they were eventually ready to shove off.

With the boat anchored at the dry beach, Todd killed the twin Honda 250hp outboards and put on his waders. He disembarked the same way Jessie had, with a splash, and made his way to the dry sand. He had grabbed a gunwale ladder before dropping over the bow, and he strode now for the beached Bayliner with the ladder firmly gripped in his left hand. His right hand remained ready to pull his .45 GEN4 Glock from the hip should he need it.

The vessel had Washington numbers on the bow. He wondered if this was the vessel on the APB list that had been involved in the killings near Yakutat. It fit the general description, but there were a lot of these boats around. Todd had known Wayne Barrett, the Harbor Police officer killed in the incident at Yakutat. He hadn't known him well, but they had sat at the same table at an inter-agency conference in Anchorage six months before, and had had a brief conversation. He'd seemed like a solid law enforcement officer. Sad that he was dead—and killed the way he had been.

The boat was leaning heavily to starboard, the side Todd approached. He leaned the ladder against the hull, pulled his cell from his breast pocket, removing it from the Ziploc bag he used to keep it dry. He took a picture of the vessel, then a closeup of the registration numbers. He then surveyed the exposed hull for damage, walking fully around the boat and noting any scrapes or stress fractures that might indicate the vessel had been in trouble. He found a punched depression two feet off the keel on the portside, just ahead of where the sleek hull sloped back to the flatness of the main hull. He took a picture from several angles, then probed at it with his gloved hand. The fiberglass felt soft under pressure, and he guessed the boat had been taking on water fast enough that whoever had been running it felt they would have to run it aground to keep from sinking.

"Find anything?" Jessie hollered from his station at the anchor.

"Yep. She must have hit a rock," he shouted back. "I'm going aboard. You have your radio?"

"Of course," Jessie replied. He knew the drill. At first sign of trouble, or if anything didn't sound right, he would call the Coast Guard on the handheld VHF.

Todd grabbed the gunwale ladder and hooked the curled top over the Bayliner's gunwale. It would be almost impossible to board the deck without the ladder; the gunwale was a full foot above Todd's head. He'd selected a spot to board just aft of the cabin, at a point least visible from the inside should anybody be waiting to take a shot at him.

Before mounting the ladder, he knocked hard on the hull.

"Alaska State Troopers! Anybody aboard?"

He waited, then tried again. No answer.

This was precisely the kind of situation that made his wife hate his line of work. She understood him and his dedication to the job very well, but that didn't keep her from worrying constantly about him. A situation like this was precisely the kind where cops found themselves walking into a barrage of bullets. He thought of Keri with her short strawberry blonde hair and blue eyes that could be either cool and calming, or icy and stern, depending on her mood. Her classic

Norwegian features bespoke strength and resolve, both characteristics Todd would quickly affirm that she had.

His wife was an admirable woman, and very capable of taking care of herself. Character, honor, and strength were important to her—all qualities she sought to instill in her Tae Kwon Do students at her small martial arts school, but this did not detract at all from her worry for her husband.

He smiled to himself, thinking of Keri. She was nothing short of amazing to him. She'd moved to Alaska not knowing anybody, simply because she loved the outdoors and wanted to experience the Last Frontier. They'd met when he'd checked the fish catch she and her friends had hauled ashore, and told her she was in violation of having taken one too many White King Salmon. He'd told her he was willing to overlook the infraction if she agreed to dinner with him. She'd agreed, and they'd had dinner, and wound up together for the night. When they'd awakened the next morning, he confessed that she hadn't had any White King Salmon.

She forgave his deception on the grounds that he was amazing in bed. She'd told him that if he wanted to remain forgiven, he would have to repeat this ritual regularly. Six months later, Todd and Keri were married.

Now, four years later on the beach in Growler Bay, Todd Benson mounted the ladder and boarded the vessel. The aft deck was a mess. Beer cans littered the starboard quarter, piled up at the lowest point on the leaning deck. It was a nice boat, in good condition— probably less than five years old. Above him, he heard the four powerful engines of the C-130 approach and hum deeply as it passed a few hundred feet away, giving the crew a good view of Todd as he inspected the decks of the boat. Nothing outside seemed amiss or out of the ordinary.

He tried the aft entrance, a small sliding glass door that opened to a small dinette and galley, with the helm station just forward. Again, nothing seemed out of the ordinary, other than a high number of empty beer cans that the occupants hadn't bothered to clean up.

He paused and listened, and drew air through his nostrils, particularly attentive for the smell of decaying flesh. While temperatures in this part of Alaska rarely exceeded 75, a boat sitting, buttoned up in the sun, could get warm enough to speed decomposition.

Smelling none, he proceeded. Something did smell stale, though – not just the dirty jacket and flannel shirt thrown on the table, but something else faint and familiar. He approached the ladder down to the forward stateroom cautiously.

"Hello?" he tried again. "Alaska State Troopers. Anybody on board?"

No answer. He pulled his flashlight and shined it down into the passageway and the cabin beyond. He could see bedclothes shoved to one side of the bed, white sheets exposed over most of the bed. The splattered pattern there was enough to tell him something very wrong had happened there. He held the flashlight on the exposed sheet as he descended the ladder and entered the stateroom.

Dried blood. And a lot of it. He shined the light around the compartment. The flashlight beam took in the bulkhead, carpet, and two night stands on either side of the bed. All of it with signs of blood and a struggle.

Clearly, this was not going to be a routine vessel grounding.

He stepped to the port side and opened a door. A small closet, filled with hanging clothes, greeted him. He went to the twin door on the starboard side and opened it. Inside was a small bathroom/shower combination. Blood was smeared half way up the shower's bulkhead, and had gathered in a pool in one of the aft corners of the floor. It appeared completely dried. From the amount and the way the smeared blood was dried onto the bulkhead, Todd guessed that a body had been stowed in the shower while the boat had been underway, the blood still flowing from the body. It would have had severe trauma to the torso, possibly the head as well.

But there was no body now.

He turned and inspected the cabin more closely. The carpet on the starboard side was stained dark with dried blood, such a quantity that Todd guessed the person who had lain there had bled to death rather than died under a beating or other trauma. Perhaps she or he had been knifed or shot, but not resulting in immediate death. He inspected the bulkheads closely, and found no evidence of bullets. If at the close range inside the boat shots would have been fired, it was highly probable the bullets would have exited the body and left evidence in the bulkheads or bedding. Very likely, he concluded, there had been two bodies. One stowed in the shower – god only knew why – and the other left to die on the carpet next to the bed.

The reported Bayliner off Yakutat returned to his thoughts. If this were the boat in question, then they were looking for someone who had murdered at least five people. Todd shook his head, marveling. Why?

Two things Todd knew for sure: At least one person had been killed in here, likely two, and both bodies had been disposed of. He went topside again and inspected the cabin. There were a few more unopened beers in the fridge and the fish hold the owner had apparently used as a cooler for his beer. The owner of a boat would throw empties away, though, so it was likely that all the empties were left by the killer or killers. Using the empty cans as a gauge of time, Todd concluded that the killers had been on board after the murders for several days. They probably wouldn't have kept the bodies on board for long, so Todd ventured a prediction that whoever was killed, their bodies would never be recovered. There simply were too many places to dispose of them.

If this were the boat from Yakutat, Todd began deducing, and was registered in Washington, it may have traversed the northern Gulf to get here. In all likelihood, the murders that took place on board had taken place prior to Yakutat, then. The reports from the Yakutat Police Department had stated that the Bayliner subjects had been in the process of loading provisions as well as money from the larger cabin cruiser—Todd reached back in his memory for the vessel's name. Fun N Games. The Fun N Games. Two elderly people shot in view of Wayne Barrett as he approached. And then Wayne had been shot in the throat while in pursuit.

In rough seas. The report had also said that the wound, a bullet from a high-powered sniper rifle, had not been fired at close range. Todd tried to envision the scene. The shot had come from forward, perhaps fired at Wayne while he was in pursuit. The shooter might have been on the fantail of the Bayliner, which would provide the smoothest ride for firing a shot, but it still would have been pitching seas and a distance.

Whoever killed Wayne Barrett was one hell of a good shot.

Todd stood upright while thinking all this through. He looked around the cabin again. The killers had taken some pains to make sure the main cabin was clean of any blood that might have been deposited while they were removing the bodies from below. They would have had to have taken them out through here, and despite the mess, there was no sign whatsoever topside that any murders had taken place.

Whoever did this had planned on the possibility of being boarded. Or visited. Perhaps they had planned on visitors, but didn't want them to know about the murders.

Todd quickly ruled out that the measures to cover up had been taken as a caution against being boarded by Wayne Barrett—or a Coast Guard or Trooper boarding. Any such boarding would certainly have included all spaces on the vessel, anyway, even if a routine safety boarding. And if for Wayne boarding . . . that would have been pointless, since Wayne had witnessed the murder of the elderly couple. No, Todd, reasoned – these killers had intended to have visitors after the on-board killings, and not random visitors.

Todd strode toward Jessie after disembarking the Bayliner.

"Anything odd?" Jessie asked.

Todd grimaced and nodded. "We need crime lab folks out here," he said as they walked toward the line leading to AST 32067. "A lot of blood in the stateroom . . ." He looked back at Jessie's stunned face. "And I do mean a lot of it. No bodies, though. We need forensics for this one."

When he'd gained AST 32067's bow and lifted himself aboard, he quickly grabbed the mic on the encryption HF radio, hailed the regional office in

Glennallen, and requested a team be dispatched from the crime lab in Anchorage.

An hour later, after satisfying himself that the killers hadn't hiked further up into the island, Todd went back on board the beached Bayliner and placed a small camera and motion detector, hidden under the aft gunwale. If anybody got on board the Bayliner, they would have it all recorded. He then disembarked the vessel and signaled Jessie to get ready to get AST 32067 underway. On board, he started the motors while Jessie drew in the remaining anchor line with the windlass and began to secure the anchor.

"Might as well keep that handy," Todd told him. "We'll be anchoring a couple hundred yards off."

Ten minutes later, they sat eating granola bars— all that Todd had on board this trip was a box of granola and power bars—and sipping warm cola.

"Why don't you get a cooler?" Jessie asked. "And buy some decent soda," he added, peering at the can's side. "What the hell is this stuff? Never heard of it."

Todd gave him a blank expression.

"No signs of anybody in the brush, eh?" Jessie asked.

Todd shook his head. "Didn't expect any, though," he added.

Jessie waited.

Todd went on. "I think they would have stayed on the boat, or nearby, until they heard us. Then maybe they'd go into the brush. And they would have left plenty of fresh signs, including footprints."

"That's right," Jessie said, suddenly realizing there had been no footprints at all. "So, maybe these guys either headed onto the island or a boat picked them up before the last high tide?"

"You're catching on." Todd paused. "Not onto the island, though. There was plenty of food and water on the Bayliner."

"And beer," Jessie noted.

"And beer," Todd repeated. "No reason to go into the wilderness. Better to wait for someone to come along."

Several minutes passed. The sun had dropped behind the mountains on the west side of the bay, leaving Todd and Jessie in a protracted evening shade. Todd looked at his watch. 7:48. The sun wouldn't be down for another three hours, and it wouldn't get fully dark, with solstice only three days away.

"Where do you think they might be?"

Todd thought for a moment. "South," he said. "On a fresh boat."

"Do you think the owners of the new boat are alive?"

"One can hope," Todd replied drily, but doubtful. Then he added, "There is a chance they wouldn't want to kill them."

Jessie looked puzzled in the dim light inside the cabin.

Todd nodded toward the Bayliner. "They ran aground once. Maybe they lost confidence in navigating these waters."

"Maybe they need the owner to pilot the boat," Jessie said, catching onto the hope.

As the evening wore on, Todd watched the minutes on the clock. Jessie was falling asleep. Periodically, Todd heard vessels hailing each other on the VHF. His eyes were getting heavy, and he felt himself drifting. He pulled his AST ball cap down over his eyes and lay back his head.

The VHF continued the sporadic drones of voices.

"Greta May, the Greta May . . . Evening Dawn calling. Pick me up, Jim?"

Jim . . . Jim . . . the word echoed in Todd's head.

His eyes shot open, and he pushed his cap back up on his head.

"Shit," he said.

Jessie startled. "What?"

Todd jumped to the helm station and picked up the encrypted HF mic.

"Glennallen, 32067."

He waited. The garbled answer came. "Go ahead, Todd. What's up?"

"Has the Kimberly Marie turned up?" he asked, his voice tense.

"Stand by," came the reply. Then, "Nope. She hasn't. Apparently she's a charter—has clients waiting at a Valdez hotel. Not good for business," the trooper in Glennallen said.

"Call the Coast Guard," Todd told him. "We need to find that boat."

Skipper's Oath

Chapter Four

Pot Shots

Several hours before State Trooper Todd Benson called the Coast Guard, Mattituck had indeed maxed his clients out and taken them back to Valdez Harbor early. It had been his lucky day, apparently, as three clients had landed respectably sized "yellow-eyes," another had taken in a ling cod a mere inch-and-a-half short of trophy size, and all had maxed out with two halibut each. All the halibut had been between 45 and 55 pounds – perfect eating, and with 85 percent of a halibut being edible meat, this meant his clients were driving home to Fairbanks with just over four hundred pounds of halibut steaks. They were a happy group, and didn't complain a bit about being dropped at the dock at 4:20pm.

Mattituck had Ernie do a quick washdown while he walked the clients up and got them set up with a fish cleaner.

"These guys will get you more meat than I could," he said, smiling and patting Dale Paulsen on the back. "This guy's the best and fastest here," he added.

He then ran up to the Harbor Quick Stop across the street from the Harbormaster's Office and picked up two pre-wrapped ham and cheese sandwiches, four cans of soup, two gallons of water to supplement what he had on board already, and several beef jerky packs. He added a loaf of bread and a jar of peanut butter. All foods that, while light, would sustain him for a few days should he need the option.

Back at the DeeVee8, Ernie had wanted to go with Mattituck, but Mattituck insisted he would be fine. His crewman helped him cast off and stood watching as the DeeVee8 backed out of her slip and Mattituck nosed her toward the fuel dock. An hour later, he was barreling southbound at 35kts through the Valdez Arm—Glacier Island and Growler Bay no more than a couple of miles to the starboard. Mattituck looked at the digital clock on the dash next to the GPS. It was 5:58 p.m., plenty of solid daylight to make Zaikof Bay, where he hoped to find Jim Milner safe and sound. Better yet, maybe he'd pass the old timer on the way down. If Jim had been dropping off deer hunters on Montague Island, he might just see him on the way down.

Mattituck slowed DeeVee8 to 20kts as he approached a line of bergie bits, smaller bits of ice broken off icebergs as they moved away from their parent, the mighty Columbia Glacier tucked up at the head of a bay directly north of Glacier Island. The glacier, receding at an alarming rate under climate change, now left a trail of icebergs and bergie bits that all mariners did well to respect by slowing down.

Two and three foot chunks of ice bumped against the DeeVee8's thick aluminum hull, and Mattituck slowed to 12kts in response. A fiberglass boat would need to be more careful, as the ice could punch holes or crack that material, but aluminum was far more sturdy, the reason why so many boats in Alaska, particularly fast boats, were aluminum hulled. There was no reason to test fate, though, and Mattituck felt better with the 12kts.

On the other side of the ice belt, Mattituck pressed the twin throttles forward and smiled inwardly at the guttural hum of the twin Volvo-Pentas as they pushed the DeeVee8's hull up on step, partially out of the water where she could gain speed without sacrificing much fuel. It was all about water displacement, when it came to hull design. The less water a boat pushed out of the way, the greater the speed and fuel efficiency. And the best way to not push water was to get on top of it.

Once the DeeVee8 was "on step," as it was called, Mattituck eased into the hydraulic captain's seat and hooked his boots on the foot brace on the bulkhead under the helm. The vessel eased into a gentle rolling over the southbound seas, less than one foot high and smooth under the light breeze.

He grabbed a Coke from the small cabin refrigerator—he wanted the caffeine—and settled comfortably back into the seat, feeling the hydraulics absorb every lift and drop of DeeVee8's bow as she knifed her way through the open Sound toward Montague Island and Zaikof Bay. And hopefully, Jim Milner.

Almost two hours later, Montague Point came on screen on both the GPS and radar as the DeeVee8 approached. The first inlet off the eastern end of the island would be Rocky Bay, then next and directly south would be Zaikof Bay, where he hoped to find Jim Milner. From the moment he'd seen the Kimberly Marie two days before, something hadn't sat very well in Frank Mattituck's gut. It wasn't much, but with Jim not replying to Mattituck's call, together with the overdue vessel report, Mattituck suspected something was amiss. Jim had been a steadfast friend since Mattituck had moved to Valdez seven years before, and they'd spent many evenings on the stern deck of the Kimberly Marie, just as they had the other night. How many beers had he tipped back with Jim, just passing the evenings away, not alone?

"DeeVee8, DeeVee8, this is the Happy Fitzgerald."

Mattituck nearly jumped at the radio. That was Todd Benson and the State Trooper boat.

"68 and back, cap'n?" he asked, knowing that whatever Todd was calling about, it had to do with Jim Milner. And since he was calling under his self-adopted code name, he didn't want others to hear. Six-eight and back meant to reverse the numbers, so Mattituck dialed the radio to channel 86.

"Happy Fitz, this is DeeVee8."

"Hey, Frank," came Todd's voice. He sounded tired.

Mattituck looked at the clock. 8:01 p.m.

"I'm in Growler, looking at a beached Bayliner. Can't go into details on unsecured radio, but something's amiss. Are you looking for our friend? Over."

Clearly Todd was taking extra precautions against being heard.

"Yes, I am. Anything new?"

"Just what I told you. Things aren't right. Something happened not too far away that has everybody searching. And with the last report of our friend, it could be tied together. Over."

Todd's efforts to alert him while being vague was not lost on Mattituck.

"Roger, got it." Mattituck thought about what Todd might know. *Fuck*, he thought. *Wish he could tell me.*

"Frank, be careful. If it's tied together, you could be walking into a real mess."

"Okay," Mattituck said.

"No, Frank. I'd advise waiting until I can get there. Ease back and anchor up someplace. I can be there by morning. Over."

Mattituck paused, watching the marker for the DeeVee8 on the GPS. She inched closer and closer to Zaikof Bay. He could anchor up either inside of Green Island, or in Rocky Bay, he thought. He broadened the view on the GPS so he could see Zaikof Bay as well as Rocky Bay, Middle Point jutting out between them.

He shook his head.

"Naw," he said into the mic. "I'll take a peek and see if I see him."

Silence. Mattituck knew Todd was thinking how to reply.

"Frank," came Todd's voice. "I strongly advise against that. I can't emphasize that enough. Do you get my meaning? Over."

"Yep, read you loud and clear, Happy Fitz."

"Anchor up and wait 'til morning, okay?"

"Nope. But I'll be careful."

"Frank, no. You need to anchor up and wait."

Mattituck liked Todd Benson very well—he was not only a great cop, but he was the kind of guy Mattituck could see himself having a pint or two with. In the end, though, Todd's a cop, Mattituck thought. And cops live by rules. And they love to bark orders. Fuck orders, he thought.

"Tell you what," Mattituck said as he adjusted the range on the radar to 6 miles to fix a distance to Montague Point. "I'll just peek, then anchor. How's that?"

Another silence, then, "Okay. But radio me as soon as you're headed to anchor. Over."

"Roger, Wilco," Mattituck returned cheerfully, enjoying his little victory over authority. Not that Todd had much choice.

Fifty miles away, Todd was working to control his anger. He hated when Mattituck did that. While the two didn't know each other all that well, Todd knew him well enough to read him. Frank's cheery tone meant he had no intention of complying. As much as Todd liked Frank Mattituck, he had to remind himself this is an Alaskan charter boat captain. Guys in Alaska tend to thumb their noses at authority—particularly when they didn't see a legitimate reason to comply. And charter boat captains are notorious for having classic Alaskan sentiments. Trooper Benson knew this all too well.

"Frank . . ."

"You're breaking up on me now, Happy Fitz," Mattituck interrupted, lying. "You're breaking up," he repeated, to make sure Todd heard him. VHF radios are one-way radios, meaning that if you transmit on top of somebody talking, they can't hear you. Mattituck repeated it a third time to make sure Todd heard him.

"Roger, DeeVee8. I copy. I'm breaking up. If you can hear me, I repeat my last: Take a peek, then report back and head for Anchorage to await me for the morning."

Mattituck suppressed his annoyance. Who the fuck is he to tell me what to do? he thought. He pressed the mic button sporadically and spoke broken words a foot or so from the mic, so it would sound broken.

Todd came back through loud and clear. "DeeVee8, I repeat. Take a peek, then report back to and head to anchor. Copy?" he waited for a reply. "Frank, do you copy?"

Mattituck rubbed the mic on the leg of his Carhartt's, opening and closing the mic as he did so. On the air, it would sound like broken static. He smiled at the old trick.

Todd's voice came again, loud and clear. "DeeVee8, it sounds like you're getting out of range now. If you can hear this, I will be there well before dawn. As soon as I'm relieved, I will make way south and call you."

Mattituck didn't reply now.

After a few minutes, AST 32067 transmitted one last time.

"Happy Fitzgerald clear of the DeeVee8, switching back to channel one-six. Out."

Mattituck had continued without slowing the DeeVee8 until he approached Middle Point, and Zaikof Bay just beyond. The sun had set to the northwest, and was on its slow arc under the horizon that kept its rays shining, albeit in diminished light, as it dipped down and then back to the horizon to rise again around 3:30 a.m. At summer solstice, it never got completely dark in this part of Alaska. Dark enough for good coverage when needed, but not completely dark. A person could hike without a flashlight.

Nonetheless, the DeeVee8's running lights were on as she rounded Middle Point and began a slow turn into the bay. Mattituck reached for the binoculars on the dash, and pulled them from their case. He scanned the bay, and fixed the lenses on a white superstructure about two miles up the bay, near the end and to the right.

The Kimberly Marie.

Mattituck could hear Todd in his inner ear. *Okay, Frank, it said . . . you found her. Now go anchor up in Port Etches across the entrance, if you want, but get the fuck out of here.* One part of Mattituck recognized that to err on the side of safety, it'd be better to have somebody else around. But the bigger part of him said he could handle this just fine. And then there was the fact that he simply tended not to follow directives from people who think they have authority over him. There probably was no real danger anyway.

The DeeVee8 held her bearing without easing up on speed. Mattituck wanted to keep the appearance of a vessel that was headed into Zaikof on its own accord, and not appear like she was looking for anybody. He set the radar to 3 miles, and noted that the Kimberly Marie was only a few hundred feet from shore. She appeared anchored off a beach where Mattituck had set ashore several times before when dropping off hunters. He smiled and eased back in the hydraulic seat, now motionless as the DeeVee8 glided on the smooth, protected waters of the bay. The prow of the vessel slowly rose and fell with the physics of moving at high speed over the water.

The beach lay near the end of the bay, to the right. It was a very pronounced, straight-lined beach that a dredging crew could not have set up better for hunter drop-offs. While Mattituck had never observed Jim Milner dropping hunters, this was the standard beach for the drop-off on the east end of Montague Island, and seeing the Kimberly Marie anchored there gave Mattituck a sense of assurance that Jim was fine. Why she was there and overdue to pick up a set of clients, Mattituck couldn't even guess. But perhaps Jim had thought he could squeeze in a quick trip between runs, but had had engine trouble or something—it was hard to tell.

In any case, Mattituck felt sure his friend was okay.

He decided to approach the Kimberly Marie and tie-up alongside for the night. With luck, Jim had put a hunting party on shore and was looking for a friend to share some beers on the stern deck.

Todd had been deeply disappointed with the radio conversation with Frank Mattituck. The last thing he needed was for Frank to approach the Kimberly Marie and get into trouble. He sat almost sulking on the aft bench of AST 32067, listening to Jessie's soft snoring, the young man's head craned sharply to the right and leaning on the bulkhead next to the forward passenger seat. How could he sleep that way? Todd wondered.

Todd looked at his watch. 11:37 p.m. In his last encrypted communication with Glennallen, he'd been informed that the forensics team would be flying out of Anchorage at 4:30 a.m., when the light and weather were favorable for a helicopter. They were expected on scene at the beach in Growler Bay before 6:00 a.m.

What could possibly happen here overnight? Todd wondered. He knew the killers were long gone, and nobody was ashore. The beached Bayliner lay tiredly leaning to her side on the beach, alone and unable to digest the evidence of what had transpired in her belly. Todd felt a sudden wave of sadness. He was tired... the sadness was a dead giveaway. He was always prone to these tendencies when he was on a murder case. While he was adept at keeping himself from thinking of the victims—the lives they had been living, full of hope and perhaps joy—the deprivation of these things from the victims' lives left Todd with an inexpressible emptiness.

Frank Mattituck eased back on the twin throttles and heard the throaty hum of the Volvo-Pentas ease down. The stern of the DeeVee8 dropped as the hull came off step and began displacing more water. The vessel's aluminum bow dropped next and settled into a soft 12kt pace, several hundred yards from the Kimberly Marie. He pulled out the binoculars and trained them on the Kimberly Marie's stern as two figures emerged. They looked a bit rough, both unshaved with the dark-skinned, grimy appearance people get out in the weather without showers for several days.

Mattituck came close, then backed the throttles to bring the DeeVee8 to a complete stop. She lulled, dead in the water, the Volvo-Pentas barely audible as he slid the side window open to hail the men on the Kimberly Marie.

"Ho, there!" he yelled.

The taller of the two men waved back.

"Where's Jim?" Mattituck added, feeling suddenly cautious.

The shorter man gestured toward shore. "He's with some of the other hunters, ashore."

Mattituck tensed. Then why, he wondered, is the dinghy secured on the transom of the Kimberly Marie, sideways on her right pontoon resting on the swim deck? This was where a mariner secured their service dinghy while underway—not when anchored and ferrying back and forth to shore, as Jim would be doing with a hunting party.

The man read Mattituck's silence and added, "my brother and I here're a bit too beat for gallavantin' around chasing deer. So we came back out to rest."

There was a significant age difference between the two men. Possibly fifteen or twenty years, if not more. No way could they be brothers. Besides, Mattituck thought, they don't look anything alike.

"Ah, yeah . . . Hunting can wear you down," Mattituck replied, careful not to show his suspicion. "Have Jim give me a shout when he's back on board, would you? Have a good one!"

"We'll be sure and do that!" the man shouted, waving.

Mattituck began to throttle up, but the taller man hailed him. He throttled back down, barely making way in the water. Mattituck nodded to show he was listening.

"I'm actually thinking I'd like to go back ashore," the taller man said. "Don't know how to run this here skiff," he said, gesturing to the service dinghy.

Mattituck debated a moment. "How'd you get back out to the boat, then?"

The shorter man shot an angry glare at his partner. They looked at each other, obviously tripped up.

After a moment's pause, the shorter one crouched and reached under the gunwale. Mattituck was shocked when he saw the man come back up with a .45 and take aim at the DeeVee8. Instinct took over. Mattituck pushed both throttles forward and heard the heavy engines growl to life, as if happy to jump into action. He was careful not to throttle up too fast and cause the props to cavitate. He could feel the long aluminum hull vibrate under the sudden pull of salt water under her hull as the props bit into the now-frothy sea and pushed it backward from underneath the boat.

A tell-tale white flip of water ten feet out his starboard window made clear the man on the Kimberly Marie was firing at him. The man didn't seem to be a great shot, falling that far short of his target.

He cranked the wheel hard to port and eased slightly on the throttle, knowing a sharp turn increased the chances of cavitation, and therefore risk in damaging the props. He wanted to spin the DeeVee8's back to the Kimberly Marie, offering the best protection for Mattituck as it would put the entire vessel's cabin between him and the gunman.

A bullet ripped through the aluminum superstructure several feet behind him as the Kimberly Marie slid to the starboard quarter and slipped rapidly aft. Mattituck straightened the wheel and increased throttle, then looked forward to see what his heading was. He was headed nearly straight up toward the end of the bay. This was not the direction he wanted to go, but it was better than exposing himself to gunfire.

He heard the loud ping of another bullet, this time much further down. The reverberation seemed amplified, and made him cringe. He looked to where he thought the bullet had penetrated, but couldn't see any damage. He hoped it wasn't along the water line.

Another ping, this one with a dulled sludgy sound. That one was definitely below the water line.

"Fuck!" Mattituck muttered. "How the----?" How were bullets penetrating from the side?

Maybe he was wrong about how good of a shot this guy was. He seemed to be hitting precisely the right spots.

Mattituck craned his head to gain a view out the port quarter window, around the obstructed view where the head was located at the rear portside, where it opened out to the fish deck. The Kimberly Marie was in clear site, nearly abeam on the port side. Mattituck was momentarily confused. Was the Kimberly Marie underway? No, he realized. He'd over compensated the turn and brought the DeeVee8 full around in the turn.

Another bullet ripped the aluminum hull, just above the water line, then another slightly lower, followed by a third, forward of the other two.

"Fuck!" Mattituck cursed. This man was clearly not a bad shot after all. In fact, he was planting hole after hole in the DeeVee8, all along the water line. If the guy was this good of a shot, why wasn't he aiming for Mattituck? Maybe, he thought, the guy can't see me through the dark tinted windows.

Just then, two more rapid shots took out the windows on the port side, exposing Mattituck. He could now clearly see the Kimberly Marie and the men on the stern deck, the taller man with a rifle—probably one of Jim's—that he was loading. The rifle had a scope. Once he was ready with that, there might not be any escape.

Mattituck thought quickly, trying to think of an escape. With several holes in the hull—how many had there been?—there was no way he could risk running back out into the Sound, where the rougher seas would undoubtedly send water flooding into the boat at a rate his bilge pumps wouldn't keep up with. He was now trapped by the DeeVee8's limitations, unable to leave the smooth waters of the bay, where he could keep the water from funneling in too fast . . . as long as he kept the DeeVee8 moving so the hull was higher in the water, she wouldn't sink.

Now he realized what the gunman had been doing—ensuring that Mattituck could not leave the bay. He probably couldn't get any kind of view through the windows, so he'd focused on keeping Mattituck contained.

And with the rifle . . . Jim kept high-powered hunting rifles on board. Mattituck would not be safe anyplace in the bay. He was now running the DeeVee8 at 30kts, hoping the speed made for a more difficult target. He wouldn't be able to keep this up for long though, especially since the DeeVee8 was probably taking on water. He had to think of something to do.

He reached for the VHF mic, and realized the radio had been silent throughout the ordeal. He hadn't even heard vessels on the Sound hailing each other. He glanced at the faceplate and saw that the lights were dead. He tried clicking the mic. No sound. He checked the power button and found it in the "on" position. He slid the side window back and reached up for the antenna just above, and felt jagged metal where the mount was. The antenna lay back on top of the cabin, useless. His fingers felt three other bullet holes in the slanted side-roof of the DeeVee8's cabin.

When the fuck had those got there? he wondered.

The gunman must have taken several rapid shots while Mattituck was throttling up the first time, taking the antenna out while at short range to prevent Mattituck calling for help. As if Bad Luck wanted to be sure, one of those shots had penetrated through the roof and lodged into the VHF radio unit itself, rendering it useless.

By now, the DeeVee8 had circled around southward and was nearing a rocky south shore of Zaikof Bay. He pulled the wheel to starboard to make sure he came nowhere near any submerged rocks in the potentially shallow water. As the DeeVee8's bow came around, nearly setting a course for the Kimberly Marie, the safe landing of the sandy beach on the north shore caught Mattituck's attention. This was the standard dropping point for hunting parties on this end of the island, but Mattituck did not like the idea of having to pass by the Kimberly Marie, which lay between the DeeVee8 and the safe beach.

He looked up the bay to the end, wondering if there were other sandy beaches up that way. He reset the GPS range to check. He studied the nautical depth readings that came up on the screen, and noted black stars closely situated along most of the shoreline. Rocks. This was the way the National Oceanic and Atmospheric Agency, NOAA, indicated various rocks on nautical charts, warning mariners not to approach the area. One could not assume that each star indicated an individual rock. It could very well be marking many rocks in proximity to each other. Two or more stars likely meant numerous rocks spread throughout the area.

He shook his head. No way was he going to try that. He wanted to make sure that if he were going to run the DeeVee8 ashore, it was a safe place where he could salvage his boat. He turned to the radar and set the range to two miles so he could see how far the Kimberly Marie was from the safe beach. She lay anchored about a third of the way from his current position to the beach.

"Further evidence something's wrong," he said to himself. Clearly the Kimberly Marie had not anchored with any intention of accessing the beach for deer hunting. She had anchored randomly.

Mattituck picked up the binoculars and checked the Kimberly Marie again. The gunmen had stopped firing at him, but were watching the DeeVee8 closely. Perhaps they were waiting for a better shot at him. Or maybe they were waiting to see what he would do. Either way, they didn't seem worried enough about Mattituck escaping, and felt that time was on their side.

What of Jim? Mattituck allowed himself to consider where his friend might be. It was possible that they were holding him prisoner below. That would mean there would be at least one more of them, as someone would need to keep Jim under guard. But what would be the purpose of that? Why take an old man hostage and steal his boat?

Was it related to the scene Trooper Todd Benson had come on in Growler Bay? And Todd had mentioned another situation someplace that might be connected.

All speculation, Mattituck thought. *I have a real situation here.*

Studying the radar and the GPS, he decided he could circle around the Kimberly Marie to the east and come up along the north shore. He knew that shore pretty well, and was confident that he could keep close to shore and also stay off the rocks. This would maximize his distance from the Kimberly Marie, keeping him close to a half mile away—a fairly safe distance from the apparent marksmanship of the Kimberly Marie's occupants.

The wide arc around the Kimberly Marie would also give him the ability to lock the wheel and gather some needed gear for going ashore. He thought about what to do. He had a hand-held VHF radio in the storage bin under the dining bench in front of the head, but it would not transmit over the land on either side of the bay. He would need to get atop a hill to get any range on the weaker radio. VHF, Very High Frequency, was a line-of-sight radio signal that could have a range of seven miles or more, but not if any significant obstacle lay between the transmission and receiving points.

Mattituck steered the DeeVee8 toward the mouth of the bay and throttled up to a cruising speed of 27kts. He then turned the binoculars toward the Kimberly Marie. The men were obviously concerned, but made no attempt to fire at him. Very likely, Mattituck reasoned, they knew he wasn't making a run for open water. They were probably just very attentive to whatever he might be up to.

Satisfied the DeeVee8 was holding steady steerage, Mattituck felt sure that if he set the wheel in a slow turn to port, there was little current or wind to take her off course. He reached under the steering column and locked the wheel in a slow five-degree turn to port, and set to work. First, he grabbed an internal frame backpack he kept on hand for hunting clients that might need one. He made sure the water filter he kept in the outer pocket had all its parts, in case he needed to filter water while ashore. He grabbed two flashlights and backup batteries, not that he would need them in the Land of the Midnight Sun, but in those twilight hours, it was dark enough to twist an ankle among roots or on the open muskeg fields that were plentiful on the island.

He then packed the hand-held VHF and its backup battery, and set to work in the galley, gathering enough food to stay on the island for several days, if he ate light. He then opened the First Aid bin under the starboard passenger bench, which contained ten Coast Guard certified PFDs—Personal Flotation Devices, more commonly known as life vests—and five good-sized, well-stocked First Aid kits. Mattituck had learned long ago that one could not have too many of these, and that they were well worth the investment of keeping packed with updated medicines and materials.

Last, he worked the combination on the small gun locker bolted to the bulkhead next to the captain's seat. Inside were a flare gun and two hand guns: a .38 Smith and Wesson, for shooting halibut, and a black Glock model 37, a .45 caliber hand gun that while Mattituck wasn't a gun freak, was as beautiful a weapon as he'd ever seen. He took the flare gun and flare pack, and the Glock along with 2 extra ammo clips. Although he'd bought the Glock largely just because he liked it, he had justified the purchase by saying it was as good a defense against wildlife as any handgun might be. He also had a small rifle locker aft, where he kept a slug-bearing 12-gauge shotgun and 3 Winchester 70 deer hunting rifles. These he ignored as they would be too cumbersome for the fast-climbing he intended.

In the end, however, he decided that under the circumstances it might not be a bad idea to sling one of the Winchester 70s over his shoulder. Just in case. He donned the belt and holster for the Glock and tucked the matte-black weapon into its place, then checked the slow circle the DeeVee8 continued to maintain without flaw.

Todd had radioed Glennallen his concern of what Frank Mattituck might be up to, along with his suspicion that foul play may be afoot on the Kimberly Marie, and related to the current case in Growler Bay. The supervising lieutenant at HQ Anchorage had agreed that the Growler Bay scene was likely secure, particularly with the camera mounted on the Bayliner, and that the compelling need was for AST 32067 to divert to Zaikof Bay. Todd had awakened Jessie, fired up the twin Honda 250s, and pulled anchor.

As soon as they had cleared the mouth of the bay and steered the fast rigid hull vessel toward Valdez Arm, Todd had begun trying to call the DeeVee8, but had no luck. After clearing Glacier Island and steering a straight-line course for the eastern end of Montague Island and Zaikof Bay, Todd had tried again. Again, with no luck. He then hailed the Coast Guard on channel 21 and asked them to put out a call for assistance. Before they did, however, they immediately tried calling the DeeVee8 themselves, likely from the VHF tower next to Hinchinbrook Lighthouse, nearly straight across the Entrance from Zaikof Bay.

When they got no reply, they tried hailing passers-by.

"Any vessels transiting Hinchinbrook Entrance, any vessels transiting Hinchinbrook Entrance, this is United States Coast Guard Area Anchorage, United States Coast Guard Area Anchorage, over."

A reply came almost immediately.

"Coast Guard, this is the Motor Vessel Danish Sun, over."

"Cruise ship," Todd said to Jessie. Jessie nodded, sipping coffee he'd just made.

The Coast Guard switched the cruise ship to channel 22-Alpha, the Coast Guard-to-public frequency. Todd followed on the secondary radio.

"Danish Sun, Coast Guard, over."

"Go ahead, Coast Guard."

"Captain," the Coast Guard voice said, displaying standard mariner protocol on initial contact. "Request you attempt to establish contact with the charter boat DeeVee8 on channel 16 as you pass Zaikof Bay. The vessel was last reported in the bay and has now been reported missing."

"Roger, Coast Guard. Wilco." Then silence. Todd kept the secondary radio tuned to 22-Alpha.

Several minutes later, he heard the Danish Sun hailing the DeeVee8 on channel 16. With no reply, they repeated the call several times for the next 10 minutes.

"Coast Guard, Danish Sun, channel 22."

"Go ahead, Danish Sun."

"No contact with the DeeVee8, Coast Guard, but there are two vessels near the end of Zaikof Bay. One is a sizeable white cabin cruiser. The other looks like it might be a charter boat, a bit more than 30 feet, with a painted yellow hull and a silver superstructure. Might be an aluminum boat."

"Roger, Danish Sun, thank you."

"There's something else, Coast Guard."

"Roger, sir. Go ahead."

"That charter boat looks like it's run up pretty high on the beach--like it ran aground at a high rate of speed."

A momentary pause. "Roger, Danish Sun. Copied. Are there any signs of immediate danger, other than a possible grounding?"

"Negative, Coast Guard. It looks pretty quiet up there, but it looks like the cabin cruiser might be rendering assistance. Her dinghy was in the water and appeared to be making way for the charter boat."

Todd tensed.

"Roger, Danish Sun. Anything else?"

"Negative, Coast Guard. Danish Sun, clear of the Coast Guard, shifting back to channel 16 and channel 12, northbound Hinchinbrook Entrance."

"Another boat aground?" Jessie asked. "What's up with that?"

Todd shook his head. "Dunno. Guess we'll find out when we get there."

Todd was particularly concerned that the DeeVee8 was run aground. This did not bode well at all. He wished Frank Mattituck had listened to him and anchored in Rocky Bay or some other safer place.

He set a waypoint in the GPS for a point outside Zaikof Bay, just to give a course to steer. When the purple band appeared, the GPS's course for them to steer, Todd turned to Jessie.

"You slept a couple of hours," he said. "I probably should, too. You okay to pilot? Rested enough, I mean?"

Jessie nodded. "Yeah . . . sure."

"Okay. We have a couple of hours before we get there. Wake me up if anything unusual happens, and well before we get to that waypoint."

"No problem," Jessie said as Todd stepped off the captain's seat. Jessie settled in, resetting the radar range to six miles. He heard Todd settle onto the crew bench behind him, and noted the snoring within three minutes.

Skipper's Oath

Chapter Five

Pursuit over Muskeg

After Mattituck had run the DeeVee8 aground, he had quickly donned all his gear and made his way to the bow. He unclasped the anchor and switched the free release on the windlass, then heard the dull thump of the anchor hitting the sand below. He pulled approximately thirty feet of line from the windlass, then set the lock so no more line would pay out. He then tossed all the gear to the sand over the bow, some five or six feet below. Not a significant drop, but with all that gear on his body, he'd be risking injury if he tried to jump with it on.

Having jumped ashore, he lifted the heavy anchor and ran it as far up as he could toward the line of marsh grass at the top of the beach. He then dug its claw deep into the sand. When high tide came, he wanted to be sure the DeeVee8 would stay put.

He pulled the binoculars from his vest pocket and brought the Kimberly Marie into view. The shorter man, the marksman, was watching him through a pair of binoculars while the taller man appeared to be trying to put the 8-foot service dinghy into the water. It appeared they intended to give him chase.

He turned and headed up the beach to the tall grass and the tree line beyond. He knew this beach well, and knew there would be a trail through the brush someplace to his left, but he wanted to get into the grass right away for two reasons: to remain a difficult target should Marksman Shorty want to take a shot, and to make it harder for his pursuers to find the trail, now that it looked like they would be on his tail.

Once in the tall grass, he knew he would become invisible, and with luck he would be able to lose the pursuers, make high ground, then circle back. *But then what?* he wondered as he crossed carefully into the grass. What did he think he was going to do if he ran up against these guys face-to-face? The marshy grass squished and sank under his footsteps. He had switched into hiking boots before jumping off the DeeVee8, so the marshy ground would not seep into his shoes and get his feet wet – greatly increasing the risk of blisters, to say nothing of the irritating discomfort of wet shoes. All of which might slow him down.

As soon as he was sure he was out of sight from the water, including any detection of the grasses moving as he pushed through the tall shoots, he cut immediately left and made for the trail. From the beach, the trail was very difficult to find. Everybody who landed on this beach knew to make their way to the head of the beach, then walk along the edge of the tall grasses until you saw the tell-tale indentation of the trail head. From even a dozen feet down, it was impossible to find. Mattituck hoped that his pursuers would follow where he entered and quickly lose his trail. The marshy ground erased footsteps within seconds, and Mattituck took great care to avoid bending any shoots to give away the direction he'd gone. If nothing else, this ploy could buy him valuable time and distance.

Ten minutes later, he was on the firmer ground of the well-trod trail, crossing from the grasses into the low scrub brush, and then into the . A short distance into the , a small knoll raised the trail to a spot where he could observe pretty well behind him without being seen. He paused as soon as he crested the knoll, and turned to survey the terrain behind him. He couldn't see the DeeVee8 as she was over the grassy edge of the beach head, where the sand dropped to meet the water's edge. But he hadn't expected to see his boat.

Further, however, he could see the Kimberly Marie anchored in the distance. She had shifted on her anchor with a change in the currents of the bay. The tide had changed, and was now headed out of the bay, pulling the Kimberly Marie to the opposite direction she had been while the tide was still incoming and rising. This was a good sign for the DeeVee8. It meant the high tides for the next few days would not pull her off her anchor on the beach. She would lay where she was, awaiting his return.

A pang at the memory forced a sudden exhale. Running his beloved boat up on the beach had been alarming and violent. He'd run her at 37kts as he approach the sandy beach, then cut the engines as the big boat barreled in. If he'd had outboard motors, he could have raised them to prevent damage to the props, but the DeeVee8 had twin diesels amidship, with shafts passing through the hull aft to the twin propellers beneath the transom. While the shafts ran through guard molding along the bottom of the hull, there would still be severe damage to the propellers, and likely the shafts as well. The hull, other than the bullet holes, would be fine. The beauty of the aluminum hull was that they were extremely difficult to damage. At worst, there might be some dings and dents.

As the DeeVee8 had approached the beach, Mattituck had killed the engines and then ducked beneath the helm, buttressing his body as securely as he could against the forward bulkhead to minimize injury when the boat came to a rasping, violent stop.

But nothing could have prepared Mattituck for the scraping, grinding sounds of the hull gliding on dry sand, the raucous din of every loose article on board flying forward and smashing into whatever lay in its trajectory. Mattituck had imagined the props digging into the sand, helping to stop the vessel's sleek hull from gliding through and over the sand, much like she was designed to do in the water.

When the noise and shaking had stopped, the DeeVee8 was hard aground and completely motionless. Mattituck had found himself partially buried under a pile of loose life jackets, plastic cups and plates, extra jackets and boots, and every other article that he had thought was well secured. It spoke of the violence of the beaching, as all these items had remained secured in very rough seas many times.

Now, standing on the knoll in the , Mattituck shook his head slowly and wondered how the fuck he'd gotten into this.

Not listening to Todd, to start with, he thought to himself as he scanned the water with his binoculars. Todd Benson had warned him of the danger, but he'd just barreled forward, riding on his own stubbornness. *Hubris*, he thought, reminiscing back to his college English class. *They call it hubris. What was the definition again? Overweening pride?* The hero suffering from hubris almost always had some kind of fall, sometimes his death. *I hope to fuck that isn't the case here*, Mattituck thought as he tucked the binoculars into their case, adjusted his pack, and headed onto the trail into the spruce.

Todd kicked and struggled with his arms to stay afloat. He'd wished he didn't have his boots on—or his pants, for that matter. Both were dragging him down, the pants saturated with salt water and the boots filled. Each kick of his legs felt heavy, requiring ten times the effort it would have taken to keep himself afloat if he hadn't had the damned boots and pants on. What had happened? He had no recollection of how he got in the water. He must have fallen overboard or---

He felt the cold water overtaking him. His legs were growing tired. His vision slipped beneath the surface, and he kicked hard to get above it. He couldn't feel whether his face was out of the water or not, as the 43 degree water had numbed his skin. He tried opening his eyes, and blinked. Air. It was air. He drew in a gulp of air, then felt himself being pulled down again by the water weight.

He felt something pulling at his sleeve, hard and insistent. Shark? At first, he hit at it, then felt cloth. He grasped at it and pulled, trying to pull himself back to air.

"Todd! Todd! It's me! Jessie!"

Todd's eyes sprang open to the reddened light inside AST 32067.

Safe... dry....

"Damn...." he muttered.

"You were *out*, man," Jessie said. "It took some real shaking to get you awake."

Todd nodded. "I'll be all right in a minute."

He hated that dream. It had been a few months since the last one, but damn! he thought, it really panicked him every time.

He sat up and looked around. The sun had set and left behind a deep twilight. He turned his attention to the dim glow of the GPS as he got up to take the helm.

"We're close to Zaikof, about 3 miles," Jessie said.

"Good. Thanks."

"Want some coffee? I know I'm not supposed to leave the helm, but I made another pot a while ago. Figured it might help when you woke up."

Todd looked at him and nodded.

"That and I wanted more," Jessie added with a smirk.

"Yeah, that's about more like it," Todd said, smiling.

As they cleared Middle Point and began a slow turn into Zaikof Bay, Todd pulled the binoculars from their case. Zaikof Bay is a straight inlet, so anybody at the mouth has a clear view all the way to the end of the bay. This is how the Danish Sun had been able to see the Kimberly Marie and the DeeVee8, and how even in the twilight Todd was now able to see all the way up the bay. The Kimberly Marie was easy enough to pick out in the near-darkness, with her white hull and white superstructure. She was sitting right of center of the bay, apparently anchored, although with no anchor lights – no lights of any kind.

Todd shook his head. "Jim Milner is not aboard that boat," he said. "He would have set the anchor lights as soon as he dropped anchor."

Jessie had the second set of binoculars and was scanning the shoreline.

"Unless he's being held hostage," Jessie proffered.

Todd mulled this over. "Could be," he finally replied. "But most cases where boats are stolen in Alaska, either the owner wasn't on board when it was stolen, or the owner is killed and disposed of." He looked at Jessie. "A lot less trouble just to get rid of them . . . and a lot of places to do that and never get caught." He gave a sweeping motion with his head, indicating the waters and land surrounding them.

Jessie nodded, then went back to the binoculars. "There's the DeeVee8, up on that beach used for deer hunter drop-offs."

Todd noted where Jessie was looking and trained his own binoculars in that direction, quickly picking up the slightly lighter aluminum superstructure in the twilight.

"No sign of anybody moving there, either," he finally noted. "Wonder what's going on."

He hated this kind of situation. No doubt, whoever was commandeering the Kimberly Marie were dangerous people. He had suspected with the Kimberly Marie reported missing that this might be related to the beached Bayliner murders, and by extension to the Yakutat murders of the older couple and Officer Wayne Barrett. But now with Frank Mattituck's boat intentionally run aground, there was little reason to doubt. He would have to approach the Kimberly Marie and the DeeVee8 completely exposed and vulnerable to attack. Training told him to call for and await backup. Instinct told him to proceed. He weighed the two options.

What circumstances could have driven Frank to drive his boat up onto the beach like that? And it was clear he knew precisely which beach to run up. Had he been attacked while approaching the Kimberly Marie? Did he set out on foot? Was he being pursued?

He fixed the binoculars on the Kimberly Marie again, specifically looking for a launch vessel. There was none. He couldn't recall with certainty, but it seemed Jim Milner had a little 8-foot rigid hull that he kept stowed on its side on the swim deck, secured to the transom. And hadn't the Danish Sun reported a small dinghy headed ashore toward the DeeVee8? Jim Milner had a small kicker outboard that he mounted to run people ashore to walk around, collect bear claw fungus and shells on the beach. There was no sign of it. He scanned the binoculars to the DeeVee8.

"Do you see any other vessel with the DeeVee8?"

"No . . . no I don't," Jessie replied. "Wait, yes . . . maybe. What's that up under the bow of the DeeVee8?"

As AST 32067 moved up the bay, the view of what was in front of the DeeVee8 improved, revealing the white pontoon side of a small rigid hull service vessel. So, somebody or somebodies were ashore, he thought, probably giving chase to Frank. Question now was, how about the Kimberly Marie? Was there anybody on board?

Todd drew on what he knew of other cases in Alaska. Most of the murder cases took place in remote areas, so he made a point of keeping abreast of them in greater detail than most of his colleagues. Which is how he'd picked up on the southeast story of a stolen Bayliner—a Bayliner he was now sure was aground in Growler Bay. As the FBI had long known, most murders follow patterns, even though they are not related to each other. There were certain sociological factors that tended to be true among them. One of these was that very few murders committed in marine settings involved more than two killers, and almost none involved only one except in cases of family and friend disputes. Given that the beached Bayliner only had one sleep quarters and there had been no sign that the dinette had been folded down for a bed – a standard feature on most boats – he doubted very much that the victims on the Bayliner had been killed by anybody they knew.

That placed the odds on there being two killers. If that were true, then Todd would bet his next paycheck both of them were ashore, hunting Frank. Nobody would leave a partner behind to hold anchor watch on a vessel in order to, by themselves, chase down an experienced outdoorsman—very likely armed—into the Alaska wilderness. No, Todd concluded. All parties were ashore, and the Kimberly Marie lay empty of occupants.

One of the many things Todd loved about his State Trooper boat was that the outfitters had equipped her with Honda outboards. Despite their behemoth size and incredible power—to say nothing of their reliability—they purred as quietly as a 2-horse kicker at near-idle speeds. This made them particularly well-suited to Todd Benson's line of work, and very handy in just this kind of situation. While it wasn't completely dark, it was dark enough to give good cover unless somebody was expecting to see you. And Todd suspected nobody expected to see him.

"We'll leave the Kimberly Marie for now," he announced to Jessie. "I very much doubt anybody's aboard. I think there are probably two of them, and they're ashore chasing Frank Mattituck."

Less than twenty minutes later, Todd was ashore, running from the water line to the DeeVee8 in a low crouch. He had a respectable amount of gear in a small pack: flashlights, a spare pair of binoculars, compass, a handheld VHF radio to back up the one clipped to his belt, water, light outer wear for weather, a fleece vest for warmth as a precaution, and several power bars. Outside the pack, he carried a Colt AR-15 rifle over his shoulder to complement the Gen4 Glock 22 on his hip, binoculars, and water. Anything else he might need would probably mean he needed to come back to shore anyhow, so he hadn't bothered.

As he came along the starboard side of the DeeVee8, he lit the flashlight to look her over. He immediately noticed a bullet hole in the aluminum hull, just below the painted yellow belt that ran all down her side. He leaned back to gain a better view of the superstructure of the vessel, expecting to see shot-out windows. At first he saw no sign of gunshots up that high, and concluded that the killers—presumably panicked and firing at the DeeVee8 when she approached—were terrible shots. This didn't fit his theory that these guys were the killers of Wayne Barrett. But then he noticed the VHF antenna hanging over the front windshield, dangling by its cable. Its base projected out over the starboard gunwale several feet forward of where Todd crouched. He stood up and approached, noting three or four bullet holes next to the base of the antenna mount.

Someone had targeted Frank's antenna.

He quickly revised his assessment of the killers, and decided they had to be pretty good shots to take out an antenna. Marksman level. Good enough shots to match those who had picked off Wayne Barrett in rough seas.

His attention turned back to the bullet hole in the hull, and only then did he notice a line of them along the side. Weird, he thought, trying to figure out how such a good shot would repeatedly hit lower than his target.

Unless, it hit him, the target wasn't Frank. He realized then that all the shots were at or near where the water line would have been. Like any vessel that was ported in a slip and kept in the water all season, the DeeVee8 had a green film of algae along the bottom that curled up along the bottom of the sides, clearly marking her waterline. Why had they targeted there?

An eery nagging led Todd to the thought that the killers had been more interested in keeping Frank from going to open water than killing him. Again, why? Did they need him to navigate the Kimberly Marie? Did they want the boat? But surely, he thought, if they wanted the boat, they would have shot Frank and motored over and taken the DeeVee8. No, there was some other reason. A reason that meant they needed Frank alive.

Todd passed along the stern and up the port side, only then noticing the shot-out windows along the port side. Maybe they had been shooting at Frank afterall.

Todd shook his head, baffled. Well, he thought, it wouldn't be the first time psycho thinking had baffled a law man.

Once Todd had finished surveying the scene of the DeeVee8 and convinced himself the killers were not lying in wait in the grass above, he signaled with the flashlight to Jessie, waiting at the helm of AST 32067, VHF-ready to relay any distress calls. Todd waved his arm in a circle above his head and pointed to the mouth of the bay, knowing there was enough light to see his gesture. In response, AST 32067's twin Hondas kicked into reverse idle and backed the boat away from shore. As soon as the bow spun back and pointed up the bay, Todd heard her gearing shift forward. She idled forward, then gently picked up speed to 5kts, per Todd's earlier instructions. He watched as she puttered away, knowing that at the one-mile mark, Jessie would take her up on step and speed around to anchor just inside Rocky Bay, the next bay north, and await Todd's call. He wanted AST 32067 well out of sight.

He made his way, crouching, along the hull of the DeeVee8 to the bow and cautiously peeked around to the service boat from the Kimberly Marie. Judging from the tracks from the water line, two men had taken pains to drag the small boat all the way up to the DeeVee8's hull and tried to keep her as much out of sight as they could. Why they would bother was beyond Todd, as the DeeVee8 beached would be enough to attract concern from any passers-by.

He noted three sets of footprints headed to the grassy marsh at the head of the beach. One would be Frank's, the other two the suspects'. Todd stepped back to the starboard side of the DeeVee8, the opposite side from the footprints and dinghy. He pulled the outerwear from his pack and bunched it around the butt of the AR-15, then taped it loosely with the hunter's duct tape he always had in the pack. Like the redneck story goes, anything can be fixed with duct tape. Todd smiled to himself as he started up the sandy beach, carefully rubbing out his tracks with the make-shift broom until he reach the tall grasses thirty feet uphill.

Once there, he unwrapped the outergear, folded it roughly, and stowed it in the pack. He then made sure no sand was on the rifle, and slung it back over his shoulder. While he was an excellent tracker, he didn't bother in the grassy marsh, especially in the twilight. He knew where Frank would have headed from here—to the trail at the left of the beach. He quietly made his way through the six-foot grass, attentive to any sign of the two men ahead. Unconsciously, his right hand dropped to the state-issued Glock to make sure it was there.

He noted the sky was getting lighter and checked his watch and confirmed that the sun was on its upward rise.

Montague Island was a popular deer-hunting destination for outdoorsmen from all over the Lower 48. Both this island and Hinchinbrook Island across the Entrance were known for high deer populations as well as favorable hiking ground for hunting. On this end of the island, the beach he was now traversing was the choice drop-off point largely because it afforded easy and quick access to the long, narrow island's interior muskeg fields. There, the spongy muskeg made for relatively good visibility for miles, as it lay low and—once a hiker figured out how to spring along its sponginess—easy to hike over open terrain. There were low scrub brush stands everywhere, providing plenty of cover for a hunter wanting to lay in wait for prey. The plentiful deer population and relative inaccessibility of both islands drew many hunters.

And where there were deer, there were bears.

Todd always kept his ears and eyes alert while on land in the wilderness. There were both black bears and brown bears—grizzlies—just about any wilderness area one might be in, and coming across a hungry black bear or a grizzly protecting a kill site instantly jeopardized a person's safety. On this particular island, because so many hunting parties entered and exited on that same beach, a well-maintained trail had been established. This gave most hunters new to Alaska the illusion of safety, but they were quickly warned by their guides that all wildlife in addition to humans enjoyed an easy walk along a trail.

Frank would know this, of course, but Todd found himself wondering about the killers. How well did they know Alaska? The beached Bayliner had been registered in the state of Washington, so it was a strong possibility the killers had stolen the boat down and brought it up to this part of Alaska to escape.

No, Todd thought as he strode briskly along the trail. That theory didn't fit the report from the Washington Crime Bureau, which had run the registration numbers and followed up with a wellness check on the registered owners in the Seattle area. They had learned from neighbors that the owners had taken the boat on an extended vacation up the Inside Passage to Juneau, Alaska, and hadn't expected them back at any particular time, although they were overdue calling in from Juneau.

It had also been discovered that the owners had been a retired couple prone to long trips in protected waters with their beloved boat. No way the owners would ever have crossed the Gulf, thought Todd—not even along the relative safety along the coast from Glacier Bay to Prince William Sound. He also figured that it was very unlikely that the killers had been on board up the Inside Passage through Canada and Southeast Alaska. And if the owners had been due to call from Juneau when they arrived, it was likely the killers had boarded the boat someplace in Canada or Southeast Alaska. Someplace south of Juneau.

As Todd gained the trail through the marsh and into the spruce, he paused and watched ahead into the darkened shadows of the woods. Valdez was technically the edge of the rain forest designation, a demarcation for a dominance of conifer trees as opposed to deciduous, which grew north of the rain forest zone. With what he could guess about the killers, he decided it might be best to assume they knew something about Alaska in general, most likely were from Southeast, and probably knew little or nothing about Prince William Sound. Still, they probably had enough survival skills to make do.

Again, Todd thought it best to use extreme caution with these guys.

He decided to get into the cover of the woods and proceed carefully. Hopefully by the time he made the muskeg fields on the other side, there would be full light and sunrise. If the killers were continuing ahead of him, he would be able to see them pretty easily. He might even be able to see Frank, if he weren't too far ahead. Even if he didn't see Frank, perhaps he would be able to figure out where Frank was leading them.

In any case, he had no doubt that Frank was intentionally leading them somewhere. Where, and for what purpose, he had no idea. Survival for sure. But there was good reason to believe Frank knew what had befallen his friend, Jim Milner. Was Frank the type to seek revenge? Would he intentionally lure these guys ashore and then take them out? Todd knew Frank as well as any charter boat captain, perhaps better. He was a good man, Todd was sure, but he also knew Frank could be unpredictable and prone to angry outbursts. Like the fight a few days before with Toby Burns. Sure, Toby had provoked him, but it sounded like Frank Mattituck had been more than willing to finish the scene with ruthless calculation.

This situation was far more provocative than the one with Toby Burns. And if Frank knew these guys were responsible for the death of a good friend, and then had the killers in his sight . . . And the bullet holes along the hull of the DeeVee8 had indicated that these men had been out to kill Frank as well.

Yep, Todd thought, *an angry Frank is capable of luring these men into the wilderness to avenge Jim Milner.*

Todd picked up his pace. He was now unsure of whether he wanted to catch up to protect Frank from being murdered, or from murdering.

Mattituck paused at the edge of the grove of spruce that had given him much-desired cover thus far. He was fairly certain his pursuers were a fair distance behind him, but he would be exposed on the musket fields for well over a mile with only a few low stands of scrub brush here and there. Here, the trail gave way to the wide open country, a point where hunting parties tended to strike headings to the hunting areas their guides had pre-determined. Most of the ground had varying depths of muskeg, but there were also large patches of open field with hard ground beneath. He would have to move swiftly.

He surveyed the terrain ahead, looking for a high point from which he could call for help on the handheld VHF. He thought from memory there had been a high hill to the north or northwest, but other than a few low hills of less than 200 feet, there was nothing but spruce, muskeg, and open field. The mountainous part of the island ran along the southern part of the island in a line from southwest to northeast. He was far less familiar with that terrain, and wasn't sure whether there were gorges before he reached the mountains. All he really needed was a few hundred feet to get a good line-of-sight signal.

There was an almost round hill directly west of him—toward Green Island—at the end of a longer hill stretching to the northeast. While the long hill it was attached to was barely more than a protrusion above the spruce at its base, the round hill stood relatively tall at probably five- or six-hundred feet. It lay four or five miles away, with a fair number of scrub stands along the way. Close to midway, there was a stand of trees that might give him some good cover.

He raised the compass to his eye and set the sights to take an accurate reading. The heading would be 253 degrees, but the magnetic compass didn't read true north. The true bearing was probably closer to 265 or so, but it didn't matter for his purposes. He would be using the same compass on his return. He didn't have time to use full cross-country navigation techniques, but he sure as hell didn't want to come back imprecisely and unable to find the trail back to the beach. He wrote down the heading for the round top hill, as well as the opposite reading for the return. The reality, he knew, was that he probably would not have the opportunity to come back the same way, but it was worth noting just in case.

He tucked the compass back into the outer pocket of the pack and swung it onto his back, securing the chest clip and waist belt that would keep the weight well-distributed over the small of his back. He turned back toward the trail to watch and listen for several moments. Satisfied there was nobody closing in, he turned to the round top hill, drew a deep breath, and set out onto the muskeg field.

Two hours after Todd Benson had set out onto the trail leading into the spruce, he broke out of the woods on the eastern edge of the muskeg fields. He had kept a good clip moving along the trail, ears and eyes alert to any signs ahead that he was catching up to Frank's pursuers. In time, he had become more convinced that all three of them were well ahead of him, and he'd picked up his pace to try to close the gap.

Now he paused at the edge of the spruce and dropped the pack and rifle to pull out the binoculars to see if he could spot Frank or the killers. It was not as easy as it seemed to pick out people walking among brush and earth-toned muskeg. Motion was hard to pick up at a distance, and most clothing was not brightly colored, so it tended to blend in with all the other shadowed splotches of brush in the fields.

On his initial scan of the terrain, he didn't see anybody. On his second scan, however, he picked up a large splotch that when he fixed the binoculars still on it appeared to be a bear—very likely a large brown bear, judging by the distance. It lay almost directly west, toward Green Island. He hoped he didn't have to go that way. It would add to the difficulty if he had to account for avoiding that bear. But nothing lay that way except a round top hill and Green Island laying alongside Montague, and only a passage between with a very rocky northern shore on Montague. That would not be a good direction for escape, so it was unlikely Frank was leading his pursuers that way.

Unless, of course, Frank's intentions were avenging Jim rather than escape.

He scanned to the south, where the mountainous range of Montague stretched to the southwest. Todd knew this terrain well, and was fairly sure Frank did, too, and while gaining altitude over one's pursuers would have a distinct advantage, there were gorges and ravines that would make that direction extremely difficult. Of course, Todd thought, he would also have a pretty good radio signal up there---

Todd stopped and allowed the binoculars to fall from his eyes. He remembered the antenna of the DeeVee8 just then, and realized that Frank Mattituck probably had a handheld radio.

The realization hit him with the forcefulness of an obvious truth.

Frank wasn't trying to draw his pursuers. He was trying to escape them and at the same time get to high ground for a better radio signal. Todd was immediately sure of this. Handheld VHF radios were far less powerful than the marine VHF radios on boats, and VHF was a line-of-sight radio signal. Any obstructions, such as mountains, could block the signal. With the DeeVee8's antenna taken out and holes along her hull that prevented her going into the rough seas of the Sound, Frank had taken to land to seek higher ground in order to call for help.

He should have known. As volatile as Frank Mattituck could be, murder wouldn't be in his character.

Todd dropped the pack again and pulled out his handheld VHF. He turned on the power and watched the radio power up to channel 16, its default setting. He tried the mic key twice to make sure it worked.

"DeeVee8, DeeVee8, can you read me?"

He waited. Hopefully, Frank had his radio on.

"DeeVee8, DeeVee8, do you pick me up. Frank, it's Todd. Can you hear me?"

Silence.

He tried three more times, then gave up. Frank probably was waiting to get to high ground before powering up. No sense wasting the battery. Todd clipped his radio back onto his belt, leaving the power on. If Frank did call for help, Todd wanted to hear it. And he had backup batteries.

Binoculars back in hand, Todd surveyed the possible routes Frank and his pursuers might have taken. To the right, the north and northeast, there were no high points to speak of, only muskeg, scrub, and a few stands. He began to scan back to the left. There were a few higher spots, but nothing that would attract Todd if he were looking for higher ground for a radio signal. He kept scanning left, and stopped at the round top hill he'd seen earlier. If Frank were heading for high ground and a good VHF signal, that would be a good choice.

He began scanning down, hoping to see a sign of Frank or the killers, although he suspected they were much closer to him than the round top hill.

He panned the binoculars' view back and forth in a grid that covered any meandering Frank or the killers might be taking. He noted that he no longer could see the bear, and made a mental note of that area, picking out a marker of a small stand of spruce as being near where the bear had been. While happening on a bear could happen any time on Montague, it was wise to keep track as best one could where the known bears were. He continued his span closer and closer, back and forth in his search grid.

Nothing.

Todd turned his attention to the ground, looking for signs of recent depressions in the muskeg, or tears that the boots might have made. He moved forward slowly, scanning the ground as he walked. After he'd covered some thirty feet, he noted a clump of overturned muskeg. The damp underside of the muskeg made it dark against the backdrop of the muskeg tops all around it. Having a clear grasp of the discoloration, he scanned ahead in a line roughly toward the round top hill, and saw more overturned muskeg. He looked to the right and left, but found no similar signs. Something or someone had clearly been through here. He followed the damp muskeg patches forward, noting it was taking him toward the round top hill.

He was beginning to think he could read Frank's mind.

After several hundred yards, he was sure of Frank's intention, and set himself confidently in that direction.

He was also sure, however, that the killers had taken the same route. Either they were good trackers, or they had spotted Frank heading in that direction. Knowing the answer to that would give another clue of how experienced these men were in the wilderness, and a better idea of what he was up against. And a better idea of Frank's chances to survive being hunted.

Skipper's Oath

Chapter Six

A Bruin Interruption

Mattituck had made good time, considering he had kept primarily on the muskeg to hide his trail. Only once had he spotted his pursuers, behind by enough distance to give Mattituck a sense of relief. He was well-armed with the Glock and the Winchester. Even at a distance, he could take out the killers if he needed to, but he would rather not. He had always been one to follow the law—except perhaps speed limits and a few other traffic laws. And when people like Toby Burns pissed him off.

These guys from Jim Milner's boat and whatever they'd done to Jim was between them and the justice system, and Mattituck had no interest in getting himself into any more trouble than he already had. As close as he was to Jim, he would not risk his future when the justice system could deal with these guys.

He thought back over the previous hours.

He had not expected to really find any trouble when he came out to Zaikof Bay. Something had seemed odd, definitely, and it certainly had crossed his mind that

Jim may have been in serious trouble, but he hadn't really thought he'd find that was the case.

He climbed a low knoll free of muskeg, huffing slightly as his thoughts meandered. *So many times*, he thought, *when you follow up on a person being overdue, or some weird circumstance that made you worried, you'd call that person and have them answer right away – all's well. Sometimes, you'd even feel stupid for it.* But now it seemed the worst-case conjectures might actually be real.

He paused at the top of the knoll and turned around to see if he could see the pursuers. He did. They were a good mile back, hiking along several feet apart. Mattituck pulled out his binoculars and found them in his sights. The shorter man was leading the way, head down and a Seahawks cap blocking his face as he picked his way through the uneven muskeg. The taller man followed, shoulders slumped like he was fatigued. He was not a thin man, whereas his partner appeared in pretty good shape. This might explain why the taller one was lagging behind. Neither had a weapon in his hand, and Mattituck surmised that the way the shorter one was moving, the pair were confident of where Mattituck was and were focused on keeping a good pace.

Mattituck turned and surveyed the terrain ahead. The round top hill looked like it might be another two miles ahead. If memory served him well—it had been last summer when he'd hiked this area last—the bigger streams ran to the left of his route, and a couple more on the right, closer up toward Rocky Bay. There was a slight elevation that ran just about where his route lay, which was part of why he'd settled on the round top to try his radio. But it also had the advantage of saving him crossing any streams.

Now, looking ahead, the route pleased him even more. It provided plenty of cleared terrain so he could keep a good pace, but also plenty of patches of scrub brush to provide cover should he need it.

Something caught his eye as the binocular view passed over one of these patches. He stopped and scanned back, stopping on a point where there was some motion. Deer, he hoped, or moose.

"Sure as fuck hope it isn't a bear," he said aloud, just to hear his voice.

He saw a brown patch of hide through a separation in the brush, and tensed. He waited to see if it would clear the brush to the left, where it appeared to be headed. A massive head emerged, and Mattituck watched the great grizzly's hide seem to shake with each heavy step it took.

"Shit . . ." Mattituck shook his head at the bad luck. The fucking bear was to the right of his intended route, crossing to the left. He and the bear were very nearly on a collision course.

He watched the bear for several minutes through the binoculars. It stopped periodically and sniffed at the air. It was hungry, trying to pick up the scent of any potential prey. Mattituck had every intention of not being that prey.

That thought stopped him short.

What if his pursuers became an interest for the bear? That would present a formidable obstruction for them and buy him a good chunk of time.

But how? . . .

He didn't exactly have a side of raw beef handy to bait the bear. He wasn't even sure how he'd attract the bear's attention anyhow—he was too far to be sure he was upwind, although the slight breeze he felt did put him generally upwind of the brawny grizzly. He watched as the bear stopped again to snuff at the air. Its snout turned side to side, gauging the strength of whatever he was smelling. The snout gravitated more in Mattituck's direction, and he realized the bear had picked up his scent.

He felt his stomach tense as he maintained watch to see what the bear would do. It was looking his direction now, but seemed to be focused slightly to Mattituck's right. Maybe the bear had poor eyesight, as Mattituck felt completely exposed standing in plain sight. In reality, he was probably much harder to pick out than he felt like he was, particularly since he was stock still. A movement down the knoll and to his right startled him with its silence. A deer stepped out from behind a small patch of scrub, silent as she stepped over the muskeg.

His bait.

Instinctively, he drew the Glock and fired. The deer bucked and jumped forward, and for a moment, Mattituck thought he'd missed. But then the deer faltered while trying to bolt to the left, and dropped onto the muskeg, kicking at its loss of balance, its eyes wide with fear and bewilderment.

Mattituck swung the binoculars back to his eyes and to the bear. Despite the distance, the grizzly had seen the deer and its tell-tale death throes. It was standing on its hind legs to afford a better view, sniffing at the air. Had it seen him? Mattituck wondered.

The bear dropped to all fours and started toward him. At first, Mattituck thought the bear was walking, from the way its hide shimmered in waves under the steps. Then he noticed the way the head and buttocks were alternating in height, and realized that the bear was running right toward him.

He prayed to god the bear hadn't seen him, and would cross the deer before it reached him.

He bolted to his right, hoping to ditch behind the scrub brush before the bear saw him, in the event it hadn't already. There was a good chance it had only noticed the deer, he thought as he lost his footing in a sudden sharp drop, sliding on a rare stretch of exposed dirt. The slide took him the rest of the way down and behind the scrub brush patch, the opposite side of where the bear had been running toward him.

The deer had died in an unusual display. More often than not, they dropped straight down when shot in the heart. Unless, he didn't hit it where he'd intended. This was, after all, the first time he'd shot a deer with a handgun. Nonetheless, it had bolted and leapt in a way that made a tasty attraction for a hungry bear, Mattituck imagined, so with luck it would stop at the deer and claim it as his kill.

The patch of scrub provided excellent cover, each conifer bush standing six to eight feet high, and thick. This allowed him to walk upright. There was no way of cutting through there, though, even if he'd wanted to. As it was, he was happy to circumnavigate the patch to keep away from the bear. If he was lucky, the big grizzly would get to work eating dinner and not even notice him passing by a quarter of a mile northeast.

A few minutes later, his boot steps silent on the muskeg, he heard a low grunt followed by a sudden rush through some brush, complete with dried branches cracking and breaking. Then he heard a soft yelp. Clearly, the deer wasn't dead when the bear pounced on it. Not his best job taking down a deer, he thought, but for all the cruelty of the animal's death, it had worked out perfectly for Mattituck. The bear would not move from the kill until his stomach was overfilled and satisfied. Or if there were a threat to its kill site. After filling its belly, the grizzly would then move off a short distance and sleep, then get back to work stuffing himself on the carcass when he awoke. The only thing that could distract the bear from its kill was an intruder.

Mattituck hoped the two pursuers would be those intruders.

Where the deer had been downed was a perfect spot for Mattituck's hopes. He had been atop the knoll, where he'd been watching the bear in the binoculars, when the deer stepped out from behind the brush and been taken down by the Glock. The entire scene was hidden completely from his pursuers, and a mere twenty or thirty feet below the knoll. The sharp incline of the knoll on the side the pursuers would come up was sharp enough that they would climb the short steepness quickly . . . too late to avoid alerting the bear.

With luck, the bear would attack.

This hungry brown bear would very likely want to protect its kill and attack Mattituck's pursuers the minute they appeared on the knoll. They would have to act quickly and get shots off, or at least one of them would be mauled.

The sounds from the other side of the scrub patch were horrific and unnerving. Mattituck's gut went cold with the thought of being the victim of such a powerful, merciless beast. He tried to move quietly along the edge of the patch, circling around with it as the brush gave way to the north, then toward the northwest. He guessed he was a good quarter mile from the bear now, and increasing the distance as he moved along.

He paused to see if he could pick up the pursuers behind him. No doubt they had heard the Glock fire, and might pause to try to figure out why Mattituck had fired a weapon.

"Damn," he whispered. He wished he had thought of that before.

They might see him moving around the patch and follow suit, missing the bear entirely. On the other hand, there was no way in hell he would have lay low that close to the bear.

He had no choice. He'd had to move and risk being spotted.

He stepped behind a straggling branch from a conifer scrub and scanned behind with the binoculars. He had risen up another small knoll that gave a good view of the field he'd passed through. He spotted the two men walking, still over a mile behind. He was surprised to see them still moving at a good pace. Hadn't they heard the Glock? Could his luck be that good? Then he remembered he'd been up wind of the bear. Bad for being near a bear, but good for cutting the range a loud noise could be heard at a distance. Perhaps they hadn't heard the gunshot after all. Even if they had, it hadn't seemed to give them pause.

Mattituck let the binoculars hang from his neck as he continued his hike around the brush patch. He would want to check on the bear periodically, although now he was sure the bear would not take interest in him unless it felt he was a threat to its claimed kill.

Mattituck had no intention of challenging the bear, and made a straight course for the round top hill.

Todd never heard the Glock. Like the killers, he was upwind of Mattituck, and a good share farther away. But he also had been in a low part of the muskeg field, more than two miles behind Frank. With no mountains to echo the gunshot, the sound waves continued unheeded in their ever-expanding waves outward, not to return and report their origin.

What was different now for Todd was that he'd spotted the two killers heading in precisely the direction he suspected. Now it almost didn't matter which way Frank Mattituck had gone, though Todd had no doubt they knew where Frank was headed and were in hot pursuit. Todd's prey, however, was the two killers.

Frank Mattituck was perfectly capable of taking care of himself.

He continued his trek over the muskeg, his boots crunching earth periodically over the areas that the muskeg had not taken over. Whenever he reached a high point, he unsheathed the binoculars and checked on the two killers. Usually he did not see them, likely because they were traversing a low point, but he saw them frequently enough that he knew he was still on their trail. They were keeping a good pace, but Todd seemed to be gaining on them, very likely because the taller of the two seemed to be struggling a bit on the hike. Was he wearing down, or did he have an injury? Todd wondered. He grimaced and eliminated the possibility of an injury – he would not have even left the beach with an injury or defect. Still, if the man were fatigued, this was useful for Todd to be aware of. It told him who to focus on when he caught up.

Soon he came alongside a patch of conifer scrub that required him to cut to the left and up a knoll that promised to afford a good view ahead. He climbed the slow hill, his boots sinking into deeper muskeg. He was climbing the knoll on the north side, which had less sun and allowed the muskeg to grow more thickly.

It was less than twenty minutes after Mattituck had stopped on a low hill and checked on the bear with his binoculars that he heard the screams.

They were preceded with two quick shots, and quickly fell silent. Another shot sounded, then silence. Mattituck scrambled up the nearest knoll and searched back with the binoculars to the kill site and the bear. He saw a man running back toward the beach, occasionally losing his footing on the muskeg and falling. He watched the man for several seconds before spanning back toward himself, to the kill site area.

He saw the low beige spot in an upward concave that would be the deer's carcasse. A hoofed leg was protruding toward the clouds, but there was no bear. He lifted the binoculars slightly and sighted the haunches of the grizzly, shaking slightly as the bear stepped sideways. The back of its head shook, as if it were shaking at something. Mattituck was aligned perfectly with the bear's spine, so he could not see around the wide body of the bear to see what he had in front of him. He could hear nothing at this distance. The screams were the last thing he'd heard.

Then he saw a hand grabbing at the bear's left ear, and another hand pounding at the top of the bear's head. The bear's head gave a violent shake, and the hands fell away.

Mattituck lowered the binoculars. Even though he'd made possible this trap, he took no pleasure in the fact that it had worked. In fact, he felt a very strong sense of regret and guilt. It would have been far more humane to have simply lie in wait and bushwhacked both his pursuers than leave the man to this kind of fate.

He turned and crouched over, nearly vomiting onto the brown spongy muskeg. His equilibrium went awry, and he careened to the side before putting out a hand on the ground to steady himself.

Mattituck was an experienced outdoorsman who had seen much death in his life. But nothing could prepare even the toughest of men for what he had just witnessed. Dying was one thing. Being mauled by a grizzly was something else entirely. A circle in Dante's hell must have been reserved for this kind of suffering.

Not sure whether he was still in danger, Mattituck pushed upward and gained his feet. He did not want to look again, but he needed to see whether the other man was still pursuing him. He raised the binoculars, bracing himself. The bear was walking slowly back to its deer, its bloodied face clear in the midday sun. Whether it was the blood of the man or the deer could not be guessed, but at least it had left off the man to return to its meal. The fact that the attack on the man—in keeping with most grizzly attacks—was in defense of the kill site was probably all that would give the fallen man a chance at life.

He raised the binoculars and found the other man, no longer running, but still making way back toward Zaikof Bay. He paused as Mattituck watched, turning toward where he had left his friend. The man stood for several moments, then started toward the kill site. He stopped, apparently listening. Clearly, the man didn't know what to do. The man pulled his rifle off his shoulder and started toward the kill site again. It looked like he intended to shoot the bear. If Mattituck's memory were accurate, he'd heard three shots at the time of the attack. Now it was clear that those shots had come from this man, the shorter of the two—the marksman who had plugged precise shots into the DeeVee8.

Mattituck considered. If this man had fired shots, there was little doubt in Mattituck's mind that at least one bullet had found its mark in the bear. But bears that size did not come down easily. The bullet—or bullets—had probably only made the bear more angry, and likely intensified the attack on the taller man.

The memory of the hands and the screams began to seep into his consciousness, and he fought them back, pushing them down into the subconscious. Mattituck had his own survival to attend to.

He pulled the VHF out of his backpack. This man needed help. Now. If there was any chance of a signal . . .

"Mayday, Mayday, Mayday, this is the DeeVee8, channel one-six, over."

He waited.

"Mayday, Mayday, Mayday, this is the DeeVee8, channel one-six, over," he repeated.

"Vessel calling Mayday, this is United States Coast Guard Area Anchorage, over."

A wave of relief swept over Mattituck.

"Coast Guard, I'm on land—on Montague Island, due west of the end of Zaikof Bay. I just witnessed a man being attacked by a bear, over."

"Roger, DeeVee8. Copied. Are you on scene?"

"Roger, Coast Guard . . . about a mile to the west."

"Roger, Sir. Is the attack still under way, over?"

"Negative, Coast Guard. The bear appears to have been protecting a kill site. It attacked the man, but is now back at its kill site."

"Roger, DeeVee8. Copied. Is the victim moving, over?"

"I can't tell, Coast Guard," Mattituck said, fighting back the relief that he was actually now talking to help. "It's too far away."

"Copied, DeeVee8. Stand by one."

Mattituck sat down and waited.

"DeeVee8," came a new voice. "AST 32067, over."

Todd! Mattituck jumped at the handheld.

"Todd," he blurted, "where are you?"

"My best guess," came the answer, "is about two or two-and-a-half miles behind you."

Thank god! Mattituck thought. Ho-lee shit! Todd only a couple miles back? How the fuck had he pulled *that* off?

"AST 32067, DeeVee8, this is Coast Guard Area Anchorage. Switch channel two-one, over."

Both replied in the affirmative, and switched.

"AST, DeeVee8, this is Coast Guard Anchorage. Be advised, a helicopter will be enroute your location in approximately 45 minutes."

"Roger, Coast Guard. This is AST. Has the team been dropped at the previous location? Over."

"Roger, AST. Team dropped, and helo nearly returned to Elmendorf. She will refuel and launch as soon as able, over."

"This is AST, roger."

"DeeVee8, this is AST, over."

"I'm here, Todd."

"You know about the two behind you, right?"

"Yes. Only it's one now. The other one is headed back your way."

"Copied, Frank. Thanks."

"I was headed to high ground to try to call you on this handheld," Mattituck continued. "I guess now I can double back. Except I have this bear in my way now."

"Roger—copied that. Maybe cut back around to the north? But do come back this way," Todd said. "I may need your help."

"Copied," Mattituck said.

"We have the remaining –"

A shot rang out. Mattituck, being downwind now, heard the shot clearly.

"Todd?"

Silence.

"Todd? Come in, Todd. Are you there?"

Silence. Another shot rang over the scrub brush and muskeg. Mattituck raised the binoculars toward where he thought he'd last seen the short man.

Nothing.

He lowered the binoculars to the other man—the downed one. He saw the bear, head raised from the carcass of the deer, looking in Todd's direction.

"DeeVee8, DeeVee8, this is Coast Guard Anchorage, over."

"Go ahead, Coast Guard."

"What's going on, captain?"

Mattituck paused. "I wish I knew."

The Coast Guard was silent.

Mattituck added, "I was trying to coordinate with AST 32… 32- whatever. Todd, I was trying to talk to Trooper Todd Benson, and I heard two shots. Then silence."

"Copied, DeeVee8. Do you have visual, over?"

"Negative, Coast Guard, they're too far away. Or down below a knoll. I can't see them."

"Roger, DeeVee8. Copied. You mentioned another person, over?"

"Yes, that's right," Mattituck replied, dropping the protocol. "There were two chasing me, and apparently Trooper Benson was behind them. I witnessed the brown bear attack one of the men pursuing me, and the other one running back the other way, apparently toward Todd."

He paused.

"Now there's silence. I don't know what happened. I'll circle back."

Mattituck heard a new shot fired. Then two more, then a series of shots. Todd was in a firefight with the short guy.

Mattituck reported this to the Coast Guard, then began running back the direction he'd come, careful to stay well north—to the left—of the grizzly and his kill site.

Todd heard a shot close by, then saw the short killer on a knoll just west of him. He could hear Frank calling him, but there was no time to reply. He pulled the Gen4 Glock from his holster. He would have preferred the A-15, but there wasn't enough time. He raised his weapon toward the knoll and fired off a shot. It was returned by two quick shots, one whizzing past him no more than a couple of feet away.

Todd quickly assessed the terrain around him. If he was going to engage in a shootout, he needed better cover. The news of the bear attack had surprised Todd.

How the *hell* had that happened? he wondered. What were the odds of a bear taking out one of the killers?

There was a small scrub patch forty feet to his right, to the north. He glanced back at the killer on the knoll and, seeing that the man was crouched and looking back toward Frank, Todd broke in a dead run for the scrub. A shot rang out, and Todd dove behind the low brush as he approached. His shoulder hit the soft muskeg and he rolled over onto his belly. He peered for an opening in the brush in the direction of his assailant. The brush was thick, and he could not see through to the other side.

He paused to think, the conversation between Frank and the Coast Guard in his ears over the VHF. Todd wasn't listening. His entire being was focused on the gunman ahead. He decided to fall back.

Skipper's Oath

Chapter Seven

Hunter Becomes Hunted

As Mattituck came abreast of the same scrub stand he'd earlier used to keep himself safe from the brown bear, he heard a shot ahead. He stopped and trained the binoculars in the direction of the shot. He heard another shot, then one further away, presumably in return. A moment of silence, then three more shots, two from the nearer gunman, and one from the farther.

Todd was in a gunfight with the remaining gunman.

Mattituck pulled the Winchester from his shoulder and took the safety off, then patted his vest pocket to make sure he had backup ammo ready. He checked the binoculars again, but could see nothing. More gunfire, then several moments of silence. Mattituck could picture each man moving around scrub brush, trying to avoid becoming a target, but seeking a target in his opponent, pausing periodically to take a shot at the other.

He paused to see if he could hear anything of the grizzly, but could hear nothing other than the occasional shots ahead. He ventured away from the scrub patch and onto the open muskeg, sporadically walking across dried grass and pebbly earth. As he made his way into the open, gaining on the gunshots, he paused and looked back toward the grizzly's kill site with the binoculars. He could see the brawny brown back, curved over either the deer or the man. When he panned left with the binoculars, he saw a patch of blue denim lying some twenty feet up a small knoll from the bear.

The downed man. Clearly, the bear was at work on the deer carcass, not the man. He got on the radio and relayed this information to the Coast Guard, along with a more accurate description of the location of the man.

"Roger, DeeVee8. Copied. Can you tell if the victim is alive? Over."

"No, Coast Guard. I can't." He looked in the binoculars again. The denim lay precisely in the same place. "He hasn't moved. But I have a pretty good view of an entire leg, and I don't see any blood. The bear is at work on the deer—its original kill site."

"Roger, DeeVee8. Copied."

"There have been shots back toward Zaikof Bay, Coast Guard," he continued. "I think AST 32-whatever is in a shootout with the other gunman."

A pause.

"Roger, DeeVee8. Copied."

Another pause.

"DeeVee8, request to know your intentions, over."

Mattituck thought about this. He hadn't thought about what exactly he was going to do. He was just moving back toward Todd and the gunman.

"I don't know, Coast Guard. But I'm headed back toward Todd."

"Roger, sir."

Another pause. Obviously, there was somebody else directing the conversation, and the radio operator was merely relaying questions.

"Are you armed, DeeVee8?"

"Roger, Coast Guard. I'm in very good shape that way."

A more prolonged pause.

"DeeVee8, Coast Guard. Roger, sir. Please keep us apprised, over."

"Roger that, Coast Guard. I definitely will."

He hooked the radio onto his belt loop and started off in the direction of the gunshots, the Winchester rifle ready and gripped tightly in his right hand, level to the uneven ground. As he took longer strides over the terrain, he took periodic glances over his right shoulder to make sure the bear remained where it was—although there was very little chance of attack now, since the bear would see he was clearly moving away from its meal.

Todd had fallen back to a small stand of spruce a quarter mile farther than the scrub patch he'd been behind when he engaged the killer. Here there was much better cover. The tall spruce created a darkened area beneath them that the gunman would be unlikely to see into very well. He had hiked in a solid fifteen feet into the relative darkness of the mini-forest and planted himself behind a fallen tree that lay nearly flat to the ground beneath it, yet the top of which was about belly high if Todd had stood next to it. Perfect height for him to crouch behind with the AR-15. Better yet, the spruce cupped around him in a concave, the apex of which he was situated. Again, the wildnerness gods seemed to be with him. This concave meant there were no tree trunks obstructing his view, but it placed him well within the safe darkness of the trees. The approaching gunman would have a very difficult time finding Todd a target.

He dropped his small pack behind the log, to his left, and used it as a table for staging what he needed. He lay the GEN4 Glock with two backup clips next to it, then the radio—volume reduced so that it couldn't be heard more than ten feet away—next to the clips. Finally, he leaned the AR-15 adjacent to the pack, against the log. He brought the binoculars to his eyes and kept watch for the figure he knew would soon appear over the slight ridge to the west.

The low ridge was not even high enough to block the view of the round top hill Frank had been heading for, but it was high enough to block the view of anybody walking more than fifty or so feet beyond it. Since he didn't know where the gunman would appear, he kept a constant scanning watch along the ridge, back and forth, back and forth. After five minutes or so, he decided the gunman must be lying in wait for him, and Todd pulled two power bars out of his pack along with a bottle of water. He kept watch on the ridge as he ate and drank.

Mattituck hadn't heard any shots for at least twenty minutes. He didn't know what time it was, but he guessed the Coast Guard helicopter might be getting ready to be airborne by now. The muskeg he was traversing had given way to more solid earth, making it easier for him as he hiked back toward Todd and the bear victim's partner. The bear was nearly a mile behind him, so he felt very safe in that direction, but up ahead, the stopping of the gunshots presented Mattituck with the mystery of where exactly the gunman ahead was.

He guessed that the gunshots had been well over a mile ahead when he'd been circling around the scrub patch next to the grizzly. Assuming that Todd and the gunman were moving back toward Zaikof Bay, Mattituck probably wasn't any nearer to them than he had been when the shots had been fired. In fact, the silence probably meant that both Todd and the gunman were on the move.

Nonetheless, Mattituck slowed as he approached the area he guessed the shots had been fired in. He felt almost more nervous than when the two men had been shooting at him and the DeeVee8 in Zaikof Bay. At least there, he knew where they were and what they were doing. Here, he had no idea whether Todd and the gunman were even moving, let alone how far ahead they might be. Mattituck didn't want to lose ground if they were moving, but he also didn't want to come up too quickly on the gunman from the Kimberly Marie and end up a dead man. No doubt, the gunman was jumpy after seeing his partner mauled by a bear.

His thoughts drifted toward the DeeVee8 as he picked his way along the muskeg-covered terrain. The downside of an aluminum hull was that true punctures in the hull were very difficult to repair. Unlike a fiberglass-based hull, where a hole could be plugged and resin patchwork done to make the holes disappear completely, aluminum would need to be prepared— jagged edges from the bullets ripping through sanded down—then the holes filled with a slow weld-bead process, and finally sanded smooth. Even then, there would be discoloration on the bare aluminum, making it clear that repairs had been done. Where the holes had penetrated the yellow paint along the DeeVee8's hull, fresh paint would cover it, but the bare aluminum repairs would detract from her value should Mattituck ever want to sell the DeeVee8.

Not that he would. DeeVee8 meant too much to Mattituck. The boat had significant value far beyond her being the perfect charter boat. Mattituck allowed his thoughts to settle on the memory of the DeeVee8's naming.

It had been the vessel's first overnight trip. Mattituck had taken Derek, his nephew, on the trip as a belated 8th birthday celebration. At that point, the vessel had not yet been named, and Mattituck had only had the boat out for trial runs. He still had the Knot Skunked, the boat Mattituck had used to form Sound Experience Charters. He intended to keep running the smaller glass-ply sport fisher until he was completely comfortable with the new boat's handling. Once he started using the Knot Skunked's replacement, he'd considered expanding the business and hiring a captain to run the older boat, but kept thinking that it would be far easier to keep on as a one-boat company. Besides, he thought, he could use the money selling the Knot Skunked to help offset the loan for the big new boat, with her price tag of $315,000.

In the end, however, he couldn't sell the Knot Skunked. He loved the smaller boat. When he put the word out he was looking for an employee captain to run the Knot Skunked, Scotty Porter had come recommended by several. As he got to know Scotty, Mattituck quickly learned the guy was a lot like him – very good with kids, completely focused on the clients' preferences, and an amiable and fun personality. After a few runs fishing with Scotty, he'd hired the man and had never regretted the decision to expand Sound Experience Charters.

So when the new boat had arrived, Sandy had flown Derek over to visit his Uncle Frank and see the new boat while she worked later nights on a special project. Mattituck, being the spontaneous type, had decided when he picked up his nephew at the airport that they should break in the new boat with an overnight fishing trip—just the two of them—to Naked Island. It would be a delayed birthday celebration in honor of Derek's 8th. Derek loved reeling in his own fish, so Mattituck took him to target "chicken" halibut at a reliable spot for the smaller fish.

While anchored up inside the island's MacPherson Passage, he had thought of "DeeVee" for Derek Vincent's initials while he and his nephew played Uno at anchor. He'd floated the idea with Derek, and the boy had beamed with pleasure that the boat would be named for him. Very likely, it meant much more to the boy that his uncle wanted the boat connected to him. The number 8 had then been added by Derek, inspired by the 8th birthday trip. When they sounded out D.V. 8, the word "deviate" was what they heard, and the name stuck.

The next weekend, while Mattituck was visiting his sister and nephew in Anchorage, Derek had helped Mattituck pick out the lettering from a vinyl lettering company online, and then helped his Uncle Frank put the name on the boat the two weekends later when Derek and his mother came to Valdez to see Frank. The letters had arrived in the mail several days previously, but Mattituck had saved putting them on until Derek could be there.

"I'll bring over a nice bottle of champagne," Sandy had told him prior to the trip.

"What for?"

"To properly christen the boat, you dweeb. Didn't you know you're supposed to break a bottle of champagne on the bow when you launch a new boat?"

"This one's already in the water," he had said.

"We're going to do this right," she had answered, ignoring him.

There was no arguing with Sandy. Mattituck even went the extra effort of loading the new boat onto its 3-axle trailer and pulling it out of the water, just so that they could act as if it were being launched for the first time. He, Derek, and Sandy had had a quick ceremony on the boat ramp, and then backed the boat back into the water. She had even brought a broom and dustpan to clean up the broken glass.

Sandy had straightened, her head high as a queen.

"On this day," she pronounced in as formal a tone as she could muster, "June the ninth in the Year of Our Lord, two thousand and twelve, I hereby christen thee the DeeVee8, vessel of great fishing and reliability, and whatever other good fortunes are supposed to befall a dream boat of this magnitude."

This had triggered a hearty round of laughter in all three, amidst gawkers impatient for them to clear the boat ramp so they could get their boats in the water. Mattituck had then climbed into the driver's seat of his F-350, and backed the newly christened DeeVee8 into the water, champagne dripping from her bow and mingling with the briny sea.

Now, hiking back toward the DeeVee8, Mattituck was surprised by the strength of his resolve to never sell the DeeVee8. The suddenness of being shot at earlier was now setting in with a shock Mattituck hadn't expected. A brush with near-death can do that to a person, certainly, but there was something more here for

Mattituck that caught him by surprise. It wasn't so much the thought of his own death that carried the shock value, but rather the thought of having nearly lost the DeeVee8. With the memory of the overnight trip with Derek, Mattituck was realizing that the DeeVee8 represented something about his relationship with his nephew that up to that moment had been buried in his subconscious. It represented family.

He paused next to a scrub bush and checked on the bear again. He was now too far beyond the knoll to see over its crest, and there was no sign of the bear, though he was sure it was still filling its belly on the deer.

All he knew for sure, he thought as he continued his trek back toward Todd and the gunman, was that he did not want to lose the DeeVee8. Ever.

Todd continued to scan the ridge, beginning to doubt himself that the killer would appear. What if the man had decided to abandon pursuit and diverted to the south to seek another route back to Zaikof Bay? There was no doubt the man would want to get back to the Kimberly Marie and try to make a getaway, although it might be pointless. The Kimberly Marie was such a slow boat that it would be like making a bank robbery getaway on a moped.

Would the killer even think of that?, Todd wondered. His thoughts returned to the question of how experienced these killers were. Had the crime they'd committed been a mistake, some other plan gone awry and resulting in the murder of the Bayliner's elderly owners. Perhaps the killers had then panicked and were on the run simply because they didn't know what else to do. Certainly there were plenty of cases Todd had read where this seemed to be what drove criminals to run for as long as they could until caught.

He scanned the ridge again, deciding that if the man didn't appear in the next few minutes, he would radio Frank to await the Coast Guard helicopter to pick up the bear victim, and then he would make as fast a way as he could back to Zaikof Bay and await the killer to show up at the Kimberly Marie.

A movement far to the right, across a slight depression over the muskeg field, caught Todd's attention, and he turned the binoculars to get a better view. Close to a mile to the northwest, he made out a head moving north, away from Todd's current location. He pulled up the mic for the handheld VHF.

"Frank . . . Frank. This is Todd. Pick me up?"

He waited a minute.

"Yeah, I have you loud and clear. What's up?"

"Are you moving north or northeast? Along a stand of tall spruce to your left?"

There was a moment's pause.

"Nope. No, I'm not. I'm headed almost directly west, toward where I thought you are."

It must be the killer, Todd thought.

"Frank, head back to the bear victim, but keep your distance. Wait for the Coast Guard helicopter and make sure they get that body. Don't try anything with the bear unless it gets onto that victim. If it does, shoot it. Okay?"

"Roger. Are you coming this way?"

"No, I'm going to follow our friend. Looks like he's headed to Rocky Bay."

"Roger. I'll catch up to you after the Coast Guard comes."

Todd hadn't anticipated that. With the DeeVee8 out of commission, though, Frank had little choice.

"Okay, Frank. We'll touch base after the helo departs."

Todd clipped the VHF to his belt and began re-packing his gear. He watched the killer for several minutes before stepping out of the shadows of thespruce. The man wasn't even checking his back trail. Most likely, he was assuming that Todd had headed back to Zaikof Bay or he was laying in wait, in vain, someplace along the way. To the killer's mind, Frank was probably still running away from him to the west. That left nobody to trail him. The man's gait and confidence in not checking behind seemed to confirm these assumptions. All Todd needed to do, then, was stay close enough to track the killer and make damned sure the killer had no clue he was being tracked.

Skipper's Oath

Chapter Eight

Death of the Innocent

Frank headed in the opposite direction for the second time in as many hours. What a bizarre turn of events. First, the leisurely cruise south through Prince William Sound with the thought that he was only checking on a friend whom he would find safe and sound, relaxing with several bottles of Rainier or Killian's Red beer on the rear deck of the Kimberly Marie. Then, being fired on—something that had only happened once before in his life—resulting in the near sinking of the DeeVee8, then beaching her and setting out on foot to call for help. Help showed up then, uncalled and on foot behind Mattituck's pursuers, whom Mattituck had managed to set up for an attack by a grizzly.

You can't make stuff like this up, he thought.

Now, he was hiking back to the scene of the bear attack after circumnavigating that same kill site to help an Alaska State Trooper who had ended up in a gun battle with the second of Mattituck's pursuers.

Just what in the fuck was going on, anyhow? he wondered.

As he approached the knoll of the bear's kill site, he readied the Winchester and leaned it against a rock while he checked the Glock .45. Satisfied all was ready, he replaced the Glock in its holster, safety off and the holster unclipped so he could draw the weapon quickly if needed. He then started up the knoll with the rifle at his shoulder, pointed ahead.

He crested the knoll, and took stock of the scene before him. Some forty feet down the slow decline, he saw the bear still at work on the deer. He was vaguely surprised that even a creature as massive as this grizzly would not yet be filled, but there it was, still tearing at the deer carcass as if it had just begun. Twenty feet closer, the man who had been one of his pursuers an hour or so earlier now lay perfectly still. His body was slightly twisted, the right leg crossed haphazardly over the left. His right arm lay straight out, the sleeve of the plaid shirt ripped and pulled down to his hand. Mattituck could see a gash along the upper arm, although the bleeding appeared to have stopped.

He couldn't see the man's face, nor his left arm. It may well have been that the arm lay under some of the torn up muskeg, hidden from Mattituck's view. The top of the man's head was in plain sight, however, and the hair was severely parted at a gap that clearly cut into the man's scalp. The greatest injury, however, was at the man's right shoulder, also well within Mattituck's view. The shirt was torn and the shredded bare skin exposed. It was a pulpy, bloodied mess that Mattituck imagined could easily threaten a person's life. He tried to survey the wound as best he could, but he was not an EMT. His charter boat license required that he be First Responder certified, but he lacked the experience to recognize— especially at a distance—whether or not the man likely would be dead from these wounds.

As he surveyed the shoulder wound, however, he saw no clear signs of blood loss, and saw the same lack of evidence on the muskeg under the man's shoulders. Could it be the man survived the vicious attack? Mattituck recalled the violent shake the bear had given the man that had made the hands fall away from the bear's head. He couldn't imagine anything surviving such a radical, sharp-toothed shake.

He held the binoculars as still as he could and watched the man's chest. After a few moments, he felt sure he was seeing a slow rise and fall. The man was breathing.

Mattituck dared not approach the man with the bear only twenty feet beyond. In fact, if the bear saw him where he was, it would likely view him as a threat to its kill, and would attack.

Mattituck raised the Winchester to his shoulder and took aim. He was almost directly abeam of the great bear and had a clear side shot to the animal's heart. The problem was that the Winchester was a deer rifle. He would have to make the shot on the first attempt, or he would be in trouble. He planned out in his mind how he would take one more shot with the Winchester if the bear didn't drop, and then pull out the Glock and be ready to hit the magic spot at the front base of the throat, above the rib cage—another direct path to the heart.

The Winchester jumped in his grip, before he had a chance to reconsider. The bear's hide quivered at the bullet's entry, and the bear swung to its left, toward Mattituck. The bear paused a moment, then began to step toward him. Mattituck fired the Winchester again, hitting the bear again in almost the same spot. Mattituck could see now he'd hit his mark.

But the bear continued unaffected. It seemed to gather its thoughts, and then took a step toward him. The Glock was now in Mattituck's hand, the right hand cupped around the butt, index finger on the trigger. His left hand gripped his right wrist, steadying his aim. His mind acting automatically, he popped off three quick shots, each hitting the bear below its chin, passing the bottom of the snout and entering its body at the base of the throat.

The great brown bear stopped, then attempted another step forward, faltered and fell, its front legs buckling under it. The eyes of the great animal seemed surprised, as if it couldn't imagine losing its ability to charge. The great girth of the snout hit the muskeg ground with a dull thud.

The massive grizzly was dead.

Todd heard the Coast Guard Jayhawk helicopter approaching Montague from the northwest, inbound from Elmendorf Air Force Base in Anchorage, some 90 air miles away. Almost an hour earlier, he'd heard shots fired from the bear site and had called to check on Frank. Frank had shot the bear, he reported, and had dressed the mauled man as best he could.

"He's still alive?" Todd had asked, surprised.

"Yeah, hard to believe, right? He's in pretty bad shape, but he's breathing and there's actually not all that much bleeding. His left shoulder is mutilated—I think the bear must have gnawed at it or something. But it must've missed all the major arteries. Other than that, he's got a very nasty looking gash on the top of his head. It goes all the way to the bone, and it's pretty long. I think that might be where he lost most of the blood he's lost. But again, not as bad as it could have been."

Todd had thought about this. If the man survived, they might be able to piece together a lot of the mystery. That is, if they could get the man to talk.

Todd had signed off the radio with Mattituck re-emphasizing that he would try to catch up to Todd when the Coast Guard hauled the man away.

Now, as he watched the helicopter zero in on Frank's position a couple of miles away, he thought what a shame it was that the bear would be left behind. It was a prized target for hunters who drew the lottery to hunt them, and from what he could tell, this one was a prize specimen. If they didn't have a life-crucial medevac to do, he imagined the Coast Guardsmen would haul the bear back with them.

Todd broke from watching the approach of the helo to check on the killer ahead. He'd been letting the man gain distance, trying to hang back enough so that Frank could catch up before dark, but now he'd have to close in on the man before he reached Rocky Bay. There was no telling what the killer was up to, especially heading for Rocky Bay instead of Zaikof Bay, but Todd imagined there might be a vessel or two anchored there, like there normally was. He didn't want to see this man commit another murder.

He found the killer paused in an open field, turned back and watching the Coast Guard helo as it descended to the site where his partner had fallen to the bear. The killer watched for several moments, in no rush to continue.

He's probably wanting to make sure the helicopter doesn't try to find him, Todd thought.

As the helo hovered a hundred feet above the ground, a Coast Guardsman appeared in the side door and was lowered by the hoist. He was in a cage-like stretcher used for rescues. The stretcher and its occupant disappeared out of sight behind the terrain.

Todd turned his binoculars back to the killer ahead. The man had resumed his trek for Rocky Bay, no longer concerned with the helicopter. He seemed to know that the helicopter wouldn't bother with him when it had his partner—dead or severely wounded—aboard.

Todd pulled the VHF to his mouth.

"AST 32067, this is AST Ashore."

A moment later, Jessie replied.

Good, Todd thought with relief. He was in range, still anchored near the mouth of Rocky Bay. Jessie was very good at following precisely what Todd wanted him to do.

"I need you to come up the bay and ID any vessels at the end. Then I want you to back off a half mile or so and hold a position mid-bay. I may need you."

"Roger," Jessie replied.

"And keep alert for any movement on shore. One of the subjects might appear in the next half hour or so, and well ahead of me."

"Roger, will do. Anything else?"

"Nope. Just keep alert and be ready to get the boat to me," Todd replied.

"Will do."

Todd put the radio away and re-checked the killer's position and heading. He was continuing at a good clip, still making way for Rocky Bay. Either the man knew exactly where the Bay was, or he was good at random decisions.

Todd let the binoculars hang at his chest and began a leisurely pace in pursuit. With Jessie covering the bay, there was no need to give hot pursuit.

Frank stood next to the Coast Guardsman who had strapped the victim into the stretcher and watched the injured man rising toward the hovering helicopter. The downwash was powerful, and he had to blink continually to maintain his vision. Finally, the stretcher was pulled into the side door, and within a two minutes the cable was being lowered again, this time with a shoulder harness to retrieve the Coast Guardsman.

"Are you sure you're not coming with us?"

Mattituck shook his head. "I'm going to catch up to the State Trooper. He's chasing down that guy's partner, and he asked me to join up with him."

The Coastie nodded. "All right. You have VHF. Call us if you get into trouble."

"Right," Mattituck nodded. "Will do."

He watched the man slip into the harness and signal the hoist operator above. Instantly, he zipped upward and disappeared into the belly of the Jayhawk. The copter's nose dipped as Mattituck heard the pitch of the rotors change, and the helicopter picked up lateral speed and began to ascend, turning as it did so toward Anchorage.

Mattituck watched until the sound of the helicopter was barely audible, then he called Todd on the VHF to tell him he was on his way.

Skipper's Oath

Chapter Nine

The Importance of Location

Mattituck caught up with Todd Benson over 90 minutes later. It was now evening, and Mattituck realized he'd been awake for well over 24 hours. Closer to 32 hours, now that he thought about it, as he'd had a charter the day before. "Wow," he said to Todd as he approached the waiting Trooper. "It's amazing what adrenaline will do."

Todd looked puzzled.

"Yeah," he replied. "Whatever you mean by that."

Mattituck chuckled. "Just that I haven't slept since yesterday morning, but I feel fine."

Todd looked at him with a blank expression.

"Rocky Bay is just over that ridge," Todd said, ignoring whatever thoughts Mattituck had. "My crewman was anchored at the mouth of Rocky Bay, ever since I went ashore. So I called him a while ago and had him run back up the bay, here, and ID any vessels anchored. I told him to run back out half way and hold position."

Mattituck nodded. "Up Rocky Bay?" he asked.

Todd again looked at him blankly.

"Just making sure you didn't mean Zaikof Bay," Mattituck added.

"Of course I mean Rocky Bay," Todd said, annoyed at being interrupted.

"So we have this guy bottled in," Todd continued, gesturing ahead toward Rocky Bay. "Jessie— my crewman—is keeping watch along the shore for any sign of our guy. As soon as he shows up, Jessie'll call me."

"Sounds good," Mattituck replied. "And this Jessie was clear on Rocky Bay, right? I mean, as opposed to Zaikof."

Todd shot him a dark glare.

"Okay, okay. No need to get pissy," Mattituck grumbled with irritation.

Todd turned and started for Rocky Bay, and Mattituck followed. They set off for the ridge at a fast pace, despite the fatigue of their bodies. The terrain up this way was easier than back on the muskeg fields. While there were as many scrub and stands, there was little muskeg and the ground was firmer, making each step more efficient as they hurried up the ridge.

When they crested the ridge, they could see Hinchinbrook Entrance ahead and Prince William Sound stretching in the distance to the left. Rocky Bay, a short stocky bay compared to the much longer Zaikof Bay, pointed from the open water almost directly toward them. The end of the bay lay right below them, the shore less than a quarter mile below.

"What the---?" Todd uttered under his breath.

Mattituck followed his line of vision to the bay, but didn't see anything out of the ordinary. Near the mouth of the bay, he could see a boat making good headway out into the Sound, headed northwest.

"What's wrong?" he asked.

Todd merely shook his head, his eyes scanning the bay.

"Where the fuck is he?" he asked, almost more a statement than a question.

"Who?"

"Jessie. He's supposed to be right there," he pointed to a spot generally mid-bay.

Todd grabbed his VHF and hailed his boat.

"Roger, AST Ashore. I'm here," came the response.

"Where?!" Todd's voice was tense and raised.

A pause.

"Right where you told me to be. I'm holding mid-bay in Zaikof Bay."

"What?!" Todd yelled without keying the mic.

He looked at Mattituck incredulously.

Mattituck shrugged. "Told you," he said flatly.

Todd ignored him and keyed the radio.

"Zaikof? What the hell are you doing in Zaikof? I told you to come up the Bay and----" his voice trailed off.

He looked at Mattituck. Mattituck looked away with feigned innocence.

"You thought I was calling you from inside Zaikof, didn't you?"

Jessie's voice was hesitant over the radio. "Yeah. Yes, I did. Where are you?"

"The end of Rocky Bay," Todd said drily. He was dead quiet, the muscles in his jaw working.

"Shit!" he shouted to the bay. He quickly scanned the shoreline with his binoculars.

Mattituck watched him, unsure how to help.

"See anything?" he finally asked.

Todd shook his head, the bill of his AST ball cap swinging widely. His binoculars panned to the mouth of the bay to the retreating vessel throwing a white wake as it moved quickly out of the bay.

"Fuck," he said with resignation, his voice low.

Mattituck, while only an acquaintance of the Trooper, had never heard the law man swear.

"You think the guy we're tracking is on that boat?" he asked, nodding toward the barely visible boat now making a left turn into Prince William Sound.

Todd grimaced.

"Only one way to find out," he said. "We'll track his footsteps down and see where they lead. If they lead to the edge of the water, then I guess our pursuit's over."

He put the binoculars away as Jessie called over the radio.

"AST Ashore, AST 32067."

"Yeah, go ahead."

"I'm sorry, Todd. I thought you meant Zaikof."

"I know, Jessie. It's okay. Just swing around here and pick us up."

"Roger," came the reply. "On my way now."

With AST 32067 not due for 15 minutes, Mattituck followed Todd down the face of the ridge toward Rocky Bay. Tracking was something Mattituck had never mastered, although he wasn't bad according to many guides he knew. But his skills were obviously nothing compared to Alaska State Trooper Todd Benson's. Was it something they taught them in the academy? he wondered. Or was this something Todd had learned from his hunting guide father and older brothers back in Wyoming?

"Where'd you learn to track?" he finally asked.

Todd was nearly hunching over the ground, alert to signs Mattituck could see when pointed out, but missed on his own. A bit of moist soil here, a bent devil's club stalk there.

"My mother's family," he answered. "I used to spend summers with her after my parents divorced, back on the Rez." He stopped and stretched his back, then looked at Mattituck. "My Mom was Hopi Indian."

"I didn't know that."

Todd chuckled. "I'm only ribbing you, man," he said. "My Mom was Hopi and I did spend most of my summers with her there during high school, but that's not where I learned to track. I just like to play up the stereotype."

"So you're Hopi?" Mattituck asked.

Todd nodded. "Half, about. At least as far as we know," he smiled. "The other half is Norwegian. Vikings," he said, a tightness in his voice. "The pillager and the pillaged, war-monger and peace-lover, all mixed up in one," Todd chuckled.

Mattituck couldn't tell if the tone was bitter or not. "So where did you learn to track? Your dad? You told me once that he was a hunting guide. Wyoming?"

"Yeah," Todd said, "that's right—Wyoming. And yes, my Dad was a hunting guide. He was an avid hunter and a helluva tracker. He could track a soft-pawed bunny through a mile of grass." He started back down toward the shore. "There's really not much to it. Just a matter of knowing what to look for."

When they reached the sandy beach, the trail was more obvious. There were boot steps everywhere within a forty foot area. Todd followed them around a bit to a spot where some of the steps were covered by a flattish spot.

"He sat down here on the sand." Todd looked toward the water. "He was facing the water, probably waiting for something. A boat, most likely. Maybe he'd been flagging down an anchored boat. That fits the boot patterns over there. Then when they were coming for him, he sat and waited."

Todd pointed to where the heels of the boots had dug into the sand while the man waited, seated. "See? He'd been waiting for several minutes."

He looked around along the edge of the water.

"I'll bet . . ." Todd's voice trailed. "Yep. There," he pointed to a spot where a line was cut into the sand at the water's edge. It appeared to be etched by a keel forced onto the beach. "That's a boat, not a dinghy. They nosed their boat up to shore to pick him up."

Mattituck was confused. "You mean someone was supposed to pick him up?"

Todd shook his head. "No. Looks like he waved them down." He indicated the boot prints all over the beach. "I'm sure of it. They probably thought he was stranded, and came to help him. They nosed up to the beach and picked him up."

A full minute of silence.

"And then what?" Mattituck asked.

"That's as far as our reading of the story goes," Todd said.

"You think he was on that boat headed out?"

"Yep. There's little doubt."

"Shit . . ." Mattituck said.

"Yep," Todd answered. "And she's way too far gone to even try to follow."

"And I sure as fuck couldn't identify that boat," Mattituck said, gazing up the bay toward Prince William Sound.

"No way we could," Todd replied. "And it turning left does us no good. Any boat headed out of here goes north. Could be anywhere by the time Jessie picks us up and we get to the mouth of the bay."

"So we're screwed," Mattituck's voice trailed.

"That about sums it up," Todd said.

After Jessie had picked them up in AST 32067, Todd had piloted the Trooper boat back around to Zaikof Bay to check on the DeeVee8 and inspect the Kimberly Marie. They had put AST 32067 against the sandy shore next to DeeVee8 and locked her up. They moved her anchor up the beach and tied it off to a tree next to the grassy marsh at the head of the beach. The DeeVee8 would undoubtedly stay put until a salvage operation could retrieve her. Todd, wanting to make sure his newly solidified friendship was secure, and as a means of saying thank you for the help Mattituck had given, hid a monitoring camera under her port gunwale to make sure the DeeVee8 was well protected. Then, the three had re-boarded the AST 32067 and idled out to the Kimberly Marie.

Todd maneuvered the Trooper boat alongside the Kimberly Marie. Jessie tied up the port lines to the Kimberly Marie's starboard side, and Todd and Mattituck boarded the 72-foot cabin cruiser.

Mattituck couldn't fight an eerie feeling as they made their way aft to the stern deck, where the sliding glass door providing entrance to the cabin was located.

All seemed as it should be. Todd had been leading the way, and drew his sidearm as they approached the aft deck. Mattituck instinctively crouched and followed suit. He drew his Glock, still on his hip, and followed the law man.

Certain nothing was amiss on the aft deck, and still hearing nothing from inside, Todd crossed the aft deck and approached the rear cabin. The sliding glass door afforded an easy view of the interior. Again, all seemed still and quiet. He pulled at the glass door, and it slid easily to the side. Todd stepped in, followed by Mattituck.

The cabin also seemed normal.

Todd turned to Mattituck. "You know Jim well, right?"

Mattituck nodded.

"You tell me. Let me know if anything seems odd."

Mattituck nodded. "Other than the door being unlocked, all seems normal so far."

"He wouldn't have left that unlocked, eh? Even if he was on board?"

"No way. If he were on board, he would have met us. My guess is he's not here," Mattituck said, a sinking feeling growing inside him. "Or worse . . ." he added.

Todd fixed a stern gaze on him, then nodded understanding.

They advanced forward to the helm station. Mattituck paused.

"Something's not right," he said.

Todd waited.

"Can't put my finger on it. But something else is not right here," Mattituck indicated the captain's station.

Todd nodded, and they proceeded down the ladder to the staterooms. They passed the galley, where nothing seemed to have been touched, and continued to the forward cabin—which Mattituck said was Jim's cabin. Todd took his time canvassing the space, pointing the flashlight to each darkened corner. Nothing here seemed out of the ordinary.

They proceeded through the remaining three cabins, all to the same end—nothing unusual.

As they ascended the ladder to the main cabin, Todd asked Mattituck if he'd put his finger on what seemed amiss at the helm station.

"Well," Mattituck started. "He's not here, to start with. That's really weird. He would not let his boat be here without some sign of where he was. And sure as fuck not unmanned and unlocked."

Todd acknowledged this with a nod.

"But it's something . . ." Mattituck approached the helm, "here . . ." he said finally.

He sat in the captain's chair. The GPS was still on.

"That's it," Mattituck said, pointing. "Jim would never leave the GPS or the radar on at anchor. Never."

He and Todd watched the radar scope circle round and round, reading the shore line and vessel traffic around. Few captains left the radar on at anchor—there was no reason for it. Leaving the radar on was something only some captains did to alert them to any approaching vessels, although there really was no point in doing so. It drained the batteries when the engines weren't running. And there was even less reason to leave a GPS on, though they burned hardly any electricity. Unless it's a charter boat captain wanting to make sure the anchor was holding, there was simply no reason to leave that on.

"Nope," Mattituck said with finality. "Jim wouldn't leave his helm station this way." He looked at Todd, his expression white. "I don't think Jim would have left the Kimberly Marie this way. Not if he were alive."

As further evidence that Jim Milner was missing, likely to an undesired end, Mattituck had noticed that the key to the Kimberly Marie was still in her ignition. The fuel key and a soft spongy yellow smiley face—a flotation device to keep the keys on the surface in the event a person dropped them in the water—were the only other things on the key ring.

They sat in two lounge chairs on the aft deck of the Kimberly Marie, much as Mattituck had done so many evenings in port with Jim Milner. Never had he guessed he'd be sitting in this chair under these circumstances.

The State Trooper was clearly in no rush. They sat several minutes in complete silence.

"How do you feel about piloting the Kimberly Marie back to port?" Todd finally asked.

Mattituck nodded. "Fine."

Several more minutes passed, contributing to the air of there being no rush for anything . . . not even conversational turns.

"All right," Todd eventually replied. "I probably should get back to Growler Bay and see what the forensics team has found. But no rush on that."

Mattituck's neck stiffened. "The what?"

Todd looked at him. "Oh, shit. That's right. You don't know anything about all that."

Todd filled Mattituck in on finding the beached Bayliner and the pools of blood.

Mattituck tried to absorb this. "So you're thinking that somehow Jim picked these guys up?"

Todd nodded. "You have to admit—a lot of coincidences in the last 36 hours or so if they're not connected."

Mattituck had to acknowledge that.

"Yeah, I suppose," he admitted. "Shit . . ." his eyes were fixed on a non-descript point on the deck. "I can't . . ."

Todd waited for him to finish. Mattituck didn't.

"There's more," Todd said. "The Bayliner matches the description of a boat involved in the murder of an elderly couple and a harbor police officer on the Gulf just outside Yakutat."

Mattituck nodded. His expression was vacant, and Todd knew the man was trying to process the likely reality that his friend had been murdered.

A few minutes passed.

"Did you say Growler Bay?" Mattituck asked.

Todd nodded.

"That's where Jim spread his wife's ashes," Mattituck said.

"Did he go there often?" Todd asked.

"Often enough to make it very likely he picked these guys up there. That doesn't bode well for Jim, does it?"

Todd shook his head slowly. "I'm afraid not."

"But what happened to him? I mean, if they killed him, there's no sign of it here," he gestured around the Kimberly Marie.

"Nope. Sure isn't." Todd let a moment pass. "That's part of the mystery. Part of what we have to solve."

"We?" Mattituck asked.

Todd smiled. He hadn't even noticed the inclusive pronoun. He realized suddenly that he had fallen into viewing Frank as a kind of partner. He looked at the charter boat captain as the man gazed reflectively out toward Hinchinbrook Entrance. *Yes*, Todd thought, *I could trust him.*

He'd known Frank Mattituck as an acquaintance, and had always liked him more than others in town, and certainly more than other charter boat captains. He knew Frank had a highly developed set of ethics—he'd seen that. But this chase across Montague today had shown Todd what Frank Mattituck was really capable of.

"If there were a need," Todd ventured, "would you be willing to help out?"

Mattituck glanced briefly at the Trooper, then back out over the water. He had never wanted to be involved, not in anything that wasn't his business. And he sure as hell had never seen himself working with a law man. He preferred to hold off on his own, and avoid authority at all costs. That's part of what drove him to Alaska—the land of rebels. And it was part of why he worked for himself.

"What's that mean?" he asked. "Help out how?"

Todd was looking at him, a serious expression on his face.

"As in, if I needed help pursuing this case, would you be interested in helping out?"

Mattituck was quiet. When he was younger, he'd carried a firm belief in right and wrong, and always taking a stand for what's right. He'd always been committed to standing up for people when they were wronged, even getting into fights in his school years because he was defending a kid being picked on. He hadn't thought of things like that in some time now.

What had happened to him? he wondered. When had he become such a loner?

Now, thinking of good ole Jim Milner, of the elderly couple off Yakutat . . . an anger arose inside him. He could feel it starting to bubble and seethe. He sat up in his seat and looked at Todd.

"Yeah. I'd be happy to if you need me."

"Good," Todd replied. "I may need help on this one."

They sat several minutes in silence. It was a perfect evening. The Kimberly Marie lay in the shadows of the bay, but the low hills along the south side of the bay were awash in the golden hue of an Alaskan sunset. The temperature was warm, around the mid-sixties, and there was no breeze. Under different circumstances, the two men would have been enjoying the quiet, perhaps sipping beers and exchanging fishing stories.

"Well," Todd said, finally. "There are 3 good staterooms below, without touching Jim's. We're all tired. I say we secure AST 32067 alongside for the night, button up the Kimberly Marie, and get a good night's rest. I'll head back to Growler Bay in the morning, and if you're okay with it, you can take the Kimberly Marie back to Valdez."

Mattituck nodded. "Sure. Then what?"

Todd considered. "After I check in on the forensics team, I'll head in to port and call Anchorage. See how that bear wrestler's doing. If he lives, he'll be our only shot at catching up with the other guy."

He looked at Mattituck.

"I'll look into deputizing you. It's been done before, and I'm sure you'd be approved. Are you sure you're willing to commit to this?"

Mattituck looked at the last of the sunlight on a peak to the southeast and watched it fade upward off the tip of the mountain.

"Yes," he said. "I'm very sure."

The next morning they were up early, and after a quick breakfast of eggs and bacon they found in the galley, AST 32067 cast off with Todd Benson and his crewman, leaving Mattituck alone to captain a vessel he never expected to captain. He watched the trooper vessel barrel off toward the mouth of Zaikof Bay, leaving a long thin line of white-churned salt water in her wake. Todd had established an hourly radio watch with Mattituck, meaning they would touch base each hour on the hour to make sure Mattituck was safe. The Kimberly Marie would be an easy target to try to recapture, should the killer take it in his mind to do so.

Mattituck seated himself in the captain's chair and turned the ignition. The twin Caterpillar diesels jumped to life, a low rumble ensuing itself on the tranquil bay. The DeeVee8, laying ashore as if trying to inch her way to the marsh at the head of the beach, lay askew and immobile. She seemed utterly helpless, leaning to one side. From this distance, she appeared only beached. The holes in her hull were not visible, and other than the shot-out windows on her port side, she seemed perfectly ready to take to her next charter full of happy, anxious anglers who had saved pennies most of the year to take to the seas in pursuit of halibut and the Alaska fishing adventure.

A wry smile appeared on Mattituck's lips in the midst of the stubble along his cheeks. His gold eyes reflected the yellow band along the DeeVee8's hull.

"I'll be back, baby," he said to her under his breath. "I won't leave you here."

He flipped the toggle switch for the "anchor up," and listened to the whine of the windlass as it pulled the anchor up from the sea bottom. Knowing he was plenty of distance from any hazard to the Kimberly Marie, Mattituck left the helm to exit aft and walked along the starboard side to the bow. There he awaited the appearance of the anchor over the bowsprit, killing the windlass directly on the winch and then securing the anchor to its cradle on the point of the bow. Then he clipped the backup pin to make sure the anchor didn't drop accidentally should the windlass fail. Satisfied that the Kimberly Marie was ready for sea, he made his way aft, re-entered the cabin through the sliding glass door, and took his place at Jim Milner's helm.

A 72-foot cabin cruiser was no row boat. She was a hulk of a vessel, and worthy of the greatest respect in handling her. Mattituck pushed the dual throttles forward and felt a soft lurch as the propellers bit into the briny sea. He turned the helm to port and felt the stern swing right as the Kimberly Marie began to make her way to the port side. In a few moments, she was pointed to the mouth of Zaikof Bay, and Mattituck spun the helm to right and straightened her on a course for Prince William Sound. The massive vessel, elegant and graceful in her slow and sure way, began to gain speed. When she reached twelve knots, Mattituck eased the throttles and settled the twin Cats into 2400rpm. He had no idea what her "sweet spot" was, but this felt right.

Mattituck checked the fuel levels of both tanks, and found them uneven. This was another sign that Jim had not been running the Kimberly Marie; he always switched the tanks approximately half way on a long run to keep the vessel balanced between the two tanks—one on the port side, and one on starboard. Still, he had plenty of fuel to run back to Valdez. Probably enough for two more trips to Montague afterward.

He waited until he was sure the heading he had on the helm was accurate on the glass-smooth bay, then dropped down the ladder to look for coffee in Jim's galley.

It was going to be a long, slow ride back to the Port of Valdez.

AST 32067 made good time north with an incoming tide that put the currents in her favor. As she came within three miles of Glacier Island, on the other side of which was Growler Bay, Todd hailed the forensics team on the VHF radio. The team had been ferried out to the beached Bayliner by a chartered crew boat. They had been on scene most of the previous day, but had ceased operations and returned to Valdez several hours early due to a scheduling conflict with the pilot boat. Now they were scouring the Bayliner for finger prints and anything that might carry the murderers' DNA. Very likely, Todd, thought with a smirk, they would have plenty of DNA samples just from the empty beer cans. The question would be whether or not the killers had DNA samples on file.

Todd slowed AST 32067 as they came along the eastern end of Glacier Island. A long string of white dots, occasionally punctuated with large white ice bergs, stretched all the way north and into Columbia Bay. AST 32067 began to bump her way through the bergie bits, each metallic thud and bang riding Todd's nerves. Despite a solid night's sleep aboard the Kimberly Marie, Todd could feel the effects of sleep deprivation. For him, it quickly manifested in his mood. Every crewman he'd ever had could tell when Trooper Benson was short on sleep.

It took nearly an hour to gain the mouth of Growler Bay, and Todd's thoughts had meandered over what he'd learned about Frank Mattituck in the last 48 hours. He had always had a positive opinion of the man, but felt he hadn't really known him until now. Perhaps that was always the case, when a person goes through a trying ordeal with another. There were certainly those who felt that you never could know a person's character until you've been through something difficult or traumatic with them. That idea had been the subject of many research studies—many of which Todd had read himself. Soldiers in action were favorite research subjects, teasing out the belief servicemen had that nobody understood them like their brothers and sisters in action. Many felt they could not fully trust others.

Certainly, he felt he had a very good read on Frank Mattituck now. The man did have a military background, Todd had already known, and there was the character-indicative way that he had stepped into his nephew's life when the boy and his mother had been abandoned by his father before the boy was even born. But this trip put Frank into a category of men that Todd felt he could truly trust and rely on. To be sure, Frank's friendship with Jim Milner accounted for his concern and sailing to Zaikof Bay to check on the old man, but it didn't account for the grit of a guy who kept his cool under fire—literally under fire—and who lured his pursuer's into the wilderness.

And then he had managed to use a bear to act as an ally for him. That took talent and grit.

But the way Frank Mattituck had stuck with Todd without second thought nor concern for himself weighed very heavily in Todd's newfound surety of the substance of Frank Mattituck. This is a man, Todd thought, that I want to cultivate a good relationship with. Not only could Frank be useful to Todd in his trooper duties, but Frank was a guy Todd felt sure he would enjoy knowing and working with. Rough around the edges, and with a reputation of being often surly and quick-tempered, Frank Mattituck was a solid guy.

Todd felt sure his decision to have Frank help on this case was a good one. If the investigation took him to any coastal towns, he'd get a lot further looking like he was hanging with a friend than barreling in as the State Trooper trying to find someone. A lot of people in Alaska—particularly those from someplace else—had things they were running from. This made them a little less willing to talk about other people and where they might be. Live and let live was a dominant theme in Alaskan life. Great way to live, but it makes being an effective cop a little tougher. Mattituck looked the part of the Alaska outdoorsman, and clearly he had what it took to handle himself if things got rough. But what Todd liked most about the idea of having Mattituck come along was that he knew Mattituck had his back.

Chapter Ten

Goose-Whacked

Mattituck was anxious to get across Orca Bay. He'd been plugging along at 12 kts for the past three hours, and getting beat up the entire time. Orca Bay was notorious for this. It was a long, wide bay that ran inside Prince William Sound from Hinchinbrook Entrance eastward almost all the way to Cordova, a small fishing town that was accessible only by sea or air. After he'd cleared Zaikof Bay and turned north, the ocean swells made for a very gentle, lulling ride. But when he'd reached Orca Bay, the winds were howling unhindered from west to east with an angry howl. He'd seen plenty of these seas, but the DeeVee8 and the Knot Skunked both made short time of the bay and got he and his clients to smoother waters quickly. Not so, the Kimberly Marie. Although, Mattituck had to admit, she rode the seas far more smoothly than either of the smaller charter boats.

He decided to follow his familiar route inside of Goose Island, across Port Fidalgo, and through Tatitlek Narrows. There were fog banks hanging along the darkened land masses to the northeast, past Knowles

Head toward Port Gravina to the east, but north and through the passage between Knowles Head and Goose Island looked clear. Through the binoculars, he could see a gillnetter working the dropoff along the western edge of the sandy underwater plateau south of Knowles—prime halibut territory, but overfished. It was a favorite of many Valdez locals because it was as close to the Gulf as most could get due to limited fuel range or inability—or unwillingness—to cross Orca Bay and brave the Gulf of Alaska.

As he approached the east side of Goose Island, the high knobby land mass of Knowles Head to the starboard beam, he could see a smaller pleasure boat sitting dead center in the passage. He would have to navigate around them, but why they were sitting in the middle of the passage was beyond him. Until the silver salmon started to run, it was pretty dead fishing in there. Some rock fish like Irish Lords, not even good enough for bait, but that was it.

He fixed the binoculars on the gillnetter, now to his port side. There were two crew aboard, busy readying the nets. Likely, they would be venturing off the west side of Goose to chase some pacific cod.

Mattituck raised his coffee cup to his lips, his left hand lightly on the helm holding the course steady. As he entered the passage, which only afforded a few hundred yards' width for him to navigate, the pleasure boat came about and began making slow steerage toward the Kimberly Marie. She was a smaller boat—probably 24 feet or so, but she had a cabin that was likely comfortable for four people inside. She had a decent fish deck, and a port-holed bow of the type that had a V-type bunk arrangement below and a head tucked into the point of the V. It was a common type of boat for this part of Alaska, and a great choice for the private angler wanting to fish salmon or bottom fish, like the halibut or yellow-eyed rockfish.

As the vessel continued on a straight line for him, Mattituck kept an eye on its approach both through the binoculars and on the radar, keeping track of her distance and her heading. With no change in her course for several minutes, he steered the Kimberly Marie to the starboard side, the standard passing for vessel headed in opposite directions, and made the change in course extreme to make clear his intentions.

To his surprise, the boat steered to port in response, keeping itself in front of him. If he kept on this course, he would run out of navigable water.

"Okay, buddy . . . if you want that side, you can have it," Mattituck said to the windshield.

The vessel then turned back to starboard, again putting itself in his course.

Mattituck picked up the mic from the VHF.

"Vessel headed southbound in Goose Passage, this is the Kimberly Marie, over."

No answer.

"Vessel southbound in Goose Passage, this is the Kimberly Marie, northbound. What are your intentions, captain?"

Still no answer.

The distance between them was closing fast.

Just then, the telltale ping of a bullet passing through glass—always quieter than one would think—announced itself on the port side, opposite the cabin. It was immediately followed by a plastic thud on the aft bulkhead. Mattituck noted the hole in the port windshield, surrounded by the tight lines of a spiderweb shattering, though the glass held around the small hole.

Instinctively, Mattituck dropped to the deck. He could easily steer the boat from down there, with the radar and GPS screens in easy view without putting his head into the view of the windows. He crawled aft to the bench at the dining table behind the captain's station and found the Winchester deer rifle. He checked the chamber and made sure the safety was set, then crawled back forward to check the other vessel's location on the radar. It was tracking to the port side now.

Perfect, Mattituck thought. He found a heading that would keep him well of the rocks, and locked the helm. He then crawled to the aft deck. The aft deck was partly covered, with a nice sized bulkhead running from five feet inside the cabin to three or four feet along the open aft deck behind the sliding glass door. Mattituck took a position inside this bulkhead, and was pleased to see that he could see through the cabin to where the other vessel was. It would be a couple of minutes before she came into range.

Mattituck didn't need to wonder very long before he figured out who was on board the small sport fisher. If it were anybody else, he would hesitate to plan taking any shots at her. After all, maybe the shot was a mistake—a careless swing of a halibut pistol with the safety off, maybe. But given the size of the boat, and the recent adventure on Montague, Mattituck had no doubt this was the other killer.

He warded off being curious what might have happened to the owners of the sport fisher. This guy had a pretty clear pattern already.

One more reason not to worry about who he hit with any shots he took at the vessel.

He readied himself, grateful to be ambidextrous. He sometimes swore he was a better shot with the left trigger than the right, but the surety of the targets at the shooting range consistently said that while he might be close, he was still a better shot from the right. Nonetheless, his left trigger finger would do very well, he was sure.

As the sport fisher came into range, he could see the figure at the port side window. The man was using a handgun, although Mattituck knew he had a rifle. Why would he be using the handgun?

Mattituck was careful to keep the barrel of the Winchester as far back as possible, just above the gunwale and immediately aft of the port bulkhead. He took a quick aim through the scope and fired off a single shot. He saw white fiberglass spray off the top of the sport fisher's cabin. He worked the bolt, then took aim again, this time taking out the port window just aft of where the man was now trying to duck—probably hindered from doing so by the passenger seat he was kneeling in front of.

The man didn't do what Mattituck expected. Instead, he crossed to the starboard side and the helm, and thrust the throttles forward while cranking the helm to the starboard side.

"Dumb move," Mattituck muttered.

No doubt, the man had instinctively turned the vessel that way thinking he would be turning away from the Kimberly Marie. That was true enough, but it would also turn the vessel's stern openly to Mattituck while moving the sport fisher out and away from the Kimberly Marie. This would give Mattituck a clear shot at the man—unprotected—inside the cabin, which was open at the rear.

Mattituck readied the rifle.

He fired the first shot into the cabin, too far to the left. The man jumped to the deck and the sport fisher careened madly to the right. Mattituck realized that the boat wasn't gaining headway like it should. The water frothed at the stern, and he realized the boat's propellers were cavitating and unable to get a bite on the sea water.

Mattituck fired a second shot, and he saw the cushioning of the captain's seat fly into the air as the bullet ripped through. He saw a hand reach for the throttles and ease back, allowing the propellers to do their purpose. The boat lurched forward as Mattituck worked the bolt and fired another round. He couldn't tell where this one went, but he knew he would quickly lose accuracy with the speed the boat appeared to be gaining.

He stood up straight and strode to the helm of the Kimberly Marie. He first checked her course on the GPS and saw that she had drifted off course to the port, away from the rocks. On the radar, he could see the sport fisher was quickly receding. Checking it with visual, he could see she was quickly running out of range of Mattituck's rifle. He decided to focus on as many details as possible on the boat, hoping to track her down later.

The first thing he checked in the binoculars was the transom, to see if there was a name on the boat's stern. All he could see to the right of the twin Yamaha outboards were the letters "-SER." Lifting the binoculars to the side, he confirmed that she had a dark blue hull, and a white superstructure. That would help, since most boats that size were all white, unless aluminum. This one was clearly a glass-ply or fiberglass, not just from the appearance, but from the way the white had sprayed with the first bullet hitting the top of the cabin.

He could see "rocket launchers"—round tubes mounted in an upward angle to stow fishing rods—lined along the rear of her cabin roof. This was a standard arrangement, keeping all of the angler's fishing rods in easy reach should she or he want to swap out. There was also wood trim around the cabin edges aft, but it looked like the interior had plenty of wood trim as well. There was a small dinette to the port side behind the forward passenger seat, and the small hatch leading to a lower bow cabin, likely where there was a V-bunk arrangement, as Mattituck had guessed.

Feeling he had enough details, he found a small notepad on the dash in front of the radar. He wrote these details down as he regained his course for Valdez. He watched the sport fisher darting north, and as it cleared the north end of Goose Island, it banked hard left and rounded the line of rocks that stretched northward, the underwater continuation of the island.

The Kimberly Marie was making good headway now as Mattituck pushed her to the point of the big Cats vibrating under the midships decking. He held her at that speed, about 18 knots, hoping to get a view of which direction the sport fisher headed in. As he neared the landmass at the northern edge of the island, nowhere near being able to round the rocks that jutted a quarter mile to the north, he saw the sport fisher scooting back south on the other side of the rocks, and then a few minutes later disappear behind the land of the island.

Mattituck decided to take a chance on the man not having his radio on. He had seen enough evidence with how the man handled the boat to tell him he was dealing with someone that was not entirely comfortable running a boat.

"Gillnetter on the south end of Goose Island, the Kimberly Marie, over."

The answer was immediate.

"Yeah, this is the Lisa G, over."

"Switch to 12, please. One-two."

"Roger, switching."

Mattiuck worked the dial.

"Lisa G, Kimberly Marie, over."

"Roger, Kimberly Marie. Go ahead."

"There's a 24 foot sport fisher coming down the west side of Goose. Can you tell me which way he's going when he comes down your way?"

"Roger. No problem. Stand by."

Mattituck made a turn for Tatitlek Narrows as he cleared Porcupine Point and entered Port Fidalgo.

"Kimberly Marie, Lisa G."

"Go ahead, captain."

"Yeah, she came barreling down all right. She made a left turn up Orca Bay, toward Cordova."

"Roger, copied. Thanks."

"Did you want the vessel's name?"

Mattituck couldn't believe his luck.

"Roger that, Lisa G. You got that?"

"Yep. She has the name 'But Chaser on her cabin and the stern."

Mattituck smiled, shaking his head. Obviously, the owner of the sport fisher was a halibut enthusiast with a sense of humor.

"She doesn't have a VHF antenna, by the way," the Lisa G went on. "In case you're worried about us being overheard."

"That's great, Lisa G. Thanks."

"Yeah," came the answer. "I figured I'd want the name of a boat taking shots at me. Been there, done that."

"Yeah?" Mattituck answered, surprised.

"Yeah. You know how those herring openers can be," came the reply.

"So I've heard. You guys live a dangerous life," Mattituck said with genuine respect.

"Sometimes. Anyway, good luck finding him. He's still steering straight up the bay. He's headed out more toward the middle of Orca, so I doubt he's headed anywhere but Cordova."

"Thanks again, captain. I owe you. I'll look you up sometime."

"Roger that. I'm homeported in Cordova. A couple of beers will do next time you're down my way."

"I'll make a point to come your way," Mattituck promised, meaning it.

"Lisa G, clear of the Kimberly Marie. Switching back channel one-six."

Mattituck settled into the captain's chair, astonished at his luck.

Once he was clear of Tatitlek Narrows, Mattituck decided to try contacting Todd Benson. He quickly raised AST 32067, calling Todd's code name Happy Fitzgerald on Channel 16, and they did the double-switchback on the channel number to avoid being listened to.

"You there, Todd?" he asked as soon as he'd dialed in the frequency.

"Yeah, how are you doing?"

"Good. But I nearly got bushwhacked back by Goose Island. Got goose-whacked, I guess," he chuckled into the mic.

"Bushwhacked?"

Mattituck could hear the perplexion in Todd's voice.

"Yeah, you know, when someone tries to knock you off."

Silence. Then finally Todd answered.

"Why the hell didn't you call me?"

"I tried in Fidalgo, about an hour ago, but no answer."

"Okay," Todd replied. "I'll be back in port in a couple of hours. When are you due in?"

Mattituck looked at the chart, noting he was a little more than half way. He noted he'd been underway close to three hours. Six hours from Zaikof.

"Pretty close to that," he said. "Probably a little later."

"Roger. Call me when you get in. I'll come see you."

"Will do. See you then."

Mattituck tuned back to channel 16, his thoughts playing back the exchange with the killer on the 'But Chaser. There could be little doubt it was the killer who'd been chasing him on Montague. The man who had a part in what was seeming more and more like Jim Milner's death. And the people near Yakutat. Probably the death of others, too. The boat he and Todd had seen departing Rocky Bay was about the size of the 'But Chaser, and like that sport fisher, it seemed to Mattituck that the boat zooming out of Rocky Bay had had a blue hull and white cabin, just like the 'But Chaser. Certainly, that little sport fisher had the outboards to push her fast. Those twin Yamahas on the stern had looked to be 175hps or 200hps. A boat that size would probably move along over 40kts if she wanted to.

Once he straightened his course toward Rocky Point, where he would need to make his next turn toward Valdez, Mattituck locked the helm and dropped back into the galley to brew more coffee. As he descended the ladder to the galley, he thought of what a beautiful yacht the Kimberly Marie was. He'd been on the boat many times, and had noticed her grace and beauty, but something about the way his hand slid smoothly along the wood handrail—mahogany, was it?—filled him with a pang of sadness. He wondered how many times Jim had descended this ladder with this same appreciation.

Merely a week before, Jim had been living his life, his biggest concern being the weather he might encounter on his next charter. He might have been running the Kimberly Marie with a full complement of passengers, all enjoying lunch and wondering what Alaskan sights they might take in during the afternoon. Maybe Jim would be taking them to Bull Head to see the sea lions, and perhaps a humpback or two nearby. He'd be bantering and joking with them, answering their questions and sharing his love of Alaska.

All without a clue of what was about to befall him in the coming days.

What the fuck?, Mattituck wondered. He thought of the two killers.

"Sons of bitches," he muttered, suddenly angry.

Skipper's Oath

Chapter Eleven

Midnight Disturbance

Todd arrived in his Alaska State Trooper uniform at the Kimberly Marie's slip as Mattituck was securing the lines for a long-term mooring. He was doubling up the stern line when he heard boot steps on the wooden pier.

"Hey," Todd said. "Give you a hand?"

"Sure. You can get the bowline. I'm just doubling them up in case she doesn't move for a while."

"What are you going to do without the DeeVee8?" Todd asked, hopping aboard the Kimberly Marie and strolling forward along the starboard side to retrieve the end of the bow line. He ran it through the forward eye in the gunwale, passed it to his hand atop the rail, then tossed it to the pier to secure to the bit.

Mattituck waited until Todd was back in earshot.

"Well, I have the Knot Skunked still running. So her clients will continue. Business as usual, I guess." He thought for a moment. "Haven't really given it much thought, come to think of it. I suppose I can keep the

DeeVee8's clients on the dates the Knot Skunked was going to be in port—run her 7 days a week."

Todd hopped onto the pier.

"You going to bump your Knot Skunked captain and run her yourself?"

Mattituck considered this while Todd secured the bow line to the bit, and joined him on the Kimberly Marie's aft deck. Taking the chair facing aft next to the one Mattituck occupied.

"Nah," Mattituck finally said. "Scotty needs the money. I'll keep him on and take a few days off. I can run the Knot Skunked when Scotty's off."

Todd nodded. In Todd's mind, this spoke to Frank's integrity. Most captains would take the employee captain's spot, potentially leaving the guy in a lurch.

"Want a beer?" Mattituck asked.

Todd smiled. He sat forward and pulled off the Alaska State Trooper jacket and the shirt with the badge beneath. He then took off the bullet-proof vest and removed the gun belt. He sat down in his white tee shirt.

"I'm off duty now, so yes, that'd be great."

Mattituck smiled and disappeared inside the cabin, returning with two brown bottles of Killian's.

"Amber okay?"

"Absolutely," Todd smiled, accepting the cold bottle with a deep gulp.

They sat several minutes in silence, enjoying the sunshine and the cold beer.

"When will you be taking the Knot Skunked out?"

Mattituck seemed to run the days in his mind, pursing his lips.

"Ummm . . . Saturday. Three days."

"Three days off," Todd echoed. "Can you sit still that long?"

Mattituck laughed. "You know me that well, eh?"

Todd smiled. "I looked into the deputizing, if you're serious about helping me out."

Mattituck looked at him, surprised. Todd dipped his head at him and grinned.

"So you meant tag along with you on the investigation?"

Todd nodded, the grin faded to show he was serious.

"Wow," Mattituck said, thinking it over. He thought about his bank account. He really didn't need to be running charters. Business had gotten ahead two years ago, and he'd been stockpiling the profits ever since. He certainly could take some time off if he wanted to. Then his thoughts turned to Jim Milner, and his earlier anger returned. He thought about the elderly couple near Yakutat, and the cop these guys had killed.

And Todd was giving him a chance to be part of solving whatever happened to Jim.

"Hell yeah," he said. "I'll come along."

"Great. If you want, I'll have our office arrange a salvage for the DeeVee8. You can just concentrate on helping me."

Mattituck's and Todd's gazes locked. An understanding seemed to pass between them.

"So you need to deputize me, huh?" Mattituck chided.

Todd laughed. "Well, actually, it really is something like it. You need to come back to the office with me."

"Do I get a badge?" Mattituck joked.

"Yes," Todd said. "You do."

Three hours later, post showers and dinner, Todd rejoined Mattituck on the Kimberly Marie. The two had agreed that it might be best to maintain a presence on the Kimberly Marie, at least while it was convenient to do so—meaning while they were in town and Mattituck was available to stay aboard. Particularly this first night back in port, it was important to be aboard in case the killer from the 'But Chaser tried to access the boat. Although the report had been that the 'But Chaser was clearly Cordova-bound, one could not be too careful. And clearly the killer had been lying in wait for the Kimberly Marie. For whatever reason, the guy wanted either the boat itself or something on it.

At the Alaska State Trooper office, Todd had asked Mattituck if they could discuss the "Goose-whacking" and the case in general over more beers aboard the Kimberly Marie. Mattituck had agreed, eager to know more about the beached Bayliner and what Todd was thinking might have happened to Jim Milner. For all the time that had passed, they still hadn't had a chance to piece together details, nor to get the full story each of them had experienced. Mattituck was especially keen to know what Todd's law enforcement expertise was making of all this. He also wanted to know what the plan was for the next several days.

A break before meeting on the Kimberly Marie also gave Mattituck a chance to touch base with Scotty Porter, his employee captain, letting him know what had happened and that he was leaving the logistics with the clientele to him. He gave direction for Scotty to use both crewmen as much as he could, perhaps having them alternate the fishing trips with cleaning the boat post-charter. This would keep both crewmen employed as much as they could keep both young men busy. Mattituck had then made arrangements for the stranded DeeVee8 clients to go fishing with other charters.

As Todd Benson and Mattituck settled in the chairs on the Kimberly Marie's aft deck, beers in hand, they began to fill each other in on what each had seen. First, Todd wanted to know why Mattituck had approached the Kimberly Marie in Zaikof Bay, knowing something was amiss.

"That's just it," Mattituck replied. "I really didn't think anything was wrong. I guess, anyway. I mean, I really thought I was going to find Jim aboard, landing deer hunters. Everything A-okay, you know?"

"But I told you to hold back. I had good reason for that."

"Yeah, I know that now," Mattituck countered.

"I really wish you'd just trusted me," Todd said.

"It wasn't a matter of trust. It was just having no fucking idea what you'd found in Growler Bay. I didn't know what you knew, and you didn't tell me."

"Like I said," Todd said, unwavering. "I wish you'd just trusted me."

Mattituck nodded. Todd was right. It really did come down to trust. He'd dismissed Todd's request and gone with his own view of things. And he'd been wrong.

"You're right," Mattituck said finally, allowing his eyes to follow a sloop entering the harbor.

Todd nodded. "How much do you want to know?" he asked, knowing most people don't want the gruesome details.

"About what? What you found?"

Todd nodded.

"How much do you want me to know? I mean, isn't some of it confidential or something?"

"You're deputized, and you're officially on the case. I want you to know everything." He looked observantly at Mattituck. "I guess what I really want to know, Frank, is if there's anything you want me to hold back. Like details about Jim Milner."

Mattituck was quiet as he watched a skiff idle by, the lone older man at the outboard on his way to check shrimp pots, most likely. He thought of Jim Milner dead, and the hot anger rose again in the base of his throat. He fought the emotion down.

"I'll be all right. We were pretty close, but I'll be fine."

"Okay, then," Todd said, and brought Mattituck up on everything he'd found on the beached Bayliner, including the blood, and what he knew about the boat and its owners. He told Matittuck about the fact that the elderly owners, residents of Bellevue, Washington, were now missing. He shared with Mattituck that while there was little doubt the blood in the Bayliner belonged to the missing owners, they would not know for sure until the DNA tests came back.

"How do they do that, anyhow?" Mattittuck asked. "What do they have to compare it to?"

"There's plenty of DNA stuff on the Bayliner— hair in the brush, residue on toothbrushes, that kind of stuff. But even that, we don't know for sure whether that DNA is theirs or someone else's. The definitive evidence comes from DNA samples from things in their home in Washington."

"Ah," Mattituck said. "That makes sense. I'd forgotten we know who they are."

Todd inwardly noted the 'we' in Mattituck's comment. He smiled.

A few more minutes of silence contributed to the relaxed ambiance of the evening.

Mattituck asked, "How long does the testing take?"

"A week or two on the outside. Sometimes less. They tend to rush it in active investigations." Todd took two long gulps of his beer, finishing it, then got up. "Mind if I grab another?"

"Of course. Bring me one, too."

Todd disappeared inside the cabin.

Mattituck watched an older couple carrying groceries to their Ranger Tug, tied up on the next dock over. They were not dressed at all like Alaskans, the woman in white shorts, green polo shirt, and a white bucket hat; her husband in beige topsiders without socks and plaid shorts with a blue polo shirt. Mattituck didn't recall seeing their boat before. Very likely visitors from the Lower 48, on their retirement voyage through Alaska. Although, he had to admit, those tug-style cabin cruisers were pretty nice. Slow, but very sturdy and cool-looking little yachts. They tended to be styled in very traditional nautical themes, with ship's clocks, portholes, and wood trimming reminiscent of the old-style cruising yachts and ships. Mattituck allowed himself a moment of imagining a relaxed, care-free retirement before his thoughts turned to Jim and Louise Milner and the retirement they'd been robbed of.

"What do you think happened to Jim?" Mattituck finally asked.

Todd was quiet for several minutes. Mattituck waited, sipping his Killian's and watching the retired man pass grocery bags from the dock to his wife on the stern of the tug.

"Well," Todd started, tone heavy. "I guess I'd say to start that there's really no doubt in my mind that Jim's dead."

He watched to see how Mattituck would react. But the freshly deputized charter boat captain didn't flinch.

"I think," Todd continued, "that these two clowns killed him when he approached the beached Bayliner to help them. It didn't happen on the Bayliner or on the beach," he added, "and there were absolutely no signs of anything here on the Kimberly Marie."

"So how do you know Jim's dead? How'd they do it?"

"Everything adds up to that. The fact we don't know exactly how they did it, or where, doesn't change that. Where would Jim be, if he's alive? Why didn't he turn up in Growler Bay? Why were there no signs—I mean zero—that anybody had gone further onto the island than the beach?" Todd considered before continuing. "No, he's dead all right. My best guess is that they killed him while he approached them in the service boat. He anchored the Kimberly Marie to help them, launched the service boat, and they shot him or knocked him on the head while he approached. Now that he couldn't give them a fight, they dragged him into the water, and finished him off there so there wouldn't be a mess in the service dinghy."

He watched Mattituck. When he didn't react, Todd went on.

"They'd learned on the Bayliner what a mess killing someone can be, so with Jim they kept it as clean as they could. I'm thinking they intended to kill him as soon as they saw the Kimberly Marie coming up the bay. They were probably watching as he came up the bay, and had a pretty good idea that Jim was alone. They signaled him for help, and when he came ashore to help, they killed him as cleanly as they could. After he was dead, they probably dragged his body back out to the Kimberly Marie—alongside the service boat, probably—and put him on the swim deck aft until they could sink him or ditch him someplace else."

Todd paused, thinking about this last point. Mattituck surprised him by pitching in.

"No ditching him," Mattituck said. "They would have to sink him somehow before they exited Growler. Too much chance of being seen outside the bay. And I like your idea that they had him on the swim deck. Easy to wash that down after they sank him."

Mattituck suddenly got up and walked up the port side to the bow. Todd waited. A few minutes later, Mattituck returned.

"I don't know why I didn't notice before," he said as he sat back down. "But Jim's shrimp pots are gone. He kept them up forward of the cabin windshield." He looked soberly at Todd.

Todd shook his head at the thought. He wanted to hear Mattituck say it to be sure they were on the same page.

"And . . . ?"

Mattituck went on. "Shrimp pots are weighted. They'll hold on the bottom until you pull their lines and bring them up. If you have no lines, it's unlikely the pots will ever come back up. And if they do, all the bottom critters will do away with whatever edibles are inside. Except bones. But if there are no lines, the pots would probably never be found."

Todd was following, but wanted to hear Mattituck play this out.

"Frank, you can't fit a body in a shrimp pot," he said.

Mattituck shook his head. "Not all in one piece, you can't."

Todd nodded, and took his time with a few more sips on his beer. He and Mattituck sat in silence, enjoying their beer.

"You're already making one hell of a deputy, Frank."

After Todd had left, Mattituck buttoned up the Kimberly Marie and went below to the port cabin, where he'd slept the night before. He liked that he'd tied up the Kimberly Marie starboard-side-to so that his cabin faced the water and not the dock. He preferred privacy and distance from the crowds.

He killed all the lights and stripped down to his shorts, then crawled under the top sheet. He had a good buzz going, having sat with Todd for two hours and a 12-pack of beer after they'd exchanged details about what each knew in the case. Their conversation had wandered to casual topics: Summers on the Hopi reservation for Todd's high school years, Mattituck's closeness to his now-passed mother and his sister, interspersed with fishing stories and thoughts on life in Alaska.

He lay back on the bed, light from a light post on the pier across the channel shining faintly through the porthole onto the bulkhead opposite. The water lapped lightly at the hull, blown by a slight breeze along the surface and causing a small ripple that threw itself against the boats in the harbor.

His thoughts drifted as he slid toward sleep. The lapping water combined with the slight motion of the

Kimberly Marie, nudging against her bumpers between the hull and the dock. The sound calmed Mattituck's agitated spirit, drew the latent anger out of him. The temperature was perfect, and he occasionally felt the cool, reassuring tufting of the breeze that found its way through the open porthole to his lightly covered body. His eyes opened every few minutes to the light spilling from the light post, and he noted the breeze and lapping again as the alternate world of dreams slowly began weaving a combination of thoughts and memories, lulling him more and more toward a dreamlike state. The lapping of the water was even, consistent. The breeze drew across the bed in an uneven pattern that seemed to rock him like a father's arms. The light of the light post spilled, the lapping gently provided a dreamy sound against the hull, and the thoughts and memories came and went, like the turning of the tide, in rhythm with the breeze gently brushing his body from the porthole, dreams and thoughts and lulling patterns of water lapping . . .

He awoke with a start. He lay still, his heart beating. Everything seemed as it had been. The light from the light post on the pier; the breeze pulling across the cabin through the open porthole; the water lapping gently at the hull, just as it had when he fell asleep.

Nonetheless, Mattituck knew something wasn't right. Something was not the same.

He lay still, trying to decipher what it was.

Nothing. Silence. Motionlessness.

Or was it? His mind stilled, and he observed. He fixed his eyes on a vacant spot and cleared his mind, just as he'd been taught when young by his jujitsu instructor. His senses instantly heightened, and he kept his mind clear and focused. The motion of the boat was not just from the lapping water, and the breeze was not strong enough to move the Kimberly Marie the way she was rocking now.

Someone was aboard.

He raised his upper body silently at the thought, sitting up in bed.

After he had been still for a moment, and detecting nothing more than the surety of the change in motion, he swung his legs over the side of the bed and pulled on his jeans, then reach for his shirt. He thought better of this; he could be more stealthy in just his boxer briefs. His hands groped in the dark for the Glock. Finding it, he gripped it in his right hand, and got to his feet.

Instinctively, he stayed low, crouching alongside the bed. For a few moments, he didn't move. His eyes were fixed on the overhead, as if he could see through to topside and at whoever might be there. Hearing nothing, he moved quietly to the door, nervous to turn the handle for fear it might squeak. He cursed himself for not taking notice of things like that before, in the event he'd later need to exit quietly.

In the passageway adjacent to the galley, he paused and listened. He estimated it was somewhere around 1:00a, as it was nearly dark—the darkest night got this time of the year. One could hike trails without a flashlight this time of year, but it was dark enough to make it safer to use one. Now, he placed a foot on the bottom rung of the ladder and lifted his weight upward. He paused again, ears attentive and remaining still to see if there was any unusual movement in the boat. Though a large boat, a person stepping at the edges could cause the Kimberly Marie to list under a person's weight.

He was high enough after two more steps upward to see out the sliding glass doors at the rear of the cabin. The Kimberly Marie, because she was a larger vessel, tied up along a longer pier with no slips. This was where the small ships and larger commercial fishing boats also tied up, abeam of the pier and end-to-end until the pier filled. When that happened, they would begin to tie up outside of each other, doubling and tripling up.

Mattituck held still a moment. Beyond the after deck, over the transom, he saw a small sportfisher had tied up behind the Kimberly Marie. Was it the 'But Chaser? he wondered. The smaller boat's hull was below the Kimberly Marie's gunwale, so he couldn't see the vessel's name nor the color of her hull. It was too dark to see much detail.

While still listening for any sounds aboard the Kimberly Marie, Mattituck looked over what he could of the small boat. It did look very much like the 'But Chaser. He craned his neck at the top of the ladder to see more of the boat without exposing himself. She was tied up far enough behind the Kimberly Marie that he could see the top of the bow. It did have a dark hull, like the 'But Chaser.

But why? Mattituck wondered. Why would the killer come all the way up here after heading toward Cordova? Or had he? Perhaps he had cut down toward Cordova just to throw him off. Or maybe to get around to the other side of Goose Island and south so Mattituck had less chance of identifying the boat.

As he mulled these possibilities, the Kimberly Marie suddenly listed gently but sharply toward the dock. The way the motion—ever so slight—moved the big yacht told Mattituck someone had stepped aboard forward, up near the bow. Mattituck would have to gain the upper deck and peer over the dash to see. While there still had been no sound, the way the Kimberly Marie now nudged against her bumpers along the pier told him someone was moving far forward on the boat. Only steps at the narrow part of the deck on the bow could cause a boat to move that way, due in large part to the tapering of the hull beneath.

He took the last two rungs of the ladder and stepped onto the main deck, between the helm station and the passenger seats on the port side. He kept his head low as he peered over the dash to the bow. There, hunched over a point three or four feet back from the bow, was the dark shape of a figure. While the confirmation of what Mattituck had felt was no surprise to him, his heart rate instantly jumped, and he could feel the sudden pressure behind his eyes. He took several slow breaths to calm himself as he watched the figure moving, apparently fumbling with something on the deck.

Mattituck forced his tensed muscles to relax. He knew that in order to be quickly responsive in his actions, he had to keep his body at the ready, but in a relaxed state. He decided to wait to see what the man was up to.

After a moment more of fumbling with whatever he was doing on the deck, the man straightened wobblingly. He stopped after straightening to a full standing position, and waivered a moment. He then took a laborious step to the port side and stopped again, apparently making sure he caused very little motion on the boat. He swayed, then stepped back to steady himself.

Mattituck's brow raised slightly, trying to make sense of what he was watching. The figure did not seem steady at all. Had Mattituck perhaps shot him earlier during their exchange? Was the man injured or dazed?

Why had he tracked down the Kimberly Marie? Was there something on board that he'd left behind? *Come to think of it,* Mattituck thought, *when the killers were last on board, they thought they were going to give me chase, kill me, then get back on board. It could well be that they left something on board.*

Mattituck thought this over as he watched the man standing stock-still, holding on to the Kimberly Marie's railing. It made sense. It explained the "goose-whacking" as well as his determination to get to the Kimberly Marie. And it was easy to imagine the killers might have left something on board. He decided the man must be trying to retrieve something they had stowed in one of the fender lockers on the bow.

As he watched, the man tried to take a turn to his left, toward the rear of the Kimberly Marie, and lost his balance. The man's hand shot out to the port rail to steady himself, then he sat down on the raised center deck that was immediately above the forward stateroom below. The man did not appear to have a weapon on him. He either had assumed the Kimberly Marie was unoccupied and came aboard unarmed, or he had a gun—or knife—tucked into his pants.

Convinced the man wasn't going to move for a few minutes, Mattituck made his way aft, grateful that he was still in only boxer briefs and bare feet. The only thing on his person beside the shorts was the Glock, tightly gripped in his right hand. With his left hand, he quietly slid the glass door open and made his way to the starboard deck. He moved forward, quietly placing one silent foot in front of the other until he reached the starboard window next to the helm station inside.

He peered around the forward edge of the Kimberly Marie's super structure, her gracefully sloped windshield in front of him. The figure still had not moved. The man sat facing the port side, away from Mattituck, his head down. He was otherwise completely still.

Mattituck advanced, completely silent and careful to make his way slowly so that the Kimberly Marie remained motionless under him. He kept the Glock trained on the man's back as he moved cautiously forward. Still, the man didn't move. Mattituck stopped, watching and listening. Several docks over, he could hear the laughter of several people, partying late into the night. If they kept that up, they would have a visit from the watchman at the harbormaster's office.

Mattituck heard a familiar sound from the figure that was completely out of place. He listened again. Was that wheezing? Maybe Mattituck had shot him in the upper torso earlier and the man was bleeding in the lungs. No, Mattituck quickly dismissed that. Any shot like that would have landed the man in a hospital or a morgue by now. He continued listening. The man did not move. He remained perfectly still, sitting with his head down. Mattituck could now see his rib cage extending and distending with each breath, as though he were breathing deeply.

He heard the wheezing sound again, in rhythm with the breathing.

Suddenly, Mattituck realized what he was hearing. He shook his head in disbelief. It was snoring. The man was snoring. Apparently, he'd fallen asleep after sitting down, not even bothering to lie down on the raised superstructure alongside him.

Straightening up confidently now, Mattituck took two more steps toward the man. He came close enough to see the man well, but far enough that he was safe from any knife swings.

"Get up," he said evenly.

No response. The man continued snoring softly.

"Get up!," he said, his voice raised slightly.

The man snorted, and his head came up. "Huh?" he said.

"I said get up."

The man straightened and turned toward him unsteadily, reaching out to the railing next to him. His head wobbled to the side. Mattituck could see his eyes in the dim light from the pier, unfocused and unable to keep steady on Mattituck.

"Who're you?" the man asked, slurring his words.

"I was just about to ask you the same."

The man noticed the Glock. "Hey! What goes on here?!" he said, surprised. He shook his head, trying to clear it.

"You're not in a position to ask questions," Mattituck said. "Who are you?"

"Put the gun away, man. I ain' doin' nuthin'." The last word was dragged out with the long vowel of a person either drunk or high.

"What the fuck are you doing here?" Mattituck barked.

"Jim lets me sleep here when I'm . . . when I've had a coupla too many at the Crow's Nest up there," he said, indicating the popular pub and lounge overlooking the harbor.

Mattituck relaxed at the man mentioning Jim. Clearly, the man was drunk, and more clearly he was not the killer from the 'But Chaser.

"How do you know Jim?" he asked.

"I've known Jim fer years . . . fuuuck. We go waay back, man."

"Wait a minute," Mattituck said, catching enough light to get the first good look at the man's face. "I know you, you're---" but he stopped himself from finishing with *the town drunk*.

The man was continuing, not having heard Mattituck's interruption.

"Waaaay back," he was saying. "I useta help him here on the Kimberly Marie." He looked around admiringly at the yacht. "She's a beaut, ain't she? Shiit . . . I love this boat. Wish it were mine. Jim's a lucky fuck. I've tol' him many a time what a fucking lucky fuck he is." The man paused, apparently passing an uncomfortable and silent belch. "I useta be Jim's first mate."

Mattituck was surprised at this. All he'd ever known of this man was sighting him in town, walking drunk, or hanging around the Crow's Nest. Rumor was that he was from a family with money, and that they'd left him a good house up by the high school and a bundle of cash to take care of him for the rest of his life.

The man chuckled, continuing.

"Well, not like his wife was the first mate, yuh know what I mean?" the man burst into a series of guffaws that seemed to make breathing difficult. He stopped and looked hard at Mattituck. "D'you know Louise?"

Mattituck ignored the question. He didn't have time for this shit.

"So Jim let's you sleep here? Where?"

"Wherever, man. Ush'lly right here. I was just tryin' to get a blanket he useta keep fer me in that forward hatch there." He burped loudly, swaying slightly, then sat down. "Ain't there. Put somethin' else there, looks like."

"Why not come inside and sleep?"

The man shook his head. "I like sleepin' out here. Riiiight here," he said, bringing his pointing finger all the way to the deck next to him. "Right here," he repeated, allowing himself to keel to his side and lie down.

Mattituck put the gun away. He checked the forward hatch. The blanket was there, shoved back behind a black backpack. He pulled out the backpack and the blanket.

"Here you go," Mattituck said, not bothering to disguise his annoyance.

He tossed the blanket to the drunken man as he passed by. He carried the backpack to the aft deck and into the cabin, where he switched on a light. He grabbed a flashlight and exited to the aft deck and onto the dock. He turned to the sport fisher behind the Kimberly Marie and walked cautiously to her, the Glock still in his hand, ready.

When he was close enough, he saw that the lamppost on the pier shone enough light on the small boat that he could clearly read the name under the forward starboard window.

"Dark Horse," he read out loud.

To make sure, he shone the flashlight along the cabin, checking for the damage from his Winchester earlier in the day. Nothing. The boat was in great shape, and not a scratch on her. She had only a single Honda outboard. Clearly not the 'But Chaser. Mattituck relaxed, his hand with the Glock dropping to his side.

He returned to the Kimberly Marie's cabin, to the backpack he'd left on the table. He unzipped the main pouch and looked inside. There were four or five zipper bags with a white substance, two larger zipper bags filled with marijuana, and interspersed among them bundles of one hundred dollar bills.

He didn't bother to count them. There were plenty there to spell trouble. He zipped the backpack closed again and went below to retrieve his cell phone, then came immediately back topside. He activated his cell and searched the contacts.

He found Todd Benson's cell and pressed the call option.

"Hello," came the groggy answer after three rings.

"Todd?"

There was a pause. "Yeah. What's up, Frank? What time is it?"

"You need to come down here right away. I found a backpack with a lot of interesting goodies in it."

Chapter Twelve

The Cordova Connection

State Trooper Todd Benson arrived at the Kimberly Marie more quickly than Mattituck had thought he would. After calling him, Mattituck had started a pot of coffee, thinking they both could use a little pick-me-up. Todd stepped aboard, a pair of jeans and white tee shirt and sneakers. He came through the open sliding glass door into the cabin and smelled the coffee brewing.

"Who's the stowaway?" he asked when Mattituck came up the ladder from the galley.

"Oh, some old friend of Jim's. Apparently, he sleeps out there when he's too drunk to drive home or something." He handed Todd a mug full of black coffee. "If you want milk or sugar or something, it's down below."

"Naw, I'm good. This is fine." He gestured toward the man asleep outside on the bow. "That'd be Earl Darick. Friend of Jim's and Jim lets him sleep on board when he drinks too much. Which is most of the time, by the way."

"Yeah, he told me all that. I didn't recognize him right away. Didn't know he was a friend of Jim's, but I recognized him from staggering around town," he said coldly before going on.

"So he was rummaging around in a forward hatch, looking for a blanket. I guess Jim kept one up there specifically for this guy so he could sleep up there."

He shook his head at the weird arrangement.

"Yeah," Todd said. "I've seen him asleep out there a few times. I guess he sleeps out there so's not to wake Jim."

"I'm guessing, yeah. Sounds like it was a standing invitation, and like I said before, Jim would not leave the boat unlocked, ever. So rather than the guy waking him up, Jim apparently kept a blanket up there so the guy could just come aboard and snooze without disturbing anybody."

He took a sip from his own mug, then continued.

"So anyway, after all that came clear, I went up to that hatch to get the blanket for the guy, and found this backpack." He indicated the black backpack lying on the dining table. "Take a look inside."

Todd rose from the passenger seat he'd been in, across from Mattituck sitting at the helm station. He unzipped the bag and looked inside. A slow whistle emerged from his lips. He pulled out each white pouch and lined them up off center on the table. He then pulled out the two large bags of weed and set them next to the white powder bags. He then began stacking the bundled bills.

"Sixteen bundles," Todd said, then sat down on the dining bench.

Mattituck joined him, careful to set his mug well away from the backpack's contents. He didn't want any question of where his hands were floating around.

"That's a shitload of cash," Todd said.

"I'd say. What's the white stuff?"

"Won't know until we have it tested."

"You don't taste it and know?" Mattituck asked, half joking.

Todd fixed an even gaze at him as an answer, then turned his attention to the outer pockets of the backpack. He pulled out a toothbrush and a tube of Crest, deodorant, a small leather New Testament, and a pack of gum. These were lined up alongside the bundles of hundred dollar bills. He unzipped the smallest pocket on the outside of the middle pocket, and pulled out only a single business card. Todd read it, then looked at Mattituck.

"Did you say that sport fisher that took shots at you today headed toward Cordova?"

"Yeah. That's what the gillnetter said."

He showed the card to Mattituck. Next to a totem logo were the words *Copper River Inn, Eyak Lake, Cordova Alaska* and an address for the Copper River Highway and a phone number. Handwritten on the side were the letters *P I N* followed by the number 116.

Mattituck absorbed this and looked up to meet Todd's gaze.

"Feel like a trip to Cordova?" Todd asked.

"Hell yeah," Mattituck replied without hesitation.

Todd nodded. "Good. We'll fly down tomorrow. I'll call you when I know when our ride picks us up."

"Ride?"

"Coast Guard. If they fly us down, we can get there without alarming anybody. There's a Coast Guard Air Station next to the Cordova airport. They fly my air support," Todd said. "I'll call them tonight and see when they can fly up. Usually they pick me up on their regular patrols, so it'll be before noon."

"All right," Mattituck replied.

"That'll give us both a little time to get some sleep. Matter of fact," he pulled out his cell. "I'll call them now so we can set our alarms and get to sleep sooner."

After arrangements were made for a 9:30a pick up at the Valdez Airport, Todd inventoried the contents of the backpack on an Alaska State Trooper evidence slip, and sealed it in an envelope. He then had Mattituck sign and date on top of the seal of the envelope, and Todd did the same.

"You get some sleep," Todd told Mattituck. "No telling what awaits us down there. But 16 bundles of either cocaine or heroin tell me these guys are attached to something big. This thing is taking on a whole new set of circumstances. Just putting together those bundles and the card, I'm thinking these guys are delivery men for a drug operation. The card looks like a drop-off point. Could be one of many."

He looked at Mattituck.

"I wonder if they had a drop in Yakutat. A couple of other points in southeast, probably."

"Wouldn't they want to keep a low profile, though?"

Todd nodded. "Again, good detective thinking. You're wondering why the killings, then, right?"

Mattituck nodded.

"Again, a lot of mystery. My experience is you just keep following leads, and it eventually all comes together. It's like pulling a loose thread on a jacket. Eventually you get to the source."

"Yeah, if the jacket doesn't come completely unraveled by then."

Todd grinned. "Yeah," he replied. "There is that. Listen, I have to swing by the office and lock this up in the safe. Be sure to bring your badge. We'll be undercover, so it's vital you have that badge and your ID."

Todd repacked the backpack as he finished. He nodded at Mattituck and strolled off the Kimberly Marie, disappearing up the dock with a substantial load of drugs and over $865,000 in cash.

The Coast Guard MH60 Jayhawk helicopter had flown Todd Benson and Frank Mattituck almost in a straight line to Cordova, flying through deep passes between jagged peaks to get them there as quickly as they could. After they arrived at the Coast Guard Air Station in Cordova, a petty officer drove them the half mile to the airport to pick up a car rental Todd had arranged. On the five-mile drive into town, Todd brought Mattituck up to speed on other pieces of the investigation.

The man mauled by the grizzly had been transported to Providence Hospital in Anchorage, and while he had been stabilized, he was still in bad shape.

"The bear's teeth punctured the skull in several places, but luckily for the guy there's no brain damage that they know of. He is in a coma, though, and they're not sure if that will be long or short term. The muscle damage to one arm and his shoulder and chest is severe and will be a long time healing. The bear apparently didn't hit any major arteries or anything, but the guy has hundreds of stitches all over his upper body, neck, and head. The guy's lucky."

Mattituck listened closely, shaking his head occasionally at the details.

"Apparently, he's stable enough that they moved him out of ICU and into a regular room, although right across from the nurse's station. We have a watch on him, of course," Todd said. "And we have a phone trace going for any calls from Cordova to the hospital."

Mattituck shot a glance at the trooper. "You can do that?"

Todd smiled. "Technology is amazing, isn't it? Yes, we can. I'm thinking that if our buddy went to Cordova for some meeting or something, he might try to call his partner in the hospital."

"He probably knows how the guy's alive, I'd guess," Mattituck offered. "The story's all over the news."

"Right," Todd replied. "So we're going to start with this Copper River Inn and see what we can find out. I have no idea how to approach this, but we'll start with the hotel desk. Maybe this pin number means something to them."

"Okay," Mattituck said thoughtfully. "Do you think it might be a room number?"

Todd considered this. "Could be. Hadn't thought of that. The P I N written on it made me think it was a pin number for something. I was thinking we just walk in and hand them the card. See how they react, or if they do something with it."

Mattituck nodded. He pressed the button to roll down his window, but nothing happened.

"Can you unlock the child thingy?" he asked Todd, who was driving.

The rental was a decade old SUV with a worn velure interior of some off-beige color, two-toned where many hands had altered the color.

"Doesn't seem to work," Todd said. He turned on the air conditioning to try to move the stale air in the vehicle.

"So what happens when this guy wakes up?" Mattituck asked.

"The one in the hospital? We question him."

"Well, yeah," Mattituck said. "That's what I figured. But what do you think will happen to him?"

"Depends on our investigation, primarily what happens with the DNA tests from that Bayliner."

"But there's no clear tie from these guys to that murder, is there? I mean, we don't know for sure that they were even there. The Kimberly Marie showed up in Zaikof without Jim, and only these guys there, but we don't really know the Kimberly Marie even came from Growler Bay – or that Jim had been there."

Todd glanced at Mattituck as they rounded a curve and Eyak Lake came into view.

"Yes, that's exactly right. Good attention to detail there, Frank. Comes right down to it, I have no proof these guys were at the Bayliner in Growler unless the DNA comes back positive on the guy in the hospital." He started watching for the hotel sign. They knew the Copper River Inn was along the lake someplace on the highway.

"But there were traces of those guys all over the Bayliner," Todd continued, "and now we have the toothbrush of one of them," he added, referring to the personal items in the backpack. "We'll be able to put them together."

"You don't have any doubt it was them?"

"None whatsoever. Been at this too long to believe in coincidences like that. Courts and churches might give people the benefit of the doubt, but it's my job to make connections and follow logical conclusions."

He slowed the SUV and moved onto the shoulder, nosing the beaten vehicle toward a gravel parking lot. An aging wooden billboard marked the parking lot as belonging to the Copper River Inn, the paint showing wear at the edges. Cordova saw a lot of rain—condititions that were unkind to a wood sign.

The building was a long, two-story motel style establishment of the type built across the Lower 48 in the 1960s. Each door was exterior, opening onto a walkway facing the parking lot. The paint on the building matched the wooden sign in both color and condition. Presumably, the selling point for the motel was Eyak Lake on the back side, where the main windows of each room likely had a view of the lake and mountains on the other side.

Todd braked the SUV to a stop in front of a separate office on the left end.

"Well, here's to lucky fishing," Todd said as he grabbed the backpack, filled with clothes to replicate how it had looked with the drugs and cash. He had wanted to make sure all looked normal to whoever might be waiting to see them. He had filled Mattituck in on this part of the plan as well.

"How do you know they don't know what those other guys look like?" Mattituck had asked.

"I don't," Todd had replied. "But it's a hunch. Why else is there a pin number on a business card? My money's on they don't know who is coming for the dropoff or pickup or whatever is supposed to be happening."

They entered the office door, to a dingy room with worn carpeting and an ancient motel TV bracketed into one corner where the desk clerk could watch.

"Help you?" asked an overweight middle-aged man sitting at a desk behind the counter, his tree-trunk legs sprawled out the sides of the chair. He wore a brown flannel shirt with a blue fleece vest.

"Hope so," Todd said. He leaned on the counter and pulled the business card from his chest pocket.

The man swayed with each step, and stopped two feet short of the counter, his eyes fixed on the card. He looked closely at Todd, then looked Mattituck up and down. Mattituck was several feet behind Todd, looking around the room. The man swayed the last two steps to the counter and picked up the card.

"You're late," he said.

Mattituck almost jerked his head up, but kept it even and consciously gave no visible reaction. He couldn't tell how Todd reacted, but he was sure it gave nothing away.

"Well, you know how it is," Todd replied.

"Yeah, well, that crossing over the Gulf is no easy run, that's for sure." The man's fat cheeks worked around his mouth, laboring to form each word.

Todd merely nodded and waited.

The man watched him for a moment, seemingly reading him. Mattituck could feel his stomach tense. An awkward moment passed, and Mattituck felt sure the man knew something was wrong.

"Someone was here yesterday," the man said. "Tried to pass himself off as you." He watched Todd without expression, then shifted his gaze to Mattituck. Mattituck turned to him with a pretended interest, guessing that this would be how someone would react who was the right person, but had just heard an imposter had come before him.

Todd didn't miss a beat. "What'd he say?"

"Not much. He was pissed, though." The man kept his gaze on Todd's eyes, reading him. "Any idea how the fuck he'd know anything about you coming?" His eyes shifted back to Mattituck.

Mattituck pursed his lips—keeping with his imagined character—and shook his head slightly, still looking mildly surprised.

"No fucking clue," Todd said, his voice tense. He was acting, too, Mattituck realized. "But it gives me half a mind to call this shit off."

For the first time, the man looked alarmed.

"Oh, shit, man . . ." his voice rose a pitch. "There ain't no need to do that." His tone was almost pleading.

Todd didn't answer. He stood for a full minute, impervious. The fat man became increasingly agitated.

"Hey, man—c'mon. I'm sure it was nothing."

Todd looked back at Mattituck, as if consulting, then turned back to the fat man.

"That guy might've been a narc or something," he said.

"Naw," the fat man gave a nervous laugh. "No way. He didn't seem anything like that."

"What'd he look like?" Todd asked.

"Shit, I dunno. Shorter than you two. Brownish hair, a bit longish. You know, not to his shoulders or anything, but longer than yours," he said to Todd. "He warn't too old, maybe upper twenties or early thirties, but a rugged face, you know? Like he's been outdoors a lot. He looked like he's pretty buffed, too, you know? Like he goes to a gym or something." He paused a moment, remember. "Oh, he had a scar on his left jaw, right along here— "

Eddie drew a line on his jaw, just above the bone and running length-wise from a couple of inches in front of the ear toward the chin.

"He was stubbly. But clean, y'know? Like he was unshaven and dirty because he's been out in the bush or on the water or something. But normally keeps himself pretty spiffed, you know?"

He watched Todd for a response. Getting none, he continued.

"He had this look to him, a look in his eye. Like he was super intense or something, you know? And the way he got angry, like he was about to go off. That's why I say no way he was a narc. No way."

"Those undercover guys don't exactly come in looking clean cut," Todd said. "They don't look like a street cop, like I do," he said with a nasty smirk. He fixed the fat man with a mean gaze.

The fat man chuckled nervously. "Look, man," he said. "Look!" he said, suddenly hopeful. "If I were in on anything with the cops, would I have told you about the guy?"

Todd turned again to Mattituck, then back to the fat man. Mattituck shrugged non-commitedly.

Todd smiled at him, then returned his face to the mean grimace. He turned around and fixed the fat man with the same mean gaze.

"That's true enough. But are you sure there's nothing going down?"

"Dead sure, man. Dead fucking sure." He looked nervously past them. "Man, if there were anything weird out there, I woulda seen it. No place for narcs to hide out there."

Todd ignored this.

"Where was this guy from?"

"He didn't say," the fat man's cheeks worked. "Can I have my stuff, man?"

"What do you have going here that you need that many kilos?" Todd asked him suspiciously.

"Hey, man. The point guy said you wouldn't ask no questions, man. The less we know about each other, the better."

Todd held his gaze on him. "Yeah, well, things have changed with this guy poking around your place. What's your operation?"

Mattituck had always known Todd was good at his job, but this was like watching a completely different person.

"Just small time shit, man. Fishermen and youngsters looking for a good time, that's all." He gestured to the town around. "Ain't much to do around here, y'know? It's just small-town fucking Alaska, man. Ain't no Disneyland and shit around here. Dudes and chicks gotta make their own fun. With a little help, that is," he grinned at Todd.

"You said the guy was pissed. What else did he say?"

"He just tried to get me to go through with the deal, but fuck man—no way without that card," he said, nodding at the business card on the counter. "No fucking way. I ain't going to prison."

"He say anything else? Try to convince you he was us?"

"He knew there was supposed to be two of him, you know. I mean, he said that right off. But again, without the card—I told him to fuck off, that I didn't know what he was talking about."

The fat man hesitated.

"He said he was going to go talk to his partner and he'd come back with the evidence."

If this guy had known about it, he would have also known about the business card."

He was quiet for a moment, reflective.

"No," he finally said. "He has no clue what 'the evidence' is, nor where to get it. He's going to be desperate to talk to his partner. And since he checked in on him, he knows he's still in a coma, so it'd be worthless to fly up there. I'm predicting the manifest from Alaska Airlines will show no purchase this morning."

Mattituck mulled all this over.

"Why a cash purchase?" he asked.

"Not likely he has a bank card or credit card," Todd said. "So he'd be buying a ticket with cash. And he wouldn't have been able to do that until this morning, just before the flight." He shook his head. "But I'm sure he didn't fly. He'll be on the 'But Chaser down here at the harbor biding his time until he can figure out how to get this pickup done."

They drove through town in silence. Mattituck was always struck by the classic Alaska coastal town look Cordova has. He loved the old-style buildings lining Main Street, with their 1970s store fronts and almost no uniformity between the buildings. Towns like this didn't even exist in the Lower 48. His eyes rose to the line of sharp peaks behind the town, and deciduous trees perfectly straight on even the steepest angles. There were wisps of clouds about two thirds of the way up, hugging tight along the trees and adding a cozy and lazy feeling to the mystique that was Cordova's.

Todd pulled to the sidewalk suddenly, and Mattituck saw that he was pulling up alongside a police officer.

He rolled the rear passenger window down as the officer recognized him and stepped over to speak with Todd. He put his face in the downed rear window.

"How's it going, Howie?" Todd said.

"Good, good," the man replied. He was an older, dignified looking man in his lower 50s. He sported long sideburns, of the type they called 'chops' in the 70s, and a very rugged complexion.

"What brings you to town? Investigation?"

Todd nodded at him. "Yeah. No uniform's a dead giveaway, eh?"

"Something like that. Anything I should know about?"

"Not yet. If it becomes something for you, I'll let you know."

"All right, Todd. Sounds good. Let me know if you need anything."

Todd nodded again. "Definitely. Have a good one."

They pulled back onto the road and continued to the harbor.

"Howie's the Chief of Police for Cordova," Todd explained. "I more just wanted him to know I'm here. If anything weird happens, he'll call me just in case it's related to what I'm working on."

Mattituck nodded.

As they pulled in to a parking spot in front of the harbormaster's office, Mattituck thought of the times he'd overnighted here with the Knot Skunked and the DeeVee8, renting a guest slip for the night each time. Usually, it was when he'd dropped off a hunting party on Hinchinbrook Island, and had a day or so to visit friends. He had an old college buddy in Cordova, an artist who was apparently making a pretty good living selling his paintings in art shows in Seattle, San Francisco, and Los Angeles.

There was also a young woman he'd met at the Fisherman's Widow, a pretty damned good pub-style grill and bar he'd found his first trip to Cordova, but he doubted she had much interest in seeing him now. They had become very close, very quickly. She was intelligent, beautiful, and had an amazing sense of humor. And she understood him and his inner struggles, his sometimes aloofness and disengagement. *Monica Castle*, he thought as his mind conjured her face. But as things got more serious, they had both found the distance more and more frustrating. Or more truthfully, Monica was more patient—it had been Mattituck who was frustrated. And something in him seemed . . . reluctant? No, that wasn't quite the right word. Distant? Too trite. Hesitant. Yes, that was about right. He had become more hesitant, almost to the point of feeling frozen; like the relationship was poised to move on, but he couldn't. For whatever reason, he just couldn't make that conscious choice to throw himself headlong into another relationship.

Another relationship . . . He began to mull this, but turned his thoughts to how he'd increasingly let time go by between calls. And the visits—he'd all but stopped coming down, and he couldn't remember inviting her up to Valdez. Things had died down between them, and now it had been a few months since he'd reached out to her.

Monica Castle. Deep brown eyes. Jet black hair, long and straight. Smooth, brown complexion. Her lips came to mind, and he thought of how they felt when he kissed her.

Thinking about her had come on unexpectedly, and he felt an unidentifiable pang deep inside him. Her smile danced into his memory, and the thought of that sparkle in her brown eyes tugged at him. He wondered if maybe she would want to hear from him. *No way*, he told himself. *Why would she?*

Chapter Thirteen

Two Steps Behind

Todd and Mattituck entered the harbormaster's office, and looked around. A long counter stretched across the room midway, cutting off the visitor's area from the work area on the other side. Three desks were visible and a private office to the rear left of the area. Nobody was visible.

"Hello?" Todd hollered.

"Yeah—be there in a minute," came a deep voice from the private office.

"Tom Graffinino, the harbormaster," Todd said to Mattituck.

"Where's his help?"

"He's always short-handed. He's a gruff guy. A bit hard to work for, I hear."

A tall man emerged from the back office, grimy Carhartt overalls and a cowboy shirt. He had a weathered face with deep-etched wrinkles that obscured his age. Many guys with weathered faces looked older than they actually were; and there were a lot of such guys in Alaska.

"Hey, Todd!" the man exclaimed, his face breaking into a broad smile. "What the fuck brings you to Cordova?"

"Well, that's part of what I came to see you about. You have a boat called the 'But Chaser in harbor? Probably came in the last few days, maybe a guest slip, but I'm not sure the boat's not home-ported here."

The burly harbormaster got on the computer on the counter, and typed with his two index fingers, pounding hard on the return key when he'd finished an entry.

"Yep," he said. "Slip B-21. Lemme see here," he reached for a logbook. "She's in port as of an hour or so ago."

"Thanks, Tom," Todd said and turned for the door. "We'll have to catch up another time."

"No problem, amigo," Tom replied, overly pronouncing the word ah-meeee-go.

Todd turned right as soon as he was clear of the door. He knew exactly where he was going. They walked along the walkway leading around the harbormaster's building, and down the ramp to the first set of floating docks in the harbor. Mattituck found himself looking ahead, trying to spot the 'But Chaser. There were too many boats, though, and judging by the slip number, B-21, it would be well down the dock on the other end.

As they neared the end of the dock, passing slip B-13, Todd dropped back next to Mattituck so he could speak quietly.

"We're going to approach bold, so we don't attract attention as we approach. Be ready with your handgun. As we hop aboard, draw your weapon and be ready. You have your badge, right?"

Mattituck nodded.

"Good. Here we go."

He kept his pace and Mattituck followed. Now they could see the 'But Chaser was there, backed into her slip, the twin Yamaha outboards raised to keep the propellers out of the water and free of algae growth. All appeared quiet.

Todd quickly stepped aboard as he drew his GEN4 Glock and Mattituck dropped into the fish deck right behind him, his own Glock in his right hand and ready. He slid the safety off.

The 'But Chaser rocked under the weight of their boarding. Todd quickly looked inside and saw nobody in the cabin. He tried the aft cabin door and it opened right away. He looked back disgustedly at Mattituck.

Mattituck nodded. It didn't seem the killer was aboard, so leaving a boat unlocked in a harbor was pretty stupid by any standard.

Todd disappeared inside and Mattituck followed. The boat was small. The cabin had a small dinette with a horseshoe bench on the port side, and a two-person passenger bench at the windshield in front of it. On the starboard side, there was a galley at the rear, just behind the helm station. Todd stepped over the open hatch to the forward berth area and peered below. There was a pair of bunks in a V into the bow, with a small toilet situated between them.

There was nobody aboard.

Both Todd and Mattituck relaxed.

"What now?" Mattituck asked.

"We get off board right away. No telling when he might come back. Then we wait. We'll find a place we can keep an eye out for the guy, and we wait until he comes back."

Tom Graffinino let Todd and Mattituck set themselves up for a watch in the second floor office, which had windows in all directions and afforded an excellent view of the entire harbor. But in particular, they could see the 'But Chaser sitting in her slip, silent and asleep. They drew up chairs and loaded borrowed mugs with borrowed coffee. "No, not borrowed," Tom had said in his deep gravely voice. "I don't want that back. Just the mugs." He'd laughed drily as he went down the stairs to the main office.

Since this was Mattituck's first stakeout, he had no idea what to expect, but he did not expect it to be such a long period of nothingness. At first, he and Todd talked about the case, trying to piece together what they knew with whatever might be behind it all. They retraced all that had happened, from Jim Milner's apparent murder in Growler Bay, to the chase on Montague Island and subsequent bear attack and escape of the 2nd suspect, to the discovery of contraband in the bow of the Kimberly Marie, to the discovery of an apparent drop-off point for drugs in Cordova.

Todd also folded into the narrative all that may have happened prior to the killers' arrival in Prince William Sound. The stealing of the Bayliner and possible murder of its owners, then the murder of the couple off Yakutat along with the subsequent sniper shot that took out Officer Wayne Barrett.

"So if we fold in what we know outside of our own experience," Todd said, "this unfolding story becomes more and more interesting. We know that an older couple left Puget Sound and took a cruise on their Bayliner up the Inside Passage, bound for Juneau. Somewhere along there, they run in with these two guys who kill them and take their boat. I know, I know —" he said to Mattituck's near protest, "we don't know if the owners were killed or what happened to them. Bear with me. The mystery to me before today was why they ran the thing all the way across the northern Gulf of Alaska over this way."

"Maybe they were just trying to get as far away as they could," Mattituck inserted, "and thought it less likely to be chased up this way."

"That's more or less what I had been thinking. Up until you found the backpack on the Kimberly Marie. That threw me for a bit of a loop. Far too much in the way of drugs for personal use, and far more cash than any two-bit drifter has on him." He took a long sip of his coffee. "Dead giveaway that these guys are mixed up with something much bigger than they are."

Mattituck nodded. "Drug dealers?"

"Not direct dealers, no. That's what I had been thinking. But today made it clear they're delivery boys. That's it. The Copper River Inn is an exchange point. So that's clear enough. But if you fold in the cash in the backpack, that looks a lot like they've already made at least one delivery. Cordova wasn't the first exchange."

Mattituck absorbed this while he scanned the harbor with the binoculars. Todd continued sipping his coffee, slouched in an office chair with his feet propped up on a low file cabinet under the windows.

"It doesn't seem likely," Mattituck said, "that Cordova would be the last stop, either, then."

Todd looked at him and smiled.

"You really were a good choice for a deputy," he said. "That's exactly right. Think about the fact that the guy in the hospital had a stash of drugs and cash that the other one might not have known about. For him to lift

that much junk and cash without the other guy noticing--
-" he shook his head to emphasize his point. "Nope. No
way Cordova's the only stop. I'd bet that the first stop
was Valdez," he said.

"You think so? Why?"

"What were they doing up at Growler Bay?"

Mattituck nodded. "Hey," he said, his tone
lifting. "What if the stops are in no order. If Valdez were
the first, and they hit rocks near Growler, they must have
been heading over to Whittier for the next stop."

Todd nodded. "You know, I didn't think of that.
I was only thinking about them coming out of Valdez,
and with today's events, I assumed Cordova was the next
stop. Whittier makes a lot more sense, though. Maybe
Cordova was next after that."

"But that hotel manager said we were late,"
Mattituck said.

"Which is why I was thinking Cordova was
supposed to be before they got that far north."

"Then why did they bypass it?" Mattituck asked.
"They couldn't have fucked up and just passed it by . . .
could they? Like missing their turnoff or something?"

Todd shook his head.

"No." He thought for several minutes.
"Something doesn't add up. What does add up seems
pretty outlandish."

"Try me," Mattituck said.

"Well," Todd began. "What if the guy in the
hospital was the actual delivery man, and the one we're
chasing now was an add-on for the trip?"

"What do you mean?"

"We know from your discovery of the backpack
and what we heard from the hotel manager that this guy
didn't seem to know what drops were happening when.

Probably didn't even know what drops were being made. So, he was along for something else."

Todd let that sink in.

"This guy's well built—keeps in shape. And he's a hell of a shot. You saw as much, but think about picking off Wayne Barrett in rough seas. And then think about how this guy seems willing to kill at the drop of a hat."

Mattituck felt lost. "I'm not following. Sorry."

"No, I wouldn't expect you to. Like I said, it's a long shot, but it's all that really makes sense."

"Okay," Mattituck said. "Who is he?"

Todd raised his binoculars and fixed them on the 'But Chaser as he answered like a child giving away a secret.

"Hit man."

Eddie Etano had argued long and hard with the owner of the Copper River Inn to install a security camera system around the hotel that could be monitored at the front desk. The owner, Albert Campbell of Twin Falls, Idaho, was a wealthy banker who was also an avid hunting and fishing enthusiast, had bought the Copper River Inn largely as a tax write-off, but one that he could also use as a home base for his extended hunting and fishing expeditions in Alaska. He had hired Eddie to manage the 24-room, two-story motel and Eddie found the job suitable for his more-or-less lazy lifestyle. It also worked well for his "second job": selling small quantities of marijuana and available drugs; and "renting" out rooms at a healthy profit as exchange points for a larger drug ring.

This latter operation involved booking a room periodically for a guy named Isaac, from Los Angeles but with a Seattle cell number. He would call and book a room several weeks in advance, and Eddie would mail a business card with a room for a set of dates to a provided Post Office box in various cities. On the first of the set of dates, an unidentified man would come in and introduce himself as Isaac's cousin, and Eddie would give him the key to the assigned room. The man would return a few minutes later with the key to be given to whomever came with the business card with the assigned room number written as a pin number, always a different person or pair of persons. Isaac seemed to prefer pairs. The "P I N" written on the card was supposed to throw off anybody who might accidentally come across the card—such as DEA, FBI, or police.

This operation had been going very smoothly for almost a year, with as many as five exchanges in some months, and never fewer than two. Eddie was making more money through this side business than he was from the management position. Since Eddie lived in the bedroom and kitchenette off the office and was the only one who worked the front desk, it was easy to keep suspicion at bay. The entire staff consisted of Eddie and three maids.

Eddie peered into the split screen monitor of the security camera system. The system allowed for all eight cameras to be displayed at the same time in a split-screen option, or to rotate through the cameras at a pace set by the operator. Right now, Eddie had the split-screen option selected.

He blinked wearily and rubbed his puffy cheek-encased eyes with a thick finger, and peered again into the screen. He'd been uneasy since the mean-looking motherfucker had stopped in demanding the key without the business card. Eddie knew that undercover narcs from the federal agencies often were mean-looking sons-of-bitches, so he was wary of the unshaved, icy blue-eyed man with the scar just above his left jaw-line. There was an underlying--- underlying something about the guy that left Eddie feeling like he wanted to shiver to shake off the eeriness in the man's eyes. It was an emptiness in those eyes. A void of some sort. Like the man had no soul, Eddie thought.

Then the other two guys came in earlier today *with* the business card, and Eddie at first was glad he hadn't given in to the first guy's demands. But when he'd mentioned the earlier visitor to these legit exchangers, they'd kind of freaked out and said they wanted to lay low and make sure before they did the exchange.

This had only increased Eddie's misgivings. If *they* were freaking out, why the fuck shouldn't *he*? he thought.

So he'd taken to watching the security cameras. Obsessively.

"Pro'bly overkill," he muttered to himself. He often talked to himself in hushed tones, the result of years in relative isolation from others. He never left the hotel, not even for grocery shopping. He had one of the maids do his shopping for him for an extra three hours of pay. Not that it was difficult work. Usually, the grocery list consisted of various frozen prepared foods. Pot pies, dinner trays, boxes of frozen burgers, or frozen pasta meals—anything that could be popped into the microwave. And soda. A lot of soda. He also drank a lot of beer, Rolling Rock was his favorite, but that was brought to him by his marijuana buyers.

He turned now from the screen and disappeared into his small room. While the kitchenette was small, it had a nice, large refrigerator that allowed Eddie to stay well-stocked in both his frozen meals and his Rolling Rock. He opened the refrigerator door and grabbed two of the green bottles, then stepped back out to the office, twisting off the cap of one of the beers as he stopped in front of the screen. He tipped back his head and allowed the fluid to drain into his mouth, swallowing as fast as it came. He paused when the bottle was half gone and gazed at the cameras. He shifted uncomfortably and let a loud belch escape.

A movement at Cam 5 caught his eye, but was gone before he could focus on it. It seemed to have been at the right side . . . so, Eddie thought, that would mean moving toward . . . he struggled to remember. Cam 3. Was that it? Yeah, that was it, he thought confidently. Another movement caught his eye at Cam 1.

"What the fuck? . . ." Cam 1 was right outside the front office.

The door flung open, hard enough to bounce off the wall behind it.

"Who the fuck are---" Eddie's angry voice trailed off. It was the mean son-of-a-bitch who'd come in for the exchange. The first guy with the empty soul.

Eddie watched the man. He moved his knee up under the counter to see if the shotgun were where he'd rigged it. He could feel the butt, firmly in place. He had a .38 in the drawer under the computer as well, just in case. The shotgun he'd rigged up so it was lying on the top shelf under the counter, to the right of the computer, and pointed at the door. It was secured in place on either side with 1"x1" pieces of wood that he'd screwed onto the shelf to hold the shotgun in place. While they lay next to the shotgun in strategic places to hold it steady even with a kick, he'd left the top open so he could pick it up and cock it for another shot from the shoulder. The whole idea of this shelf rigging was to give him one good shot about waist high on anybody standing in front of the counter.

The mean SOB stood staring him down for a moment, his face unflinching and his eyes a steely grey.

"Give me the key," he said flatly.

The problem with the jury-rigged shotgun was the safety. The trigger was rigged for him to bump a lever with his knee, and it would fire right through the thin paneling on the outer side of the counter.

But the safety . . . shit, he thought. *How do I take the safety off without being obvious?*

The man stepped forward into the room, and Eddie saw a chance to try something. He looked up over the man's head at the TV mounted at the ceiling to the left of the door. Sure enough, the man turned to see what Eddie had looked at so suddenly. Eddie reached down and flipped off the safety while the man's head was turned.

Suddenly, the man raised a gun and shot out the TV. The sudden loudness of the shot made Eddie jump, and he felt inside that he'd lost his nerve. He knew in that moment he couldn't fire the shotgun. Fear gripped him.

"I ain't fuckin' around here," the man said, his voice smooth and even. "Give . . . me . . . that . . ." and then his voice raised to a shout that made Eddie again jump – ". . . *FUCKING KEY!!!*"

Eddie stood frozen. He felt like his legs and hands had lost contact with his brain. He wanted to move, but he couldn't.

The man took three quick strides toward him, gun pointing at his chest. Suddenly, the hand with the gun shot out and Eddie felt the barrel of the gun clip his forehead. It didn't seem like it could carry such force, but it did, surprising Eddie as he fell to his knees behind the counter.

In that moment, as if not seeing the SOB broke the freezing powers he apparently had, Eddie found courage. He reached up in the thousandth of a second that his knees hit the floor and pulled the trigger of the shotgun. The blast was deafening in the small room. Eddie's ears rang and he felt like he could hear nothing—perhaps never would again.

He felt the vibration of the SOB hit the floor, more than heard it.

As he struggled to his feet, Eddie caught a glimpse of the hole the shotgun had blasted through the paneling. He reached with his left hand and pulled the drawer with the .38 open. His hand touched the cold metal just as he heard a gunshot from the other side of the counter.

"Fuck!" he heard himself burst in surprise more than pain. He thought for sure he'd been shot, but he didn't want to take his eyes off the other side of the counter. All he knew was he was still on his feet. Another shot rang from the other side, and he realized the man was firing from the floor. Maybe Eddie's shotgun had found its mark.

He had the .38 in his left hand now, his writing and firing hand. He moved as quickly as he could back toward his room, walking backward and praying to high heaven that he didn't trip over anything. He did not take his eyes off the counter.

The SOB's head popped up suddenly, followed by his shoulders. The man was swinging the gun upward as he rose to his feet. Eddie had the advantage, as he'd kept his gun up while he backed toward his room. He fired a shot that tugged at the man's sweatshirt, and Eddie saw the man's gun come level and flash a quick light at the end of the barrel. Next thing he knew, Eddie was lying on his stomach, unmoving. He knew without question that he'd been shot that time. He was afraid to move, and unable to feel where he'd been shot.

"Fuck . . ." he whispered.

He heard footsteps come around the counter and flip up the entrance panel. The footsteps approached, crunching debris on the tile floor with each step.

"The key," the man said, his voice unchanged from earlier. "And the room number."

Eddie closed his eyes.

"I know you're conscious, dickhead. Didn't fucking shoot you bad. Just knicked your head," he said, his voice cold and unconcerned.

Eddie kept his eyes closed.

The man kicked the bottom of his feet, making him jump uncontrollably.

"The room number, goddammit!!!" the voice was bellowing, and Eddie jumped again.

"O-one s-s-sixteen. Keys are on hooks in the box on the wall."

"That's a good little pussy boy," the man said. "Better not be fucking lying. Are you?"

Eddie shook his head, still lying as still as he could. He felt the throbbing in his head now.

"'Cause here's what I'm gonna do," the man waited a moment. "I'm going to take that key and walk down and make damn fucking sure the money's there. And if it ain't, I'll come back and put a bullet solid in your little pussy-shit head. Got it?"

Eddie nodded.

"Oh," the man added. "And just to make sure you don't try to grovel your way outta here or to a phone, I'm going to knock your fucking head with the butt of this here gun, so's you stay put until I come back. Understand?"

Eddie nodded.

"So, better come clean right now if you're lying. 'Cause if you are lying, I'll be back down here before you wake up and fucking blow your goddamn brains all over your cheap-shit linoleum flooring. In other words, I'm going to ask you one more time, and you're going to tell me the truth. Or you die."

Eddie swallowed hard and nodded. "I . . . I ain't lying," he stammered. "It's one-sixteen. Half way down, bottom floor."

"Okay, then. Hope you're telling the truth and you live to see another day."

The man heeled his gun hand back and brought down hard on the back of Eddie's head. His body went limp.

The man stood straight and looked around for the box on the wall. It wasn't even closed. He stepped over and found the hook for room 116, took the key with it's green plastic rectangle with the numbers 1 – 1 – 6 embossed, although the white coloring was faded where many fingers had handled it. He looked one more time at the fat Samoan lying on the floor, his head lightly bleeding from the grazed wound above the temple. He then stepped back around the counter, then, his eyes catching the security camera display on the computer monitor, he stepped back behind the counter and put two bullets into the computer CPU. He then left the office.

He strode along the motel on the first floor, walking past the stolen pickup he was driving, and found Room 116. He inserted the key and stepped into the room. On a cheap round table in the corner, he saw a black backpack. He quickly stepped to it and unzipped the main pouch. He had no idea how much money was there—those were the details that Carl, his partner now in the hospital in a coma—was in charge of. Hell, Carl hadn't even told him about the fucking "evidence," whatever the fuck that was supposed to be. He'd hoped to do this right, but Carl was still in a coma.

Now, the Whittier drop was another story. That one he did know. Even if Carl weren't awake by the time he got there, he could make that drop. Although now with how things turned out here, who the hell cared about the drop. Maybe he'd just rob the shit out of the rendezvous and forget all the others. In all, there were supposed to be five drops. The first had been Yakutat, followed by Valdez. Whittier was supposed to be the third one, and Carl had told him where the drop was and where he'd stashed the backpack for Whittier. The Cordova drop was supposed to be Number 4, and then Seward. That was going to be it, then. But he had no clue where the Seward drop was supposed to be. Maybe it'd be better just to rob the Whittier drop and disappear.

Except for the stop in Anchorage, of course. That was the real reason Norman Peck had been sent. He was only sent by The Organization when somebody wasn't cooperating and needed to be dealt with. Sometimes it was a warning, sometimes it was quick and easy. Quick and easy meant one shot, and then back to L.A. or Seattle.

Sometimes San Fran or Portland. It depended on where The Organization wanted him to be. Home wasn't a concept Norman Peck cared for anymore. He hadn't since before Afghanistan. But the operation in Monrovia was when he'd lost all perspective on life he'd grown up believing in. Now it was just one thing to the next. Didn't matter what. The Organization gave him chances to do what he did best, and that's all that remained.

Now that he had the Cordova money, he was pretty well set. He could just say fuck it to the rest and get as far away as he could. Then again, The Organization was an outfit to be reckoned with. They wouldn't take all that well to him cutting out. He shook his head with a violent jerk.

Doesn't fucking matter, he thought. *Doesn't fucking matter if I work for them or not. Where would I go? What would I do?* No, he decided. This job gave him the only satisfaction that remained for him.

What do you do with a sniper you've fucked up? He thought about this. *Let him keep sniping.*

He felt a moment of shuddering at that thought. It was too late. He was a fucking waste. Although if he had the drugs, too, that could carry him along for quite awhile. Wherever he went, he could sell that off and have more money.

But to do that, he would have to get back to the Kimberly Marie. He knew there were three more backpacks on that boat. Getting to it might be a bit risky, though.

He grinned at the thought. *But fun*, he added to himself.

He zipped the backpack up and headed out the door. He hopped in the stolen truck and cranked the noisy beast up, popped it into reverse, then pulled onto the highway and picked up speed for town. He'd get back on the 'But Chaser and get to----

"Where?" he said aloud, then laughed. "Eenie Meenie Miney Moe . . . Whittier? Kimberly Marie? Whittier? Kimberly Marie? Well for fuck's sake, I jus' can't decide!" His laugh was cut short by the flashing lights straight ahead of a cop car coming at high speed from town. Instinctively, he sat up straight and checked his speed. The police car flew past him, siren blaring. Very likely, it was headed for the motel.

"Well, shucky-fucky darn! . . . guess that means no grabbing dinner before I get the hell outta Dodge." He laughed again, elated at the feeling of being invisible and uncatchable. He punched the roof of the beat-up pickup several times, whooping like a crazed drunken good-ole-boy, then punched the gas for the marina.

Skipper's Oath

Chapter Fourteen

Wild Goose Chase

Mattituck shifted his weight as he gazed out the window with the binoculars. For what felt like the eight-hundredth time, he scanned the view back to the 'But Chaser. Nothing. The boat lay in her slip, unmoving, and nobody around. It was getting toward dusk now, and he wondered where this guy could be. He shifted his weight. His right leg was stiff from the position he'd been half-crouching in. It started to buzz.

"Fuck—leg's gone to sleep."

Todd started from a near-sleep. "Yeah?" He struggled to sit up. "Forgot to tell you this is the boring part of the job."

"No, really? I was hoping for something more dull down the road to top this."

Todd's cell rang with Bob Marley's *I Shot the Sheriff*. Mattituck chuckled.

"I have that set for most of my law enforcement network," he said with a grin as he pressed the answer tab.

"Hey, Howie," he said into the phone and listened. "At the – did you say the Copper River Inn?" He fixed a meaningful look at Mattituck, and signaled with his hand to gather their things. "Yeah . . . Wow. Okay, we're on our way." The chief on the other end said something else. "Yes, it's related, I think. We'll be right there." The chief said something else. "No, we don't know who the guy might be, but we've been on his tail from Glacier Island to Montague, half way to Valdez, and back down here." He listened to the Chief. "Look— we'll be right there."

Mattituck was already heading for the stairs. Todd grabbed his GEN4 and strode for the stairs as he tucked the Glock into its holster. As they reached the bottom of the steps and crossed the harbormaster's work area, Todd called for Tom Graffinino.

"Yep—what's up?" the gruff man said, stepping out of his office.

"Do me a favor . . . keep an eye on the 'But Chaser and call me if you see anybody get on board."

"Anybody? Or the guy who booked the slip?"

"Both."

"You got it."

"But don't try to be a hero, okay? Just call me."

After they had jumped into the rented SUV and started at high speed toward the Copper River Inn, Todd filled Mattituck in.

"They just got a call," he said, referring to the Cordova 911. "Shots heard at the Copper River Inn. Just a few minutes ago. Howie has three units coming in from both directions. He expects to get there in time to keep everybody contained. But you'll want to be careful, and stay behind the SUV when we get there. I don't need you getting shot."

Mattituck just listened.

"Okay?" Todd looked over at him. "Frank?"

"Yeah, okay."

Eddie lay on his stomach for several minutes after the SOB's footsteps passed through the front door. No more than two minutes later, he heard a rough engine start up—it sounded like it was running open exhaust, so was probably an older vehicle. He heard the Wrrrrr of the vehicle in fast reverse, then the gravelly sound of tires spinning on the dirt parking lot. He listened to the tires catch on the pavement with a small chirp, then the sound of the small engine as the vehicle sped away toward town.

Feeling safe now, he struggled to get up. He needed to call 911, and started thinking through a story he could feed the cops about what happened. The SOB came bursting in and demanding all his cash, Eddie thought. Then when he shot at Eddie, Eddie returned fire with the shotgun and a shootout followed. Or was that too cliché? he wondered.

He tried to think of another more plausible story. Maybe the guy came in looking for someone—a drug dealer maybe . . . no, Eddie quickly dismissed that one. How does he know about the drug dealer, the cops would ask. No. Too risky. He mulled, his head pounding as he reached for the phone. The SOB had shot out the computer with the security system, so he was free to make up whatever story he wanted, but it still needed to make sense.

And keep them from suspecting Eddie of anything illegal.

Sometimes, they say, something close to the truth is best. So, maybe the guy came in demanding the key to Room 116. Eddie would say he has no idea why, but the man was insistent and drew a gun. When Eddie held his ground, saying that room was rented, the guy opened fire. Eddie liked this story. It rang true—and if anything looked suspicious at Room 116, it would jive with this story.

"Cool," he said out loud and nodded his big bushy-haired head. It occurred to him that this story made him look a bit of a hero, too, protecting his clients even in the face of danger. He smiled and picked up the phone, grabbing a tissue and touching it to his head to check the injury.

Just then, he heard a siren approaching from the direction of town, then another one from the direction of the airport. Apparently, somebody had already called 911.

Trooper Benson and Frank Mattituck rounded a corner and saw ahead the dirt parking lot at the Copper River Inn. As they approached at a rate of speed Mattituck suspected was above the safety range of the SUV, they were surprised to see the two Cordova Police cars standing outside, lights flashing.

"Either they're moving in on someone, or the show's over already," Todd said.

He steered off the pavement and into the dirt parking lot, sliding to a stop in front of the office of the Copper River Inn. Simultaneously, they jumped out with guns drawn and approached the door. Inside, they found one of the officers treating a wound on the fat manager's head. Cordova Police Chief Howie Long was standing in front of the seated manager, writing notes.

Eddie Etano looked up blankly at Todd and Mattituck, then froze when he recognized them as the drug dealers that had come in earlier that day. *What the fuck were these guys doing coming in with cops swarming everywhere?* he wondered.

Howie Long looked over his shoulder at them.

"Hey, Todd," he said.

"Todd--?" Eddie said before he could stop himself. "What the--?" The realization came to him that Todd and Mattituck were narcs.

Howie turned back to Eddie. "You know these two?" he asked with a smirk.

Eddie's body sagged slightly. "I ain't sayin' nothin', man."

"Well," Howie continued, "you can finish the description of this shooter."

"Yeah, okay," he said, watching Todd and Mattituck cross the room.

Todd stepped around to the back of the counter, careful not to crush any evidence. He crouched under the computer screen to look at a shotgun lying in what appeared to be some sort of bracing system that was screwed down to keep the gun from moving.

"Hey!" Eddie shouted suddenly. "What the hell you think you're doing back there?"

"It's okay," Howie said. "He's one of ours."

A siren was approaching from town.

"Okay," Howie said to Eddie. "I got enough for now. We gotta get you to the hospital." He nodded to the officer, who then took Eddie's arm and started guiding him out the door. "I know where to find you."

Todd's head popped up from behind the counter. "I'll be visiting you in a while," he said to Eddie.

"Yeah, I'm sure." Eddie's voice reflected both resignation and sarcasm. Then he was out the door to meet the ambulance.

"So what happened here?" Todd asked Howie.

"Eddie—that's the manager who got clipped on this head with a bullet, Eddie Etano. He's a Samoan guy who took a liking to being here. He passes himself off as Alaska Native pretty much to everybody. Even most of the Eyak tribe think he's Athabascan, from up around Healy. We know the truth because we've had him up on marijuana charges. Some sources say he's supplying, but we haven't caught him yet."

Todd nodded, not revealing what he and Mattituck knew.

"So anyway," the Chief continued, "he says this guy came in demanding the key to Room—" he looked at his notes, "--- 116. Eddie said the room's rented, so he can't give him that room. Offered him another. But the guy was insistent and drew a gun. Then when Eddie still refused, he started shooting the place up. Eddie has this shotgun rigged up—" he indicated the gaping hole shot through the front paneling of the counter--- "under there. He reached down and fired the thing at the guy. He thought the thing had ripped the guy in half, but grabbed his .38 anyway. It's right there," he said. The gun lay on the counter in an evidence bag. "He grabbed it just in case, Eddie said, and then the guy got up and fired at him. One of the bullets grazed his head above the temple. Knocked him down, and he played dead. Then he heard the guy come around the counter and grab the key from the box up there on the wall." He nodded toward the key box on the wall behind the counter.

Todd nodded. "Have you checked Room 116 yet?"

"Nope. You got here pretty quick after we did."

"What if the shooter---"

"Oh!" Howie interrupted. "Forgot to tell you Eddie said he heard the guy tear off in a car or something. He guessed something older. Said it sounded like it was running with open exhaust, it was so noisy."

Todd shot a look at Mattituck. Mattituck nodded.

"Thanks, Howie. We gotta run."

"You going to try to chase the guy down? He's in town or beyond by now. No way you'll --- unless you know where he might be," he said, a question mark hanging in his tone.

"He might have a boat in the harbor. That's where we were when you called, but he wasn't there."

"Okay. You better go check it out. Lemme know what you find out," the Chief said.

"Will do." Todd gestured around and toward Room 116. "Likewise."

"You can count on it. We need to work together on this one, it sounds like."

"Definitely," Todd said, and bolted out the door with Mattituck close behind.

"You drive," he told Mattituck as they approached the SUV.

Tom Graffinino stood at the head of B Dock, ready to stop the guy who'd rented Slip B-21. Sure, Trooper Benson had told him only to keep watch, but Graffinino had spent well over half his life paying no attention to what any fucking authority told him to do, and even now only did when he had to. Or if it were to his advantage. In this particular case, neither applied. Not in Tom Graffinino's view. This motherfucker in Slip B-21 had told him he'd pay when he left.

"Harbormaster Graffinino ain't nobody's fool," he said aloud, taking a deep drag off his unfiltered Camel.

He didn't have to wait long. Tom heard an engine with a muffler problem pulling into the parking lot above the harbor. He looked up and caught a glimpse of a beat-up Toyota pickup—the edges of its hood and doors rusting out—nose into a parking spot overlooking the boats. Its single headlight went dark, and Tom heard the door creak loudly as the driver got out. A moment later, he saw his man from Slip B-21 turn onto the ramp down to the floating docks.

The man saw Tom as he turned from the bottom of the ramp toward B Dock. Tom stood up straight and flicked his still-lit cigarette into the water.

"What's up?" the man asked casually. He sure didn't look like a guy worried about being chased by a State Trooper.

"Not much," Tom replied. "Heading out?"

The man paused, surprised.

"Why you ask that?"

"You said you were paying on your way out. So if you're heading out, you owe me."

"Naw, I'm not heading out." The man started again, intending to step around Tom.

Tom, standing 6'4" with a solid 240lb build of very little fat, stepped in the man's path.

"How 'bout we step into the office and just square up for now anyway."

The man stopped. "Maybe later," he said flatly, an unveiled threatening edge in his voice.

"It was a statement, not a question," Tom said evenly. "I'm a salty old fuck, used to dealing with some pretty rough fishermen. I don't aim to fuck around with you here, son."

The man took the last word as condescending, and tensed with anger.

"Ain't your fuckin' son, old man. Get the fuck outta my way. I'll get your damned money later."

Tom didn't see the fist jab into his gut with surprising force. The seasoned harbormaster had spent 15 years in Alaskan logging camps, and 20 more on fishing boats. He was no novice in the world of scuffles. But never had anybody laid a hand on him without him seeing it coming. Until now. The force of the blow bent him slightly forward before he could control it. He started bringing his fists up, forearms ready to block, but it was too late. Tom did see the next shot from the man's left just before it landed hard on his right cheek, a straight tight jab. His head jerked back, although his neck muscles kept his head from snapping completely backward.

Those blows were no logging dick's untrained swings. This guy knew what he was doing.

The next blow came from the man's right fist, cutting across on Tom's chin with guided missile-like precision. There was no way to stop the impact of such a hit, coming from the side angle, and Tom's head snapped to the right. His body followed and he lost his balance. He landed on the wood dock on all fours, his head going fuzzy from the force of the blows.

Shit, he thought from a detached place in his mind, three blows and I'm on my fucking knees. This guy knows what he's doing.

A force between his shoulder blades forced his chest and face to the splintery wood. He grimaced, his cheek pressed hard against the planks. He felt cold steel against his ear.

"Now, old man. I'm going to have to say goodbye for now. But first . . ." Tom felt the man push something into his shirt pocket. "That should be more than enough to cover my slip fee. The rest is to pay for silence. I may need to come back here, and I expect there will be no reason to be nervous coming back. Understand me?"

Tom saw no reason to argue. Not with a gun at his ear. He nodded.

"Good," the man said, his voice calm and untaxed, as if hitting a man with that kind of force did nothing in the way of wearing him down. "Now I have to be sure that you'll let me out of the harbor without further—how do the fancy shmucks say it?—without further *incident*," the man pronounced the last word with sarcastic emphasis. "Sorry about this blow from my gun, old man. But it's better'n a bullet, yes?"

Before Tom could respond, everything went black.

When Todd and Mattituck arrived, Tom Graffinino was back in the Harbormaster's Office and the 'But Chaser was out of the harbor and getting up on step in the channel, northbound.

Mattituck paused and peered through the late evening twilight, trying to see Slip B-21. Todd continued into the office.

"Anything?" Todd said to the back of Tom's head.

Tom was seated at a desk with his back turned. He kept writing on a ledger and didn't reply.

Mattituck came through the door. "What the fuck? Where's the 'But Chaser?"

Todd turned in surprise.

Tom, not moving, said calmly, "Ain't she there?"

"Slip's empty. She's gone."

"Why didn't you call me, Tom?" Todd said, anger in his voice. "I was counting on you."

"Your mistake then," was the only reply. "My ex could tell you that." He kept writing on the ledger.

Todd stared at the back of his head for a moment, then turned. "Let's go," he said to Mattituck.

Outside, he told Mattituck to drive. "I have calls to make."

"Where to?" Mattituck asked.

"Airport."

Mattituck backed the SUV onto the street and put it in gear, headed through downtown and to the highway out toward the airport.

Todd dialed up the Glennallen AST office.

"I need the Coast Guard helo," he said when the officer on duty answered.

"Okay, stand by. You're in Cordova?"

"Yes, that's right."

They rode in silence while Todd was on hold. Mattituck didn't bother to drive fast. If they were going to get a Coast Guard helo, it would catch up with the 'But Chaser in no time. He thought what a hell of a story this would make to tell his nephew, Derek, when he saw the boy again. He smiled at the thought of his nephew. How many times had Derek told him about cop shows and movies, and his Uncle Frank told him the storyline was outlandish and unrealistic. Now here he was in the middle of an unfolding story that had more crazy twists and turns than those crazy cop movies.

The Glennallen officer came back on the line.

"Todd?"

"Yes, I'm here."

"No can do. They're on Search and Rescue west of Montague. SAR trumps LE ops," he said, referring to Law Enforcement.

"Shit. Don't they have two choppers there?"

"Other one's in Kodiak for some electronic swap-out or something."

"Just my luck," Todd said. He thought for a moment. "AST 41448 still here?"

"Yes, of course. Where else would it be?"

"Just checking." He held his hand out in front of Mattituck and made a circle with his upturned index finger, signaling to turn around.

"Okay," he said into the cell. "The 'But Chaser's running out of town, probably north. We're going to grab the boat here and see if we can find her. The suspect did some damage at the Copper River Inn down here, but he got past the harbormaster, I guess. He was supposed to call me if the guy showed up."

"Tom Graffinino?"

"Yeah."

"Par for the course. You should know that."

Todd nodded, even though the officer couldn't see him.

"I know. I just keep hoping for better."

"Your mistake," the man said.

Todd chuckled sardonically. "Funny, that's what he said."

"Sounds like Tom. He really doesn't give a shit about anything."

"You know him?"

"Yeah—I was hired from the Cordova Police. I've known Tom a long time. He's a guy out for his own interests. He has trouble keeping employees, you know."

"So I've heard. All right. I'll check back in with you once we're underway on the HF radio."

After hanging up, he brought Mattituck up to speed. "Helo's are all gone, so we'll have to take the 41-footer." He looked at Mattituck. "You know we have that one down here?"

"Yeah, but it's always been a bit of a mystery. Why two boats and only one Trooper on the Sound?"

"Faster sometimes to fly here and take a boat from here. Plus it gives us another boat for when we bring back-ups down, or are working on a case where we need two boats. Mostly, though, we use it to help with fishing openers. We bring an officer down from Anchorage or Fairbanks, and we work in tandem."

"Well," Mattituck said. "Lucky it's here."

Todd was quiet a moment.

"Yeah," he said finally. "It's starting to look like we're going to need a lot of tools for this wild goose chase."

"This guy's really something, isn't he?" Mattituck proffered.

Todd nodded. "Not many like this guy. He's either really skilled, or he's lucky as hell."

"Or both," Mattituck said, and turned off the highway back to the marina, passing the Harbormaster's Office to the Prince William Sound Science Center, where the State Troopers shared a small dock with the marine research center.

Skipper's Oath

Chapter Fifteen

So Close

State Trooper Todd Benson was seeing immediate payoffs to having deputized Frank Mattituck and having him along on this strange case. Now, as they cleared the breakwater and entered the channel, Todd turned the helm over to Mattituck so he could work on the case itself. He sat on a bench seat at the table in the aft cabin and began to put down some notes while making calls.

This case was turning into one of the strangest of Todd's career so far. Not only were there new revelations at almost every turn, but it seemed like they were constantly two steps behind the suspect. They had pieces of the suspect's motivations, and some indications of what he was doing and a hint of where one future move might be. But these all amounted to pockets of unconnected information that were not very helpful for anything other than keeping them just outside of arm's reach of the suspect.

It also seemed that at every major turn in this evolving saga, someone was getting hurt. All but the bear incident were due to the loose suspect's disregard for anybody who got in his way.

Todd thought of this last observation, and his earlier comment to Frank that this suspect was either incredibly lucky, or highly skilled and experienced. He thought about how the man had found his way across Montague's eastern end, tracked a potential victim, and then found a way to another bay when things went awry. He then figured out how to commandeer another boat, then ambushed Mattituck and got away again. He was able to navigate the boat to Cordova and locate a drop that he apparently didn't have all the information for, and then came back and skillfully—if perhaps messily—obtained what he set out to get.

He tapped his pen on the table and looked forward. Frank Mattituck was sitting high at the helm, navigating the channel at their cruising speed of 28 knots. Frank was a skilled boat operator, and Todd was glad to have him running the boat.

"You want some coffee?" he asked.

Mattituck, intent on the radar due to the darkness, nodded. "That'd be great."

Todd got up and crossed to the small galley. Since he was usually the only one who used this boat, he knew there was a can of coffee, and some dry and canned goods. The small galley was equipped with two propane stove tops, a small refrigerator, a sink with faucet. Behind the galley was a small head. AST 41448 was well-equipped for overnight trips, which was what Todd usually used the vessel for.

After he got the coffee brewing, he sat back down at the table and made calls while he still had the Cordova cell range. He needed to check in with Glennallen, consult with the Area Captain in Anchorage on a plan of action, and see how Suspect 1, the victim of the bear attack, was doing. With luck, he was out of the coma so he could be interviewed for any information that might help their case.

Mattituck was watching a vessel on the radar that was approximately 5.8 nautical miles ahead of them. It looked approximately the size of the 'But Chaser, and was moving along at a speed consistent with the cruising speed of a double outboard vessel that size. The problem was that it was scooting straight up the western channel – the preferred channel that cut inside of Observation Island—which had what looked like a tug and barge chugging northbound in the channel. The western passage was narrow enough that navigating around a tug and barge could be limiting, but the M/V Chenega, an Alaska State Ferry, had announced it was about to transit southbound in the western passage. Normally, this would make Mattituck choose the east channel, but that would cost AST 41448 valuable time in her pursuit of what Mattituck was hoping was the 'But Chaser.

In taking readings on the radar, it appeared that the AST 41448 was gaining on the 'But Chaser by about four or five knots. Not a lot, but perhaps enough. Having to go around Observation Island, however, would set them back.

Todd brought him coffee in a wide-bottomed mug with rubber on the bottom, perfect for boating. He took a sip of the strong blend and felt it warm him on the way down.

"Thanks—that's perfect."

"No problem," Todd said and went back to the table.

"I'm going to cut through the west channel even though there's a bit of traffic. I don't want to lose ground on this contact. I think it might be the 'But Chaser."

"How far ahead?"

"About 5.7 miles now. She's rounding the point into Orca Bay now. We'll lose sight of her until we get into Orca as well."

"Well, nice thing about being a Trooper boat," Todd said, "is you can announce your presence as being in a hurry. With that contact rounding the point, you won't alert them. The switch for the lights are labeled, on the left of the helm."

Mattituck located the switches for the light bar and siren. He switched the lights on but kept the siren off. In the near darkness, the lights would let the ferry and the tug know who they were so they needn't worry about collision. With pleasure boaters, you could never tell how experienced they were, nor whether they even knew the rules of the road. Unlike with cars and trucks, there are no licenses or training required for pleasure boaters.

As they overtook the tug and tow, and the Chenega became more clear in the decreasing distance, Mattituck thought about how odd this moment of calm was in the midst of the pursuit of this killer. Todd was busy gathering information for the unfolding case while Mattituck quietly navigated the channel, turning slightly to starboard now to make a port-to-port passing with the Chenega.

The Alaska State Ferries, technically named the Alaska Marine Highway System, was exactly that: a marine highway. They were the main mode of transportation between many communities and the only link to the asphalt highway system that could be followed to the Lower 48. Their blue hulls with a gold stripe along the top of the blue, giving way to a white superstructure, were a welcome and beloved sight for Alaskans. Now, as Mattituck watched the twin hulled fast ferry approach, his memory floated back to a trip to

Cordova with Sandy, Derek, and Monica Castle. Monica had spent the week with Mattituck in Valdez, and with Sandy and Derek coming to visit for the weekend, they had all decided it would be fun to take an overnight trip to Cordova and see where Monica lived. Mattituck had booked the ferry tickets as a relaxing mini-trip. Going anywhere on the ferry was relaxing and scenic.

Monica was an attorney in Cordova, and had lived most of her life there. Mattituck and she had a slowly-developed relationship that started when they were introduced at the popular restaurant, The Fisherman's Widow, by a mutual friend. They had established a fast rapport that quickly grew into something more. Mattituck had been guiding a hunting team that didn't want to spend very many nights in tents on Hinchinbrook Island, so at the end of each day, he ferried them to Cordova where they stayed in a hotel, then headed back to the island and a day of hunting early the next morning. The next evening after meeting Monica, he'd found himself thumbing the napkin with her number on it. Finally, he'd given in and dialed her. They had a late dinner together at The Salty Bovine, a would-be steak house that served far better burgers than anything else. Not a fancy first-date by most standards, but suitable for the setting and lifestyle they both lived in a remote and beautiful land.

Beauty, Mattituck had always believed, often lay in places others didn't want to venture to. That made the beauty all the more beautiful, to his thinking. It was like a hidden, magical cove that nobody else knew about. A guy wanted to drop anchor and stay there forever.

That's what Alaska was to Mattituck. And that's what Monica had become.

Now, as AST 41448 skirted along the portside of the nearly-idling Chenega, all these memories came to him in powerful waves. It felt as though the significance of that trip had increased over time, but Mattituck knew this wasn't the case. More likely, he thought, the events of these past few days changed his perspective on things. Something about being shot at and then chased down by a ruthless killer gave a guy a new way of seeing the world around him. Not just the world in an empirical sense, but the world in an experiential sense—in the way a guy lived his life in it. He'd thought he had found the perfect life by coming to Alaska and running a charter boat business. He could keep the negativity and bullshit at bay. And working for himself . . . it was a nice life. But something about the last few days made it pale somehow. And now, thinking of Derek—of family, and what's always been important—it suddenly felt like he'd built a castle in the sand. He smiled at the cliché, thinking that Monica Castle was not a castle made of sand. She was the real deal. So what was the problem? he wondered.

He suddenly wanted to see Derek and Sandy, spend time with them and hold them. Since he and Sandy's mother had died three years earlier, she and Derek were really the only family he had left. They had uncles and aunts spread out over the Lower 48, but they had met very few of them, and felt close to even less. He and Sandy only had each other. And Derek.

But the memory stirred by the Chenega and that weekend in Cordova seemed to envelope Monica into that circle as well. Truly, Mattituck had never met anybody like her, and neither she nor he had wanted to end their relationship. The reality though, they had agreed, was that they were both place-bound. She had an established law practice in Cordova that her father had built over a thirty-five year period, and it and the house she lived in were all he had left her. She simply couldn't walk away from that. And Mattituck couldn't move the charter business to Cordova. That would be professional suicide. Valdez was on the highway system, and so was a prime launching point for a fishing charter company. Cordova was far too remote, and accessible only by sea and air. And so, they had decided to see each other when it worked, but agreed that a long-term, permanent outcome was probably not going to happen.

Which, now that he thought about it, was a weird way to end a relationship. Ending it without really ending it.

Mattituck looked back at Todd, speaking on the cell with someone—after listening a moment, he realized it was the hospital.

Todd shook his head at Mattituck when he noticed the charter boat captain looking back quizzically.

"He's still in the coma," he said, still on the phone.

Mattituck nodded understanding.

"Hey," Todd said, getting Mattituck's attention. "How far to Salmo Point?"

Mattituck looked at the GPS, then at the radar and reset the range finder.

"Less than 10 minutes."

Todd nodded acknowledgement, then went back to the conversation on the phone.

Mattituck went back to his thoughts. It had both surprised him and not surprised him that the past few days' events had triggered a desire to see Sandy and Derek, and that mixed in with them was the desire to see Monica again. He thought of her black hair and smooth olive complexion. Her father was full Eyak, and her mother Russian, although she seemed to have inherited more of her father's features than her mother's. She had warm brown eyes, and a smile of perfectly straight and white teeth that were framed with lips that he loved to look at and to feel against his. Her jawline, like so much of her, was perfect in his eyes. He loved her. He knew that. And he knew that she loved him.

He decided he would call her when all this settled down. It had been a few months since they'd spoken, though. Maybe she was seeing someone. Maybe the last thing she wanted was a call from him.

The contact on the radar that might be the 'But Chaser pulled his attention. He rubbed the stubble along his jaw, then pushed the thoughts of Monica out of his head. He peered into the radar and noted the Chenega was well astern, and that Salmo Point, the turning point for entering Orca Bay, was quickly approaching. He was anxious to see where the 'But Chaser was, and how much they might have gained on her.

"So the guy at the Copper River Inn, the manager," Mattituck started.

"Yeah," Todd answered immediately, "I've been thinking about him, too. I suspect we'll get a lot of info out of him."

Mattituck laughed. "Did you see his face when we walked in?"

Todd shared the laugh. "He was pretty surprised. I think it took a little bit for him to realize who we really are."

"Too bad we couldn't talk to him." Mattituck thought for a moment. "What if he skips out? I mean, he knows we're going to come back, right?"

Todd thought for a moment. "It's hard to say what goes through these guys' minds. If he's smart, he's figured out that we could have had him arrested, but didn't. We had enough on him to bust him."

Mattituck's brow creased. "I'm confused. What do you mean?"

"You know about informants, right?"

Mattituck nodded.

"Do you know how they become informants?"

Mattituck shook his head as he watched a seiner coming around the point, and steered starboard to allow a wider berth. This reminded him of the flashing blue lights, and he reached down and shut them off.

"Well, they become informants much like this. You have them nailed, but they're the small-time compared to what you're after. So you get their help, and they're willing to give you the help because they figure you're going to nail them if they don't help."

"So you're thinking he'll be there when we come back?"

Todd nodded. "Yep. Unless, of course, we catch Suspect 2 here and it's unnecessary. Although then the hotel manager can be used to ID Suspect 2 and make it a sure thing we nail his hide."

"Comin' up on the point," Mattituck said.

Todd got up and joined him, standing next to the helm station. His gaze was intent on the radar. As they came around the point, they picked up first a larger contact a mile or so beyond the point, bound for Cordova. There were three other contacts, or larger land masses, near the north side of the opening into Orca Bay. As they cleared the point and had an open radar view of the end of Orca, they could see two contacts in the middle of the bay. It would be a moment or two more before they could tell which direction the vessels were moving.

"That further one is our contact," Mattituck announced. "The other one is moving too slow."

"Well, you must be better at reading this than I am," Todd said. "I'm still trying to get a read on them."

"Set your eyes on a contact when the radar passes over it, then as it cycles around, you can see if it moves, which way, and roughly how fast. Remember, radar only reads the contact when it's pointed that way, and it circles around."

Todd knew how radar works, but he hadn't tried this trick. He tried it now. It worked. By looking at one contact, he could detect the movement of all the contacts around the one he locked his eyes on.

"Pretty good," he said.

"They're both headed away from us. I'm guessing we've gained a half mile on him." He set the radar range on the forward-most contact and read the measurement. "He's 4.8 miles, so we've gained almost a mile on him in just that time."

"Do you think he's slowed down from what he was doing back in the channel?"

"Yeah," Mattituck replied. "Definitely. I'd guess he feels safe now and is wanting to save fuel."

"I think you're right."

"It's a bit of a haul over to Whittier," Mattituck added. "And that's a small boat. His range is probably limited. Add to that he has twin outboards, which is great for speed but sucks down the fuel almost twice as fast. Even if he fueled up in Cordova, and there's no doubt he did, he's going to want to try to maximize his fuel efficiency."

Todd thought about this. "But that's not his boat. He won't know the most efficient speed, will he?"

"He might, if he's a resourceful guy. He might google those Yamahas and search their fuel efficiency.

Most manufacturers give estimates for different sized vessels, so he'd have a pretty good idea."

Todd watched the radar, then peered out the forward window and grabbed the binoculars from the dash. He pointed them forward, locating the 'But Chaser and the nearer vessel. It was pretty dark at this point, though, and all he could see was the white stern light on the closest boat.

"I think he's running darkened ship," Todd said. "Which isn't a bad idea." He reached down and flipped off the toggle for the running lights.

Mattituck smiled. "Good move. And he doesn't have radar, so we have him at a disadvantage."

Todd was staring at the radar screen. The beacon bar ran around the screen three full times before he commented.

"I think we're gaining on him," he finally said. "Judging by your trick."

Mattituck set the range finder and watched the beacon run around.

"Yep. Definitely. He's 4.1 miles away. We're closing on him, and fast."

Todd reached for the mic to the High Frequency radio and turned on the scrambler. He then dialed the frequency to the working Alaska State Troopers frequency and hailed the Anchorage office. When they responded right away, he reported their position and status in the pursuit of the 'But Chaser.

"Do we have any information on the owners of the 'But Chaser?" he asked.

"Affirmative on that," the voice sounded like it was filtering through a fish aquarium, the result of the scrambling device. "It's registered to a Jonathon K. Wattings. He has a wife, Kimberly J., and two kids aged

4 and 6. Their address is Cordova. We've requested a wellness check on them. Cordova Police have stopped by the house twice with no responses at the door. We're working on places of employment."

"Roger, thanks," Todd replied.

He hung up the mic and stared out the windshield. Mattituck held their course, noting that they were quickly closing the distance between them and the slower vessel ahead. He steered a course slightly to the right of the vessel, wanting to make sure they lost no distance on the 'But Chaser. In a few minutes they would be clearing Channel Island on the starboard side, and the rocks off the far end of it. He could already see that the 'But Chaser had made a slight turn to the right, keeping in the channel as it passed the rock off the small island.

"I'm going to pass this vessel on the right, and that should keep us closing in on our guy."

Todd nodded.

Mattituck noted the stern, chiseled expression on the trooper's face.

"Do you think the whole family had been out?" he asked Todd.

Todd shrugged. "It's starting to look that way."

He was quiet for several minutes.

"This is the part of the job I hate," he said, his voice barely audible.

Mattituck maintained a respectful silence.

"When shit happens to kids . . ." Todd's voice trailed. "Fuck. There are no words, you know?"

"Do you think he would have killed them all? Kids too?"

Todd didn't give a direct reply.

"You said you saw nobody on board except this shithead, right?" That was all the answer Todd offered.

People talk about the aura a person can give off, and Mattituck noted that Todd's aura at the moment was one that demanded privacy. He turned his attention to the 'But Chaser ahead as AST 41448 overtook the slower vessel behind the 'But Chaser. He could see now it was a gillnetter, probably headed out for a fishing opener. He took a reading of the 'But Chaser on the radar: 3.8 nautical miles.

Now it was just the two boats running without lights, but the one in pursuit had the eyes of radar while the pursued was simply trying to be as invisible as he could be. They were westbound in the eastern end of Orca Bay now, running to the right of the commercial shipping lane. Mattituck was now sure that the man running ahead of him did know how to run a boat, and how to steer by the marine GPS. He was making a straight line to the end of the rocks that run south from Sheep Point that had the 'But Chaser keeping as straight of lines as possible. It was a tactic any smart boat operator made when he was pushing the limits of his fuel tank.

He took another reading on the radar: 3.2 nautical miles. They were closing in on him fast.

Mattituck glanced at Todd. He was still in his dark place.

"All we can do is catch this guy and see him pay for what he's done," he said to the trooper, thinking of the family the man running the 'But Chaser had likely murdered.

Todd seemed to snap out of his trance.

"Yeah," he said, his voice low. "It really gets me, though. Sometimes I think I'm not cut out for this shit." He looked at Mattituck. "It's too fucking depressing sometimes, y'know?"

Mattituck nodded.

Todd took a reading on the radar. "Wow . . . only 3 miles ahead now. We're closing in pretty fast."

Mattituck nodded again.

"When he gets to Gravina Point, I predict a slight right turn," Mattituck said, sharing his thoughts. "I think he's keeping as short a distance as possible to conserve fuel. He must be trying for Whittier."

Todd nodded. "Seems likely."

They rode in silence. The seas were relatively calm, with a low easterly swell of less than two feet. AST 41448 took the seas well. She was a much heavier vessel than AST 32067, and so had less tendency to bounce over the top of the waves. Instead, her deep Vee hull cut through the waves and the boat road fairly evenly.

Todd took another reading.

"We are really cutting the distance: 2.7 miles. Has he slowed down?"

"I'm thinking so," Mattituck replied. "Again, trying to conserve fuel. Plus, he's likely keeping an eye back this way. But it's pretty dark right now, and we're running without any lights. He can't see us."

"That's right," Todd said, smiling.

Mattituck could see him thinking. He waited.

"Here's what we're going to do," Todd said finally. "When we're half a mile back, we'll call him on Channel 16 and let him know we're here. I have to give him a chance to give up."

Mattituck shook his head.

"I know," Todd said. "This is what sucks about being the good guys. You know he won't give up, though. So we'll keep darkened ship and close in. I'll be forward with the assault rifle."

"You have an assault rifle?" Mattituck asked, genuinely surprised. *Well, why wouldn't a trooper have an assault rifle?* he realized.

"When he doesn't stop, I'll open fire," Todd continued.

Mattituck took a reading: 2.4 miles.

They again rode in silence, rocking as AST 41448 gently rolled over the angled seas. They were now about half way to Gravina Point, and Mattituck noted the slight right turn the 'But Chaser took as it rounded the point. Just as predicted.

"Nice call," Todd said, also watching.

Fifteen minutes later, the 'But Chaser was directly south of Red Head and making way for Knowles Head, near where the killer had tried to bushwhack Mattituck at Goose Island.

He took a reading on the radar: 1.2 miles.

Just then, AST 41448 faltered. Mattituck noticed it first, being at the helm. Just as in a car, the driver always feels best what the car is doing—the same was true in a boat. There was a scaling back of the humming of one of the engines, and the boat began to pull to the port side.

"Something's wrong," Mattituck said, reading the gauges on the dash. "I think it's the port side engine."

Todd was at his side, reading the tachometer. It was reading 1600 and dropping. The cruising RPM had been 3200. The starboard engine held steady at that RPM. Mattituck was now having to heel the helm heavily to the starboard side to compensate for the loss of the propulsion on the port side. The RPMs on the port engine dropped to zero. Mattituck could now feel the drag caused by the dead propeller on the port side. He imagined the blades on the propeller, flat against the water, acting as a brake.

"Fuck," he said. "We're losing serious speed here."

They could visibly see the 'But Chaser was beginning to pull away from them.

"Here, take the helm," Mattituck said.

When Todd's hand was on the helm, Mattituck grabbed a flashlight that had been on the dash and half ran to the rear deck, looking for the hatch to the engine compartment. He pulled the ring in the deck up and turned it, unlatching the hatch and pulling it upward. The noise of the remaining engine doubled, and Mattituck could smell oil and diesel. He lit the flashlight and shined it into the compartment, leaning down so his head was inside.

He was looking for any sign that would explain the engine failure. He also had a faint hope that maybe a spark plug wire or something had come loose. He scanned the huge engine, admiring the large block and cleanliness of the engines and the compartment. AST 41448 was a well-maintained boat, to be sure. Whatever happened was not due to lack of care.

Seeing no signs of anything he could try fixing, and no manual start for the engine, he closed the compartment and returned to the cabin. He noted on the GPS that they were now only making 19 knots, and slowing. As the bow of the boat dropped deeper in the water, the hull displaced more water, increasing the impact of the lost engine exponentially.

"We're screwed," he said.

"Yep. Looks that way."

"Fuck . . . We were so close, too."

Chapter Sixteen

Aimless Until Needed

Earl Darick awoke in the sunlight splashed across the bow of the Kimberly Marie. He lay for a moment, soaking in the rays and allowing the warmth to continue warming his skin and his soul. He smiled with his eyes closed, grateful to be alive another day, but with a dark corner of his mind wishing he wasn't alive to greet this new day. He fought back the darker thoughts and allowed himself to just be. Breathing, and aware of this beautiful thing called the sun.

He shifted his weight uncomfortably. He must have been sleeping in one position—on his left side, on the hard cabin top of the forward cabin of his friend's big yacht. He thought of Jim Milner, how the man always took care of him. Another thing to be grateful for, Earl thought to himself. Good friends. If he'd had a drink handy, he'd toast his old friend. Maybe Jim was aboard, come to think of it.

Earl forced himself upright, letting the blanket Jim always kept in the forward hatch for him fall to the side. He looked around. Everything was familiar. The bow of the Kimberly Marie, the slip she was moored in. The regular vessels all around. The mountains skyrocketing behind Valdez. The clean fresh air, he thought as he drew a deep breath. There was no air like the air in Valdez, that was for sure, he thought.

He stood up and stretched, then folded the blanket and returned it to the forward hatch. He walked along the port side decking to the aft deck and peered in the sliding glass window. No movement. No sign of life, in fact.

"Where are you, Jim?" he asked, his breath briefly steaming the glass.

He sat in one of the chairs on the aft deck and waited. Maybe Jim had run up to the grocery store. Or went to grab some breakfast. Usually he was aboard, and Earl and Jim always sat for a bit after Earl awoke and chewed the fat. It was a regular thing. Sometimes Jim would give him some breakfast, usually a cheese omelette—Jim was really good at omelettes—made with that damned cheddar cheese he loved so much. Earl didn't much care for that particular brand of cheese, but beggers should not be choosers. That's what Earl always said, and he was a man who lived by what he said.

He waited nearly two hours. When there was still no sign of Jim, he decided he'd better walk on up to his house and see what he might have for food in the pantry. His house was a smallish three bedroom, built right after the '64 Earthquake, that his parents had built when the new town was established. His family had survived the shaker, and Earl and his sister had been little tykes when it hit. *How old had he been?* he wondered now.

"Lessee," he muttered quietly, thinking. "1964. March 1964. I was born in '54, July the fifth, to be exact. . . . so that'd make me. . . ." he stared off for several minutes.

"Well," he finally said. "Fair enough to round me off at about 10, I suppose."

He was now walking past the Harbormaster's office, crossing the road and heading up toward the grocery store. His house was up near the hill side. And he'd forgotten why he had been thinking about the Earthquake. He walked along, enjoying the sunshine and smiling at the tourists he came across.

After filling his stomach with toasted bread and Jiffy peanut butter, the smooth variety, Earl had gained some more sleep on his couch with the useless programming of afternoon television in the background. When he awoke, it was past dinner time. He got up and showered, then headed for the Crow's Nest, where he could get some dinner. Dinner and drinks, that is, he thought with a smile.

Many Valdez residents wondered how he made a living. He didn't, he always told them. His parents had made his living for him. They had been landowners of a stretch of land that was needed to build the pipeline up near Paxson Lake, north of Glennallen. That had set them up for life, so well that it had set Earl up for life as well. His sister, God rest her soul, had died in a car accident when she was 21. Earl had never married, and as far as he knew, he had no family after his grandparents, who had lived someplace in Mississippi, died. He'd had an uncle and aunt as well, but they had moved long ago, and Earl had lost track of where they might be.

That left Earl. Just Earl. No wife, no kids, no family, and no job. Except the job he'd had with Jim Milner. But he'd kept the little house he and his parents and sister lived in. And then he had been Jim Milner's first mate for—how long? Shit, Earl thought, how long had that been? Nine years? Twelve? He really didn't know. Sure, Jim had paid him, but Earl couldn't even tell you how much now that a few years had passed.

A shadow of sadness crossed over his face. Then Jim had let him go. Too much drinking, Jim had said. Oh, Earl didn't blame him, of course. Jim had kept him on long past when Earl became more or less useless— that's how Earl now put it in his mind, not how Jim had said it. Jim never said stuff like that. He was a good guy, Jim. He'd wanted for Earl to clean up, but he never called him a drunk like others did. No, Jim would never have done that. But eventually, Jim had had to let Earl go.

"I don't blame him," Earl said under his breath as he approached The Crow's Nest.

Five or six hours later—Earl couldn't have told you how many—he stepped out of The Crow's Nest and made his way to the railing overlooking the marina. The lights were on, even though it wasn't completely dark yet. He leaned heavily on the wooden rail, swaying slightly as he tried to steady himself. The lights swam for a moment, then Earl closed his eyes. He thought of walking home, but decided he had indeed gone past the threshold that said he should sleep on the bow of the Kimberly Marie. He opened his eyes and looked out at the pier the Kimberly Marie tied up to, down at the end. He just wanted to make sure she was tied up there before he walked all the way out there. Sometimes, Jim was on overnight cruises, so it was always best to check before walking.

She was there. Earl decided to wait and steady himself before walking.

"Shit," he said quietly. "If I wait for that, I'll be here all night. Right here at this here railing. Right here."

He straightened and started making his way to the head of the docks.

Twenty minutes later, he was pulling the blanket out of the Kimberly Marie's bow. He more crawled than walked to his favorite place on the port side bow, atop the VIP cabin below. He lay down with his head on the cushioning velcro'ed to the top of the cabin for people to bathe in the sun. Normally, he lay on the harder surface and only used the cushioning for his head, but tonight, he scooted his body up and lay full on the cushions and pulled the blanket over himself.

He lay on his back and stared at the brightest of the stars, the only ones visible in the incomplete darkness. He smiled, a warm breeze drawing across his body and tugging at his hair.

This is the life, he thought as he drifted off to sleep.

The Kimberly Marie shifted, and Earl Darick's eyes opened.

He lay still, staring at the stars. It was dark now. But why had he awakened? He never did that. Not even when late parties were shut down by the Harbormaster.

The Kimberly Marie moved slightly under him, and he thought Jim Milner must be up and moving around inside. It had been several days since he'd seen his old buddy, and he hadn't seen him at all since the Kimberly Marie had returned to port.

He sat up. *I haven't seen Jim at all this time in port*, he thought again.

He got up, but something made him stop. Something was different. No lights on inside the Kimberly Marie. No sound. What had made her move? he wondered. Something was wrong, he thought. *Shit, you dickhead*, he scolded himself. *You're reaching that paranoia stage they say you hit after so many years of drinking like I have*, he thought.

The motion of the Kimberly Marie renewed, and Earl knew for sure someone else was aboard. But something impressed on him the need to be cautious. Call it paranoia, he thought, but why take a chance?

He moved quietly and slowly to the port side, the side opposite the dock. He crouched and waited.

The Kimberly Marie continued to rock slightly. A sound aft caught his attention, and he realized he was in view of the window from the inside. If someone were inside, or were getting inside, they would see him. He moved further aft and crouched again. His ears attentive. He heard the sliding glass door opening, and realized what he'd heard was the grating sound of a glass cutter.

Someone was breaking into Jim's boat.

The *fuck* you say, he thought, suddenly enraged. Nobody breaks into my friend's boat! He started to make his way aft. He had no idea what he might do, and he really didn't care. *What the fuck do I have to live for?* he wondered vaguely. *I'm just a fucking drunk.*

He paused.

But I'm a loyal drunk, goddammit.

He suddenly pictured Jim below, asleep in his cabin. Fuck, what if this intruder came upon Jim? Would he kill him? Jesus, Earl thought, and made his way further aft. He had to get inside and stop this burglar.

He peered around the bulkhead, hanging partially over the aft deck. He could see inside the cabin clearly, and he saw the figure of a man hunched over the bench of the dining table. He had pulled out one of the storage bins under the bench seating, and was fumbling with something black. Black cloth. He peered in. A black backpack.

Earl looked around for something to use as a weapon. He didn't see anything. He peered back into the cabin. The man was still fumbling. Whatever it was he was fussing with, it was caught on something or stuck. Earl thought of the gaff hook that Jim always kept under the port side gunwale. A gaff hook would make a formidable weapon. But how to get far enough aft to grab it before the man came out?

He peered back inside. It occurred to him that he was not acting like a drunk. Not at all. His head was clear, his thoughts lucid. He was not about to let this fucking thief rob his friend, or worse yet, harm him. The man was walking around, apparently looking for something. Earl seized the opportunity to take three quiet steps aft, reach under the gunwale, located the gaff hook, then stepped to the side of the cabin entry where he could watch the intruder. There, he waited to see what the intruder would do.

The man pulled a Leatherman knife from under the captain's chair, and started back to the storage bin where the black cloth was caught. It appeared he intended to cut it loose.

"Fuck!" the man muttered. "Goddamn rust." He tried to force the rusted Leatherman open, but it wouldn't budge.

Then the man was walking forward, toward the ladder down to the galley . . . and toward where Jim was probably asleep. Earl acted quickly. He stepped into the cabin, the gaff poised and ready, and strode quietly after the man.

"What the hell? . . ." the man said in alarm.

But Earl was upon him, and swung the three foot handle length around and brought the gaff hook in a flash at the man's body. The handle stopped short with a thud. The hook had found its mark.

Earl stepped forward and yanked at the hook. It pulled at something heavy. It was definitely in the intruder's body. Where exactly, Earl had no idea – everything was moving too quickly. He pulled again and evoked a pained grunt from the intruder.

"You fucking son of a bitch!" the man said in a low growl.

Earl saw a movement as the intruder grasped something from his waistband. Almost too late, Earl realized it was a gun.

A gun! he thought. *Fuck! I hadn't thought of a gun!*

His reflexes took over, and his arm was swinging again. This time, the gaff bounced off the man's head, and he fell down the ladder to the deck below. The gun clattered to the deck under the helm station. Earl watched it slide against the bulkhead, a couple of feet out of his reach. It was a mistake to look away from the intruder, though, and Earl suddenly felt the handle pulled out of his hand. He swung his head around and saw the man struggling to reverse the gaff handle, but the ladder's opening was too narrow to turn around a 3-foot handle.

Earl could hear shouts from someplace outside, and he saw from the glance the intruder made toward the aft cabin door that he'd heard it as well. He dropped the gaff to the deck below and lurched upward, grasping at Earl's pants.

Earl kicked at the man, landing blows to his face several times.

"Help!" he yelled, hoping to hail the voices. "Help! Help me!"

He got his footing and lunged for the aft cabin, barreling through the open doorway and onto the aft deck. He heard the intruder fumbling for the gun. Fear gripped Earl, and he almost froze. He forced himself to move his legs. Several people were running toward the Kimberly Marie from down the dock. Earl climbed onto the gunwale, and realized too late that he was on the wrong side of the boat—he was on the water side.

How the *fuck* did I do *that*? he cursed.

Just then, a blast and a flash filled Earl's consciousness. The intruder had fired the gun at him from the open cabin door. Earl felt nothing, but instinctively he knew his best bet was to react like he would a brown bear: play dead.

Earl let go of the gunwale and allowed his body to fall overboard. He went over the side of the Kimberly Marie, splashing into the icy cold water. Again, instinct played well in him, and he squelched the urge to react to the cold. He forced his body over so he lay face down in the water, turning his head to the side. A moment later, presumably after the intruder looked over the side to check him, he heard footsteps gain the deck and run further down the dock. He could hear several people shouting at him, but they were not pursuing him nor approaching any closer. Clearly, they had heard the gun shot and were keeping under cover.

Slowly, Earl lifted his head and made his way back to the Kimberly Marie, palming his way to the swim deck aft. He pulled himself onto the swim deck and sat a moment, catching his breath. Farther down the dock, he heard an outboard start. He concentrated on breathing evenly, then looked over his body to make sure he hadn't been shot. He had not. The guy had missed him completely. And apparently, Earl's acting job had been convincing.

He heard the outboard down the dock click into gear, and a boat emerged to idle out toward the mouth of the harbor, then opened up in fast retreat to escape the marina.

Earl got up and stood on the swim deck, his head completely clear. He climbed over the transom back into the Kimberly Marie. He found the gaff lying on the deck in the galley. There was blood on the hook two inches up from the tip of the hook. He crouched to look down to the deck, and saw several droplets of blood.

He straightened up and climbed the ladder, then followed blood droplets onto the dock, noting drops of blood every few feet. As several people approached, asking if he was okay, he decided he'd better report this to the Harbormaster.

Chapter Seventeen

The Recruitment

AST 41448 had made its way back to Cordova with only its starboard engine. Frank Mattituck and Todd Benson had made the run back in almost complete silence, dejected at having come so close to catching—or doing away with—the killer. The strangest part about it, Mattituck had thought, was that the killer very likely had no idea how close he'd come to being stopped. They had watched the radar screen in dismay as the 'But Chaser had pulled away into the distance.

When reality had impressed itself irrevocably on them, Mattituck had steered AST 41448 out toward the middle of Orca Bay so that they could track the 'But Chaser on radar, hoping to see where the killer was headed. When the 'But Chaser appeared to steer inside of Goose Island, the route for Valdez and not for Whittier, they were uncertain where the man was headed. At first, Todd had thought that maybe he was going to stay inside of islands to avoid rough waters, but Mattituck had reminded him that the boat was trying to conserve fuel and wasn't likely to steer a longer route just to avoid rough seas.

They had been forced to speculate. Todd had predicted that they would get a report from the Harbormaster's Office in Valdez that the Kimberly Marie had been broken into.

"I think there are more stashes on the Kimberly Marie," he'd pronounced. "With more drops planned, I bet he's headed back to pick up the junk for the drops."

"But this guy doesn't give a shit about delivering product—he just stole the money in Cordova. Why wouldn't he do that at the other drop sites?"

"He only stole that money when he didn't have the stuff to drop," Todd explained. "And remember that he'd already scoped the motel out and got a good read on the manager. Our suspect can't assume it'll go that easily at the other drop points."

Mattituck nodded. That seemed true enough.

After they'd reached Cordova and moored AST 41448, Todd's cell announced a voice mail waiting. Todd pressed the screen and held the cell to his ear. He nodded at Mattituck.

"Harbormaster wants me to call him, no matter how late."

He pressed more options.

"Good morning," he said. "It's me, Trooper Benson." He listened, nodding occasionally. "Valdez Police are investigating? All right." He listened a couple of minutes more, the Harbormaster apparently telling him the whole story. "Yeah, I think we came across that guy sleeping there the other night." He listened again. "Yeah, he's on the level, I think. Just a friend of the owner's. Okay, thanks. Let me know if anything else turns up."

Todd hung up and told Mattituck the story.

"Your sleepy drunk friend was sleeping on the bow of the Kimberly Marie again. A visitor came aboard

271

in the middle of the night and broke in through the aft sliding glass door. Remember this is all within a couple of hours of us losing the 'But Chaser."

"Plenty of time for that boat to get to Valdez from where we lost sight on the radar," Mattituck agreed.

"Exactly," Todd said. "This guy was rummaging around looking for something, and Earl—your drunk—got the itch to be a hero and took a swing at the suspect with a gaff."

Mattituck's eyes widened. "He took a swing at him?"

"Apparently. And the gaff hit home somewhere, because there was quite a bit of blood. The intruder shot at Earl but missed, but Earl was smart and played dead, falling into the water over the side. It apparently fooled the suspect. The shots got some attention, and the suspect had to leave in a hurry. Apparently, he left without whatever it was he'd come to get. But he left in a sport fisher tied a little way down from the Kimberly Marie. The boat fit the description of the 'But Chaser."

They were silent a moment as they secured AST 41448 and walked to the SUV.

"What now?" Mattituck asked.

"We pay this motel manager a visit. See if we can get a good description of this guy—or whatever else the manager knows." He looked up from securing the bow line to steel bit on the dock. "He's in the hospital."

"But he recognized us as the ones who'd come in for the exchange, and then as law enforcement."

"That's precisely why I know he'll talk to us."

"Your budding informant," Mattituck said with sarcasm.

"Textbook," Todd said with a smile. "Watch."

When they arrived at the Cordova Hospital the next morning, Eddie Etano was in stable condition with a concussion from the blow of the bullet that had grazed his head above the temple. They found him in his room, shoveling large spoonfuls of scrambled eggs into his mouth, pausing long enough to take bites off an English muffin smothered under a layer of red jam. His heavy jowls worked at the bites, but came to a stop when he raised his brow and saw Todd and Mattituck enter his room. He put down his silverware, holding them in his gaze.

"I was wondering if you guys would come around," he said.

"Here we are," Todd said cheerfully.

"I ain't sayin' nothing."

"Sure you are, Eddie. You're going to help us because it's better than the alternative."

Eddie watched him untrustingly.

"Come on, Eddie," Todd continued. "You're not going to make me go through the whole 'We need some information' bullshit, are you? You know what we're here for, and what we need."

He watched Eddie, his smile unwavering. Eddie said nothing. After a moment, he went back to chewing and scooping in more eggs.

Mattituck was struck by the sheer bulk of Eddie's body. The hospital blankets rose from the edge of each side of the wide bed in a high smooth arch under Eddie Etano's multiple chins. Mattituck found himself wondering if there were a weight limit for a hospital bed.

Todd turned, and spotting a chair against the wall near the door, he stepped over to it and dragged it loudly to Eddie's side.

"We have plenty of time." He smiled again at Eddie. "You can work with me, or you can sit there and wonder when I'll run out of patience and start taking away privileges. Or we can cut all that bullshit and just work well together."

Eddie stopped chewing and looked at him, genuinely interested.

"Privileges?"

Todd nodded. "Yeah. There's the privilege of freedom. There's the privilege of not being harangued continually by law enforcement operatives even when you are free—and that might not be all that often in the coming months, by the way---" This comment clearly gave Eddie pause. "--- and there's the privilege of knowing you're doing your part to help keep the riff-raff off the streets."

Eddie shook his head. "You're shittin' me."

Todd's smile slowly faded. "I guess I really don't have any patience today after all," he said.

He got up, followed by Eddie's dark eyes. Eddie had stopped chewing again.

Todd didn't slow down. In a moment, he was out the door, and Mattituck and Eddie could hear the rubber soles of his boots on the tile floor as he strode down the hall toward the exit.

Eddie looked at Mattituck. Mattituck shrugged and started for the door.

"Hey," Eddie said. Mattituck stopped and turned. "What's your partner going to do?"

"I have no clue," Mattituck said. "He's unpredictable when he's like this. There's been a couple of times he turned a guy into his own drug boss." Mattituck shook his head, faking a memory. "That didn't turn out all that well. I'd guess in the guy's last moments he wished he'd gone informant."

"I don't have no drug boss," Eddie said, an edge of fear in his voice.

Mattituck nodded vaguely. "Then maybe you don't have anything to worry about." He started to leave.

"Wait," Eddie swallowed, then tried to shift his mighty weight under the blankets. "I mean it. I don't work for nobody. I get a call. I set up the room. A couple of guys come in and get the key, then a few minutes later they come back with the key again. Later on, a couple of different guys come in, do the same thing." His black eyes gained a pleading moistness. "I swear, I don't know nothing more than that. I swear to god."

Mattituck nodded again. "Always two guys? Never anybody solo?"

"Nope, never. That's why I was suspicious of the guy who shot me. Well, that and the fact he didn't have that card you and your partner had. That's why I thought you were the legit pickup."

Mattituck drew his upper lip under his bottom lip.

"I think I might be confused a little," he said. "I thought you said you didn't know what these guys are doing with the room."

Eddie shifted again with a series of spastic jerks.

"No, well I ---" he stammered. "I don't. Not really. I'm just guessing."

Mattituck gave him a quick nod. "All right. Play it that way if you want. Let's see what my partner comes up with." He started for the door.

"No, wait. Listen, man. I'm telling you everything I know."

"I really don't think you are, Eddie. That's the problem. We're not interested in fucking around. We can make things easier on you, but we can also do just fine without you. We have plenty of leads, and we'll nail these fuckers pretty soon. We're closing in. And then we'll know all about it and nail your fat ass to the wall along with this other guy. It's okay with us that way."

Eddie stared, uncertain what to say. Mattituck let his words sink in.

"We don't really need whatever you have to catch this guy. See, his pick-up buddy is in a hospital in Anchorage, in a coma, and when he wakes up he's likely to talk. In whatever he says, I'd wager something about you will spill out one way or another. And when it does, we'll have no mercy for you. But even if the guy doesn't wake up, we've already pieced together enough to catch this guy soon enough."

He bored a cold gaze into Eddie's eyes.

"And again, when we do, you'll be fucked. Nobody's going to protect you, Eddie. Whatever you have would just make our job quicker and easier . . . and probably safer. As a memento of gratitude, we bestow some leniency on those who help us out. Follow my meaning?"

Eddie swallowed and nodded.

"You look like maybe you're thinking more clearly now," Mattituck said. "To quote The Clash, 'should I stay, or should I go?'"

Mattituck delivered the quip without expression. He was enjoying playing up the John Wayne cop image. Or maybe Clint Eastwood.

Eddie sat still, unanswering.

"All right," Mattituck said, and turned for the door.

"What's the arrangement?" Eddie asked.

"Those are details for my partner. Shall I give him a call?"

Mattituck could see beads of sweat on Eddie's forehead. He nodded.

"Make no mistake, Eddie. There's no going back. You fuck us up on this and you're dead meat. If my partner comes back and you waver, you're fucked. Understood? If I call him back, you gotta come completely clean. You're not in a negotiating position, Eddie."

He watched Eddie for a response. Finally, Eddie nodded solemnly.

Todd entered the room several minutes later, and Mattituck could see Eddie Etano tense.

"So, you want to help us out?"

Eddie stared at the mound of blanket curving over his torso.

Todd looked at Mattituck. "I thought you said---
"

"He was," Mattituck interrupted. He looked at Eddie. "Well?"

"Okay," Eddie said finally.

Todd nodded. "Okay. So why don't we start with the drops. How do those happen?"

Eddie explained that with each drop there were two men, nearly always different guys, who came in first. They would present a business card with the pre-determined room number on it, written with Eddie's own hand, and Eddie would give them the key. Several minutes later, they would return with the key and leave.

Anytime in the next day or so, another pair would come in with the same room number on a business card, and the same thing would happen. Several minutes later, they would return the key, and that was it.

"Nothing else happened? So you would return the key to the box and that was it? So you set a room aside for free?"

Eddie shook his head. "No. The rooms were always pre-paid. I get a package, pretty much always one of those little boxes that checks come in. Inside, there's some cash and a PO Box number to send the business cards to, along with the dates for the two exchanges. It's always first date for the drop, and then a first date for the pick-up. They're usually a few days apart, but it varies. I think because some pairs come in by air and some by boat. But anyways, I'm supposed to keep it open-ended and make sure nobody goes in the room until after the pickup."

"How much cash?"

Eddie smiled secretively. "Enough. Covers the hotel and a small fee for my efforts."

Todd nodded. "How often are these exchanges?"

"At least once a month. Usually two, though."

"Okay." Todd was quiet for a moment. "The way the shooting went down wasn't, I assume, as you told the Police Chief."

Eddie looked out the window.

"It's okay," Todd said. "I have an . . . arrangement to propose. It'll mean you can tell me the truth and not worry about consequences."

Eddie's wide face turned back to Todd.

"You've watched TV, right Eddie? Cop shows and shit like that?"

Eddie nodded.

"So you know what an informant is."

"I didn't think those were for real."

"Oh, they are," said Todd. "It's not a bad arrangement. I mean, I could bust you, but you're not really doing that much harm out there. But the people you do business with are another story. So, I'm fine with looking right past you at them. Get my meaning?"

Eddie nodded.

"But it depends on mutual trust, Eddie. I need to get good, solid information from you when I need it, and you need to never breathe a word of our working relationship—ever. To anybody."

"Okay, I could be cool with that." He was quiet for a moment. "In those shows, the cop shows. . . ."

"Yeah?"

"Informants get paid, right?"

Todd chuckled. "No, Eddie. Remember that shows are largely fiction. No, what informants get is freedom. And a pretty good degree of protection. Your financial situation is solid enough through your business partners."

Eddie looked at him solemnly.

Todd handed him a card with his cell number on it.

"Text or call anytime you think I might be interested in something."

Eddie put the card on the side table and nodded.

Chapter Eighteen

Chance Meeting

It was close to 8:30 p.m. when Todd Benson and Frank Mattituck exited the elevator into the main corridor at Cordova Hospital. Mattituck felt almost like a different person—like a cop. It was freeing, in a way. Like he was given a chance to try on a new skin, a new personality.

Sandy would have liked him to do that. As much as his sister loved him, she did not hold back on her opinion that he could be an asshole. He called it an unwavering commitment to truth, but she always waved this off.

"That's an excuse for being an ass," she would say. "Ironically, it's a way of *hiding* from the truth that deep inside, you're hurt. You've built up walls between yourself and the world, all so that you won't get hurt. And in the process, you wind up hurting everybody around you. Maybe that's why you're running a tad short on friends," she'd said that last time they argued over this.

The last point bit hard, and left him wondering if she might be right. But once back in Valdez, hanging at

The Crow's Nest with plenty of interaction, he'd allowed the thought to fade.

Now, as he and Todd made their way to the front of the Cordova Hospital, he suddenly thought of Monica Castle and how he'd let things fade away with her. Was it possible Sandy was right? Was he building walls around himself?

Like a slap, Janelle popped into his head, and something in him recoiled as the pain of her memory crept in. He shook his head at how much he'd trusted her, thought she was it. And certainly that she was loyal. But then those pictures . . . and her deceit was captured and sent to destroy his belief in people.

Fucking Janelle, he thought. *Cheating fucking bitch--*

But then Monica pressed into his thoughts. Her smile, her warm eyes. There was something different in her—something very different from Janelle. Whatever he'd told himself while with Janelle, he had to admit there was something amiss there that he'd always known, although not consciously. Hindsight is 20/20, they say, and it certainly was here.

All the more reason to protect against that shit happening again, he mused bitterly. Nonetheless, Monica held her spot in his thoughts, rebutting everything he was trying to convince himself was true about the deceitful, untrustworthy nature of human beings. Maybe a few exceptions—Mattituck could name a half dozen for sure—but by and large, good reason to keep distant from people.

He forced his thoughts to the present.

He wasn't sure which part was more surreal: that only a few days ago he had been running fishing charters, or that he was now full-board law enforcement, chasing down a murderer. And deputized, no less. The two worlds felt so radically separate that he felt like two people. The duplicity felt vaguely like deceit.

He glanced over at Todd Benson, walking beside him in the hospital corridor. He'd make that list of a half-dozen, Mattituck thought. There was nothing false in Todd. Or it seemed, anyway.

Cordova is a town of no more than 2500 people, so it shouldn't be a surprise to bump into someone you know. But the sudden appearance of Monica Castle walking through the entrance to the hospital nonetheless took Mattituck by surprise. The surprise was accentuated by the fact that he'd just been thinking of her. Perhaps it was also the thoughts of the dichotomous lives of charter boat captain and deputized trooper that caused the illusion, but the illusion carried the full force of surprise bordering on shock. Her long black hair framed the shape of her olive face, and when her warm brown eyes met his, those pure white and perfectly straight teeth drew into that smile that always immediately pulled him into her.

"Hi, Frank!" she said, genuinely happy to see him.

Somehow, he'd expected her to be angry with him. For what, Mattituck would have been hard-pressed to guess. But it had been some time since he'd tried to call or to text her. Doesn't that always piss off women? he wondered.

"Monica," he said far more even-keeled than he felt. "I've been wanting to call—"

"Then why didn't you?" she smiled at him, her gaze genuine and warm.

"Uhhh . . . You know." As was typical for him, he opted for the straightforward and honest truth. "I have zero excuses. Just---"

"I know," she said with a nod. "I get it. Ninety miles." There was no accusation in her voice. Only the acknowledgement of reality.

Mattituck nodded vaguely.

"Yeah," he said, his tone lower. "Ninety miles."

"So what have you been up to? Besides charters, I mean."

He shook his head. "That's about it. Lots of water and fish. You?"

She shifted her weight and stood straight. "You know. Law."

"You look really good, Monica," he said suddenly. "Happy."

"So do you, Frank." Her eyes continued to smile at him, her gaze steady. "And I am happy. Not as happy as a few months ago," she said suggestively, "but happy enough to get by."

Mattituck held her gaze. "Well, maybe that happy will come back." He felt suddenly hopeful.

"I hope so. I miss it. A lot."

A few moments of silence sat between them. Not awkward; just there.

Finally, Mattituck spoke. "So what can a couple of people do about ninety miles?"

Monica smiled.

"Well," she said. "I suppose they could ignore it. At least for the time being."

Mattituck's hand moved instinctively forward before he could stop it. Monica reached out in response, and their hands joined. Mattituck had always loved the way her hands looked and felt, slender and shapely and with perfect color. A feminine strength resided in those hands, and Mattituck loved that. Everything about them came back in a comfortable, familiar flood. For both of them.

"What do *you* think a couple of people might do about ninety miles?" she asked in return, her hand still in his.

Mattituck nodded. "Definitely. What you said."

"Good," she said. "How long are you in town?"

Mattituck looked over his shoulder at Todd. Todd had moved to a respectful distance, beyond earshot. He stood looking out a window, waiting.

"I'm not sure. I'm working with the State Troopers at the moment."

Monica's head drew back in surprise.

"State Troopers?"

"Yeah. I've kind of become . . . well, deputized."

"What?" she said with completely unbridled surprise.

Mattituck nodded. He felt like they had never been apart. As though they had just fallen asleep in each other's arms the night before, and were now catching up on each other's day. Nothing to hide, everything to share.

"Deputized? I didn't even know they do that."

"Apparently they do. Long story." He paused, reflecting. "Damned good story, in fact. I'll need to fill you in."

"Please do." She looked into his eyes. He knew in that exchange that she was feeling exactly as he was — as though no time had passed since they were last together. Just as he had so many times with Monica Castle, he sensed a link between them that was beyond anything he thought possible between two people. He scolded himself at the thought – again, just as he had done so many times before. That kind of stuff was all trumped up by people selling books or astrology readings. Soul Mates and Twin Flames, and all romantic connections governed by the magical. He told himself it was all crap, and tried to push the thoughts out of his mind.

"Call me when you know your schedule, Frank. Okay?" Her lips held the smile, but her head tipped slightly to the side, changing the effect of the smile. Mattituck again felt the connection. Something deep in his chest knew exactly what she was feeling.

There was much different with Monica than it had been with Janelle. None of the . . . what was it, exactly? Not distance . . . lack of connection? Lack of transparency?

"Nothing's changed for me, Monica," he surprised himself by saying.

"Me, too," she said, then stepped forward and kissed him lightly. "Cut the nonsense and just call, okay, Mattituck?" She lingered a moment, and he could feel her breath on his lips. He smelled her skin, light and pleasant, and yearned to kiss her again. Her smile rose higher on one side as she drew back, and he knew everything was as it was.

Yes, the back of his mind churned, with Janelle there had been a lack of transparency, and definitely a lack of true connection. There had been a lack of truth. With Monica, everything seemed true. Was true, he corrected.

He smiled broadly, feeling a tad goofy. "Okay, Castle. Will do."

"Good," she said. "You better."

Todd held the door open for Mattituck. When they were clear of the building, walking toward the rented SUV, Todd finally spoke.

"She's pretty hot," he said.

285

"You're a married man," Mattituck rebutted, banter clear in his tone.

"Not for me. For you. I mean, don't tell me anything you don't want to, but she's hot, and she obviously really likes you."

Mattituck kept pace to the SUV. "You sound surprised."

"I am," Todd said truthfully. "I am."

Mattituck let it go.

"So what's next, boss?" he asked cheerfully.

Todd was watching Mattituck as they walked. He didn't think he'd ever seen Frank that cheerful. He had a sudden image of Frank Mattituck as a boy—full of hope and fun and kid-ness. Somehow he'd never thought of Frank as a kid. To Todd, he'd always been what they call an old soul.

He was wondering who the woman was, and what hers and Frank's relationship was. Clearly, they had a strong connection, and everything pointed to romantic involvement. This side of Mattituck was intriguing to him. If this were a long-term relationship, it explained a lot about Mattituck in Valdez. Valdez was also a small coastal Alaskan town, with a population of just over 4,000, so anybody's relationships were well-known. Sometimes, even their interests were known. And it was known in Valdez that there was no shortage of women interested in Frank Mattituck, despite his gruffness. Todd's wife, well-connected in town, shared with him all the longings of the single women.

But it was also well-known that Frank Mattituck was not involved with anybody. If he'd had any relationships in the past few years, Todd—and his wife— had no knowledge of them. This woman in Cordova was both a surprise and a possible explanation.

"All right," he said to Mattituck. "We fly out tomorrow around noon. Since our flight takes us through Anchorage, I thought we'd stop in and see how our other suspect is doing. Then we fly into Valdez and get the boat, then head out to see what we can find."

He unlocked the door to the SUV, got in, and reached to the passenger side and unlocked the door for Mattituck.

Mattituck had already been mulling over what the killer on the 'But Chaser might be doing, and he'd come to the conclusion that he was headed for the Kimberly Marie. He shared this with Todd.

"You think he didn't find whatever he was after?" Todd asked, turning the key to start the SUV.

Mattituck nodded. "He definitely didn't. He was after something with black cloth."

"Yes," Todd replied.

"The backpack at the hotel was black, right?"

Todd nodded.

"So was the one in the forward compartment on the Kimberly Marie," Mattituck added.

"And," continued Todd, "the cloth thing the drunk had said the suspect was digging for on the Kimberly Marie last night was black."

"Precisely," Mattituck said.

"You really are catching onto this job fast," Todd said with a smile.

"Thanks. I say we fly straight back to Valdez. You get on your boat and get out there. I get on the Kimberly Marie, and try to lure our guy out there. You stay close by, and then when he tries to retrieve the other backpack, we nail him."

"Lure our guy out where?" Todd asked.

"To some bay or something. Away from town where people might get hurt. I mean, the guy has already shown he'll fire his gun in port, right? And wouldn't it be a lot easier to keep an eye out if there's just the Kimberly Marie and the 'But Chaser?"

Todd nodded. "I have to admit, it's a good plan. Add to your points that our suspect would feel a lot more bold if he didn't have to make another attempt in Valdez. He's gotta feel like he's being watched for there. But I don't like the idea of having you possibly face off with this killer by yourself."

"I won't be. You'll be close enough." He fixed a hard look on Todd that made the Trooper flinch inwardly. "Besides, I can handle myself. I'll be fine."

For Todd, it was a reminder of how most people see Frank Mattituck: inwardly angry and sometimes volatile. He set his negative thoughts aside.

Todd had to admit, this plan was better than trying to keep tabs of all the people around the Valdez Harbor. And Frank was right: this suspect had already demonstrated he's perfectly comfortable firing a weapon where plenty of by-standers might be hurt. To say nothing of killing people simply because they were in the way.

"All right," he said. "I'll call for a charter flight straight to Valdez. We'll set it up for the morning."

"No," Mattituck said. "We need to get there tonight."

Todd thought of the woman with the long black hair. Didn't Frank want to see her? Then again, Frank was living up to exactly what many had Todd was a darker side to Mattituck. Brooding and insistent on his way. Nonetheless, he had full confidence in Frank. Whatever made up that darker side, Todd felt sure that Mattituck's good side would win out. And he seemed very committed to his new role.

Maybe, Todd thought, that dedication was what was driving his insistence they go to Valdez tonight. *Does is matter why?* Todd thought, *getting there tonight could only work in our favor—especially if that suspect really is headed to Valdez.*

It turned out that the Coast Guard was planning to run night fishery operations with one of the helicopters out of Cordova, so Todd and Mattituck were able to get another ride back to Valdez. Unfortunately, though, there was a storm in the Gulf and the ride was bumpy. The pilots had orders to patrol on the way to Valdez, so they kept over the water, lengthening the trip. There was a herring opener in three places in Prince William Sound, so the crew took a reading on which fishing vessels were working that opening. They relayed this information to Air Station Kodiak, then flew toward the Valdez Airport to drop off their guests. While they were away from the opener, the Air Station would run checks on all the vessels at the opening to verify current licensure and to identify any that had outstanding safety or fishery violations.

It was interesting to Mattituck to see how the Coast Guard operated. Todd explained what they were doing throughout the operation, and how they would follow up with any violating vessels from the reading. A Coast Guard cutter, usually the USCGC Long Island, would be on station in the Sound to respond to any issues among the fishing vessels, to conduct random boardings, and to follow up with any vessels found in violation of the safety or fishery regulations.

As the Coast Guard MH-60 Jayhawk circled the relatively tightly massed mix of gillnetters and seiners,

Mattituck watched out the open side door. This was only his second time on a helicopter—the first being the ride from Valdez to Cordova earlier in the week. It was nothing like he thought it would be. The massive machine, it seemed to him, shouldn't be able to fly. Airplanes and jets he understood; he could see how they stay aloft. But a helicopter, especially one of this size, was beyond him. There was a knot in his stomach when he thought about the fact that he was being held 500 feet above the water by 5 or 6 blades rotating round and round.

Nonetheless, he enjoyed the ride. He had always wondered when the Jayhawks flew over while he was on charters what they were doing and what it was like to be flying in one. Now he knew.

"Scratch this off my bucket list," he said aloud.

Todd turned to look at him, his headset making his head look alien.

"Helicopter ride?" he asked.

Mattituck nodded.

Todd smiled and nodded back.

The Jayhawk was banking sharply to the right, getting a clear view of a white seiner's name on the bow, and commercial fishing license number on the cabin. Then, in one smooth motion, the nose of the Jayhawk dipped and the copter picked up speed as it started north for Valdez. Mattituck let his head fall back to the bulkhead, and closed his eyes, suddenly weary. He felt the pull of a dreamlike state. How many hours had it been since he'd gotten solid sleep?

Mattituck awoke with the change in pitch in the rotors and the engines. He had the groggy, mist-laden feeling of having come out of a deep, too-short sleep. He closed his eyes tightly and shook his head. He opened his eyes, then repeated the routine. He opened his eyes again, to the same end. Usually, this brief regimen brought him back to alertness, but not this time. He shifted his weight, shook his head, then shifted his weight and shook his arms. Still no effect.

He noticed Todd watching him, a bemused curl at the corners of his mouth.

"What?" Mattituck asked.

Todd shook his head slowly, dipping his head as if unbelieving.

"You sure you don't want to take the night and get caught up on sleep?" Todd asked.

The Jayhawk's rotors started winding down. The crew wouldn't let them disembark until the rotors came to a complete stop.

"No way," Mattituck said. "He's probably getting close to Valdez. We need to get the Kimberly Marie underway."

Todd nodded.

"Okay," he said. "Good enough. We'll go straight to the harbor. I'll help you get underway, then I'll take AST 32067 out. It's getting pretty dark now, so I'll hold close to the north side of the Port. In the off chance our suspect sees me, he'll figure I'm out on patrol and checking the boats anchored up that way."

"Sounds good."

With that, they crawled out of the Jayhawk and made their way through the airport to Todd's State Trooper pickup waiting outside.

As the Kimberly Marie drifted slowly away from the dock, Mattituck thought of coffee. While Jim Milner had terrible taste in wine and food, he had impeccable taste for beer and coffee. In fact, all that he'd seen in Jim's galley for coffee were various blends from Kaladi Brothers, Mattituck's favorite coffee. Monica also loved Kaladi Brothers. A memory of her sleeping soundly when he'd awoke wafted into his thoughts, just as the scent of Kaladi Brothers had wafted into his bedroom and awakened her. She had lain half covered by the tossled sheets, her brown shoulder so smooth it reflected the light spilling through a crack in the drapes. He felt in memory the same vivid and focused adoration he'd felt in that moment.

She had found a flannel shirt of Mattituck's and emerged from the bedroom wearing only that. She had found him in front of the stove, dropping chopped green onions and peppers onto the makings of an omelette frying in a skillet. He looked up and smiled.

"I was going to bring you breakfast in bed."

Her smile was wide, equaled by her eyes, and the combination lit up her entire face. "Nobody's ever done that for me," she had said. "Is that Kaladi Brothers? Mmmm . . ." She had said, picking up the white foil bag of grounds on the counter and pressing her nose into it to draw in the full aroma.

Mattituck smiled at the memory. He thought about bumping into her at the Cordova Hospital, how much of a surprise to find that she wasn't angry with him. At all. In fact, it seemed like no time had passed and all was normal with them.

The Kimberly Marie seemed to be far enough into the channel to engage the throttles. He checked to make sure the running lights were on, then stepped on the foot brace in front of the captain's chair to gain a better view over the bow. She was indeed clear, and he pushed the twin throttle forward to engage the propellers at an idle. The Kimberly Marie began to make way toward the mouth of the harbor.

Mattituck began the routine for getting underway in open water, beginning with checking the GPS, ensuring it was set for the course and waypoints he had programmed in. This course would take him to Heather Bay, adjacent to Columbia Bay, and a popular anchorage due to the well-protected waters and excellent shrimping. For their purposes, it was just off the route from Valdez to Whittier—the killer's presumed next drop and pick-up. Next, he turned on the radar and set the range to 6 miles. He liked this range because it gave excellent resolution so he could easily distinguish between vessel traffic and shoreline.

Thinking of the shrimp in Heather Bay, Mattituck decided that as soon as he got a pot of the Kaladi Brothers brewing, he would double-check Jim's shrimp pots atop the main cabin, and then see if he had any bait. Shrimp was sounding very good to Mattituck right now. But then he remembered that the shrimp pots had gone missing after Jim's run-in with the killers.

When was the last meal he'd had? he wondered. He thought hard, but couldn't really remember. He knew that he and Todd had grabbed food on the run, but he could not remember his last meal.

The Kimberly Marie cleared the jetty and Mattituck felt the bow rise and fall, then he could feel the open-water swells rolling along the bottom of the big yacht's hull. Standing at the helm, he could see her white bow in the near-darkness rise and then fall, and then from bow to stern, a lifting of the hull that was even and steady. It was a gentle motion, like being rocked in a father's arms just before bed.

"Jim? . . ." a voice tentatively called from below.

Mattituck's feet nearly slipped off the foot support. He froze, unsure of how to move and whether to reply.

"Jim?" came the voice again, a little more boldly.

"Who's there?" Mattituck replied, glancing over his shoulder to the dinette, where he'd laid the Glock. He took two quick strides to retrieve it.

"It's me, Earl. That you, Jim?"

Mattituck saw a face at the bottom of the ladder. It was the drunk who had been sleeping on the bow. He felt his shoulders ease.

"You said your name is Earl?"

"Yeah. Where's Jim?" he asked, recognizing Mattituck.

The guy still didn't know what was, to Mattituck, very old news. A pang of sadness swept through Mattituck.

"You know how to make coffee?" Mattituck asked him.

"Shit yeah. What kinda question's that?" Earl retorted, clearly annoyed.

"There's some Kaladi Brothers down there. Can you get a pot going? Then come up here. You have a lot of catching up to do."

The face remained.

"Okay. But where's Jim?"

Mattituck watched Earl's face.

"Look, I've been a friend of Jim's for quite a while," Mattituck said. "We were pretty tight. I know you and he were as well –"

"What do you mean 'were'?" Earl said, his voice tightening.

"Earl . . . Jim's dead."

Silence.

"Dead . . . ?"

"Well, we don't know for sure, but yeah, I'm pretty sure."

"We?"

"I'm Frank Mattituck. I'm a charter boat captain, but I also work with the State Troopers at times. Well, I actually just --- well, anyway. We're trying to catch Jim's killer."

Earl shook his head, trying to clear it. Mattituck could see this was all too much, too fast.

"Jim? . . . dead?" Earl's face turned back to Mattituck. "How? What happened?"

"We're both going to need that coffee. Brew that up and then I'll fill you in. Meantime, it looks like you'll be riding along to see if we can catch Jim's killer."

Chapter Nineteen

Luring Bottom Feeders

Mattituck had finished two cups of coffee by the time they reached Entrance Island. They had approximately two hours left to Heather Bay, and Mattituck estimated they would be there around 1:00am. He had told Earl most of the story of what he knew of Jim's killer, what probably happened to Jim, and why Mattituck and the State Troopers believed Jim was in fact dead. What Mattituck did not share were the particulars of the beached Bayliner and its missing owners, the murders of the elderly couple and Officer Wayne Barrett off Yakutat, and the likelihood that Jim Milner had navigated the Kimberly Marie up Growler Bay and met an untimely end.

"That's about right, I figure," Earl reacted to the story. "Jim was always runnin' up Growler Bay. No doubt in my mind, anyway, that he'd of run up there. And if that beached boat was full of blood samples, and then the Kimberly Marie wound up in Zaikof without Jim aboard . . . well, I reckon there ain't any doubt."

He sat at the dinette, nursing his coffee.

"Poor Jim," he said finally. "Shit," he said suddenly, his head popping upright. "If Jim's dead, what happens to the Kimberly Marie? I mean, Jim ain't got no family. And he has clients comin', I'm sure."

"I don't know, Earl. I suppose we'll find out soon enough. But how did you end up below? I thought you like sleeping on the bow."

Earl explained that while he did normally sleep on the bow of the Kimberly Marie, his run-in with the killer the night before had made him nervous. He'd decided that it was safer to sleep in one of the staterooms below.

"Why sleep on board at all?" Mattituck queried. "I mean—don't you have a home?"

"Oh, yeah—hell yeah, I gotta home. Up near High School Hill." Earl sulked a moment, turning to look out the window. "Guy thinks I ain't got a home." He turned back to Mattituck. "Whattaya think, I'm some homeless drunk? I ain't no homeless drunk. I come from good stock."

"Okay, Sorry. I didn't mean it that way."

Earl was quiet a moment, then nodded, accepting the apology. He looked like a child who had just been assured his parents didn't think he was a bad kid.

"So why not just go home?" Mattituck asked.

Earl took a packet of sugar from the bowl in front of him, tore it open, and poured the sugar into his cup.

"I dunno," he started. "Gotta remember I was on this boat a long time. I was the first mate. I ran the boat a good chunk of the time."

Mattituck nodded.

"I was good, too. There was times Jim didn't have to worry none about anything. I could run the boat and he could catch up on his sleep." Earl was watching

Mattituck closely, anxious to see approval—or respect. "Coupla times, Jim had somethin' going on or had to make a supply run to Anchorage, and he left the boat for me to watch. Sent me out to pick up hunters on Hinchinbrook once, even."

Mattituck looked at him. After a moment, he smiled and nodded.

"I'm kinda attached to the Kimberly Marie, you know?" Earl went on.

Mattituck nodded.

"But even more so, Jim. I've always been close to Jim. We were like brothers." His eyes began to glaze. "I had no idea where Jim was, but I did know somethin' wadn't right. That's why I wanted to be on board."

"Makes sense." Mattituck met Earl's eyes. "It's obvious he had a lot of confidence in you, Earl. And anybody Jim has confidence in, I do."

Earl's shoulders seemed to straighten, and a hidden smile crossed his features.

Mattituck grabbed the mic to the VHF radio.

"Happy Fitzgerald, the Happy Fitzgerald, this is the Kimberly Marie, over."

Todd answered right away.

"Kimberly Marie, Happy Fitzgerald. Wanna go to six-eight?"

"Roger," Mattituck replied. "Six-eight."

He changed the channel and called Todd.

"How's it going there, captain?" Todd asked.

"Roger—going great," Mattituck answered. "I'm headed out to Heather Bay and try some shrimp. I'll drop the shrimp pots and then anchor up, see what I have in the morning."

"Roger that. I'm sitting the night in Galena Bay. I'll be trying for some yellow-eye off Bligh in the morning."

Mattituck knew Todd wasn't in Galena. They had decided that they would call each other periodically to increase their radio presence, thereby increase the chances of the killer overhearing them and knowing where the Kimberly Marie would be. He knew that Todd was criss-crossing the Port of Valdez, looking like he was doing vessel checks but was really trying to locate the 'But Chaser.

"Any luck today?" he asked Todd.

"Yep. I landed one, all right."

Mattituck thought about this. It meant Todd had sighted the 'But Chaser. But where? And why hadn't he called to let Mattituck know—and to make sure the killer knew the Kimberly Marie was underway?

"Well, dammit," he said into the mic, "why the hell didn't you call and tell me?"

There was a moment of silence as Todd thought about how to remain cryptic. Mattituck studied the radar, looking for vessels aft. There appeared to be four, but he couldn't tell yet whether they were moving or not, let alone which direction.

"I called as soon as I could, buddy," Todd chuckled as he said it to add an element of humor.

"Ah, sure," Mattituck said back, keeping their conversation masked. "You just don't want me to know where the fish are."

"Oh, hell, man," Todd retorted. "You don't need me to tell you any such thing. The fish follow you wherever you go."

Mattituck was surprised. And impressed. That was a brilliant way of telling Mattituck that the 'But Chaser was already following him.

"Ha ha ha!" Mattituck laughed into the mic. "Okay, okay. What about you? Any fish follow you around?"

"Hell, no! I have to chase those sons-a-bitches down. I'm usually a pretty good ways behind 'em, though."

Again, Mattituck was impressed at how much Todd was telling him without giving anything away. It sounded like the 'But Chaser was following the Kimberly Marie, and AST 32067 was a distance back, but following. Probably to make sure the killer didn't see him.

"How do you do that?" he asked. "I've never been good at chasing fish down. I rely on pure dumb luck."

Mattituck marked each of the four contacts aft of the Kimberly Marie to start tracking them. He needed to know which one was the 'But Chaser.

"Oh, you know . . . I sit in one place for a while, waiting and waiting, then scoot over to another hole. Sit and wait there for a while, then jump over to another hole. On and on like that, and eventually I hook 'em and reel 'em in!"

Mattituck shook his head, glancing over at Earl's baffled expression. He's keeping hidden in coves and behind points of land, Mattituck thought. Then when the 'But Chaser is too far to identify AST 32067, he runs to a point closer and then stops and waits for the 'But Chaser to move further along. No wonder Todd was so good at what he does.

"Roger that. Okay, well, happy fishing. Maybe I'll see you in the morning."

"No doubt. I'll come over and raid your shrimp pots . . . after you have them all aboard and cleaned already!"

"Ha! If you want to partake, you'll have to be there early enough to help out."

"Oh, I'll be there in plenty of time, my friend. Not to worry."

"Catch you later. Kimberly Marie clear of the Happy Fitzgerald, switching back to 16."

He switched the radio back to channel 16, thinking about the last part of their exchange.

They were coming up on Potato Point, at the southern end of the Valdez Narrows. When they passed Potato Point, they would be entering Valdez Arm. The southern end of Valdez Arm was where Bligh Reef was, the now infamous rock where the Exxon Valdez oil spill changed the ecosystem of Prince William Sound and destroyed many lives among those who lived in south central Alaska.

"Who was that you was talking to?" Earl asked.

"Todd Benson, the State Trooper."

Earl's brow clenched up. "I know Todd Benson," he said. "You guys running under cover or somethin'? Why'd he call himself the Happy Fitzgerald? And what was all that business about fishing and shrimping and what-not?"

"Yes to the under cover. And that conversation was kind of code so we know what's happening while not giving any clue to the suspect what we're doing. We want him to think I'm a sitting duck."

Earl watched him evenly for a moment.

"Wait. You mean you're expecting this guy to come after you?"

Mattituck nodded. "He already is. He's one of these boats back here. That's part of what Todd was telling me."

Mattituck continued tracking the four vessels behind the Kimberly Marie.

"Todd doesn't know I'm aboard, does he?" Earl asked.

"Nope," Mattituck said without looking up. "And we're going to keep it that way. We can't let the suspect know I'm not alone."

He turned his head and fixed a somber gaze on Earl.

"You might be the trump card if things get ugly."

This visibly took Earl aback. "I ain't gonna have to tangle with that bastard again, am I?"

"Hope not. But you know, Earl—you seemed to handle yourself just fine. And we'll be taking him down together." He took a sip of cold coffee. "You're not alone."

This didn't appear to make Earl feel any better.

"We'll be fine," Mattituck said, unsure whether he was trying to convince Earl or himself.

As they approached the buoy along Freemantle, halfway down Valdez Arm, Mattituck remained at the radar. He'd isolated the contact that was likely the 'But Chaser. He still couldn't see the boat with the binoculars, as the sun had not yet begun its turn back toward the horizon. The 'But Chaser was obviously traveling without running lights. But the contact was steady to the Kimberly Marie's course and speed. What was occupying his attention now was a contact further back. At first, it was holding inside Midway Rock, in the Narrows. Then, when the 'But Chaser was three or four miles south, the contact had made very good speed over to Jack Bay across the channel. Again, when the 'But

Chaser was approximately four miles south, it made a speedy run to a small cove just north of Galena Bay.

Mattituck rubbed his eyes. He'd gotten very little sleep in the past few days, and it was catching up to him. He couldn't lose his momentum now, not so close to catching this killer. He was very sure all this would be over tomorrow, and he could sleep, but he wanted to make sure he was as rested as he could be for the big show in the morning. He was very sure the 'But Chaser wouldn't make a move until they were in Heather Bay. He looked at where they were on the GPS, and estimated another hour or more before they would reach Heather Bay. More likely, an hour and a half.

"You doing okay?" he asked Earl, who was sitting in the passenger seat on the port side. He'd insisted he was too agitated to get any sleep, so he'd sat with Mattituck and they'd made light conversation.

"Yeah," Earl said irritably. "'Course I'm okay. Why wouldn't I be okay?"

It turned out that Earl was a serious baseball fan, and his team—like Mattituck's—was the Mariners. Although Mattituck maintained that he was merely a fan of the game, he did have a few favorite teams. And a few on the list of not-favorites. Earl was a walking encyclopedia of baseball, spouting off player names and stats anytime the conversation turned to a new player or team.

"The 1992 World Series?" he would say. "Did you know that was the first time a World Series game has ever been played outside of the U.S.?"

Mattituck hadn't known that.

"And they won it, too. The Toronto Blue Jays. Took the series 4 games to 2 against the Braves. The big shot 1990s dynasty Braves. Sure was fun to watch them lose."

And on and on like that for the better part of an hour. Mattituck was starting to like Earl more and more.

Now, though, Mattituck's eyes were burning.

"You're not tired?" he asked Earl.

"Nope. Like I said. I couldn't sleep if I wanted to."

"You know where Heather Bay is?"

Earl looked hard at him. "Of course I know where Heather Bay is. You think I ran this boat and worked alongside Jim Milner for the better part of a decade, and I don't know these waters?" He huffed with annoyance. "Damn straight I know where Heather Bay is. What kind of talk is that?"

"Okay, well, I need some sleep. You know how to –" he stopped himself from asking whether Earl knew how to read the GPS. Better not to launch the man into another bout of outrage.

"I know how to what?"

Mattituck ignored the question.

"You mind steering us in? I really need to get a few minutes sleep, if I can."

"Yeah, sure," Earl said, stirring from his seat and getting ready to take the helm.

Mattituck pointed at the contact for the 'But Chaser on the radar.

"That's the enemy," he said. "I have the range finder set to him, and he's been holding pretty close to that line. Give or take, anyway. If he starts closing in on us, get me up. Okay?"

"You got it, Cap'n. Sleep well."

Earl did not look like the homeless drunk he'd impressed Mattituck as being that first night they met. He seemed focused and alert, and willing to do what was needed. Mattituck wondered if this was the Earl that Jim

Milner had trusted as his first mate. And, he continued in his thoughts as he gathered their mugs to take to the galley on his way to the stateroom he'd been using. And, Mattituck wondered, why had Jim Milner stopped carrying Earl as his first mate – or deckhand?

He carried the two mugs to the galley sink below, leaving them to be washed later, and turned to his stateroom. He closed the door behind him, and lay down on the bed, motionless. He didn't even bother to take off his shoes. The pillow was soft and embracing, and the hum of the twin diesels lulled him along with the gentle rocking of the Kimberly Marie as the magnificent vessel sliced her way south toward Freemantle Point, and around the corner Heather Bay.

Todd sat at the helm of AST 32067 in the cove immediately north of the mouth of Galena Bay. He hadn't bothered to drop anchor—here nor at the previous two points he'd lain in wait. The glow of the radar lit his face with a ghostly aura. He let his head drop backward over his back, stretching his neck and relieving the tension in his shoulders. It was beginning to get light, and he had to make sure he didn't bear down too closely on the 'But Chaser. If it got light and the suspect saw the Trooper boat, he might run. Truth be told, though, Todd was not at all sure that would be such a bad thing. He was nervous that this current plan was putting Frank at risk.

He missed having his crewman with him. Not only did Justin give him relief, but he was generally good company. And that was particularly valuable at a time like this. Justin's grandfather had died, however, and he was in the Lower 48 for the funeral. It had been lucky that Frank Mattituck had agreed to help Todd on this investigation. Although there was no way Todd would ever have asked Justin to do what Mattituck was doing.

He watched the contact on the radar screen that was the Kimberly Marie. He wondered how Frank was doing. They had been going non-stop since this whole thing had begun. The man had to be tired. *Me?* Todd thought, *I'm used to this. Ops normal.* But a civilian—that was another matter.

The 'But Chaser was holding steady on the speed and course of the Kimberly Marie, hanging back by a distance of just over two miles. He was very sure now that the suspect had no intention of trying to overtake the Kimberly Marie tonight. He looked at his watch. 2:48am. He studied the GPS and decided it was too risky to close in again. It'd be better to wait until the 'But Chaser was rounding Freemantle, and then run top speed all the way down. By then, the 'But Chaser would be steering around Round Point and heading into Heather Bay. Todd could close in before the 'But Chaser reached the Kimberly Marie even if the suspect intended to go immediately to the Kimberly Marie.

He cut the motors and flipped the "anchor down" toggle. He then set the alarm on his cell phone. His eyes heavy, he leaned back into the highback seat and closed his eyes.

Skipper's Oath

Chapter Twenty

The Elusive Bottom Dweller

Only an hour had passed since Todd laid his head back and pulled his cap over his face, but when the alarm on his phone sounded, it felt like it was a new day. The sun was on its way back up, and Todd could easily see across Valdez Arm to the high mountains across the way. This land truly was a pristine and beautiful place, he thought. Mornings on the water always hit him the same way.

He toggled to pull up the anchor, and turned the key to the Honda outboards. They purred to life. He checked the radar screen, and saw no sign of either the Kimberly Marie or the 'But Chaser. They must have rounded Freemantle already. With the speed of AST 32067, though, he wasn't concerned. He could cover that distance very quickly.

He did a quick visual check around him, even though the radar showed he was clear of any nearby vessels. He pressed the throttles forward and felt the outboards kick into gear. He continued pressing the throttles forward and felt the boat pick up speed. In a moment, the bow rose and the outboards pushed the hull of AST 32067 up onto the sea's surface—she was now "on step," as they called it. He checked his speed. He was already at 30kts, and gaining speed. He turned the helm to port and nosed the boat straight out into Valdez Arm.

While he never failed to maintain a professional outward demeanor, there had always been a bit of the giddy little boy in Todd Benson when he was doing certain parts of his job. One of them was high speed on AST 32067. This was precisely why he preferred this boat to AST 41448, which he kept moored in Cordova. Both vessels were highly useful, of course, but the speed and agility of AST 32067 more suited Todd's preferences. And the smaller boat gave him a rush.

Now was one of those times. The waters of the Arm were calm, with only a slight breeze drawing across the surface—just enough to take away the glassy calm reflection the waters were capable of. AST 32067 literally glided across the surface, slicing a nicely trimmed wake as she sped toward Freemantle. To the south, Todd could see a tanker making its way north to the Valdez oil pipeline terminal. Keeping close to the massive vessel were two emergency response tugs, required by law ever since the 1989 Exxon Valdez oil spill. Should the tanker lose steerage or power, the two tugs would be able to control the tanker with little effort. Astern of the tanker, one of the tugs was in tow, the line from the tanker to the tug an instant capability to pull the hulking tanker away from danger.

What Todd could really go for right now was a hot cup of coffee. He thought of Frank Mattituck aboard the Kimberly Marie. The yacht was well-equipped and luxurious. He pictured Frank well-stocked on coffee as he readied the shrimp pots to be placed in key spots within Heather Bay.

AST 32067 was at 48kts and riding smoothly. In good conditions such as those present now, she could top

53kts, and possibly reach 55kts. Todd pushed the throttles forward to take her to full speed. He would be on Freemantle Point in no time. He estimated he would be able to round the point and turn to the west, and then northwest, about the time the 'But Chaser was already entering Heather Bay. It had also occurred to Todd that the 'But Chaser might not approach the Kimberly Marie at all. Maybe he just wanted to see where she was going.

He shook his head. No, there was something—or some *things*—that the suspect wanted. Ideally, the timing would have been such that the suspect would have reached the Kimberly Marie in the dark, when everybody was presumably sleeping. Either the suspect would hole up and wait for a chance to approach under darkness, or he would go with an aggressive and direct attack in broad daylight.

Todd wondered what the suspect might be thinking at this point. He had to know that someone was onto him and was searching for him. After the run-ins at the Valdez Harbor, law enforcement would be on the lookout for something. Todd was sure the suspect was smart enough to know that. It was likely he understood that a State Trooper was among them. Todd also guessed that the suspect was wondering who would be running the Kimberly Marie. It was a vessel that had been involved in an incident in Zaikof Bay, so the suspect might assume it was the Trooper trying to nail him. But then again, the suspect had no idea that they knew anything about the backpacks, and he had no reason to believe that Earl was alive—last the suspect had seen the drunk, he had shot him and left him floating in the water next to the Kimberly Marie.

Todd smiled inwardly. This was his favorite part of working a case--figuring the pieces out. He nodded as he checked his speed and the radar. It was by far most likely that the suspect's thinking was the Troopers had no idea about the backpacks. Or the 'But Chaser, for that matter. Even when the suspect had tried to ambush Frank, he kept the boat at a distance and probably figured the boat had not been identified. From the suspect's perspective, he was running free and unidentifiable.

True to his word, Earl woke Mattituck when they arrived in Heather Bay. Mattituck got up, groggy, and they set the anchor and cut the engines. The silence was stunning, as was the darkness of the mountains surrounding the bay. It was still mostly dark, and the light from the horizon in the northwest, where the sun would rise in a couple of hours, was enough to illuminate the glassy water with a golden hue. Mattituck drew the sight in like the fresh, crisp air of the morning. It was quite a bit cooler here, due to the proximity of Columbia Glacier and the high number of icebergs and bergy bits.

"You go ahead and get some sleep, Earl. I'll keep watch."

"No way, man—you're tired. You go ahead. I'll stand watch." Earl was quiet for a moment. "What are we watching for? Are you thinking that crazy bastard's going to try something?"

"There's a good chance of it."

"Shit, really?"

"Yeah, shit really."

"Well, can I have a gun or something?" Earl asked, picking nervously at his ear lobe.

Mattituck did not like the idea of Earl having a gun, but under the circumstances, he wished he had something in addition to the Glock.

"This is the only gun we have."

"Jim's got a gun locker down below."

"He does?" Mattituck wasn't surprised, but he was surprised at himself that he hadn't thought that Jim would have guns aboard someplace. "Let's check it out."

Before they climbed the ladder below, Mattituck checked the radar. No sign of the 'But Chaser yet. He tucked the Glock into his waistband and followed Earl below. The man knew exactly where to go. He went straight into Jim's stateroom, and into the closet next to the private head. Mattituck paused at the doorway to the stateroom, watching.

"It's locked," Earl said, his voice muffled by the clothes hanging next to the narrow gun locker inside the closet. "Not to worry, though. I know where the key is."

Earl brushed past Mattituck and quickly climbed the ladder to the helm station. He reached under the captain's seat and pulled out a small portable tool box. Inside, he pulled open a small compartment meant to house screws or drill bits, and pulled out a small key. He hurried back down the ladder to the gun locker. The door swung open with a well-oiled silence.

"Bingo!" Earl said, peering into the locker.

Mattituck was peering over his shoulder.

"Damn . . . one's missing," Earl said, indicating two empty spots.

"There's two slots," Mattituck said.

"Jim didin' have that many rifles. Only one's gone."

"You sure?"

"Yes, sir. Sure am. Missing one is his sniper rifle, too. Got a nice scope on it an' everything."

"Sniper rifle?"

"That's what Jim called it. Guess it was like the one he used in the war. He was a sniper in Viet Nam."

"He was?" Mattituck was surprised. He'd known Jim for a while, but never knew he had even served in Viet Nam. "What kind of sniper rifle?"

Earl looked back at him.

"Whado I look like, a gun expert? I got no idea what kinda rifle it was."

"And you want me to leave you with a gun?"

"I don' know vintage sniper guns from deer rifles. Don't mean I cain't shoot."

Mattituck nodded.

"Well, where's he keep the ammo for these others?"

"I dunno."

"You know where the guns are, but not the ammo?" Mattituck asked.

"He usually has the ammo right at the bottom here. Ain't there. I don't know where else he'd keep it."

They searched the stateroom. They went through the dresser drawers, desk and drawers, and the other closet. There were drawers under the bed. Still no ammo boxes.

"Who the fuck has rifles but no ammo?" Mattituck blurted with frustration.

"Jim."

Mattituck looked at him.

"Jim didn't much like guns." He took in the unbelieving expression on Mattituck's face. "I know, hard to believe right? A decorated sniper from Viet Nam? But it's true. I think something that happened there fucked with his head. Jim hated guns. He had them because he felt he had to. He had a handgun, too, come t' think of it. That warn't in the locker neither," he said looking around at the closet with the gun locker.

"Fuck," Mattituck muttered. "Well, I guess that just leaves us with the Glock, then."

He turned and headed to the ladder. Jim Milner must have had the sniper rifle with him when he'd gone ashore in Growler Bay. That meant that he'd been killed by surprise. It also meant that the killer on the 'But Chaser might have that sniper rifle.

He checked the radar when he'd regained the main deck. Still no 'But Chaser. He adjusted the aperature and waited for the radar to cycle back around one full circle. No contacts.

"Where the fuck are you?" he asked, gazing at the screen. "You should've been here by now."

He set the range further out in hopes of seeing a contact in the mouth of the bay. Nothing. Heather Island, which lay between Heather Bay and Columbia Bay, was a very low island—almost a big sand bar with vegetation on it, really. So he looked to see if the radar would pick up any boats on the other side of Heather Island. Where the water was on the other side, there were hundreds of contacts. Ice bergs, he realized. No way he'd be able to pick out a boat over there.

He grabbed the binoculars and his jacket, and stepped onto the aft deck, then went up the ladder to the flying bridge. From there, he climbed atop the small cover over the flying bridge helm station. This had him a solid 15 or more feet above the water, and he figured he could see the other side of Heather Island from here. He scanned the water on the other side, easily picking out the white faces of ice bergs littered in Columbia Bay.

He paused. Was that? . . . He couldn't quite make it out, but it looked like the top of a boat immediately on the other side of the island, as if it were anchored close to shore. Or nosed up on the beach. A pang of panic suddenly gripped his gut. He scanned to see if he could spot anybody on the island. Of course, it could be pleasure boaters, maybe camping on the beach or the island.

He kept scanning. He could see the outlines of low vegetation, and an occasional log or rock. A tall stump at the edge of the near shore caught his attention. It looked almost like a man, but had stumped branches near the top at either side. The top of the stump was oddly rounded, though, and Mattituck could almost swear it was ---

A flash in the middle of the stump confirmed this wasn't a stump. Before he could react, something pulled hard at his right underarm. It pulled so hard at the sleeve of his jacket that it jerked him completely off the narrow flybridge cover. The pull at his jacket was so strong that it spun his body and sent him pitching sideways onto the windshield of the Kimberly Marie. He rolled twice and slid to the bottom of the windshield.

He lay completely still, hoping to look dead. That was a helluva a shot from that distance. And Mattituck knew that he was still in plain view. His only hope was to convince the gunman that he was dead.

As he lay motionless, he listened intently for any sound below. No doubt, Earl had heard Mattituck fall. Unless he'd gone to bed and was already asleep. Mattituck had no way of knowing. All he could hope was that Earl was smart enough to keep out of sight, if he was awake. He opened his eyes, and realized he was on the side of the forward deck that was closest to Heather Island. Fucking luck, he thought. He was completely in view of the gunman. He tried to see the shore without moving his head, but without the binoculars, he couldn't make anything out. The gunman, on the other hand, obviously had a scope and would be able to see Mattituck. And if he had a night scope . . .

Mattituck dared not move a muscle. His thoughts turned to his arm. He had been sure he'd been shot, but he didn't feel anything. Could it be that the bullet had only passed through the jacket's loosely hanging sleeve? It was a Gore Tex jacket, with very heavy material. Would a bullet passing through the sleeve be powerful enough to spin him and throw him off the flying bridge?

And what if the gunman planted another shot into him, just to be sure? He decided to keep to his plan of playing dead. It was his best chance. If he tried to bolt now, he was an easy shot. Better to make the gunman believe he was dead.

He waited several minutes. Complete silence. Nothing moved. Nothing stirred. Mattituck lay completely still and watched the shore of Heather Island. Nothing seemed to move, although he was not at all sure if he'd see anything if it did move. He continued to lay, unmoving.

It felt like he lay there for the better part of twenty minutes when he heard what sounded like a wake. It was the salt-foamy sound of salt water pushing white over the top of salt water. If it was the 'But Chaser, presumably who had shot at him, then Mattituck had clearly missed his chance to do something. The gunman must have run back to the boat on the other side of Heather Island and run back to the mouth of Heather Bay and in. Certainly, it was the killer and the 'But Chaser. And it was too close to try moving now.

What he did do, since his hand lay close to his hip, was reach to see if the Glock were still in his waistband. If it was, then he would defend himself and the Kimberly Marie. He moved his hand slowly, so as not to attract attention. He could hear the wake approaching from a short distance off the bow. He was clearly in view of the approaching boat. Again, he dare not move.

He inched his hand closer to his waistband, increasingly hopeful that the Glock was there. Closer . . . closer. He could feel the top edge of his jeans. Slowly, he moved his fingers along the waistband. Up along the hip, to the back . . .

No Glock. It must have fallen free when he fell. Mattituck fought to keep himself calm. He took three slow, deep breaths as the approaching boat came close to his line of vision. He closed his eyes. Even with the remaining darkness, he could not chance revealing that he was alive. He heard the boat come alongside the Kimberly Marie, then stop. He felt the Kimberly Marie list slightly to the starboard side where the boat presumably had looped a line to secure to the Kimberly Marie.

The killer was aboard. He kept his eyes gently shut. A moment later, he heard steps coming up the starboard side toward him. There was a pause when he was in view of the footsteps. Mattituck guessed the killer was looking at him. Then, just as swiftly, the footsteps moved aft. Apparently, Mattituck looked dead enough. No doubt, it helped that he hadn't budged an inch since the fall. That would be a long time for anybody to play dead. Who would? Mattituck felt lucky he had.

He could hear the killer moving around inside the cabin. It sounded like he might be retrieving the backpacks. Mattituck had found the one at the dinette, but he had no idea whether there had been more. Clearly now, there had been. After a few minutes, he could hear what sounded like back packs being tossed onto the fish deck of the boat alongside—the 'But Chaser. Mattituck considered for a brief second trying to sneak up on the killer, but then thought better of it. That was the kind of move stupid hero-wannabes make. And probably end up dead. In movies or TV, maybe they're successful, but Mattituck figured in real life it was different. He continued to lay perfectly still.

Suddenly, he heard what he'd unconsciously been afraid he might here. A commotion below. All he could hear was muffled voices, one yelling, the other placating. Then it was quiet. A moment later, he heard voices in the cabin, then more clearly as they stepped out on the aft deck.

"You going to shoot me?" he heard Earl ask.

"If you do something stupid, yeah. Fuck yeah," a gravely voice replied.

"What are you---"

"Get on the other boat," the killer ordered.

"What?"

"Get – on – the – other – fucking boat, ass wipe," the killer said, his teeth clenched.

Mattituck felt the Kimberly Marie shift as Earl presumably hopped across the gunwales, followed by the killer.

"Lay down." Then a moment later: "Lay the *fuck* down, goddammit!"

"Okay, okay," Earl replied. "Is he . . . is he dead?"

Mattituck guessed that the pause had been Earl noticing Mattituck lying presumably dead.

"No, he's sleeping very nicely. Like a fucking little baby. I'm sure he'll wake up any fucking minute, wanting his fucking bottle," the killer sneered.

Still, Mattituck lay absolutely still.

He heard the 'But Chaser's motor start. Then the click of the gear being engaged. The engine whirred up loudly and Mattituck heard the boat picking up speed toward the mouth of Heather Bay. He opened his eyes and slowly moved his head so he could see. Sure enough, it was the 'But Chaser, slicing a smooth, straight wake out of the bay. He could see the killer at the helm, half turned so he could watch Earl on the fish deck while he piloted the boat. Earl's hands appeared to be bound behind his back.

The man driving the 'But Chaser was a murderer, and had just supposedly killed another man in Mattituck. Why the fuck, Mattituck wondered, would he take a hostage?

Chapter Twenty-One

The Chase

AST 32067 made a sharp turn to the right as it passed Elf Point and entered Heather Bay. Todd sat upright behind the helm as he gained a good view straight up the bay and eased AST 32067 out of the turn and put her on a course up the middle of the bay. Several hundred yards ahead, he could see the Kimberly Marie, anchored a short distance offshore Heather Island. He scanned quickly with the binoculars, but could see no other vessels. He checked the radar, searching for the 'But Chaser, but didn't see her. He thought briefly of turning around and patrolling Columbia Bay, but decided against it.

Where was the 'But Chaser?

He suddenly realized how much he'd expected to come up behind the 'But Chaser as it approached the Kimberly Marie, and felt dumb for having put so much stock in that assumption. Why had he been so stock-sure in his expectation?

As he closed in on the Kimberly Marie, a figure emerged from the cabin onto the aft deck. The Kimberly Marie had shifted on her anchor so that her port side was exposed to Todd, and he could see it was Frank, now waving at him to approach. He slowed AST 32067 and pulled open the side window. He poked his head out, his hand still on the helm as AST 32067 eased her hull off step and deeper into the water. She slowed to 5kts as she approached.

"You okay?" Todd shouted instinctively.

"Yeah," came the shouted reply. "I think so."

Mattituck helped Todd tie up alongside the Kimberly Marie. Todd stepped up onto AST 32067's gunwale and then onto the Kimberly Marie. Mattituck clasped his hand as they came together.

"Have you seen the 'But Chaser?" Todd asked.

"Um, yep . . . sure have." Mattituck tried to hold up his right arm.

Todd saw the torn jacket and blood stains.

"What the---?"

"The guy shot me. Well, sorta," Mattituck said.

Todd was stunned.

"Shot you? What---? How did . . . ? Where is he?"

"He bolted with the 'But Chaser out of the bay about 45 minutes ago. He came aboard and took his backpacks, and then left."

"He left you alive? What happened?"

"He thought I was dead, actually. He shot me from Heather Island. Long story," he said to Todd's increasingly perplexed expression.

"Heather Island? What the hell was he doing on Heather Island?"

"I'm guessing he didn't want to attract attention by approaching. I think he figured he'd just kill whoever was on board, then all would be clear for him to come aboard without any trouble, get his backpacks, and move on."

Todd watched him, disbelief emitting from every pore of his face.

">

"Oh, two things. I think the gun he used was Jim's. There's a Viet Nam sniper rifle missing from his gun locker below. Did you know Jim was a sniper in Viet Nam?"

Todd ignored the question. "How do you know all this?"

"That's the other thing. Earl—you remember the town drunk who sleeps on the bow?"

Todd nodded.

"He was asleep in one of the state rooms when I got underway, so he's been along for the fun."

"Why didn't you tell me when we were on the radio?"

"The 'But Chaser was right behind me. I didn't want him to know there was more than just me aboard."

"Where's Earl now? Below?"

"Nope. He's on the 'But Chaser."

Todd leaned back onto the gunwale.

"Shit . . ." he said.

"Right?"

They left the Kimberly Marie anchored and locked up, and set out aboard AST 32067 in pursuit of the 'But Chaser. Since Todd had not seen her on his approach to Heather Bay, they knew that she was headed west, very likely bound for Whittier.

Todd had Mattituck driving the boat at first so he could dress his gunshot wound. The blood had dried the shirt under the jacket to his skin, requiring care and patience to expose the wound so it could be treated. Complicating this was the fact that the helm station was located—as it was most boats—on the starboard side, or on the right. Since the wound was on Mattituck's right, he had to stand in the middle of the boat, to the left of the helm, and face the starboard side while steering with his left hand. Todd sat in the captain's chair with the medical kit in his lap.

"Fuck!" Mattituck yelped when Todd pulled again at the dried shirt.

"Don't be a baby. I thought you were a tough charter boat captain."

"Fuck you," Mattituck said irritably.

"So some news for you," Todd said, then gave a downward yank to the sleeve.

"God *damn* it!"

"Your boat's been picked up and is being transported to dry dock in Kodiak."

"Kodiak? Really?"

"Good shipyard there. They'll have the DeeVee8 all fixed up and ready to go back to work in no time."

Mattituck nodded. "Thanks for taking care of that."

Todd said "no problem" as he ducked under Mattituck's arm to get a better look.

"You are one lucky guy, Frank."

Mattituck looked at him.

"You were shot right through the arm. I mean, as in all the way through." He whistled. "Wow," he added. "And you didn't know this?"

"Well," Mattituck replied. "It did knock me off my ass. Spun me around and knocked me down. I thought it had just pulled hard on the jacket sleeve."

"Bullets go *through* clothes, Frank—not pick you up and toss you."

"Well . . . but I didn't really feel anything."

"Shock."

"For hours?"

"Yep. It happens." He grinned and looked at Mattituck. "That or maybe you really are a tough charter boat captain."

"Fuck . . . off."

Todd leaned back and pulled gauze out of the pack, then dumped a clear liquid onto it. He reached up with it and began cleaning the wound. Mattituck winced and in seconds felt tears welling in his eyes. He fought back the urge to curse.

"Go ahead," Todd said smiling. "Let it all out, Tough Skipper."

Mattituck turned a cold glare at him.

"Oh, yeah," Todd said, noticing. "That says it *all*."

"Fuck you. Just. . . . fucking fuck you, fuckhead."

"This will be the only time you get to call me a fuckhead, dickhead," Todd retorted with a grin. "I'm considering it temporary insanity."

Mattituck turned his attention to the sea ahead. They were moving at 50kts, steering in an arch south to avoid the cluster of icebergs. They were fortunate in that a south breeze had been blowing for several hours, pushing the ice north, back up to the head of the bay and against Columbia Glacier. Still, bergie bits could be anywhere, and many of them were translucent, making them invisible as they bobbed in the water. Occasionally, there was a bang on the aluminum center hull as AST 32067 hit one. Normally, such transiting would be putting a boat's propellers at risk, as they were normally fully exposed on the sides and part of the bottom behind the lower unit of the outboard motor. But the Trooper boats were equipped with a prop guard that fit over the entire prop, and which allowed the water to pass through without exposing the props to debris.

Still, Mattituck figured, it was better not to tempt fate. He steered around the bergie bits he could see—at least, as best he could at that high speed.

Mattituck looked down to see what Todd was doing. He was applying temporary bandage stitches to the entry and exit holes.

"Aren't you going to sew me up like a Rambo?"

Todd shook his head. "I can't sew. I can't iron, either. And I sure as hell don't do windows."

Mattituck smiled.

"When you're done, take the helm and I'll plot us out and see if I can pick up the 'But Chaser on radar."

"Sounds like a plan," Todd replied, opening a small pill vial. "Here, take this."

"What is it?"

"Painkillers."

"I'm all right," Mattituck said, lying. The arm had been throbbing since soon after the shooting.

"Take them. It's not an option. I'm going to need you alert and undistracted."

Mattituck nodded and took the pills.

"What are they?" he asked Todd.

"Codeine boosted acetaminophen. If that doesn't help, we can try morphine. But not until the action's past."

"I won't need it."

"Ever been shot?"

"No."

"Then shut up."

They rode some time in silence as Mattituck first adjusted the radar several times to see if he could identify any contacts ahead. Unfortunately, they were not even half way across Columbia Bay and there were countless icebergs interfering. A radar could not distinguish between an iceberg and a boat—both came back as contacts. Giving up, he searched the chart tubes and found NOAA chart 16700, Prince William Sound. He grabbed a protractor lying on the dash and a ruler.

"Got a calculator?"

"Someplace, yeah."

Mattituck slouched his shoulders at him.

"Um," Todd said under the critical gaze, "try the drawer on the right of the sink there in the galley."

It was there. Mattituck sat at the tiny table in front of the passenger seat and unrolled the chart to the area between Columbia Bay and Whittier. First, he measured the distance at just under 70 nautical miles. He had estimated that the 'But Chaser had a 45 minute jump on them. Crap, he thought. Probably closer to an hour. If the 'But Chaser could make 25 or 30 knots . . . he punched the keys on the calculator. With the speed of AST 32067, they might just be able to catch up to the 'But Chaser before arriving in Whittier.

"I think we might catch him," he said.

Todd looked at him.

"Good news," he said. "I was afraid they got too much of a jump on us."

"Nope. Lucky us. Well, and thanks to your Speedy Gonzalez boat here."

Mattituck continued plotting. He tracked a time plot in red pencil for the 'But Chaser, and in regular pencil for AST 32067. He used a speed of 30kts for the 'But Chaser, and 50kts for AST 32067 for the first plot, then did another for the 'But Chaser at 25kts. As a last plot, in part for good measure and in part because he liked plotting, he did a plot for the 'But Chaser at 35kts even though he was sure she couldn't make that speed.

He laid down the pencils and protractor, and let his head fall back to stretch his neck.

"Well?" Todd asked.

"We'll catch her all right. Someplace along the crossing of Port Wells. There's a small chance it'll be closer to Decision Point, at the entrance to the channel into Whittier, but my best guess is toward the other side of Port Wells."

Todd nodded.

"Good," he said.

"AST 32067, AST 32067, this is Glennallen, over."

It was the High Frequency radio, on the State Trooper frequency. Todd unclipped the mic from the headboard and keyed it.

"Glennallen, AST 32067, over."

"Hey, Todd. Just wanted to let you know your man in the hospital might be waking up soon. His vitals have changed in the direction of coming out of it."

"Ah," Todd said. "That's good news. We're chasing the other suspect into Whittier. We anticipate intercepting him around Port Wells. Any chance of getting some air backup?"

"I'll check and get back to you. I know our helicopter is in Fairbanks. It'd have to be Coast Guard or Air Force."

"Shit," Todd said to Mattituck. "That means no gunfire from above. All they can do is watch us."

He keyed the mic again.

"I guess either will work just as well."

"Roger. I'll see who can scramble. How long until you need them on site?"

Todd looked over at Mattituck.

"An hour would be best," Mattituck said, "a little more than that at most."

Todd relayed this, then signed off.

They rode in silence for several minutes. Mattituck got up and went out to the aft deck. The ride was smooth on the protected waters between Long Bay and Glacier Island. He breathed deeply, enjoying the crispness of the salt-edge air. He closed his eyes for a moment, steady on his feet and leaning slightly toward the bow of the boat, accommodating the nose-up angle of AST 32067 as she barreled along on step. The twin Honda 250s hummed smoothly and churned the briny waters into a foam. He opened his eyes and admired the low rooster tail the motors kicked up.

His eyes turned to the starboard side, along the north side of the channel. He loved this stretch of water. The high, sandstone look of the cliffs rising crisply from the water and towering 400 feet up always amazed him. This was the only place he knew where this geologic feature was on Prince William Sound, and the look of it along with its rarity never failed to impress itself on him. Along the tops of the cliffs were thick stands of conifers, topping the beige cliffs with a dark-green spiked hair look. He smiled at the image. These cliffs were punkers.

He pulled an empty 5-gallon bucket to the cabin, turned it upside down, and sat down on it. He closed his eyes for a moment, still except as the speeding AST 32067 gently rose and eased through the water. The Honda outboards hummed in his ears, and he drew in the clean air. He opened his eyes and watched the water zipping along the other side of the boat, mesmerized as if watching the flames of a fire on a cool summer evening.

"Frank, I think we may be catching up," Todd hollered from the helm nearly an hour later.

Mattituck hadn't moved since he sat down. All the nerves in his butt were dead, it felt like, so he took a moment to stretch and kick each leg, hoping to shake the sleep out of his ass. He stepped into the cabin and walked up to stand next to Todd. He looked into the radar screen first and located a contact moving at a steady speed as it approached the big bay called Port Wells.

"This seems too early," he said.

Todd didn't answer. He just handed him the binoculars. Mattituck peered through and adjusted the focus. He immediately picked up a smaller sport fisher. It was hard to tell from straight behind, but it looked like a blue hull. It did look like the 'But Chaser.

"How long for the helo? Did you hear back from them?"

"Yeah," Todd replied. "They're finally enroute, but they're at least a half hour away."

"Coast Guard?"

"Air National Guard."

Mattituck began the work of tracking the 'But Chaser—assuming it really was the 'But Chaser. He set the range finder to the contact and waited through several cycles of the readings. They were definitely closing pretty fast on the vessel. He grabbed the calculator and began punching in estimates from the distance between AST 32067 and the contact, subtracting the distance and calculating how fast AST 32067 was moving compared to the 'But Chaser. He double-checked his figures, then put the calculator on the dash.

"We'll be on him pretty quickly," he announced.

"I figured. It looked like we were coming in pretty fast. This is a bit sooner than you'd figured earlier, eh?"

"Quite a bit, yeah."

They were quiet as they gazed ahead to the 'But Chaser.

"Want me to take the helm?"

"Yeah. Be better if we have a gun on him when we approach. I'm going to guess that he won't hesitate to shoot at us."

Todd stepped off the captain's chair and Mattituck slid on, taking the helm. He loved running this boat. It was extremely agile on the water, particularly on smooth seas like this. The rush of the speed was accentuated by AST 32067's relatively low profile on the water. Unlike the DeeVee8, which sat significantly higher with the eye level approximately 8 feet above the water, AST 32067 was closer to 4 or 5 feet. It was like driving a low profile Corvette or Maserati, as opposed to a high suspension four-wheel-drive pickup.

"Do we turn on the lights?" Mattituck asked.

"No. No reason to attract attention. When we get close and hail him, we will. Right now, I don't think we want him to speed up."

Mattituck nodded. That made perfect sense, he thought.

Todd readied two Colt AR-15 rifles. He checked their chambers, locked their magazines in place, then began loading backup magazines from several boxes of ammo he had stored in the gun locker at the aft cabin. He set the rifles on their butts within the rack between the captain's and passenger seats, and secured the arm at the top, designed to hold the weapons in place during rough seas. The rifles were within easy reach. He then retrieved two Gen4 22 Glocks from the gun locker and went through the same routine of checking and loading them. When all was ready, he handed one to Mattituck. Mattituck took the black hand gun and slipped it into his waistband.

They were closing very fast on the 'But Chaser, and as they came into better visibility, Mattituck picked up the binoculars and checked. There was no doubt now it was the 'But Chaser.

"It's her all right," he said.

Todd took the binoculars and brought the 'But Chaser into view. He set them down on the dash and went aft to a storage bin. He returned a moment later with two bullet-proof vests.

"Here," he said, holding one out.

Mattituck took it. It had never occurred to him he would wear one, but he was glad now—particularly after being shot—that Todd had an extra. He put it on awkwardly, evoking chuckles from Todd, who finally helped him put it on correctly.

"Feels tight," Mattituck complained.

"It's supposed to be." He fixed a bemused look on Mattituck. "Quit your belly-aching. This thing might save your life."

"True enough," Mattituck acknowledged.

They were well within view of the 'But Chaser now, less than a mile behind. Todd was watching the boat through the binoculars.

"Looks like he might have Earl tied up on the fish deck."

He reached to the dash under the helm and flipped the switch for the flashing blue lights. Then he reached for the mic on the VHF radio.

"'But Chaser, 'But Chaser . . . Alaska State Troopers, channel 16, over."

No response.

"'But Chaser, this is the Alaska State Trooper vessel coming up on your stern, over."

He was watching ahead through the binoculars with the other hand.

"I can see him leaning down and looking back at us," he said to Mattituck.

"'But Chaser, this is the State Troopers. Haul up and prepare to be boarded.'"

The 'But Chaser's bow began to rise, then settled as she gained a steady speed on step. She was picking up speed.

"She's running," Mattituck said. "Dumb fuck. He can't out run us."

"He doesn't know that," Todd said, still watching through the binoculars.

He adjusted the focus.

"Jesus," his voice had an edge of disgust. "He has Earl's eyes taped. Looks like duct tape."

"His eyes taped shut? What the fuck for?"

Todd shook his head. "This guy's sick," was all he said.

He picked up one of the AR-15s.

"Well, doesn't look like he's going to just pull over for us."

The middle windshield was also a door to the bow, and Todd opened it but didn't step out. He kneeled against the step to the door and took aim, releasing the safety as he did. Mattituck was surprised. Was Todd really going to shoot?

He pulled the gun up and reached for the mic. They were only 400 yards astern now. Mattituck could clearly see the low rooster tail kicked up by the 'But Chaser's prop. He could see Earl, his head steady and unturning. He probably couldn't hear anything over the twin outboards, so there was nothing to take interest in or turn his head toward.

Todd reached again for the mic.

"'But Chaser, 'But Chaser, this is the Alaska State Troopers, directly astern your vessel at the present time. Haul up and bring your vessel to a stop."

"Why even bother with that?" Mattituck asked.

"I have to. We have to give him every opportunity to stop."

He keyed the mic again.

"'But Chaser, this is the Alaska State Troopers, channel 16. You are hereby ordered to respond."

No answer.

Todd flipped a switch on the radio unit, then keyed the mic.

"'But Chaser, 'But Chaser," Todd's voice boomed from a loudspeaker outside, someplace on the top of the forward cabin. Mattituck saw Earl's head turn toward them. Clearly the loudspeaker was loud enough to be heard aboard the 'But Chaser.

"'But Chaser, this is the Alaska State Troopers," he said again, his voice booming loudly outside.

Sitting low in the fish deck of the 'But Chaser, Earl shifted and tried to gain his knees under him.

Todd leveled the AR-15 in the forward opening again, taking aim. Without further warning, he fired. Instantly, the starboard cabin window shattered and fell free.

"A warning shot," Todd said.

"Warning shot? You took out the cabin window right behind where the fucker's sitting. You may have hit him!"

Todd grinned.

"So the seas pitched the boat a little and I didn't hit my mark," he said sardonically.

Mattituck watched him, trying to read whether Todd was serious.

Suddenly, Earl was on his feet, and a gun was at his head. The killer was in the doorway to the cabin, clutching Earl close in front of him. Earl appeared frozen, afraid to move.

"Damn," Todd said. "Guess I didn't accidentally hit him." There was no humor in his voice.

Mattituck steered to the starboard side of the 'But Chaser. They were less than 200 feet now, and approaching too quickly to the stern of the 'But Chaser. He eased back on the throttle and held a speed even with the 'But Chaser's. He held steady on course and waited for instructions from Todd.

Two or three minutes passed. Nothing changed. AST 32067 held position, and the killer kept the gun on Earl's head. Finally, the gun floated out from Earl's head and moved downward slowly, then up fast, and back down slowly. Then it gestured back toward Columbia Bay. The message was clear: Get back.

"What do you want me to do?" Mattituck asked.

"Hold steady. He's not in charge here."

A minute more passed.

Todd leveled the AR-15's barrel at the 'But Chaser. Mattituck was sure the killer could see the black barrel pointing straight at him.

He could. The pistol came away from Earl's head and pointed at AST 32067. Mattituck saw a flash. He saw and heard nothing. The bullet must have flown past altogether.

He heard the pop of the AR-15, then saw the tell-tale white flip of salt water several dozen feet beyond the 'But Chaser's stern.

"Was that on purpose?" he asked Todd.

"Trying to take out the outboard," he answered.

Another pop, then another. One bullet went high again, and the other burrowed into the hull under the fish deck gunwale.

The killer responded with two more shots at AST 32067, and the port window aft crackled with the sound of splintering glass. Mattituck swung his head to look, and saw the bullet hole in the glass, surrounded by a spider web pattern of cracked glass.

Earl's body moving to the port side of the fish deck pulled Mattituck's attention back to the 'But Chaser.

"What the----?" he muttered.

The killer half lifted and half pushed Earl over the side. A huge splash was visible as his body hit the water.

"Jesus!" Todd shouted. He kept his eyes on where Earl went in.

"Cut back! Cut back!" he barked at Mattituck.

As soon as Mattituck had eased on the throttle, Todd yelled for him to come around. He was pointing at the spot where Earl had gone into the water. Mattituck swung the helm to the port, turning away from the pursuit of the 'But Chaser. Todd kept his arm extended, his finger holding the spot where Earl was in the water. Mattituck scanned the water where he was pointing, but saw nothing.

God! he thought, *he must be under the water!*

They were at a very slow speed now, perhaps 10kts, as AST 32067 turned her starboard quarter on the 'But Chaser. Mattituck couldn't believe this was happening. Were they really going to lose this guy *again*, after being so close to nailing him?

Todd was taking off the heavy vest. Mattituck looked aft to see where the 'But Chaser was. She was making good headway toward Whittier. Unless they could scoop Earl up right away and get back on the 'But

Chaser, the fucker was probably going to get away. Again.

"Do you see him?" he asked Todd.

Todd's head shook as he pulled his second boot off. He had never taken his eyes off the spot Earl had gone in the water. He stepped out onto the bow, looking intently ahead as they approached the spot.

"I still don't see him," he shouted back at Mattituck.

Mattituck was ready to disengage the props.

"Be ready to pop the clutch out when I tell you," Todd hollered.

"Ready now," Mattituck said, wanting Todd to know he'd already thought of this. It would be a gruesome end to Earl if they ran him over with the props engaged.

"Disengage!" Todd yelled.

Mattituck pulled the throttled to the mid point and felt them pop into the neutral position. He heard the pitch of the Hondas change as they went into an idle.

He removed the vest and joined Todd on the bow. They each assumed a spot forward and on each side as AST 32067 slowed in her headway, continuing forward at 2 or 3kts and slowing. Nothing. They couldn't see Earl anywhere.

Mattituck climbed over the windshields and onto the roof of AST 32067's cabin. Keeping his eyes scanning the water, he removed his boots, then shirt and pants.

As he walked back and forth across the roof of the boat, he pulled his socks off. He was now only wearing boxer briefs as he searched the waters. Earl would not survive long in these cold waters, especially with his hands bound and duct tape over his mouth and eyes. The man was underwater, unable to move, and unable to guess which way was up.

A movement about 8 feet under water caught his attention, and with lightning instinct, Mattituck dove into the water, cutting through the freezing salt water to the body he was sure he'd seen. Within a moment, his hands bumped a soft, but heavy something. He moved his increasingly cold fingers and felt cloth. Earl! He grasped at the clothing and pulled him upward. The body jerked, but then relaxed. Mattituck had no idea whether it was a death throe or if Earl knew he needed to force himself to relax in order to survive. Maybe he knew he'd been touched by someone, and knew to relax and trust the person to get him to the surface.

He pulled at the body, and drew it to his chest. Then he kicked toward the surface. He could feel his lungs beginning to scream for oxygen, and he kicked again with both legs. Slowing, they began to rise. Earl remained calm—or unconscious. Mattituck had no way of knowing which.

They broke the surface. Immediately, his legs still kicking to keep them both afloat, he reached up and ripped the duct tape from Earl's mouth. The man sucked at the air. Mattituck spun his head around, looking for AST 32067. His head bumped the hull, and he felt a hand grasp his arm.

White pain flashed through his brain, blinding him. Todd had grasped his wounded arm.

"Fuck!" he yelled.

"Sorry, buddy," Todd said. "Can't let you go yet. Bear it!" he yelled, almost into Mattituck's ear.

It helped to focus Mattituck against the pain. Todd's hand slid along his arm to his hand and pulled it upward, out of the water.

"I know it hurts, but you need to hang onto the gunwale. I need to get him aboard," Todd said.

Mattituck was trying to focus his vision, but he still could only see white pain. He focused his attention on keeping his hold on Earl with one arm around the man, and with the other hanging onto the gunwale of the boat. He blinked several times, clearing the salt water from his eyes. Finally, he could see. The pain in his arm made his entire right side numb, but he forced himself to remain focused. He watched as Todd, lying on the bow and leaning over the side, wrapped a line around Earl's body. He brought the ends of the line up under Earl's arms, creating a makeshift cradle. He tied it off in front of Earl's chest, then disappeared a moment. Mattituck felt Earl's weight lift, and he looked up to see Todd standing on the bow, pulling on the line and lifting Earl's body out of the water. With each pull, he shortened the length between his hands and Earl's chest.

After several pulls, he had Earl high enough that he was able to grasp the knot at Earl's chest and haul him onto the bow.

"You okay?" Todd asked.

A cough, followed by silence.

"Good," Todd said, apparently answering a nod from Earl.

Todd's face emerged over the gunwale.

"Okay, Frank. I'm going to pull you aboard now. It's going to hurt like hell, man, but hang in there, okay?"

Mattituck nodded. As he felt Todd grasp his underarms, he felt suddenly utterly exhausted. With a lurch, his body rose out of the water and dropped painfully onto the bow.

Then all went black.

Skipper's Oath

Chapter Twenty-Two

The Waking

Mattituck awoke to the hum of the twin Honda 250s. His vision was askew, and everything was swimming. He felt like he was floating, and the drone of the engines only contributed to the feeling. Also, the slow rise and fall of the bow of the boat. It all made him feel . . . floating. He felt happy and calm. He kept his head still, afraid to move too fast.

"Uhhh..." he said, meaning to say the word 'Todd.'

"It's okay, Frank." Todd's voice. "Lie still. We'll be in port in a few minutes."

"Man, you are my fucking *he*-ro," came another voice, drifting like a kite in a soft breeze. "You fucking saved my life!"

Must be Earl, Mattituck's brain floated the thought across his consciousness.

"Um, muh, fuh. . . ."

Todd laughed lightly.

"Can't understand you, buddy. I shot you up with morphine. Sorry. I know you don't like it. But I need to get you to the hospital without going all sour on me."

Mattituck nodded his understanding, not bothering with words anymore. He lay his head back on whatever it was on. It didn't matter to him what it was. It felt secure and firm. *Good enough for me*, he thought with an overwhelming peace. It was warm where he was, and he was being rocked with a nice purring sound. He closed his eyes and passed out again.

Mattituck awoke again as Todd steered AST 32067 into the harbor. He could hear a helicopter over head. He turned his head from where he still lie on the bench seat and saw Earl in the passenger seat, then with a slight turn of the head, Todd at the helm. His head was still swimming. Damn Todd for giving him morphine.

"I hate this shit," he said.

"What's that?" came Todd's voice.

Mattituck slowly turned his head from side to side.

"I said I really really really hate this shit."

"I know you do. I had to give it to you."

"No you fucking didn't. Jesus."

Earl was watching him.

"Man, I owe you my fucking life. You know that?"

"No you don't," Mattituck replied. "We're cool. You'd do the same for me."

"Don't matter. If I did it for you, you'd owe me your life. But it's the other way around. I swear to fucking high heaven, I will do anything for you, man."

Mattituck sat up, supporting his head with his hands on his forehead.

"No, you really don't need to. Seriously."

"Why don't you two argue about this another time?" Todd said. "Are you clear enough to talk?"

"Yeah, I'll be fine in a minute," Mattituck said.

"Good. So here's what you've missed. Interesting turn of events. Our guy in the hospital is awake. He's refusing to talk, but I've asked that we be the first to talk to him. So we're set there. Next, the helicopter came on scene, but too late to follow the 'But Chaser into port. They did find her tied up here, but our suspect was gone by then. He was tied up without even bothering to check in with the harbormaster. He just sailed in and tied up. Grabbed all his stuff and took off. I already had the police search the boat for black backpacks. None."

"Okay," Mattituck said, unsure where this was going.

"So, my guess is that our suspect has no intention of coming back to the 'But Chaser. He took all his stuff with him. Including his guns."

Mattituck shook his head with disbelief. "Again, he gets away and we have no clue where he's going."

Todd nodded. "He's one lucky guy."

They tied up at the Whittier Harbormaster slip, next to the office. Mattituck lay on the bench, still feeling like he was floating aimlessly around the ionosphere. Todd had checked his wound before leaving him to walk up to the Harbormaster's office to borrow the computer. A ground unit from the Troopers was in Girdwood and had been sent to Whittier to pick them up and transport them to the hospital in Anchorage. There, Todd figured, Frank could be treated properly while he paid a visit to the newly awakened suspect. Meantime, he wanted to start writing the reports and save some time on that later.

"They have a Trooper unit heading over to pick you up?" Glenn Carter, the harbormaster asked.

"Yeah, out of Girdwood."

Todd had known Glenn for a long time. Early in Todd's career, he had been assigned to the Kenai area, patrolling the "combat fishing" on the Kenai river. The term came from the overcrowding of anglers along the river banks, standing almost shoulder to shoulder, hoping to hook a famous Kenai River king salmon. His territory included the Kenai Peninsula from Kenai over to Seward, and north to Whittier. The time he spent in the Whittier area, on the northwestern edge of Prince William Sound, is what had made him request a transfer to Valdez when the previous Trooper had retired. The pristine nature of Prince William Sound, and the relatively undiscovered status of it, had drawn him.

Now, sitting in the harbormaster's office, summarizing the events in this case so far, he was struck by just how elusive the loose suspect was. He had escaped them no less than three times—four or five, it could be argued with a looser definition of "nearly caught." But Todd was not sure that the man was lucky. Not sure at all. There were too many indicators that the man was very experienced in the outdoors—both on land and sea—and could handle himself very well.

First of all, there was the marksman shooting of Wayne Barrett near Yakutat, and the precisely placed shots on the DeeVee8 in Zaikof Bay. Frank Mattituck had said he was sure it was the shorter of the two men who had been firing the rifle at him as he and the DeeVee8 approached the Kimberly Marie in Zaikof Bay. Todd himself had seen how good of a shot the man was as he inspected the beached DeeVee8 before chasing the suspects into Montague Island. Even a good shot could not have hit precisely where he wanted to that many times.

Second, this suspect knew his way around a boat. Even if it had been the suspect in the hospital who had navigated them north from southeast Alaska, this guy had been handling the boat and the navigation very well since. On land, the man knew how to traverse over unmarked territory, and he seemed very comfortable with being in the wildnerness.

Third, the suspect was in excellent physical condition. He had kept a nearly stunning pace as he hunted Frank, and then shifted to escaping to Rocky Bay. Which also brought up the point that the man knew exactly where he was hiking to. At the time, Todd had thought that the man had made a mistake, exiting farther north than where he'd entered the island. But now he was certain the route had been intentional. He knew that someone had been bringing up the rear and avoided returning to Zaikof Bay.

And there was the bear attack. One of the things he hoped to learn from the awakened suspect in the hospital was how exactly the bear attack had happened. When Todd had observed the two suspects pursuing Frank on Montague, the shorter one was usually leading the way. How was it, then, that he escaped the bear? If he were leading, he should have been the easier target for the bear.

Fourth, there was the escape in Orca Bay, outside of Cordova. Now, that was luck, Todd thought. If AST 41448's engine hadn't failed, they would have had the guy there. Of course, Todd reasoned, maybe a skill the suspect had might have gotten him out of that situation as well.

Finally, there was today. That was clearly skill. Purely premeditated skill. Todd had been wondering why the suspect had taken Earl hostage, but now it was clear the man was simply guarding against the chance he might be followed. With the Trooper boat right behind him, he had known that if he threw his hostage overboard, the Trooper would have to stop and rescue him. He knew his hostage was a ticket for escape.

Todd gazed out the window at that thought. How sure am I, he wondered, that the suspect didn't think he'd been identified the other night on the Kimberly Marie?

"Shit," he said aloud, the realization hitting him without warning. He then looked around to see if Glenn was looking. The harbormaster was busy working in his books, transcribing information into the computer.

I can't believe the obvious didn't hit me, he thought. He'd been so focused on the fact that the suspect had thought he'd shot Earl dead the other night, that he was overlooking the fact that the shot had attracted attention from a lot of people in nearby slips. Todd shook his head, feeling stupid. Or tired. It was a sign of fatigue. The suspect *did* have good reason to think he'd be chased today.

Todd tried to think of everything from the suspect's perspective. So he'd been aboard the Kimberly Marie trying to get his backpacks, and had been interrupted. He shot Earl—or thought he had—and seen the dead man fall overboard. The dead Earl had been shot while aboard the Kimberly Marie, and the Kimberly Marie had obviously been identified as a boat of interest to the law. There was no missing that after the Zaikof Bay incident. Very likely, the suspect knew the Kimberly Marie was being watched. If not before the supposed shooting of Earl, definitely afterward.

So again, looking at it from the suspect's view, it became absolutely certain that the Kimberly Marie was a trap. Why would a vessel so heavily involved in a murder and chase be getting underway? Todd shook his head again. Why hadn't he thought of all that earlier? The suspect knew. He'd known through the whole set-up. But that didn't change the fact that he needed to get the backpacks. So he'd followed the Kimberly Marie, then nosed up to shore on the other side of Heather Island. Shit, they'd even said in their stupid "undercover" conversation on the radio that the Kimberly Marie was bound for Heather Bay. So the suspect had had plenty of time to look at the charts and plan out his next moves. He'd had hours, in fact.

He'd nosed the 'But Chaser up to Heather Island on the other side, knowing he was invisible to radar due to the icebergs, and then walked the short distance across the island to watch the Kimberly Marie. And watch her as he obviously had. He would have had a chance to observe, completely invisible and knowing anybody on board would be watching for him to come into the bay. They never would have thought he might try to sneak up on them.

So he'd watched. He'd sat there and watched. Since Earl had been asleep below, he'd concluded it was just Mattituck aboard. When the opportunity came, and he was sure there was only one person aboard the Kimberly Marie, he'd taken him out with the sniper rifle from Jim Milner's gun locker.

A thought occurred to Todd. That meant that the man knew the rifle was a sniper rifle. He would have had to recognize while sizing up Jim's guns that this one was for sniper work, not deer hunting.

A chill ran through Todd. That might mean the suspect was a military man—or former military anyway.

He mulled this over, mixing in what he knew of the apparent skills this suspect had. He ran back through how the man had handled himself. The conditioning he appeared to have. His multiple abilities. And then another thought that had been nagging him since Howie Long, the Cordova Police chief, had told him about it. Howie had said he'd seen Tom Graffinino, the Cordova harbormaster, and Tom had taken a beating. It was noteworthy, Howie had said, because in the years the chief had known Tom Graffinino, a 240 pound, solid and tough man—a mean man, many would say—he had never known Tom to have that many marks and swelling from a beating on his face. The one time that came close, Tom had taken three men in a bar, and while they'd laid some solid shots on him, he had all three roiling on the hard wood floor within a few minutes. And even then, his face had not been as roughed up as he had the other day.

Todd sat back in the chair and rubbed his forehead.

The timing of this had been mere hours after Todd and Frank had set out after the 'But Chaser. Now, piecing all this together, Todd became convinced that Tom Graffinino had lied to him. He had seen the suspect. And the suspect had beat the shit out of him. Tom was not the kind of guy to admit that. And now, sitting in Whittier recollecting the scene just after the suspect had departed in the 'But Chaser, Todd could not remember what Tom had looked like at the time.

In fact, he couldn't remember seeing his face at all. He and Frank had only been in the Harbormaster's Office for a few minutes, and Tom had not turned around from the desk when he spoke with them. Todd had thought it odd at the time, but had been too distracted by the need to get underway after the 'But Chaser to consider it. But now, he was sure that Tom had intentionally kept his face turned away so Todd and Frank wouldn't see it. He'd probably tried to stop the suspect, and had his ass handed to him.

Todd continued staring out the window at the tree-covered mountain behind Whittier, lost in his thoughts. The more he thought about this, the more sure he was that for at least much of the time, the suspect had been a step or two ahead of them. At first, perhaps, the suspect hadn't known they were on his tail. But in the past day or so, he most certainly had. And when he'd found Earl aboard the Kimberly Marie this morning, he had probably been surprised, but turned the unexpected into an advantage. With his hands bound and his mouth and eyes duct-taped shut, Earl was no threat while on the 'But Chaser. And if the suspect found he was being pursued, he could toss the man overboard and increase his chances for escape.

And this contingency plan had worked perfectly. When he'd thrown Earl overboard, Todd and Frank had no choice but to cut off the chase and pick up Earl. The way he was bound, in fact, meant Earl would slip under water and delay them longer—hence the cruelty of the binding. The suspect had bound him that way precisely because it meant Earl would serve as an extended delay.

Todd had to admire the intelligence and adaptability of this suspect. The man was no mindless criminal. He was, in fact, beginning to fit a profile. The disillusioned ex-military man—perhaps having served a tour or two or three in the Gulf or Afghanistan—returned home to a place where he no longer belonged. If a special ops sniper, he may have become a killing machine who found himself unable to adjust back to normal life. He was now immersed in a kind of war of his own. A war of survival. Not just physical and financial survival, but psychological survival.

Todd's cell rang.

"Benson here."

"Hey, Todd. Johnson in Anchorage. We have a unit coming your way. He just passed through the tunnel and is rolling into Whittier now."

"Good, thanks."

"You said your assistant is injured?"

"Yeah, that's right."

"They're ready for him at the hospital. Smitty's going to run you in Code Red."

That meant full siren.

"Not necessary, but good speed would be helpful."

"I'll let you work that out with Smitty."

Ah, Smitty. Ben Smith. A good cop, and a good friend while Todd had been working this area. Smitty was a highway Trooper, assigned out of Anchorage, but with a patrol area that ran all along Turnagain Arm to Kenai and Seward.

"All right," he said into the phone. "Thanks."

He emailed his document to himself and erased it from the computer, then shut the computer down to make sure it couldn't be easily retrieved. A precaution. He gathered his keys and notes and headed for the door. On board AST 32067, he found Frank sound asleep. Todd wondered briefly if he had given him too much of the morphine. It had actually been a low dose, but if Mattituck really were that opposed to the stuff, and it was relatively new to his body, it might hit him hard.

He roused Mattituck, who after waking up and taking several steps, seemed to be feeling better.

"My head's a lot clearer," Mattituck said. "Shit, Todd. Don't ever put that shit in me again, okay?"

"Can't promise that, my friend. Better to make sure you'll be okay. And as crappy as that stuff might be, it kills pain and keeps people's heads in a better place."

Mattituck nodded.

"A highway unit is about to pick us up and take us to Anchorage. I'd like you to get checked out while I talk to our friend, the bear whisperer."

Mattituck chuckled at the joke. "All right."

They stepped onto the dock, Todd steadying his friend as they made their way to the road on the other side of the Harbormaster's Office.

In less than twenty minutes, they were on the highway to Anchorage, skirting Turnagain Arm at as high a rate of speed as they could manage on the two-lane, winding highway. This time of year, Turnagain Arm was often choked with tourist traffic, and it was slow going either direction. Some drivers became impatient, taking risks to pass slow motor homes, and making the Turnagain Arm stretch of highway one of the most dangerous in Alaska. There were more head-on collisions along this thirty-mile stretch of highway than nearly any place else in the United States.

They were running with the Trooper cruiser's lights on, but the siren off. Cars moved over to the shoulder and let them pass, shortening the trip into the city. After Todd and Smitty got caught up, filling in the year since they'd last seen each other, Todd turned from the front passenger seat to speak to Frank, sitting quietly in the back seat. He was happy to simply try to ward off the waning effects of the morphine.

"I think I may be working out a profile on our suspect," he said.

Mattituck's gaze turned quickly to him.

"Everything adds up to him being ex-military. And perhaps worse yet for us, he's been a step or two ahead of us this entire time."

Mattituck listened as Todd filled him in on his thoughts from earlier while working on the report. He ran Frank through all his conclusions about the suspect's abilities and conditioning, as well as his thoughts.

"Special Forces," Mattituck said when Todd had finished.

Todd watched him.

"What makes you say that?"

"It just adds up." Mattituck looked at Todd steadily, the morphine quickly wearing off. "I think you're right about him," he added.

"What do you know about Special Forces?" Todd asked.

Mattituck only closed his eyes.

Chapter Twenty-Three

The Importance of History

Mattituck was quiet the rest of the ride into Anchorage. He slouched in the back seat of the Alaska State Trooper cruiser and listened to Troopers Todd Benson and Ben Smith getting caught up. Apparently, Todd had served as a Fish and Game Trooper in the Whittier-Seward area prior to being assigned to Valdez. Mattituck watched the scenery of Turnagain Arm pass by as the cruiser sped along the two-lane highway, vehicles pulling over in deference to the flashing lights. On the right, the Chugach Mountains loomed almost straight up from the side of the road, soaring over the waters of the Arm. On the left was Turnagain Arm itself, named by Captain Cook during his expeditions to find a northwest passage to Europe from the west coast. Legend had it that he'd named the inlet Turnagain Arm because the expedition had forgotten that they had already explored this body of water before they realized they'd been there before, and so Captain Cook named it for their being forced to "turn again" to find another possible route through to Europe.

The inlet was a popular tourist attraction, particularly when the beluga whales ran up the Arm in pursuit of smelt for an easy and steady meal for a few weeks. The white whales came near enough to the highway to afford excellent views of the beautiful, medium-sized sea mammals. On the cliff side of the highway, Dall's Sheep often came down close to the highway, providing ample photo ops of the cliff-hugging animals. For those who ventured up the numerous hiking trails along Turnagain Arm, moose and other wildlife were frequent sites, and occasionally bear could be seen—although maulings from the close encounters were not as uncommon as authorities would prefer. Nearly every year, a fatal or near-fatal attack occurred on the trails of Chugach National Park.

Mattituck watched the water, noting it must be low tide, as the mud flats were clearly visible most of the way across the Arm. His thoughts drifted toward his sister and Derek. He wondered what they were doing today, and whether he and Todd would be in town overnight. If so, perhaps he could squeeze in a quick visit. It had been a few weeks since he'd seen them.

"We going to be in Anchorage overnight, do you think?" he asked Todd when there was a pause in Todd and Smitty's conversation.

Todd looked back at him. "Could be. Depends on what we find out, I guess." He watched Frank for a moment. "Need a break?"

Mattituck shook his head.

"No, I'm good. I was just thinking if we are in town, I'll try and see my sister and nephew."

"Well," Todd said. "Even if there's a need to get on the suspect's trail right away, you probably will need some rest."

"No way. I can see Sandy and Derek after we're done."

Todd watched him a moment. "Okay," he said finally. He was glad, actually. Frank was a good partner, and often had good insight and instincts. Todd wasn't sure if the case would have progressed nearly as well as it had if he hadn't had Frank along. He turned to watch the road ahead, and resumed his chat with Smitty.

Mattituck's thoughts wandered back to Sandy and Derek. He missed them. As he'd never married, they were the only family he really had. He and Sandy were the only children, and both parents had passed away—their mother most recently, just three years earlier. He loved his sister's character, her commitment to what she believed was important. She was a petroleum engineer, and had been working in Houston when their mother fell ill with lung cancer. She had been a heavy smoker when they were younger, and the two of them had pressured her to quit smoking in response to the "dangers of smoking" campaign that they had seen in school. In dreaded fear for their mother's life, they had harped on her continually until she finally agreed to quit. The habit had apparently still eventually claimed her life, although Sandy and Frank Mattituck had still felt they prolonged her life more than had she never quit.

Dorothy Mattituck had fallen ill at the beginning of the charter season, and with their father dead by a decade, there were only friends to care for her. She had never moved from Sandy and Frank's childhood home of Seattle, which while psychologically close to Alaska, was a 5-hour flight from Anchorage. Houston was further. Sandy had decided that since she had been feeling stagnant and unsatisfied with her life, she would take Derek and relocate. The oil company she worked for had agreed to an indefinite leave of absence, and offered to continue her retirement and benefits plans if she committed to returning to the company at the end of the time she felt she needed. Sandy had agreed.

For thirteen months, Sandy cared for Dorothy, and Derek had settled into a new life in a very different place than he was used to. But he had felt no painful separation from Texas. His dad had deserted his mother before he was born, having thought that he was going to be born with Down's Syndrome. He and Sandy had been in a committed relationship, but after the test came back with the news, he had urged her to have the pregnancy terminated. Because she felt this was the wrong reason to terminate a pregnancy, the couple had found themselves in a spiraling crisis in their relationship. Sandy had tried not to judge, but increasingly she questioned who he was, as well as whether she could raise a child with a man who had wanted to terminate their child because he was disadvantaged. If it had been for more general reasons, such as that he felt they weren't ready to have a child or that they were unable to support him, that would have been different. But to terminate simply because he didn't want to deal with the difficulties of a Down's Syndrome baby . . .

She had forced herself not to judge, and largely succeeded, but there remained the problem of being the parents of the child. He didn't want the child. She did. There really is no compromise in such a situation. One or the other has to give in. And Sandy was not about to give in. Not when it meant her child. Even had the father relented and stayed for the birth and beyond, Sandy felt she could never believe that he loved their child. She simply couldn't reconcile it. Not that it mattered. Her intended life partner left before they could reach any such change on either side. Very likely, he had known Sandy wouldn't change her resolve, and he was firm in his own view. First, he had moved out – supposedly to allow time for them to sort out their thoughts and feelings, and supposedly as an attempt to save their relationship. But he had suddenly disappeared without a word. No call. No notes or letters. Not even a text. Not any indication of where he'd gone.

And she had never heard from him again.

Six months later, Derek Victor Mattituck was born. A perfectly normal baby. The positive test for Down's Syndrome had been a false positive.

Frank had flown to Houston a week before the due date, mother Dorothy in tow, and mother and brother took over the daily tasks so that Sandy could rest more and await the baby's birth. The three had quickly re-established their firm relationship, just as it had been with the three of them since Sandy and Frank's childhood. Their father had never been an engaged father, and was more an authority figure who was present evenings and weekends than a loving member of the family. So the arrival of Derek, two years after Frank and Sandy's father died, had been a binding experience for the remaining Mattituck clan.

Both Dorothy and Frank were present when Derek was born, although Mattituck had refused to be anyplace other than at his sister's face, coaching her through the breathing. Dorothy was more the side-kick doctor, watching every detail of the birth of her only grandchild. All three had expected confirmation of the Down's Syndrome, and had been surprised when the boy was born free of any abnormalities.

Ironic, Mattituck had thought. The father left for fear of the syndrome, and the boy had been born normal. Sandy maintained from that moment on that the

Universe, for whatever reason, had determined the only product of that relationship would be sad memories for Sandy and an amazingly wonderful child.

Sandy had dated afterward, but only half-heartedly. She had always believed that no man would want to inherit children that weren't his own, so she was resigned to living a life without any real love interests. Her brother countered this with his own belief of how he would feel if he met a woman he really liked with a child, but she had always retorted that he was the only really good man alive. Plus, she pointed out, he didn't exactly have a good track record of serious relationships, either. He'd had to concede that point. Her bitterness, however, only saddened him all the more when it became clear that she was not simply being hurt and angry. Mattituck knew what his issues were. His sister, however, seemed truly jaded.

Horns on the highway pulled Mattituck back to the present. He looked with a mixture of annoyance and pride at a group of tourists causing a slow-down in traffic as they stood at a small turnout, four motorhomes crowded into the small pavement pad, cameras upturned to snap shots of Dall's Sheep.

Sandy's jadedness and her brother's steadfast commitment to Derek had had everything to do with Sandy moving to Anchorage. After their mother passed away, she had been offered her old position back in Houston or a new position with a promotion in Anchorage. She hadn't even needed time to decide. On the instant, she accepted the position in Anchorage. Nobody had been happier at the news than Mattituck. Except perhaps Derek, who had not liked Seattle but adored his uncle. When Sandy and Derek looked for a new home in Anchorage, they had made sure there was a room they would set up that would belong to Uncle Frank.

When they arrived at the hospital in Anchorage, Mattituck was quickly ushered to the Emergency Room to have his arm properly sanitized and dressed. While he was waiting to be seen, he thought about texting Sandy to let her know he was at the hospital, but then quickly dismissed the idea. She would worry, knock off work early, probably pick up Derek, and zoom to the hospital. She would fuss over him and insist that he come stay with them, and would fight him like a protective mother bear about going out again to help Todd Benson.

So instead, he texted Monica. Not two minutes had passed before his phone rang. Her picture appeared with the ringing on the face of his cell, and he smiled at it. It was a selfie they'd taken together from the top of Flattop Mountain during a weekend getaway to Anchorage. Their sun-glassed faces were beaming, their cheeks pressed together, and her wind-blown black hair was thrown over both their heads. Cook Inlet was spread out behind them like a nuptial blanket, sparkling in the bright summer sun.

He declined the call and texted her that he couldn't talk at the moment, and would call her after he was checked out at the hospital.

U ok? she texted in response.

Y... Fine. Loopy from morphine Benson shot me up with.

Is he the trooper?

Y

U addict. ☺ Afraid to talk to me high?

Y – Def

Won't change what I think of U.

Good, he texted back. Then, *Seems nothing can ever change what I think of you.*

As it should be <3

Mattituck felt his heart rate pick up. He smiled at the heart.

Been too long, he texted.

Agreed. When can I C U?

ICU? I'm not in that bad of shape! lol

Ha! When can I see you?

Don't know. Soon I hope.

K. I'm here.

So am I

Good. You better be. ☺

☺ *<3*

He put his phone away and looked up to see Todd watching him, a bemused expression on his face. Mattituck realized he'd been grinning while texting Monica.

"The hot one from Cordova?"

"My aunt from Poughkeepsie," he retorted.

Todd shook his head with a crooked grin. "Wish I had an aunt that could put a stupid grin on my face."

The doctor came in and Todd excused himself.

"I'm going to visit our friend while you get worked on," he said.

Mattituck nodded.

"Just don't leave me here. I'm in this through to the end."

Todd nodded with a sudden sense of relief he hadn't expected.

"I know," he said. "I'll be back for you."

Carl Elkins lay on the hospital bed and blinked at the ceiling. It hurt to move, even though they had him on some pretty strong pain meds. The last he remembered was being on that island, chasing the guy from the yellow boat, behind that crazy dickhead as he pushed hard after the guy. The man, Peck, was truly twisted. It was like he was hellbent on killing anybody who posed a risk for them. Or anybody who had something the motherfucker wanted. Like that old couple from Washington they'd met in Petersburg. The asshole Peck had decided they needed the old couple's boat, so he'd acted all nice and shit, got them all scared about the supposed rough town of Petersburg—not at all true, but the couple hadn't known that—and convinced them that Carl and he should walk them back to their boat.

When they were on the boat . . . *Jesus*, Carl thought. *Jesus Christ!* . . .

He was back in Petersburg in an instant, the drugs carrying his memory back in time. Carl had stepped into the aft deck of the little Bayliner the old couple had been traveling in. They'd been sailing all the way from the Seattle area, headed to see the old woman's sister in Juneau. They'd been sailing for two weeks, taking their time, stopping in at whatever port struck their fancy. And now, this -- *Jesus!* Carl thought.

He'd helped the old woman step into the aft deck, and then reached up to help the old man. They were such a sweet couple of old folks. Like grandparents—in fact, they probably *were* grandparents. He could see the old man now, holding his hand, then the weight on his hand and the man relied on him to support him into the boat. He was going to get some wine, he'd said as he then unlocked the cabin door and stepped in. Carl had looked up to see Peck drop onto the aft deck, then look up at him. He danced his eyebrows at Carl meaningfully, a sick grin on his face. He then stepped into the cabin, and Carl saw he had a buck knife in his hand.

The old woman, not seeing the knife, stepped in behind Peck.

Carl didn't know what to do. His heart was pounding in his chest.

This can't be happening.   This can't be fucking happening! he'd thought.

He followed the other three in, trying to think of a way to stop whatever it was the crazy fuck Peck had in mind.

Normal Peck really was a fucked up man. He was younger than Carl by a good fifteen years, and had only been out of the military for a little over a year. He didn't know much more about the guy, though, except that he'd been an Army Ranger—Special Forces—in the gulf wars. All of the gulf years, according to Peck. He'd done every tour, and volunteered for every special ops assignment available. But that's all Peck had told him, besides a lot of stories of situations he'd been in while overseas that Carl had no way of knowing were true or not.

They'd been hired by some drug boss in Los Angeles to pick up some backpacks in Petersburg, then get to Yakutat for a drop, with others in a few towns further north. The pay was fucking ridiculous, so Carl had accepted without second-guessing. The "exchanges" were elaborate. They all involved hotels that had deals with the drug boss to have a room ready for them to drop the backpack for that town in a room. There would be another backpack there with the payoff. They were to drop their backpack with the drugs off, pick up the pack with the money, return the key to the hotel manager, then get to the next town.

Yakutat. Whittier. Cordova. Valdez. Seward. In that order.

Except it didn't happen that way. All because of the fuckhead's bullshit.

Once they were in the cabin, Peck had pushed the old man toward the ladder leading down to the forward stateroom.

"Hey! What are you---?" the old man had protested.

The old woman screamed, and Peck had swung with alarming speed and nailed her above the left ear with a crushing blow. The woman's voice stopped instantly and she dropped to the deck like a sack of potatoes.

Carl's eyes were shut tight now at the memory. His head moved from side to side, shaking a "no" or in attempt to swing the memory out—even Carl wouldn't have been able to tell which. He just knew he wished it had never happened. It wasn't supposed to happen that way. They were supposed to fly.

The old man tried to grab Peck, and Peck's elbow had struck backward and caught the old man in the upper gut. Carl heard the air push out and the man gasp and he doubled over. Peck turned around and chuckled.

"Stupid old fuck," he'd said.

He had actually fucking laughed at the old man. *Laughed*. Then he grabbed the man on either side of his head and pushed him backward into the ladder well. The old man fell to the next deck down, a sickening crack as his limp body thudded on the deck below. No sound of movement followed.

Carl looked at Peck. There was a determined joy in the fucker's eyes. He could see the former Army Ranger was in a place where he could not be disturbed. He was living his own reality—whatever that was. But Carl could see it in his eyes. A look of cold, steely . . . what? Carl couldn't put his finger on it. It wasn't anger, nor hatred. Both were a kind of emotion. And Peck was completely void of any emotions whatsoever. Wherever he was in his mind, it wasn't a place that was normal.

Peck had looked at him then, and Carl knew. He was not looking into the eyes of a sane man. But he wasn't exactly insane either. It was something other than both. And completely detached from anything resembling human emotion.

So, Carl had wondered, this is what too much war—or too many special operations—could do to a man.

Peck had looked away from him, down at the unmoving old man on the deck below. The old woman had started to stir, and it brought Peck's attention back to her. He took three steps and loomed menacingly over her. He grimaced at the back of her head and she, facing the floor, tried to sit up. Peck had reached down and grabbed the old woman's blouse and began dragging her toward the ladder leading below.

"Please," she mumbled, struggling to form the words. "Please . . ."

"Shut the fuck up, bitch!" Peck yelled down at her.

Carl's memory would never be able to erase the woman's eyes as she turned her head up toward Peck, confusion and fear mixed in her soft blue eyes.

Jesus! What he was witnessing seemed surreal, like watching a second rate gore movie. Or one of those

363

Welcome to the
Palmer Public Library!

You checked out the following items:

1. Skipper's Oath : The Frank
   Mat
   Due: 8/21/17

2. The Daily show (the book) : an
   Due: 8/21/17

You saved $45.95 by coming
to the Palmer Public Library!

true crime shows. Only this was real. This was really happening.

The woman reached up to Peck, as if to be helped up by a grandchild after a hard fall on the ice.

"Help me . . . ?"

Peck stopped, and for a moment, Carl thought with relief that Peck might have changed his mind. Come to some realization of what he was doing, perhaps. Instead, his face twisted into outrage.

"What the fuck, lady?!" he half-hissed at her.

She winced and seemed to fold in on herself. But her hand remained up.

A loud slap violated the muffled close quarters as Peck slapped the woman's hand aside. He grabbed her blouse again and pulled it violently toward the ladder. The blouse gave way and slipped over her head. Her white aged body exposed with only a bra embarrassed Carl, and he turned instinctively away. It was out of respect. A woman should be respected. An old woman should not be violated.

"Pleee—" he heard, his back still turned. Then a scream.

Carl turned to see Scott half-lifting the woman by her hair. Her body slid along the deck, and disappeared into the well to the deck below. The thud was broken, presumably, by her husband's body beneath her. He could hear her voice, not quite whimpering, not quite sobbing. He saw Peck descend the ladder like a rabid hyena, the crazy grin fitting the image.

The sounds he'd heard next were something he hoped to bury in a repressed memory. He'd not lived a good life, he thought to himself. He'd committed plenty of crimes. And yes, he'd even knifed a guy back in Gainsville when he was a teen. Manslaughter, he'd been charged with. And served his time. But he'd always regretted it. What was the word? Remorse. That was it. A deep sense that what he'd done was wrong, even though he felt it was justified by the other's aggression. But this . . . This was beyond Carl's comprehension.

He heard a scream come from the cabin below, then silence. He felt he was going to throw up. He tried to take a step forward, toward the ladder, but his feet wouldn't move. He suddenly felt an odd buzzing numbness throughout his body, immobilizing him and rendering him—he thought—a coward. He knew what it was, and that word was the right word. If Carl was anything, it was honest with himself and his short-comings. He could not move out of fear. Cowardice.

Or was it? He knew fear well, too, and that's not what this was. Not now that he thought about it. It was simply an inability to react, to move. It was like his brain's ability to give commands to his body—specifically his legs—had been severed. Communications lost. A complete power failure.

But then he was at the ladder well, looking down. The woman was gone, and Peck nowhere to be seen. He could hear the shower door in the head slide shut. Or open. He couldn't tell which. He heard two more violent thuds, then the shower door slide shut. So it had been opening a moment ago, not closing, his mind reasoned. He was aware of a certain detachment in himself. He was thinking more of details such as whether the shower door was opening or closing, and—he was aware—avoiding thoughts of what was really happening.

I'd make an interesting case for a shrink, he thought. How I'm thinking of everything except what's happening. He heard the sliding of clothing, with soft weight behind it, sliding along plastic. The kind of plastic used for shower inserts. Like the one in the head below.

Then he saw Peck step into the passageway from the stateroom. There was dark liquid all over his jeans. Carl knew what it was. Or a part of him did, anyhow. But the rest of him forced the knowing Carl back into the shadows of his thoughts, and he only saw dark liquid. Peck looked up at him.

"Hadda do it," he said. "Good thing I've done this shit before. Many times. Many a fucking time. Saving our asses," he said, then nodded at Carl as if he saw that Carl understood. "Ain't no big deal."

But Carl didn't understand. Not at all. He was so far from understanding, in fact, that his mind was preventing him from comprehending what was happening. The weirdest part was that he'd known it. It was like watching a Stanley Kubrick film that you don't understand. At all. And you wish you could walk out. But you can't. You're stuck in your seat. God only knows why, but you can't fucking leave. You can't walk out. It would feel good to walk out. To get up and make your way to the aisle, stepping over legs and feet while the confusing Kubrick film keeps rolling, until you get to the aisle and you nearly trip as you break free from the tangle of seats and knees and feet. Then you walk up the slope—Carl so wished he could do this—and to the exit doors. Through the lobby. Then out onto the sidewalk, into the fresh cool air. Where reality sets in again.

Where you realize that the world in the movie theater is fake. It wasn't really happening. No matter how real it had seemed. It didn't really happen. And now you're on the sidewalk, cars driving by, the city lights washing over you and insisting they are real and the movie isn't. It was all an illusion. It was only images you saw. It wasn't real.

Peck was dragging the body of the old man into the stateroom.

"Get the motors started and cast off the lines," he barked at Carl.

"What?"

"Get us underway, man!" Peck listened for a response from out of view. "Get us fucking *going*! Under*stand*?!"

The authority of Scott's command got Carl moving. It was like being on the sidewalk outside the movie theater. It was a chance to escape the moment. It was like Scott was a movie theater usher, holding open the door to the lobby and inviting him to get out of the theater—out from the false, confused horror of the movie. And he jumped at it.

When they'd cleared the jetty at Petersburg harbor, and Peck came up the ladder, dressed in fresh clothes, Carl felt sure none of this had really just happened. How could Peck be so calm and clean if it had really happened? It had to have been something else, and maybe Carl had taken some bad drugs or something. He couldn't be sure what that fisherman he'd met in the bar had given him. It was weed, supposedly, but maybe it'd been laced with something. Something fucking wicked bad. Sure, he thought. Otherwise, how could Peck be so clean and calm.

But Carl was too old not to know a bold-faced lie when he heard one.

By the time they were in Frederick Sound, shock had subsided and Carl was again faced with reality. A mixture of fear with the realization that he was implicated in the murder of the elderly couple had already triggered a decision of survival for Carl. With his record, there was no way anybody would ever believe he wasn't on board with what had happened. He was guilty, no matter how you sliced it up. No, his best course of action was to keep moving forward and find a way out of this down the road.

Peck had insisted that they needed to dispose of the bodies, so they were looking for an inlet free of other boats. Peck's plan was to get some hefty rocks from shore, tie them to the bodies, and pitch them overboard "for the shrimp to feast on in the depths of Davy's locker," as Peck had put it, laughing at what he'd considered his clever sense of humor.

The motherfucker had laughed as if he'd told the funniest joke at the Stand-up Club. But Carl did not breathe one word of protest. He knew his best chance of survival was to play along. Bide his time until he could find a way to bail.

And that's how he'd left it until the nonsense up by Yakutat, and then Valdez. More killing. Unnecessary killing. They'd made the drop in Yakutat, but then Peck had decided when he saw a small yacht that they needed "provisions." They'd circled the boat, and presumably it had called for the law in Yakutat during that time, because a while later, a Harbor Patrol boat approached. Peck shot the yacht owners, and then senselessly shot the cop in the Harbor Patrol boat after it had followed them.

But that wasn't all. As they'd been heading in to Valdez for the second dropoff, they were coming in too late in the day, and so they'd found a sheltered bay on the chart and steered the Bayliner in, when they'd cut in too close to shore at the mouth of the bay—Growler

Bay—and hit a rock. Peck, the crazy motherfucker, ran the boat fast after they found they were taking on water. He was looking for a sandy beach—god only knew why at the time—and then found one near the end of the bay. Way the fuck up the end of the bay. And then he'd run the boat right up onto the beach.

It turned out to be the right thing to do, Peck had realized later. It gave them shelter and food until someone came along to save them. What had not even crossed Carl's mind was that Crazy Fucking Peck would murder the first person to try to help. But that's exactly what he'd done. The old man with the big yacht had put his little boat in the water to come get them, and as soon as the old man was in reach, Scott fucking decked him with wrench. Smashed his skull on the first blow. The memory of the sound of cracking bone under skin sickened him.

Now, in the Anchorage hospital, the memory gripped him. It reverberated through his brain. With each echo, Carl shifted uncomfortably. He looked around the hospital room. Nobody had spoken with him except the doctors—and they only talked about his wounds. Carl knew there was a uniformed cop outside his room, and they changed the guard every eight hours or so, so that there was always a guard. No doubt, that spelled trouble for Carl. But he had no idea how much. He recalled the chase on the island, but he had no idea whether Peck was alive or dead, caught or free. Maybe they knew about the murders, and Carl would be implicated—or blamed.

He looked around the room for something to distract him, but everything lay in its place, still and silent. He could hear voices out by the nurses' station, but nothing else. The TV remote caught his attention, and he ran through the channels several times before he settled on a sitcom re-run. But the memories continued.

After Peck had done away with the old couple, there was the problem of the bodies. Peck had insisted they would use the boat to make their deliveries. It would mean running the small cabin cruiser across the northern Gulf, but the first delivery was in Yakutat, half way across to Prince William Sound. And the small boat, Peck said, had a big enough fuel tank for them to run that kind of distance. But they couldn't have the bodies down below.

"They'll start to stink the place up," he'd said.

"How do we do it?" Carl had asked.

"Therein lies the problem, that's for sure," Peck had said, looking around for something—Carl couldn't even guess what.

"Maybe we just throw them overboard," Carl ventured.

Peck stopped looking and turned to look at him full on.

"Are you fucking kidding?" he said. "Have you ever seen a dead body in the water?"

Carl shook his head, suddenly nervous.

"Shit . . ." Peck said, and resumed looking. "Bodies float."

"Oh . . ."

"Yeah. Oh."

"Well, what if we tie something heavy to them?"

"Like what?" Peck shot back. "A block of concrete? Maybe we should just mix up some Ready-Mix and pour castings around their feet. Are you fucking kidding me?"

Carl had become increasingly uncomfortable. Murder was murder, yes. And the way this guy had knocked off the old couple—yeah, that was pretty bad. But there was something in Peck's tone now that separated the two of them. Like Peck no longer saw him as a partner on the job. He gazed out the window as he steered the boat, following the track on the GPS Peck had programmed in. He had to admit, Peck seemed to know something about everything. He knew how to run the boat, how to navigate it, how to just about do anything that needed to be done. Carl had long since stopped asking how. "Learned it in the Army" was always the answer. Carl knew lots of people who'd served in the Army, and none of them seemed to know all that shit.

His eyes drifted to the rocky shore. He sat up, squinting to see better.

"What about a rock?" he'd asked.

"You mean like a boulder-like rock? Where the fuck are we gonna get a rock?"

"Over there," Carl said, pointing.

And that's what they'd done. They had nosed close to shore, then put the little raft in the water and collected heavy, two-foot rocks. Six of them to be exact. That's how many Peck had figured they would need. Three for each body. And "figured" was actually what he'd done. Based on some standard Carl had no clue about, Peck did the math and calculated the weight needed to drop the bodies to the bottom of 200 feet of water, and hold them there.

"Why 200 feet deep?" Carl had asked.

"Optimum shrimp and crab depth."

"What? You mean for them to---?"

"Yep. We need the bodies completely disposed of. And shrimp and crab are perfect for the job. We just need to find something to wrap them in that will allow the critters to get to them, but that won't let body parts float to the surface during the—ah—during the process."

"Like what?"

"Like netting. Fish nets."

"Where the hell are we going to get---?" Carl stopped. Peck was pointing at the decoration on the rear bulkhead. The old couple, creating a nautical theme in their little retirement yacht, had hung fish netting on the wall and ceiling, spread as it followed down the bulkhead in an appearance of having been cast to the sea. Cute, Carl thought. He could picture the married grandparents, picking out exactly how to hang the old-style netting they'd probably bought at a second-hand store. And now it would be used to sink them to the bottom-feeding critters on the bottom of the sea.

"Here we go," Peck had said, holding up a screwdriver. "That's what I've been looking for. The fuckers screwed shanks to the wall and ceiling to hang the netting. No way to get it down in tact without a screwdriver."

After they retrieved the rocks, they ran the boat up an inlet and anchored, and had gone to work on the preparation. Carl had had to fight nausea at the smell of blood in the cabin below. The old man crumpled next to the bed. The old woman crammed into the narrow shower stall. Apparently, Peck had tried to put both bodies in the shower to contain the blood, but had given up after putting the woman in there, and had simply dropped the old man out of the way on the floor.

The amount of blood was astounding. There was blood still pooling on one side of the bottom of the shower, and seemed to still be flowing out of the woman's throat. Again, the brutality of Normal Peck was sickening.

"Why's she upside down?" he'd asked.

"Fastest way to drain the blood," Peck had answered flatly, as if explaining to a child how clouds move across the sky.

It had looked like the woman had been killed by stabbing, then shoved into the shower stall upside down, and then her throat slashed to bleed her . . . like a fucking deer. Carl looked away.

"I'll do the old man," he told Peck.

"Suits me."

Again, the amount of blood was stunning. The carpet under the old man had been an off white, but the entire area was now a dark reddish black, and sopping wet. Carl shook his head, wrapped the man's body in a spare bottom sheet from the closet, as he'd been instructed, and dragged him out of the state room, hauled him up the ladder, and dragged him out to the aft deck. The sheet was to cut down on the mess while moving the bodies. A few minutes later, Scott dragged the woman's body out in the same manner. They had then wrapped the bodies together in the large fishing net with the rocks inside, snug against their bodies.

"Ain't that sweet?" Peck sneered. "The little love birds all tight up against each other."

Carl was speechless.

"Get a room, you two!" Peck raised his voice at them. Suddenly, he stepped forward and kicked the nearest body. "Hear me?, you fucking disgusting horn-dogs?!"

He swiveled his grinning face at Carl, then laughed deeply. The smile left his eyes and he went silent as he saw Carl's face.

"What'sa matter with you?" he said accusingly. "No stomach? Fucking pussy! Goddamn fucking pussy!" he barked.

When Carl didn't reply, he said half under his breath. "Give me a hand getting them over, godammit. We gotta get going."

Now, in the hospital, Carl stared at the TV. He had no idea what was on. His memory was swimming with the recollections. He looked down at the handheld thing with the button to increase his pain meds. The memory of the old man in Growler Bay began to impose itself next. How they'd been rowing the body back to the yacht, Carl doing all the work while Peck got ready to secure them to the old man's big boat, anchored a short way off shore.

"Hey, look at that!" Peck had said excitedly as they approached. He was pointing at the bow of the big boat. "Shrimp pots!" he exclaimed happily.

"Yeah?" Carl replied, trying to keep his voice even.

"Shrimp pots, man. You know what that means?"

"No idea," Carl said.

Peck grinned at him. "It means getting rid of him will be a helluva lot easier than the horny old folks, copulating in their net-coffin."

"How so?"

"Easy. We send him down in parts."

"In . . . parts?"

Peck was already thinking ahead, planning. "We just need to make sure the parts are too big to get through the openings in the pots . . ."

Carl shook his head at the memory. He shook hard and fast, trying to force the memory out. He went dizzy with the violence of it. But the memory was persistent . . . The sound of the cutting, then putting pieces into the shrimp pots. Occasionally, the cutting was through ligaments, and Peck cursed through those parts, and then sharpened the knife for the next cutting session. There had only been three shrimp pots, so Peck complained near the end about fitting all the pieces and parts into them.

Finally, Carl had heard the pots splash into the water. A moment later, Peck had come into the cabin.

"Let's get this thing running."

He'd started the engines, then run the anchor up.

"You drive. I'm going to clean the deck back there."

Carl continued gazing at the hospital TV screen, lost. He pressed his eyes shut. The memories persisted. They ran through his head, over and over, mixed in with surmisings of the old people and how they'd lived. Whether or not they had grandkids that would miss them. What kinds of things they did for fun, the friends they had . . .

He looked down at the medication control, the button at the end of the device that controlled the dosage up to a maximum the doctor would allow him to have without overdosing. He picked it up and pumped the button twice, then three more times. Then he lay his head back into the pillow, hoping the meds would sweep away the memories and worry.

Chapter Twenty-Four

Revelations

Shortly after he'd pumped them in, the meds allowed Carl Elkins' memories to fade into a happy tranquility. He only slept a brief nap, though, and slid back into consciousness with his eyes closed. He could tell by the brightness under his eyelids that it was late in the day. He knew because his room faced the direction that the sun set in—whatever that direction was in this crazy "land of the midnight sun." He lay for several minutes, drawing breath and wondering what was going to happen. The bear had done a number on him, that much he knew. He had broken ribs, a broken collar bone, a broken arm, and had several punctures in his skull where the bear had bit him. And that was just the bone injuries. He was missing a large section of skin on his shoulder and chest where the bear had torn and gnawed at him, as well as deep gashes in his chest muscles and upper right arm. His neck, luckily, had been largely left alone or, the doctor said, he'd be dead.

Despite how ugly the upper torso and arm wounds were, it apparently was the head wounds that were the greatest threat to his life. An amazing thing, the body—it had shut down by putting him into a coma while his body rested and fought through the worst of it. The memories of the bear attack began to encroach, and he groaned and opened his eyes.

A State Trooper was sitting in the chair next to his bed, watching him.

"I'd say good morning, but it isn't," he said.

Carl only groaned again and closed his eyes.

"I know you're probably tired, maybe in some pain, but I won't take long. I just need a little info."

Carl shook his head.

"I'm going to venture more than a guess when I say that I know your partner doesn't give a shit about you, so what's the sense in protecting him? Especially when you have a shot at lessening any charges that come against you."

Carl's eyes opened on the trooper.

"What do you mean?"

Todd Benson drew in his lips and shook his head.

"I haven't done anything," Carl tried.

"Bullshit. Look, I'm in here with a straight deal. I'm not fucking around. I don't have the time for it. You can help me out, or I just go with my hunch and see if I nail your buddy. I'm pretty damned sure I know where to find him, so I'm not even sure cutting you a deal will help me. But it's no sweat off my nose if you serve life without parole, or get a lesser sentence."

He let that sink in.

"I'd just assume cut you a deal and know for sure where I'm headed. Again, I don't like wasting time, so it'd be worth it to me. But no doubt I'll nail your buddy's ass to the wall eventually----"

"He's not my buddy," Carl said, cutting him off. "And, not necessarily on nailing him. You don't know what you're dealing with. The guys' a fucking animal."

He pumped the meds a few times and closed his eyes.

"Oh, I have no doubt he's a hot shot," he heard the trooper say, his voice beginning to take a warpy edge.

Carl shook his head. "Seriously," he said, feeling his voice sliding off reality. "He's not fucking human . . ."

Todd watched the man in the bed. He saw him pump the meds, then close his eyes. The man's body relaxed, and Todd knew he was asleep again. He picked up the paper and went back to reading, waiting.

Reality and memories take on unusual characteristics with certain pain medications. The line between them and whatever present moment is underway often tends to become unclear. They have a way of moving from one to another with such fluid transition that a person can be in a new memory without realizing they are no longer existing in reality. As Carl closed his eyes to try to seal off the trooper from his reality, he slid along that thin line until he felt very realistically that he was reliving the hike on the island, chasing after the guy from the yellow boat.

He was struggling to keep up with Peck, the inhuman former Ranger. Norman Peck, a younger man by more than ten years, was continually chiding him for his lack of speed and stamina. Normally, Carl would tell someone like that to fuck off, along with how to do it and where. But the reality was that he was afraid of Peck. The man was about the closest thing to insane—truly insane—that Carl had ever seen. Not only had he witnessed the man ruthlessly kill three old people, but the way he went about the drug drop-offs had an air of the crazy about it as well. *Shit, he thought, even the idea of ditching the flight from Petersburg to Yakutat and taking the elder couple's boat instead—that was some crazy shit.*

Now in full coma-like memory, Carl was panting and heaving his legs over the muskeg after Peck in pursuit of the guy from the yellow boat, he was beginning to think that Peck's insanity had a focused intensity about it. It wasn't random crazy, like you tend to think of crazy, but it had a purpose. Always, everything the ex-Ranger did was absolutely clear on its objectives, and he went about it with a pit bull's tenacity.

So was it really crazy, or was it just intensely violent focus? Evil?

Carl decided he didn't care. He just wanted to get through this fucking job and back to some kind of normal life. The thought of it gave him new energy, and he found himself catching up to Peck's determined and fast-paced back.

"'Bout fucking time you picked it up!" the ex-Ranger barked at him. "We'll never catch this dickhead if we don't pick it up." Peck looked at him over his shoulder. "You do realize, don't you, that the further we have to chase his ass, the further we have to hike back to the boat?"

Actually, Carl had not thought of this. He found his pace picking up so that he was nearly on Peck's heels.

They were climbing a small knoll, and Carl found himself lagging again. Peck gained the crest of the knoll, and began the descent down the other side. Low scrub brush was on either side, and a large patch of the scrub spread over a good portion of the downward slope on the right. Peck was looking at it when they both heard a *paooooft* ahead. Both heads swung back to the slight trail through the muskeg ahead.

A large brown mass rose to what must have been 7 or 8 feet ahead of them, shaking its coat in the low Alaska sun. Both men froze. The bear stood on its hind legs at the bottom of the slope, perhaps 20 yards below them. Peck took two tentative steps backward, and Carl tried to do the same, but his legs seemed stuck. The bear dropped to all fours, then took several steps toward them.

Peck spun and bolted in Carl's direction. The speed of the man's acceleration caught Carl off guard, and his legs remained rubberized and planted. He felt cold and empty inside as Peck ran toward him. Then, finally, Carl found his legs and turned to run. He felt sluggish at first, then felt his legs find their groove and begin to pump with traction. Peck was almost astride now, but Carl was getting up to speed quickly. He dared not look back to gauge whether or not the bear was in pursuit. He had to keep his eyes fixed on the trail in front of him to be sure of his footing. He could hear Peck's steps right behind him, and felt almost that he was moving away—that he was running faster than Peck. It didn't seem possible, but they say adrenaline is an amazing booster . . . Carl almost smiled inwardly. The old joke sprang into his consciousness: "I don't need to run faster than the bear to get away from it—I only need to run faster than *you!*"

Then something came between his forward-moving back leg and the ground, and he felt himself toppling forward.

Impossible!!! he thought, confused at his loss of footing.

His head dropped forward, and he saw the walking stick Peck had been using, lying crosswise in front of his right shin across to his left foot's trajectory.

Then he was down. Somehow, his head shot upward and he saw Peck's face grinning down at him as it moved across the sky above him. Then Carl's chest hit the muskeg and his head jounced forward and his forehead bounced off the spongy muskeg.

He tripped me! The mother-fucking cocksucker tripped me!!!

He desperately lifted his head and tried to draw his legs under him. His knees moved in slow motion as he became conscious of the bear running up the slope toward him.

Jesus! *Jeeee-zusss!!!*

His right foot took hold of the muskeg, and he catapulted himself forward, but the foot slipped backward, and his knee dropped onto the muskeg, hard. Rock was beneath the muskeg, and he felt his knee-cap squarely drop with his full weight on it. A flash of pain shot through his vision, and he fell again to his chest. He could taste the muskeg in his mouth. He blinked, and saw a half-darkness, half-green, then he was whisked backward and everything went blue.

With horror, he realized he had been flung onto his back as the bear caught hold of his calf muscle, digging its claws in and gaining a solid grip on him. It pulled its powerful arm and down Carl went, spinning crazily as he came under the bear's control. He saw the bear's muzzle, then only its ears.

Again with horror, but magnified this time, he realized he could only see the bear's ears because its muzzle was at his chest.

Time slowed. Everything seemed to move from fast motion, from 24-frame, to a slow waterlogged speed, like 18-frame motion. He felt his body tugged back and forth as the bear gained a firm grip in its jaws and pulled

Carl's torso side-to-side like a stuffed toy in a Doberman's jaws.

The motherfucker tripped me so he'd escape! he thought. *He fucking threw me to the goddamned bear!*

Carl saw the open mouth of the bear above him. He saw the white teeth, the black lips framed by beautiful reddish-brown fur. Then the jaws were on his skull, and all went black.

Until the hospital. And the doctors. Everybody had made a fuss over him. Apparently, he'd been in a coma for several days. He was lucky to be alive, everybody told him.

And now, he thought as he looked again at the Alaska State Trooper sitting next to him, he was alive. Fully alive. Peck had fucking left him for dead—fucking set him up to die under the bear, for fuck's sake!—and yet he'd lived. The fucking lowlife cocksucker slow-hiking Carl Elkins had lived. Sur-*prize*, mother-fucker Ranger man!

He looked at the trooper. The man sat in his chair, patiently watching him, his notepad in hand.

Carl moved from the memory-reality back to the present-reality, suddenly unsure of how private such realities were. Had the trooper seen what Carl had relived in the memory-reality?

"It really is amazing you lived through that," the Trooper said, shaking his head admiringly.

Carl nodded. Had he been telling all that out loud?

"With these pain meds, I'm not really sure half the time whether I did survive," he said.

The Trooper smiled. "I can imagine."

Still unsure whether he'd been sharing all that out loud, or if it had unfolded only in his own memory, Carl decided to share an observation.

"So that's what happened," he said, watching for the Trooper's response.

"I think I got it," the uniformed man said, tapping his notebook with his pen. He closed the notebook and looked earnestly at Carl.

"I'm even more inclined to make sure you come out of this as okay as you can," he said. "I can't imagine what you went through. And betrayed by your partner. Sorry, but that really sucks."

Carl nodded. That was sure true, he thought to himself.

"Again," the Trooper said, "they call it a plea bargain. I call it a promise. You give me something that helps me nail that bait-thrower, and I'll do all I can to help you lighten your share of the blame."

"I really didn't take part in any of the killings," Carl said, tired. "It all just happened, and so fast."

"With a guy like this, I'm not surprised." Todd looked at the man lying on the bed. He looked genuinely scared. In that instant, Todd believed the guy really had been caught up in more than his league of crime.

"So this guy literally throws you to the bear," Todd said. "Do you really want to protect him in some empty Code of Brotherhood?"

Carl stared blankly for several moments. Finally, he shook his head.

"The man can go to an ice-cold hell for all I care," he pronounced.

The Trooper took out his notepad again.

"The next stop is Seward," Carl said. "It's the last drop besides the biggest one in Anchorage. The Anchorage ring is the biggest, but they usually do that drop separately. Mostly because it's the biggest. But for some reason, it's been put in with the smaller coastal drops this time."

"Do you know where in Seward?"

"Yeah. The Puffin Inn." He waited for Todd to finish writing. "Here's how it works," he said, and unfolded the entire operation. The business card with a code number written on it, how it's given to the manager at the desk, and then they go to the room and drop off the black backpack, and pick up one identical to it. Inside theirs were the drugs; inside the one they picked up was the money. They then returned the key to the front desk and that was it. On their merry way.

"Last question," Todd said. "You mentioned a drop in Anchorage. Where is that one going to be?"

"I don't know," Carl said. "Peck puts me on a plane and then does that one alone."

Todd thought about this.

"Okay," he said finally.

Todd took down Carl Elkins' name and closest relative information, then asked what info he had about Normal Peck. But all Carl knew about the killer was his name, that he had been an Army Ranger, and only out of the Army for a year or less.

"Question," Carl said after Todd had finished with his questions.

"Yeah?"

"The guard out there. He's keeping me in here?"

"Partly."

"Do I really look like I'm going anywhere?"

Todd shook his head. "No, you don't. That's the other part."

"Protection?"

Todd nodded.

"He could get past that guy, you know."

"Maybe, but there's a camera on your door, and two more on the nurse's station that also look down the halls."

"Cameras won't stop a psycho."

"No, but two more cops on the floor will. One watching the cameras, and another just down the hall. We have you covered."

"All that coverage is in place?"

"All except Cop numbers two and three. That'll be within the hour, because of what you've told me. The one at the end of the hall and the one at the door will be in constant view of each other. No way this Scott-the-Ranger will get to you. Guaranteed."

"Yeah, I'll keep my fingers crossed," Carl said, unconvinced.

Chapter Twenty-Five

High Noon

The resources available to an Alaska State Trooper were beginning to astonish Mattituck. He remembered the rumors about Texas Rangers being almost lone maverick agents, working alone to fight crime, and having a nearly endless amount of resources, as well as license to pursue criminals in whatever way they saw fit. Todd Benson seemed very much like that type of officer of the law. He moved here and there at will, only reporting his whereabouts and occasionally what he was working on. Otherwise, it seemed to Mattituck he was free to go anywhere while working on a case, and anything he needed was available to him.

Most recently was the Trooper highway cruiser Todd picked up in Anchorage for them to take to Seward. After Trooper Benson had finished interviewing the suspect in the hospital, he had called for a vehicle, and within a half hour, it was at the door. Todd had checked in on Mattituck and found that he was ready for discharge. The trooper had seemed relieved.

"I was afraid you were going to be admitted or something," he'd said.

"For what?"

"Hey," Todd had said, looking at him as they turned onto Arctic Blvd and headed for the highway. "Sometimes a wound like that can be infected. You must be up on your tetanus shots," he added, winking.

Mattituck smiled.

"You underestimate my superhero status," Mattituck said.

"Speaking of superheroes," Todd retorted, "this guy we're after seems pretty adept at this stuff." He proceeded to recount to Mattituck what he'd learned about Peck-the-Ranger.

"Wow," Mattituck said after he'd finished. "So maybe his getting away hasn't been so much of luck as maybe the guy knows what he's doing, eh?"

"Exactly my thoughts. We need to be very careful how we approach this."

"What are you thinking?"

"Well," Todd began. "We are pretty hard on the guy's heels. I'm going to guess he headed straight to Seward. But unless he stole a vehicle, he couldn't get there all that quickly. We know he can steal boats," Todd proffered sardonically, "but that would take way too long. From Whittier to Seward means heading back east into the Sound, then south and around the Kenai Peninsula land mass, three inlets over, and up into Seward. I haven't made that exact run, but it would be well over 12 hours."

"So by car, then?"

"If he could manage it. But a stolen car . . ." Todd paused to think it over. "I really don't think it would be that easy. There is a bus, though. And that wouldn't attract attention. If ex-Ranger Peck stole a car, or hi-jacked one, it would get law enforcement attention right away." He was quiet a moment. "No, our Peck is smart. He wouldn't risk it. The more I think about it, he'd either take the train or bus. But the train only runs to Seward once a day—and that out of Anchorage. He would have had to have been at the Portage station earlier to have caught the train. I'm laying my money on the bus."

Todd reached for his cell phone and opened the contacts page.

"What about flying?"

"Only float planes out of Whittier. It's a possibility, but I doubt it. He'd have to charter a plane, and that means showing ID." He looked at Mattituck. "I'm very sure he's on the bus."

"Okay," Mattituck said. "I'm playing devil's advocate here."

"Please do," Todd said.

"If he takes the bus down to do this exchange, how's he going to get out of Seward. There's no airport. And you've already eliminated charter flights."

"True. So again, stealing a car and traveling on the highway—too risky. Even if he gets to Anchorage and grabs a flight . . . "

Todd's voice trailed off.

"What?" Mattituck asked.

"The last dropoff is in Anchorage on this stint," Todd said vaguely.

"And?"

"Carl Elkins said that normally the Anchorage drop is separate from these others." He paused, thinking.

Mattituck waited, watching the scenery go by. This part of the Kenai Peninsula always stunned him with its conifer-filled mountains and pristine alpine lakes.

"Shit," Todd said finally. "I have a weird hunch that this guy is not the normal delivery man. It was nagging at me when Elkins' told me that Peck was to do the Anchorage drop alone." He shot a glance at Mattituck. "I mean, think about it. We've seen how good he is in the outdoors, running a boat, figuring things out, adjusting, and always keeping on track with his objective. Like a Ranger. He has his objective, and he keeps moving toward it, changing up his actions and plans as needed. Isn't that what special ops people are trained for?"

Mattituck's head jerk up at him. Todd was watching him attentively.

After a moment, Mattituck shrugged. "How would I know?"

"I don't know what else could make sense." Todd was back to talking more to himself now. "Why the added Anchorage stop? That's the question."

He looked at Mattituck. Mattituck shrugged.

"So . . . he's an ex-Ranger. He knows navigation. He knows Alaska and how to get around. Or at least knows how to quickly figure it out. On Montague, he knew what direction to go—probably knew where Rocky Bay was. He knew he was going to a different bay. And he knew that there was a good chance of flagging a boat there, and he was right, then stole it. He then lay in wait for you and the Kimberly Marie."

He looked meaningfully at Mattituck. Mattituck watched him without comment, waiting for him to continue.

"He was waiting for you, Frank. Why else was he there? He knew you would be coming back through there. And he was waiting for you."

"Why? To ambush me?"

"Yes . . . well, more to get his backpacks back off the boat. We now know he was after the rest of the drop backpacks."

Mattituck nodded. "Yeah, I can see that."

"And the guy is really skilled. He was on this trip with a partner, but at every step we've been on him, he clearly didn't need a partner. I think he was on the trip with Carl Elkins only because that's what the hotel managers expect to see."

"So you think this guy could have done all this alone, and that the Anchorage drop was added because . . . why? I'm missing that part."

Todd glanced at him.

"He's a hit man," he said flatly.

Mattituck absorbed this.

"For who?" he ventured.

"Whoever's behind the operation. Someone in Anchorage has pissed him off—the drug boss, I mean. Someone in the operation in Anchorage has crossed the big boss. The cartel. Whatever we want to call him. And he's sent in his hit man to take the Anchorage guy out."

Mattituck was quiet. Todd let the silence ride as they passed a sign: Seward, 23 miles.

"If that's all true," Mattituck said. "We'd better really watch our shit."

"We've got the Seward Police on stand by. They've called in two off-duty officers to back us up. And," he said, looking at Mattituck, "they have a plain car for us to use. We'll pick it up on the way in."

"What about your uniform?"

Todd reached to the back seat and pulled a duffel bag up.

They rolled into Seward in the early evening. The tall mountains surrounding the coastal Alaska town made it seem darker, as the sun had already begun its slow June trajectory toward the horizon. Todd drove the cruiser straight to the Seward Police station, and they met up with Chief Swanson, who was leaning on the front fender of a Seward Police SUV, chewing a toothpick, waiting.

"I've got my boys lined up and ready to back you," he said to Todd. "The Puffin Inn is over toward the marina. I've had a guy staking it out."

"Any activity?" Todd asked, following the Chief into the police station with his duffel in hand.

"Nope. Not a thing. Looks you're right about this guy taking the bus."

Clearly, Mattituck thought, Todd had already run through all his musings with the Seward Chief.

"The bus will be here at 7:25 p.m. It pulls in at the Marathon Mountain Diner, which is a block west of the Puffin Inn."

They passed through the arctic entry to the police station, crossed the lobby, and entered the briefing room behind the reception counter. Todd wasted no time changing his clothes, tucking two black Glocks into the waistband of his Levi's and putting on the flannel shirt outside of the jeans to cover the handguns. Mattituck sat on the folding table at the head of the briefing room and waited.

"I have two men called in from off-duty. One is positioned across the street from the Puffin, on stakeout duty. The other is hanging out at the diner so we know exactly when the bus comes in, and he'll try to ID our man."

"You got the description I forwarded?" Todd queried.

"Yep. This is from the other guy in the hospital, right?" the Chief asked.

"That's right."

"Okay. Pretty much fits any Tom-Dick-and-Harry working a cannery or fishing boat, but my guy is keeping an eye out."

"Well," Todd started, "in any case, we'll know when he hits the Puffin. Frank and I—This is Frank, by the way," he added, gesturing at Mattituck, "will be posing as guests at the Puffin. When the suspect picks up the key and enters the room, that's when we'll make our move."

"What's the plan?" the Chief asked.

"We'll approach him as he comes out, and ---"

"Why not just charge the room?" the Chief asked.

"Too risky with this guy," Todd returned. "We want to have him out in the open if we can."

The Chief mulled this over. "Okay," he said finally.

"I'd like your two guys to be on hand at that point. They can be at either end of the building. Wherever they are, I want them absolutely on the ready to jump in if things get ugly."

And they will get ugly, Mattituck thought. He could not envision this guy giving up . . . at all.

At 7:10p, Mattituck and Todd had driven a semi-beatup Jeep Cherokee to the Puffin Inn. Todd and Mattituck both with Trooper-issued Glocks in their waistbands, and Mattituck with a 5-inch Buck Knife in a leather case clipped to his jeans. They checked into a room that seemed centrally located, since they had no idea where the room was that Peck-the-Ranger would be making the exchange in.

As they checked in, Mattituck sized up the desk manager. He was a scrawny guy in his mid-thirties, one of those guys who has a scraggily beard and gaunt cheeks. His clothes were typical rural Alaskan town—a black Sublime shirt with grungy off-market jeans, tattoos down his arms, and a heavy silver chain around his wrist. Mattituck didn't know all that much about addicts, but this guy seemed to have all the earmarks: the gaunt appearance, vacant eyes with dark semi-circles beneath them, and teeth that appeared far too rotted for a man his age.

The Puffin Inn was a standard motel design. There were two floors in a medium-sized rectangular building, with all rooms opening to a balcony that faced the parking lot. Theirs was on the ground floor, dead center, overlooking the off-street parking along Seward's main drag. There was no way they would miss whatever action might occur.

Todd kept watch at the window, binoculars at the ready to bring in anything needing more detail. They had a good view of the Marathon Mountain Diner one block up and on the other side of the street. When the bus arrived, there would be no missing it. Because its stop was in front of the diner at the curb, the bus would have to come around the block in front of the Puffin Inn to line itself up for the stop. When it did, they would have a blind spot due the Puffin Inn placing them back at an angle from the left rear of the bus; the door to the bus was, of course, on the front right side. This was why it was important to have the Seward Police officers on station and also keeping an eye out. With so many sets of eyes on the diner, there was no way that Peck-the-Ranger would escape notice.

"I'm going to go downstairs and see if they have any coffee," Mattituck said.

Todd looked askance at him.

"I thought you only drank the good stuff. They only have dredge water in a place like this."

"With enough cream and sugar, I can down anything for some caffeine."

Todd furrowed his brow and turned back to his watch out the window.

"Don't you only drink black?"

"Yes. Except when the coffee is channel dredge."

Mattituck stepped out onto the landing and drew in the salty Alaskan air, noting the edge of a cannery in the scent. He smiled, despite the fatigue. That clean briny air always brought a smile. He turned and headed to the stairs, descended them to the street level, and made his way to the office. Two men turned from the sidewalk and crossed the short distance across the parking lot and reached the front door just as he did. The taller man gestured for Mattituck to go in first.

As Mattituck passed through the door, he tensed. Something about them. . . . . but there were two of them, and the bus hadn't arrived yet. Plus, the guy was taller than their suspect and had black hair and a beard. Mattituck hadn't gotten a good look at the other guy. Hadn't gotten a look at all, he realized. *Not very cop-like of you*, he chided himself. As he entered the office, he took the opportunity to hold the door open for the two men and size them up as they passed through. The tall dark-haired man smiled and thanked him. The other man had a ball cap on and a camouflaged jacket. Over his shoulder was a black backpack. He noticed a well-defined scar along the man's jaw as he passed by.

Mattituck tensed. In a moment of panic, he realized he had left his gun in the room with Todd. Another brilliant non-cop move, he thought.

He nodded at the man with the backpack, noting that the tall one had nothing in his hands. Between the two of them, there was only the backpack.

The man fixed a steely gaze on him and gave a curt nod in return. Although Mattituck had never been close enough to get a good look at the killer, he knew in that instant this was their guy. He thought of Todd upstairs, watching for the bus . . . . the other officers positioned around the diner, all waiting for the bus. And here was their guy, passing unnoticed while all the cops are looking, literally, the other way.

Mattituck let the door close behind them and stepped to the coffee pot. The coffee had been sitting for a few hours. The odor of burnt coffee filled his nostrils and forced him to turn his nose. It didn't matter—he was no longer interested in drinking coffee. The coffee station had become a cover for him. He had no idea what to do, but he stood in front of the small table with the coffee pot, turned slightly so he could watch the men out of the corner of his eye. He wished he'd brought the Glock. He instinctively wanted to reach down to make sure the buck knife was still in his leather sheath, but dared not. Such a move would alert the men if they saw him.

The man with the backpack stepped to the desk and handed a business card to the desk manager.

No question now, Mattituck thought.

"How's it going?" the desk manager asked, a nervous edge in his voice.

Peck didn't bother to answer. He leaned with one hand on the counter and waited for the manager to get the key to the room.

Mattituck wished he could get word to Todd. He pictured him standing at the window, waiting for the bus. He imagined the officers on stakeout huddled or leaning against a lamppost, waiting and watching while all this was happening without their even noticing. He thought briefly of how he might pull the buck knife and take the killer with the blade at his throat. But he had no idea whether the dark-haired guy was a part of this or someone the killer had picked up so that there would be two of them. Mattituck and Todd had learned with Eddie Etano at the Copper River Inn that the drop required two drop-off people. Obviously, Peck had learned the same.

Norman Peck turned toward Mattituck and watched him mixing the creamer into the pungent coffee. His gaze was cool and calculated. Mattituck knew he was being sized up.

"What brings you to Seward?" he asked Mattituck.

Mattituck stalled a moment. He hadn't expected the killer to speak to him.

"Salmon fishing."

"It's good here?" the killer asked.

Mattituck knew he was being read. The killer knew he's being pursued and was checking out as best he could anything that might be out of the ordinary. Mattituck knew he needed to give no reason for the killer to get nervous about him. He quickly abandoned any thought of trying to take the killer himself.

"Yep. Really good fishing here."

What Mattituck didn't mention was that salmon season was still a few weeks away. This was not lost on the desk manager, though, who was now returning to the desk with a key in his hand but was watching Mattituck with a wary eye.

He knows, Mattituck thought. He knows I'm lying and is suspicious.

Again, Mattituck scolded himself for the blunder. He should have known that what he said would be an obvious lie to anybody who knew when the salmon run. He fought to control his nerves as he tensed with the uncertainty of how the desk manager would react. But the man said nothing, and turned his attention back to the killer. If he suspected anything, he clearly had no intention of getting involved. More than likely, his only job was the key exchange, and wanted no part of anything bigger.

Suddenly, the desk manager turned back toward the key chest.

"Sorry," he said as he turned. "Wrong key."

Peck's head snapped around to him. His hand slipped into the pocket of the cam jacket. A gun, Mattituck thought. He has his hand on his gun.

"Here you go," the desk manager said, returning. "Room 213."

"We're supposed to be on the ground floor," the killer said.

"Sorry. This is the only room available," the manager's eyes shifted to the counter in front of him. He was afraid to look the killer in the eye. Peck's gaze bore into him.

"You're sure this is the right room?" he asked.

"Yes, of course. Why wouldn't I be? I prepped it myself."

The killer looked back at Mattituck, who was throwing the skinny red stir stick he'd used into the garbage. The killer half-turned toward him.

Just then, the door burst in with surprising violence.

"Freeze! Nobody move!"

It was Todd, Glock leveled at the two men at the desk.

The top hinge of the door had pulled free of the door frame with the kick, and the door half lay, half leaned against the wall to the side of the doorway. The silence was as complete as it had been sudden.

"Hey, man," the dark-haired man said. "I have no idea what's going on here, but I want no part of it."

Silence. Nobody moved. Todd stood low, half-crouched, the black Glock steady and trained on Norman Peck's chest.

The dark-haired man with the beard continued. "He just hired me to drive him down here is all. I don't know any---"

A shot deafened the room and the dark-haired man dropped to his knees, nearly spinning as he went down. In the moment of confusion, Peck took advantage and with his left hand pulled a handgun from his pocket and aimed at Todd. Peck was now holding handguns in each hand.

Mattituck knew all too well this level of skill and training. It was a skill—and training—he shared with Peck.

Todd, who's attention had been momentarily pulled, was a split-second slower than he would have otherwise been. He pulled the trigger on the Glock, but it was too late. The killer's gun jumped in his hand as another shot rang out, identical to the first one.

Mattituck knew instantly that the first shot had been fired from the killer's pocket. He hadn't bothered to pull the gun out of his pocket, knowing at close range that he had his target.

Todd's shot ripped the sheet rock behind the desk, missing its target. But the killer had missed the first shot as well, and it ripped through the window next to the door behind Todd. Broken glass fell to the ground on both sides of the wall. Todd was already in motion, tucking to the right while leveling the Glock at the killer for another shot. The killer, too, was in motion, taking two steps along the desk and springing upward to jump over it. The feat took Mattituck by surprise, even in the split-second of time. As the cliché goes, Mattituck thought in the back of his mind, time slows down with intense action. Or seems to.

Mattituck instinctively moved to the back of a couch as he heard something skittering along the floor toward him—the Trooper-issued Glock that he'd left in the room. As Mattituck scooped it up, Todd fired off two quick shots at the killer as the man jumped over the counter. Mattituck was struck by the man's agility. It took strength to launch one's body like that with such short lead steps.

The desk manager was no place in sight. Behind the counter, all that could be heard was the killer landing on the flooring behind the front desk. It sounded like he had rolled as he landed—another indication, Mattituck noted, of his Special Forces training. Todd was on his left knee, his right foot poised and ready to launch him into a run. He had the Glock in both hands. Mattituck braced his forearm on the table and pointed his Glock at the motel desk, watching for any sign of the killer.

A moment of silence followed. It seemed the shots fired were still echoing off the walls.

Then Peck's head popped up, followed by a barrel in front of him. Two flashes from the end of the barrel caused Mattituck to instinctively recoil. He had never been in situations like this, despite his background. Training is training, however, and became like second nature to the trained. Mattituck counted two beats, then spun and rose to his left knee. He took aim at the killer's head and fired a shot—too late. The head disappeared just before his Glock jumped. The bullet sailed into the bottom of a picture frame hanging on the wall behind the desk, causing the picture to jump off the wall and crash to the floor.

The head appeared again, higher this time as the killer rose to try to get aim on Todd. Mattituck fired two quick shots to give his friend cover.

The face of the counter and the wall behind it erupted in a starburst of splintering wood and ripped-up sheetrock. Mattituck nearly paused before firing again, at first thinking his Glock had caused all that. Then he realized several shots had been fired at the killer at the same moment, and he heard voices behind him and in the doorway.

The Seward Police officers were there.

Behind the counter, the top of a door on the back wall swung open for a moment, then slammed shut. The killer had escaped through the door.

"Around back!" Todd shouted over his shoulder as he started for the counter. "He's looking for an egress out the back!"

Two officers hurried down the walkway in front of the building. The Seward Chief appeared in the doorway, followed by another uniformed officer. Mattituck could hear approaching sirens in the background. Todd was at the counter now, leaning with his back against it. Mattituck noted that he'd chosen a spot to the side, where the front was actually a half-wall instead of panel front, providing more protection. He paused a moment, then rose and spun around with the Glock ready to fire. No shots. He checked the area behind the counter and found it clear.

He lowered the Glock and stepped over to the downed black-haired man. A pool of blood was gathering to the left side underneath him. He lay face up, his head unmoving and to the side. Todd didn't see the telltale rising and falling at the torso that indicates breathing, so he reached with his hand to the man's neck and felt for a pulse. After a moment, he looked back at the chief and shook his head. Then he started in pursuit of the killer.

"Check him and treat as you're able until an ambulance gets here," the Chief said to the uniformed officer behind him.

He followed Todd through the back door in pursuit of the killer. Mattituck followed.

Todd stood to the side of the back door and turned the knob as quietly as he could, in case Peck was on the other side. He then pushed the door and it swung open. The room on the other side was dark. Todd ventured a peek, then ducked back in case a shot were taken at him.

Nothing.

He stepped into the doorway and surveyed the room. It was a back office with a single bed along the left side and a desk sharing the wall with the door to the front desk and lobby. The desk was a mess, with papers and folders haphazardly arranged on the sides to make room for writing in the middle. Shelving and cabinets lined the remainder of the walls except for the door on the far side. From the look, it was an external door, likely giving way to the alley way behind the motel.

Todd crossed the dark room and opened the back door ajar. With no shots in response, he opened the door wider and peered through, scanning the empty alley. There were no further alarms going off in his head, so he stepped out onto the pitted asphalt among the mish-mash of garbage cans and a large green dumpster. Still, no sign of the killer.

Could it be that this guy was going to get away again? Todd wondered.

Just then, he heard shots down the alleyway, followed by shouts.

Todd ran down the alley toward the shots. As he came to a stop at the end of the alley where it spilled into the street, he heard the bus make the turn onto the main road.

I sure had that part wrong, he thought to himself. Apparently, the suspect had hired someone to drive him to Seward.

Another shot rang from down the street on the right. Todd ducked back behind the corner of the white building next to him. He stole a quick glance and saw a uniformed officer crossing from the left to the right, then another. They must be in pursuit of the suspect, he thought. He heard footsteps and turned to see Mattituck slow and join him from up the alley.

"Shots down the street, toward the marina," he said to him as he caught his breath. "Two uniformed officers are pursuing our man."

"Okay," Mattituck said.

Todd reached to his radio and turned to the general law enforcement channel. The Seward Police would have switched to this frequency as well, in keeping with standard protocol in interagency operations. He didn't know why he hadn't done that earlier, since this was an interagency operation. Immediately, he heard voices. The officers down the road.

"Okay—hold back. I'm not sure where he went."

"10-4," came the reply. Then, "I think he went over behind the hardware store."

"Is he headed to the marina? Why the hell would he be heading for the marina?"

Todd looked at Mattituck.

"A boat," Mattituck said.

Todd nodded.

"I think if we cut over across the street and go one block over, it's almost a straight shot down to the marina. Maybe we can head him off."

Todd nodded again. "I think you're right." He keyed the radio mic clipped to his shoulder.

"This is Trooper Benson. We're a block behind you, but will cut around to the north and then down to the marina. I think that's where he's headed. You two try to slow him down and maybe we can head him off before he gets there."

"10-4," came a reply.

"What makes you think he's going to the marina?" came a new voice. The Chief.

"Trust me, he is," was all Todd said.

Chapter Twenty-Six

Killer's Inferno

Todd led the way across the street and then over one block. All along the way, they saw people nervously peeking out windows, and an occasional brave soul stepping cautiously out to see if they could see what was going on. Otherwise the streets were completely clear. It even seemed to Todd that the traffic had stopped. They ran with their Glocks in hand, then stopped at a building on the corner of the next block to check the passage before running out into the open.

Todd pulled his badge and pinned it to his shirt.

"You'd better do the same," he said to Mattituck. "Don't want any do-gooders who want to help thinking we're the bad guys."

Mattituck fumbled in the inside breast pocket of his Columbia jacket. Finally, he pulled out the deputy badge and pinned it to the outer breast of the jacket.

Todd called in their position and checked the others'.

"We're a block down from where you last saw us. We have him pinned in an alley."

"Okay, good. Keep him there a few more minutes if you can."

"10-4. Will do."

"Let me know if he moves from there."

They could hear sporadic shots from two blocks over.

"Yep. 10-4."

Knowing the suspect was pinned two blocks over, they were free to run and find a position. They set out at a fast jog under nervous stares. Mattituck had become used to the bullet-proof vest the Seward police chief had given him, but now the weight of it seemed to pull and drag at him, making him feel sluggishly slow.

"He's free," came over Todd's radio. "Don't know how he pulled that off, but we just saw him run out of a building two doors down from the alley."

Todd slowed so he could respond.

"Which way?" he radioed between pants.

"Toward the harbor."

"Roger—got it."

They were half a block from the marina. Mattituck could see the array of masts and mastheads neatly lined along the docks. Although he'd been to Seward several times, he couldn't remember the exact arrangement of the docks and the pedestrian entrances. It might be difficult, he thought, to head off the killer if there were more than a couple of entrances—and he was pretty sure there were more than a couple of entrances.

They were approaching the end of the road. There was a stretch along the waterfront on the right that Peck would have to cross before reaching the marina on the north side, but there were plenty of structures to provide cover along the way. They paused and surveyed the area, particularly the open area between the next street to the right, where the suspect was likely to come out.

"I don't think we can get to the marina before him," Todd said. "We'll need to try to stop him in this open area."

Mattituck nodded, tightening his grip on the Glock. He instinctively checked the safety.

They crouched next to each other, ready to spring to action. What that action was, exactly, Mattituck had no idea. But as he glanced at Todd, it was clear to Mattituck that the State Trooper knew precisely what to do. He decided it best not to ask and simply followed Todd's lead. He watched the opening one block over where the killer had last been sighted. As he waited, a part of his mind thought once again about how these coastal Alaskan towns seemed very much alike. The climate was such that buildings and anything else exposed to the elements faced continual moisture and salt in the air, and these resulted in a kind of uniformity in appearance of just about everything. Buildings looked like they needed perpetual paint jobs, and there seemed to be sand and grit everywhere. But all of this was also what made the place so unique, so appealing and genuine.

A few minutes had passed, and Todd shifted next to him.

"Shouldn't he have come out by now?"

Todd shifted again, and looked at Mattituck over his shoulder.

"Yeah. I'd think so. Let's give it another minute, then we can start moving that way. Maybe he wasn't headed to the marina after all."

Mattituck shook his head. "No, I think he is."

"Well, maybe he's planning to take the guy's car. The guy who he hired to drive him down from Whittier."

Mattituck looked surprised.

"I'd taken that to mean drive him down in a boat."

Todd paused.

"I never thought of that," he said. "I just assumed it was a car."

"They came from the direction of the marina. If they'd driven a car, why wouldn't they drive it all the way into the parking lot?"

"Good point."

"And the timing. If he hired a car out of Whittier, he probably would have been here hours ago." Mattituck shook his head. "No, I really think they came in a boat, and that's where he's headed now."

Todd looked back at his friend. Yes, he was right. They had to have taken a boat from Whittier. And the timing would be just about spot on. Once again, Todd thought Mattituck would have made one hell of a Trooper.

They were both watching the next street over. Still, no sign of the ex-Army Ranger. Todd reached for the radio mic.

"Are you guys in pursuit? Where are you?"

"We lost him," came the reply, almost immediately.

"Fuck!" Todd cursed off the mic. "Why the hell didn't they report this?" he asked, only to Mattituck's ears. "Okay," he said into the mic. "Where did you last see him? And when?"

"Reported that earlier. When he came out that building instead of the alley and we called it in. That's the last we saw him."

"Headed where?"

The voice on the other end was becoming irritated. "I reported that earlier, too. Toward the marina."

"And are you heading this way as well?"

A moment's pause. Mattituck could imagine cursing on the other side. Interagency tension, he guessed.

"Of course. At a safe progress," came the curt reply.

"These guys," Todd muttered at Mattituck. "We might as well be on our own."

Mattituck tried to smile.

"Let's go," Todd said.

They started for the next block up. Todd explained that they would try to do a cautious sweep as they made their way back toward the area of the last sighting.

"What if he comes out another way? Like he did from the building instead of the alley?"

Todd paused. Mattituck was right. This guy was squirrely as hell. Maybe they should stay put and wait for the Seward guys to make their way down.

"You're right," Todd said. "In fact, maybe we'd be better position ourselves at that building half way to the marina," he said, indicating a long warehouse two hundred yards from where they were. Approximately an equal distance lay on the other side, between the warehouse and the marina.

"Quite a bit of open space to get there," Mattituck said hesitantly. He, too, was thinking about how the ex-Ranger seemed to always do the least expected.

"I don't think we have much choice if we want to get this guy. I think you're right about the marina. We need to get between him and the marina."

"Okay," Mattituck nodded. "I'm right behind you."

They broke in to a low run for the warehouse. They crossed the pitted asphalt of the street and jumped the guard rail on the other side, skidding on the loose sandy gravel on the other side. Between here and the warehouse, there were a few miscellaneous items — empty 50-gallon drums, an abandoned dumpster, and a 1960s era flatbed truck that looked like it hadn't been moved since it was paid off. All they could hear was the crunching gravel under their feet as they ran, leaping over the occasional tall grasses growing wild in patches all over the open lots.

Gravel suddenly kicked violently up in front of them in three spots, and before Mattituck had a chance to process why, Todd was dropping to the ground in front of him. Mattituck followed him, wondering why Todd would choose this open spot to duck for cover. They really didn't have any.

As Mattituck's body skidded to a stop, belly down on the gravel, another spray of sand and gravel kicked up ten feet back toward the town. Mattituck scanned the buildings to see where the shots were coming from, the Glock ready in his hand. He saw a flash from the abandoned green dumpster, almost an equal distance to the warehouse, and in the open lot between the town and the long structure.

How the *fuck* had the guy gotten there without them seeing him? He must have been there before they got to the end of the street among the town buildings.

But how?

One thing he knew, they couldn't stay lying here on the open ground. He fired two shots at the killer. Sparks flew off the corner of the dumpster and the man ducked back. Mattituck took the opportunity for a run.

"C'mon!" he yelled at Todd, pulling at his shirt as he rose to run for the warehouse.

He'd been vaguely aware of nothingness from where Todd was lying next to him, but only now did it register that Todd was motionless. He stopped midway in the launch to running, and crouched over Todd.

His friend was not moving. Mattituck checked his pulse while scanning his torso. There were no visible — then he saw the torn cloth of Todd's shirt, in his back on the right side, at the curve of the rib cage. He looked closer. No blood.

And no time for looking closer, he decided.

He rolled Todd to his back and lifted his shoulders off the ground. Todd's face was slack, his eyes closed. A good sign when the eyes are closed — it means the person was alive when he went down. Besides, his pulse had been strong. For whatever reason, Todd was alive even though he'd taken a shot in the back.

Then Mattituck remembered the bullet-proof vests they were wearing. The vest must have stopped the bullet, but he'd been hit hard enough that the shot had knocked him unconscious.

Mattituck grabbed Todd's Glock, dropped when he'd been shot, and shoved it into his own waist band. He then hooked his forearms under Todd's armpits, his own Glock free in his hand to pause and take shots to give them cover as he dragged Todd toward the warehouse. Each time the ex-Ranger showed his head, Mattituck paused and fired, trying to remember how many shots he'd fired and how many were now left in the magazine.

Todd was heavy, even just dragging across the graveled lot. The vest and guns didn't help. Mattituck hoped that all that theory about adrenaline giving you extra strength and speed was true. He was scuttling backward with Todd in the crook of his elbows, keeping the gun leveled at the dumpster to fire cover shots for them. Still, he was surprised at the speed he was able to make.

Adrenaline, he thought. *Adrenaline and determination.*

He chanced a quick glance over his shoulder to see how much farther they had. Not as far as he'd thought—only about 25 yards to go. Tops.

A movement at the dumpster caught his attention, and the Glock in his hand jumped instinctively. He saw dirt and sand kick up in front of the dumpster as the killer bolted out from behind the green metal bin and set out at a dead sprint toward the other side of the warehouse. Mattituck held his fire, not wanting to waste shots when the killer clearly didn't intend to shoot at him.

Fifteen yards. Ten yards.

It was a race in steps to get to cover.

The ex-Ranger was nearly behind the warehouse. Mattituck knew that as soon as the man had cover, he would pause to take more shots at he and Todd. He tried to pick up his pace. Already, his body was groaning and straining. He could feel the extra pressure in his knees with each backward step as his legs pushed in the unnatural motion, and with the added weight on top of the odd motion.

He felt Todd stir as they closed in on five yards. Mattituck shot a glance to check on the ex-Ranger, and saw him disappear behind the back side of the warehouse.

Shit! he screamed inside his head. He felt a sudden pressure inside his skull as his blood pumped hard through his body, moving adrenaline to the muscles as fast as possible. Near-panic gripped his thoughts, and everything seemed to slip into an unreal state of being. Sound seemed muffled, or blocked out completely. His vision seemed to constrict into the view of Todd's chest and belly, then legs, all sloping toward the ground beneath him as he ran backwards. Everything seemed slow and sluggish, like a repetitive nightmare, leaving his mind acute and fast, but his body slowed and dragged as if under water.

He looked behind him again. Just a few more feet.

Inwardly, he braced himself for a gunshot either on the ground, in him, or in Todd. He took two more steps. About another yard. That was it. Just one more yard.

Todd jerked awake and twisted, falling out of Mattituck's grip. He spun around to try to see who had been dragging him. His eyes locked on Matittuck's.

"What the---?"

"Here! *Here!*" Mattituck shouted at him, gesturing forward. He half-dragged, half-threw Todd to the sheltered side of the warehouse. The motion threw Todd into an awkward roll, and he stopped when he hit the wall. Next to him, Mattituck fell in an exhausted heap, fought to catch his breath, then lurched into a crouch and peeked around the corner of the building.

"What happened?" Todd asked with bewilderment.

"That fucking vest saved your ass," Mattituck shot back. "I thought they protect you completely."

"They stop the bullet, but it'll still knock the shit out of you," Todd replied, his wits coming around.

"The guy was behind that dumpster. He beat us out here, apparently," Mattituck explained. "Have no idea how, but there it is—he obviously did."

Todd shook his head and swung his legs under him. He drew a deep breath and winced.

"Jesus . . ."

"Hurts, eh?"

"I've been hit before, but this really hurts." He drew breath again. He knew he'd have to put the pain out of his mind. According to his training, no serious injury can happen with a bullet hitting a vest, so he knew it was really mind over matter. He had to pull it together. Had to.

Mattituck was peering around the corner of the building. His far arm—his right arm—was extended around the corner. Although Todd couldn't see it, he knew the Glock was in his hand, aimed at the far corner of the building.

"How's your arm?" he asked, referring to Mattituck's own bullet injury.

"Fucking hurts like fucking hell," Mattituck said, distracted.

"Bleeding, or is the dress holding?"

Mattituck glanced at his arm.

"It's fine," he said, more focused on what Peck might be up to.

"What did Peck look like when you last saw him?" Todd asked Mattituck.

"What do you mean? You're the one who took the description of him."

"No, I mean what was he doing? Was he at a dead run when he went behind the building, or was he pulling up like he was going to stop?"

"Oh. He was at a dead run. Absolutely all out."

Todd nodded. "He's not there."

Mattituck shot a glance back at him. Todd was getting to his feet and starting for the other end of the warehouse.

"What?"

"He's not there. If he were going to pull up and take shots at us, it would have looked like that's what he was going to do." He let that sink in. "If he was at a dead sprint, then he's making tracks for the marina. May already be there for all the time we're fartin' around here." Todd raised his voice as he said this, starting a jog.

Mattituck caught up and ran abreast of the Trooper. In the back of his mind, he noted that this warehouse must not see a lot of traffic. In front of the bays, green weeds reached upward unhindered, and broad-leafed ground weeds splayed out here and there from cracks in the concrete that surrounded the building. He glanced at Todd. His running was labored and slightly favoring of one side—the injured side. He imagined a nasty black bruise starting as they ran.

They came to the end of the building and stopped. Both men peered around the corner. Instantly, they saw the suspect at a dead run for the marina. On the other side of him, rows and rows of masts lined the docks. Beyond that, Mattituck could see the breakwater that surrounded the marina, giving the boats protection from the chop the wind tended to kick up, and the occasional sets of swells that entered the harbor area. It was the time of day when pleasure boaters and anglers were coming back to port. Mattituck could see boats of all types and sizes pointed toward the marina as far down the inlet as he could see.

It was a busy time in the marina.

Todd was looking at the same thing now.

"This is not ideal," he said to Mattituck. "Too many people can get hurt."

He seemed to hesitate.

"What's wrong?"

"Sometimes we have to just let it go if a chase puts too many people in danger."

He thought for a moment more.

"But not this time. Let's go!"

They set out in pursuit. Todd seemed to have a new energy, as though stopping and surveying the reality of all the people around had impressed a new urgency into him. The killer shot quick glances over his shoulder and noted their pursuit. He paused a moment, turned, and fired a shot at them. It was a haphazard shot that went astray so far off that Mattituck didn't even hear it, nor where it might have hit.

Todd didn't bother to return fire, and Mattituck followed suit. Peck was nearing the gangway to the first set of docks, and the pedestrian traffic was thickening. It appeared nobody had heard the shots nor taken notice of the chase scene bearing down on them. The killer Peck didn't appear to be slowing down for the crowd. He kept running at a full sprint, weaving between men and women and their kids, pulling off their life jackets, and groups of men carrying rods and dragging coolers filled with the day's catch.

The killer slammed into an overweight, balding man wearing dark green Helly Hansens. The man flew several feet, his torso bending as he did, until he fell into a toppling mass, taking out the legs of a nearby elderly man. The older man dropped on top of the green Helly

Hansens. By the time both bodies stopped and lay still, the killer was a solid ten feet beyond them and still at a dead run.

The ex-Ranger ran past the first gangway without slowing down nor checking where he was. He seemed intent on a particular destination. He ran full speed to the next gangway, knocking a backpack out of a woman's hand when he couldn't navigate around her. He began to slow as he neared the second gangway. It felt to Mattituck that they were closing in on him, but they were just now entering the thick of the pedestrians.

Mattituck looked up to see the killer at a full stop, a hundred or so feet ahead of them. Instinctively he knew what the man was about to do.

A split-second later, it was confirmed as Peck raised his handgun and fired two shots at them. Screams rang into the air, and the feel of the place completely changed from the end-of-day-fishing relaxation to pandemonium. It seemed that everywhere, people were spinning around this way and that, trying to see where the shot came from and who was being shot at. Guns are not unusual at a harbor, as many use them to kill a halibut before pulling the massive fish aboard. But gunshots are cause for alarm.

In front of them, people began to part a path for Todd and Mattituck as they saw the flash of badges on their chests. The killer took one more shot, then bolted onto the gangway toward the boats.

Ten feet ahead of them and to the left, a middle aged man went down, a blood stain clearly visible on his shoulder. Mattituck became aware of screaming behind him to the right, and he shot a quick look to see a woman crumpled on the ground with a pool of blood gathering on the ground around her. He wondered if it were possible for that much blood to emit in such a short time.

Anger gripped him. This guy was fucking reckless.

Beside him, Todd was barking into the radio mic.

"Bystanders down! I repeat, bystanders down! We're at the marina—ambulance and backup needed, NOW!!!"

Mattituck and Todd ran to the second gangway while the killer ran to the main floating dock, then turned right. Todd looked past him as soon as he had a track on the man, and surveyed the harbor entrance. There were a lot of boats coming in, and hoards of people on the docks and boats in their moorings.

This could get very ugly, he thought to himself.

He and Mattituck raced after the ex-Ranger. They launched onto the gangway, barreling past scared vacationers and anglers, all trying to get to safety. Some, recognizing that the two men with badges were targets, struggled frantically to get away from them and where they were going. Todd led the way across the gangway, boots clopping on the planks as they made their way to the main floating dock. Todd saw the suspect cut to the left and down a dock between slips two-thirds filled with boats. The empty slips, he presumed, were coming in as this chase was on. Again, his thoughts turned to just how ruthless and cold this man was, and all the lives that were at risk.

As they approached the dock Peck had run down, Todd and Mattituck saw the suspect slow and stop. Mattituck dropped to the decking, and Todd hurled himself into the fishdeck of a nearby sportfisher.

Todd heard two shots fired, and immediately heard the splintering of fiberglass above his head. Shards fell on his head, shoulders, and the deck of the boat he was on. The suspect seemed to be zeroing in on him more than Mattituck. He poked his head up to see where the man was, and was met with two more shots—one sailing close enough to his head that he could hear it pass, and the other into the wood piling holding the floating dock in place.

Shit! I can't even get a look at where he's going. Which – he thought – *was probably exactly the man's intention.* Instill a fear of looking so that he creates a window of time to ditch onto the boat he's bound for without being seen.

But the killer had lost track of Mattituck and wasn't attending to him. He was intent on the cop seeking refuge on the boat.

Mattituck, meanwhile, lay flat on his stomach on the deck. Only the top half of his head would be visible to where the killer stood on the dock, taking pot-shots at Todd. He peered down the dock at the man from relative safety. Once the man seemed to feel he had Todd pinned down, he turned and ran several more feet and turned to check on Todd. He shot twice more, and Mattituck could hear the shots bore into fiberglass on the superstructure of the boat Todd was on. Clearly, the killer was trying to keep Todd from looking up and seeing where he went.

And doing a good job. Todd Benson was completely pinned down.

He doesn't know I'm here, Mattituck thought with surprise. *How could he not know I'm here? It must be the crowd—he lost track of me in the crowd. Good!*

The killer turned and dropped into the fish deck of a glass-ply about 15 or 20 slips down. Since the boat was on the opposite side of the dock from where Mattituck was—on the same side that Todd was on—he could see the boat fairly well. Intuitively, he noted key features on the boat, a grey raft on top of the cabin and a Furuno radar dome; there were a line of matching red halibut poles in "rocket launchers" along the rear cabin roof.

He stayed down and signaled Todd to do the same. The killer sprang back to the dock, aimed down the line of boat transoms, and put bullets into the wood piling on the opposite side of the boat Todd was hunkered in. It was obvious now that the killer was taking care to make sure Todd stayed down and unobservant. It would have worked, Mattituck thought, and the man might have slipped away, if it weren't for Mattituck lying in watch.

The killer unmoored the vessel and jumped back into the fish deck. He must have jumped in, started the boat, then taken the shots and unmoored it. He was intent on holding the trooper down and at bay.

He disappeared into the cabin of the glas-ply. He was getting underway.

Mattituck jumped to his feet when he thought the killer had ducked into the cabin to steer the boat. Todd saw this and jumped to his feet as well. Todd fell in behind Mattituck by only a few feet and they bolted down the dock.

The Glas-ply was pulling out of its slip.

Mattituck stopped and took aim. Todd joined him.

Todd reached over, not firing, and pulled at Mattituck's sleeve.

"Don't shoot!"

Mattituck looked at him briefly, but Todd didn't return the look.

"Fuel cans on the transom—at least three."

If they shot those, they might explode, putting everybody within thirty feet at serious risk of injury or death.

They held their fire and ran down the dock. Mattituck could see Peck inside the cabin at the helm as the boat swung out into the channel, clear of its slip.

"He's going to get away!" Mattituck yelled.

Todd stopped and took aim, then paused. There were several boats coming in along that channel, one less than two dozen yards farther down. Todd took aim again in spite of this. He was not about to let this guy get away again. Mattituck took aim as well, following his lead. When Todd began firing, Mattituck fired as well. A barrage of bullets pelted the boat as the killer tried to steer the boat into a getaway.

Mattituck could see the killer exit the cabin through the door onto the forward bow as the bullets tore into the fiberglass of the superstructure and cabin. Windows shattered amidst flying white fiberglass.

Then, one of the bullets—possibly two—hit one of the gas cans, and it ignited, triggering the other two.

Like most boats that carry extra fuel in gas cans, this one had them lashed atop the transom and gunwales at the rear of the boat, exposed to view in an effort to keep them out of the way of those on board. Most boats this size did not have fuel tanks big enough to carry the owner to the halibut banks she or he wanted, and so they would pack extra fuel to compensate. Doing so made the boat a floating bomb, though. But then again, who could guess that any boat would become the focus of such a fire fight?

In a fiery and expanding brilliance of flame, the entire back of the boat was engulfed in a horrific explosion. It was far more than Todd would have guessed one gas can could pack—whatever bullet or bullets penetrated the gasoline can must have passed through to the next, and possibly another one after that. The result, no matter the cause, was stunning. The explosion expanded out in volcanic anger to several boats tied up at the dock, and set them on fire.

Todd knew from training that fiberglass could burn at just over 1000 degrees, and an explosion like that could produce enough heat to overcome that number by a half dozen-fold or hotter. Certainly enough to heat up the fiberglass cabin and hull to a sustainable burning temperature.

And it did.

The inferno deafened both Todd and Mattituck, and surely everybody else nearby. It skirted across the top of the water while jettisoning skyward in a fury of yellow and orange flames.

"Jesus," Mattituck heard himself mutter.

Todd didn't respond. He began running down the dock toward the now infernal boat. All he could see was the hull at the water line, and a ball of fire and black flame billowing upward. No way could the killer Peck survive that. No way. With the feeling of sudden deflation, of sudden silence after sustained high-decibel noise, Todd felt the intense and unexpected stop of the chase.

It was over.

After all this—days and days of chasing only to see the guy escape time and again, it was finally over.

Peck was dead, Todd thought. *The crazy fuck was finally dead.*

Mattituck followed Trooper Benson to the glasply's slip. The boat drifted in the channel between the lines of boat slips, surrounded by debris in the water, and burning brightly with threatening blue and yellow flames. The boats that had been coming in toward their slips were stopped or backing down. One boat, as Mattituck watched it now, burst into full throttle reverse in attempt to escape, nearly backing into another vessel thirty yards behind it. It was the boat nearest the flaming glas-ply, and apparently feared catching fire itself.

Mattituck and Todd stood on the dock next to the now-empty slip where the glas-ply had been tied up, trying to absorb the drifting carnage. It seemed unreal, like something they were watching on a TV screen. Except here, now, the air was salty and cool. The dock under their feet was solid in its floating wood reality. The sudden deafening silence was absolute, punctuating the feeling that the entire world had stopped for a few minutes to try to process what had just happened in this tiny corner of Alaska.

Skipper's Oath

Chapter Twenty-Seven

Alaskan Phoenix

Todd Benson sat on the transom of the Kimberly Marie with Frank Mattituck. They lounged in the morning sun, ignoring the societal ban on drinking before 5:00p . . . or even noon. The day before, Mattituck had brought the magnificent yacht in from Heather Bay after the Seward inferno, and had stayed aboard overnight. Todd, in keeping with standard procedure, was on administrative leave "pending an investigation of the events associated with, and leading up to, the death of the suspect in Seward."

"They really do that, huh? A suspension? Even when you were clearly just doing your job?"

"None of that is clear until someone checks up on my story," Todd replied, then added to Mattituck's dismayed look: "And you don't count. I deputized you and you were in on the end scene. So your testimony is a part, but it doesn't settle anything. And it's not a suspension."

Mattituck nodded understanding.

"So tell me about that black-haired beauty down in Cordova," Todd probed with a grin.

"You're changing the subject."

"Yeah, but from how you were getting all shy and coy, I'm guessing it's a good subject to change to."

"She and I used to date," Mattituck said evasively.

"Used to? Looked like things were heating up pretty well. I mean, just judging by how you looked at each other."

Mattituck gazed out toward the harbor entrance, watching a fishing seiner chug in alongside the fish-packing plant.

"We were pretty involved a few months ago."

"What happened?"

"Nothing. It just kind of ended."

"'Just kind of ended'? How does that happen?"

Mattituck's head moved side to side, slowly. "I really don't know. She's really something, so . . . you know."

Todd looked at him. "No, I don't actually."

"You said yourself she's beautiful. And she is. Ridiculously beautiful."

"And? Sorry, I'm missing the problem with that," Todd laughed.

Mattituck chuckled along. "Yeah, you're right. I don't know. She's such a good person, you know? I mean, really good. She does volunteer work. And she takes on cases at her law practice when people can't afford to pay."

Todd took two slow swigs off his beer.

"I'm still missing what's wrong. She's gorgeous, kind, involved in the community. Sounds like your kind of girl to me."

Mattituck smiled. "She's better than me."

Todd looked up. "Better than you?"

Mattituck looked away and found an eagle perched on a piling to fix his eyes on.

"So what about this suspension?" he asked Todd.

"Dammit, it's not a suspension," Todd said, a touch annoyed. "It's administrative leave. With pay."

"Don't sulk. It's not becoming of your he-man, super-cop image."

Todd laughed. "Hey, it's a couple of days paid vacation."

"Which you spend lazing your ass here on Jim Milner's boat." The quip had been intended for bantor, but it landed very differently. The tone turned somber.

"So what happens now?" Mattituck asked.

"They'll close out the investigation. Check on all the deaths—Damn! Did you keep count of how many people this guy killed?"

Mattituck shook his head. "Well," he said, "there was Jim Milner, and the people in Yakutat, then the family on the 'But Chaser he killed to steal the boat . . .'"

"Anybody who was in the guy's way."

They were silent for several minutes, sipping their Alaskan ambers.

"Know what's weird?" Todd asked suddenly.

Mattituck shook his head.

"Some drug guy was murdered in Anchorage just this morning. Two days after Seward."

Mattituck sat up. A nagging sensation came back to him.

"It's just weird because it happened at a motel in Mountain Village. So, for most eyes, it's not really weird at all. Drug shit happens there all the time. But . . ." Todd's voice trailed off for a moment, then returned.

Mattituck was watching Todd intently. "But what?"

Todd slowly shook his head. "Dunno."

"You say it happened at a motel. Did you check it out yourself?"

Todd nodded. "Yeah. The security tapes. Nothing helpful. The guy comes in, takes aim, and blam blam blam right to the heart before the motel clerk can even fall."

Mattituck hadn't taken his eyes off his friend.

Todd's cell rang, and he looked to see who it was. He motioned for Mattituck to follow him into the cabin, and answered on speaker.

"Benson?"

"Yeah, it's me."

"Johnson, here at Anchorage headquarters. I have good news. You can go back to work in the morning."

"What?"

"They've closed the case. You're off leave. Sorry, buddy—no more vacation for you."

Todd was visibly surprised. "How could they close the case? I mean, they haven't even positively ID'ed the charred body. How do they know for sure it's this ex-Ranger?"

"Hey, I was just told to call you, okay? Want more detail, you'll need to talk to the captain. All I know is the Army wanted the case closed and, well, they must have made a good argument, because that Intel Officer is at Patrick Air Force Base with that body, waiting for a transport. Case closed."

"What? Wait. Why does he have the body?"

"You know, military burial and all that. He took possession of the body. He confirmed it as the Ranger's and claimed custody."

"But how could he confirm it? They haven't had time to ID the body yet. How can they close the case?"

"Look, I don't know the details. Talk to the captain."

"All right. Well, what about the Mountain View killing? The motel one?"

"Determined it's unrelated. Oh, hey! That reminds me. The guy in the hospital who tipped you off on the Seward connection? He's dead."

"What?"

"Yeah, I know, right? Dead early this morning. The doctors are puzzled. I mean, the guy was on a great recovery, but they're thinking that maybe one of the skull punctures from the bear's teeth might have hit something they didn't see before."

"Have they checked anything else? Like his blood? Anything unusual in his blood?"

"Like what?" Johnson asked.

"I don't know, like poison, or an overdose or something."

Johnson chuckled. "No. Listen, Benson, nobody went in or out of there except nurses tending to him. There's no investigation. We had two troopers watching him. There's nothing suspicious to investigate."

"It just seems too much of a coincidence," Todd persisted.

"Benson—Todd. Listen, man, you were on that guy for days. Days, man. It's hard to believe it just ends like that. But it does—it's over. You did a great job. End of story. So go get some rest and come back and go after the next bad guy. That's how we roll, right?"

Todd hung up without answering.

"I need another beer," he said. "Two or three maybe."

Mattituck watched him with disbelief.

Todd looked up at Mattituck, his face pale.

"You're not buying all that, are you?" Mattituck asked.

"It just doesn't add up right."

"What can we do about it?"

"Nothing, I guess," Todd said. "As far as everybody is concerned, all guilty parties were either killed or arrested. It's a closed case."

Mattituck held his gaze.

"At least officially," Todd added, and took another sip of his beer.

The two men sat in silence on the Kimberly Marie, looking over her transom to the mountains across the valley. Mattituck let his gaze settle on Sugarloaf Mountain, his thoughts drifting. Todd down the rest of his Alaskan amber, then twisted off the cap of the next.

The salty Alaskan air was fresh and crisp, a testimony to the beauty of life. But the men on the transom of the Kimberly Marie sat solemn. They knew the dark underbelly of humanity was always there.

- Finis -

CPSIA information can be obtained
at www.ICGtesting.com
Printed in the USA
LVOW08s1629080217
523625LV00004B/812/P